Dear Reader,

What can you forgive in a friendship? That's the question that is central to this story, and one that has always fascinated me. Research suggests that friendship is good for us, but why do some friendships last forever, while others wither away? What happens when those close bonds are tested?

Milly has been friends with Nicole since childhood, but their lives have taken very different paths. Despite that, they have been there for each other through thick and thin, until recently when Nicole ghosted her. At the toughest time of her life, her friend wasn't there for her and Milly doesn't understand why. But then Nicole calls out of the blue, needing Milly's help. Can they find their way back to the closeness they once had?

I loved exploring the complex dynamics of a long-term friendship, and it made me reflect on my own friendships (and reach out to a few people I might have neglected a little while writing the book!).

I hope you enjoy reading this book as much as I enjoyed writing it, and that the story and the beautiful setting of the Lake District provide you with your own secret escape!

Readers love spending time with
SARAH MORGAN

'Sarah Morgan never fails to make me smile'

'Such a great author who pulls you into the book's world the moment you start reading'

'Sarah Morgan never ever disappoints'

'One of my go-to authors when I'm looking for a heartwarming, feel-good read'

'Always a treat'

'Smashes it every time, delivering romance, emotion, hope, friendship, loyalty, happiness'

'Sarah never lets us down!'

Sarah Morgan is a number one *Sunday Times* bestselling author. Eleven of her books have been *Sunday Times* top ten bestsellers, including *The Christmas Cottage*, *The Christmas Book Club*, *One More for Christmas*, *Beach House Summer* and *The Summer Seekers*. She has sold over twenty-four million books worldwide.

Sarah lives near London, England with her family and when she isn't writing or reading, she likes to spend time outdoors hiking or riding her mountain bike.

For all the latest book news, exclusive content and competitions, visit Sarah's website and sign up to her newsletter at

www.sarahmorgan.com

Sarah loves to connect with readers on social media. Find her on:

f @AuthorSarahMorgan

⊙ sarahmorganwrites

𝕏 @SarahMorgan_

P.S. Want even more great reads, giveaways and book news?
Follow @hqstories

SARAH MORGAN

A Secret Escape

ONE PLACE. MANY STORIES

HQ
An imprint of HarperCollins*Publishers* Ltd
1 London Bridge Street
London SE1 9GF

www.harpercollins.co.uk

HarperCollins*Publishers*
Macken House, 39/40 Mayor Street Upper,
Dublin 1, D01 C9W8, Ireland

This edition 2025
1
First published in Great Britain by HQ,
an imprint of HarperCollins*Publishers* Ltd 2025

ISBN: 978-1-84845-923-6

Printed and bound in the UK using 100% Renewable
Electricity by CPI Group (UK) Ltd

For more information visit: www.harpercollins.co.uk/green

To Michele Bidelspach, with many thanks.

1

Milly

Why had she said yes?

Milly sat in her car outside the railway station, although it seemed generous to call it that, given that it was in the middle of nowhere and consisted of nothing more than a single platform and a shelter. There was no ticket office. No buzz of waiting people. Just one train an hour.

It was the last place on earth you'd expect to encounter a movie star, which was presumably why Nicole had chosen it.

Milly understood the need for discretion and privacy, but still, this felt like overkill.

There was one other car parked along the narrow country road, but other than that there were no signs of life and she sat in the darkness, trying not to be spooked as she waited for the last train of the day. She'd opened the car windows, but even at this late hour it was stifling and there was no sign of the weather breaking. Back in March when it had rained every day, Milly had dreamed of sunshine, but June had brought with it sunshine and a smothering heat that made her dream of rain.

The makeup she'd so carefully applied before leaving had already melted away, but she didn't bother renewing it because what was the point? It was dark and there was no one to see her anyway. It didn't matter how she looked. But when you were meeting someone many considered to be one of the most beautiful women in the world, it was hard to resist the urge to make an effort.

Not that anyone noticed her when Nicole was around. They never had.

She sighed and checked the time.

Maybe Nicole had changed her mind. *Please let her have changed her mind.*

She'd heard nothing since that single phone call the night before. Was she wasting her time sitting here? She thought about her child, safely asleep in her grandmother's house. Milly hated asking her mother for help, and this time she hadn't even been able to explain why she needed Zoe to do an impromptu sleepover because Nicole had sworn her to secrecy. Zoe herself had protested that at thirteen she was able to stay on her own, but after all the upheaval in their lives Milly wasn't ready to consider that. Zoe was the most important thing in her life. What if there was a fire? An intruder? Having lost so much, Milly was clinging tightly to what she had left. Also she had a niggling feeling that something wasn't quite right with Zoe, but whenever she asked she was given the *I'm fine* response. Milly had cycled through the obvious things: Was it school? The divorce? Moving to a new home? Whatever it was, Zoe clearly didn't want to worry her with it, which simply increased Milly's anxiety levels.

She needed to spend more time alone with her daughter, but when you were a single working mother, time was a scarce resource.

And now she had Nicole to deal with. Friendships were supposed to make you feel better, not worse. At what point did you say *enough*?

She felt guilty because her mother had assumed Milly was finally going on a date and hadn't been able to hide her delight. "Good," she'd said. "It's been eighteen months since Richard walked out, and the divorce has been final for six months. I'm pleased you've finally moved on."

Moved on?

Milly hadn't moved on. If she'd admitted that the *last* thing she wanted was another romantic entanglement when she was still tied up in knots about the last one, she would have caused her mother even more worry, and she didn't want to do that. She kept those thoughts to herself, but the effort required to pretend she was coping well was exhausting.

All she really wanted now was to be the best mother possible to Zoe, but she was pretty sure she was failing at that too. She'd read so many books and articles on how to make divorce easier on kids the advice swirled around in her head. She was trying hard to put everything into practice. She'd been careful not to say a bad word about Richard in front of Zoe (although she used plenty of bad words when she was alone in the shower), and she tried to keep everything around them as normal as possible. She forced herself to get up in the morning and smile and pretend to be fine when she really wasn't fine at all and would gladly have spent the whole day in bed. She told herself that she was modeling coping strategies for her child, and that was what mattered, wasn't it? It didn't matter that inside her head she was a mess.

Between lying to her mother, putting on a brave face for her child and forcing herself to be polite to Richard even when he was being frustratingly unreasonable and uncaring and nothing like the man she'd married, she'd forgotten what it felt like to actually express her true feelings.

There had been a time when the prospect of Nicole coming to stay would have lifted her mood, because if there was one person in the world she could be honest with, it was Nicole. But not anymore.

What was she doing here when the last thing she needed was more emotional stress? She didn't know if she was a fool or if this was the very definition of friendship: showing up no matter what.

3

Promises made when you were fifteen didn't seem to make as much sense when you were thirty-five. They certainly hadn't meant anything to Nicole.

Hurt and tired, she reached for her phone and sent a message.

Are you on the train?

A flash of headlights caught her attention and she froze in her seat as another car approached. It drove past without stopping, and she let out the breath she hadn't realized she'd been holding. She wasn't built for subterfuge.

When Nicole had called her asking for help, she should have said no.

She was particularly frustrated with herself because she'd recently done an online course on assertiveness, thanks to a twenty-minute wait at the hairdresser, where she'd foolishly fallen into the trap of doing one of those magazine questionnaires.

If you answer yes to more than three questions, you may have a problem with being assertive.

Milly had answered *yes* to all ten questions and had decided right then and there that she needed to do something about it. Her tendency to say yes was the reason she felt pressured all the time. It was the reason she lay awake at night, stressed and hyperventilating with her to-do list racing around her brain. Her inability to be assertive was the reason she never felt able to call out Richard's unreasonable behavior. (He'd already humiliated and divorced her, so really what more could he do?) She didn't know if the way he behaved was a hallmark of ex-husbands generally, but she knew she wasn't handling it well. It had to stop. She had to change.

She was too busy to take a class in person, largely because of her inability to say no, so she'd enrolled for an online course and for two weeks had spent an hour every evening exploring ways to be more assertive. She'd learned about boundaries, about the importance of standing up for her rights and respecting other people's, she'd filled out worksheets where she'd tried out different ways

4

of saying no. Assertive, but not aggressive. *Use the I word, not you. When you do (fill in particular behavioral aberration here) . . . I feel (describe, without swearing, how it makes you feel) . . .*

She'd passed with top marks and thought that maybe this would be a new beginning. And then her phone had rung.

The name that flashed up was *Sister.*

Milly had stared at it for so long it had stopped ringing. But it had immediately started again, and this time she'd answered it, even though part of her didn't want to.

It wasn't her sister, of course. She didn't have a sister, but when Nicole's career had taken off, she'd insisted that Milly store her number under a different name. It had felt exciting at the time. Clandestine. It had made her feel special, because all of a sudden everyone wanted a piece of Nicole, and Milly had her number in her phone.

They'd been in their early twenties, but even at that tender age their lives couldn't have been more different. Milly was married to Richard and had just discovered she was pregnant. She spent her days helping her mother run the family business, a small but exclusive resort of lakeside cabins nestled close to the water in the beautiful Lake District.

Nicole, on the other hand, had dropped out of college to pursue acting seriously, and by the age of twenty-one had achieved global fame after starring in a movie about a teenager who traveled back in time to save the planet from destruction. It had broken all box office records. Milly had seen the film and agreed with the critics that Nicole had been captivating in the role, but that wasn't the point where she'd recognized just how talented her friend was. That moment had come a few months later, when Nicole had all but floated onto the stage to accept the most coveted award in acting wearing a custom-made gown that somehow managed to make her look both innocent and alluring. Her speech had been heartfelt and moving, and many of the people in the audience had cried.

Milly had cried too, and that was when she'd realized that her friend wasn't just going to be big, she was going to be huge. Because the speech was all lies, and Milly knew it was lies. She was, quite possibly, one of only two people who knew it was lies, the other being Nicole's mother, who was unlikely to be watching.

But still Nicole had made her believe every word.

Nicole had called her afterward.

"Did you hear my speech?"

"Yes, I heard your speech."

"You know the truth. People would pay you to tell my story."

Milly had rolled her eyes. *"Don't be ridiculous."*

"You have no idea how far people will go to get information on me and tear me down."

"You're sounding paranoid."

But Nicole had said the same thing a few days later when Milly had met her in her suite in a London hotel where she was staying for a premiere of her latest movie.

She'd been escorted to the room by unsmiling security guards with earpieces and overdeveloped muscles, and she'd sat stiffly on one of the white sofas in the ridiculously opulent suite, feeling out of place and desperate to find common ground with her old friend.

She remembered ten-year-old Nicole saying *One day I'm going to be famous*, and here she was—famous.

And fame had changed everything.

"Seriously, Milly, you can't have my name in your phone anymore. Someone might see it. We need to agree on a different name." Nicole had been wired, nervous, talking too quickly, sipping a glass of wine even though it was three in the afternoon. Her hair fell in dark silky waves down her back, and those famous green eyes, *eyes that made you lose your power of speech* as one smitten critic had put it, were huge in her pale face. In real life she seemed thinner than ever, and Milly, almost eight months pregnant by then, had felt like a baby elephant next to her.

She'd shifted slightly, trying to get more comfortable, which was almost impossible with a baby stuck under your ribs. "Who is going to see it? And what are they going to do? Mug me and steal my phone? I live in the middle of nowhere, Nic. I'm surrounded by trees and mountains. When I open my windows I hear nothing." That wasn't quite true. She frequently slept with the windows open, and she lay in the darkness and listened to the plaintive call of the birds and the occasional hoot of an owl, thinking how much she liked her quiet, predictable life. Unlike Nicole, she'd never had a desire to be famous, and nothing about her friend's life had given her reason to revise her opinion. "My home isn't exactly Paparazzi Central."

Nicole had looked at her with a mix of envy and pity, as if she was wondering how anyone as unworldly as Milly made it through the day.

"Indulge me." She'd put down her wineglass and taken the phone from her friend. Her slim fingers had flown over the keys. "There. Fixed."

Milly had stared at it. *"Sister?"*

"Why not? It's what we are. It's the way I feel about you. The way I'll always feel about you." Nicole had hugged her then, and Milly had hugged her back, and for that brief moment their old connection had flickered to life. This was the Nicole she'd grown up with, not the new glamorous Nicole who couldn't walk down a street without being recognized. Still, she hadn't been able to shake the uneasy feeling that their relationship was about to change in a big way, and it made her sad because nothing was more important to her than their friendship.

"You're going to forget about me."

"Don't be ridiculous." Nicole had said exactly what Milly had hoped she'd say. "You're my best friend. You'll always be my best friend, and when we're both old, you're going to come and spend winters with me in California and we'll sit on the deck and watch the sunsets and talk about that time I drank half a bottle of vodka and dyed your hair purple. You were so upset you threw my favorite bag in the lake."

Milly knew those weren't the moments she'd remember when she looked back on their friendship. She'd be thinking of all the times Nicole had walked into a room first because Milly had been too shy to enter on her own. She'd remember the patience Nicole had shown when teaching Milly how to project confidence even when she was quaking inside. She'd think about the nights Nicole had stayed over at her place after Milly's dad had walked out. The hours they'd lain awake talking about the future and what they both wanted.

And despite Milly's fears, their friendship had endured. There were frequent phone calls and messages where Nicole would send photos of herself being transformed by hair and makeup into an assassin, an FBI agent, an art thief, a superhero.

Milly had sent back photos of Zoe. Zoe at six months. Zoe taking her first steps. Zoe's first day at school. She'd sent photos of the four new luxury cabins they'd built by the lake and then felt embarrassed because Nicole owned properties around the world and Milly's cabins, modest by comparison, were probably of little interest to her.

But despite their very different lives, they'd been in regular contact until eighteen months ago when Nicole had suddenly ghosted her.

Thinking about that brought her back to the present.

Milly checked the time again. The place felt so dead it was hard to believe a train was due to arrive any minute. But even if it did, there was no guarantee that her friend would be on it. Maybe Nicole was going to ghost her again. Maybe she wasn't going to show up, and Milly would drive back home alone feeling more of a fool than she already did.

And if Nicole did happen to arrive, what was Milly going to say?

Why have you ignored me for the past eighteen months?

Where were you when I needed you?

It had happened right after Milly, Richard and Zoe had visited her in LA. Milly assumed there was a connection and had spent hours going over the holiday in her mind but couldn't identify a reason. Initially she hadn't worried because she knew how busy Nicole was, but a few weeks later when Milly had left a message telling her that Richard was having an affair and divorcing her and there was *still* no response, she'd started to worry. More than worry. Her friend's silence had hurt. It had been a bitter blow, coming so soon after Richard's betrayal.

The one person she'd always thought she could depend on, her safety net in life, had let her down.

Milly still couldn't believe Nicole had ignored something so life-shattering. When had they ever not supported each other? Some long-term friendships continued out of habit, but theirs was real. Theirs was rare and special. Until it wasn't.

Nicole's silence hurt more than it should have because not only had Milly been dumped by her husband but it seemed she'd been dumped by her best friend too, and in some ways that felt worse. It had been the lowest moment of her life. So bad that she tried not to think about it because she'd dragged herself back from the edge and didn't want to risk staring into the blackness again.

She'd survived, mostly thanks to the support of her mother and grandmother, but it had changed things. There was no more believing that Nicole would be there for her in a crisis. No more pretending that the word *Sister* in her phone was anything more than a way of disguising Nicole's identity.

Even now, so many months later, that reality hurt.

"Maybe it's me." She spoke aloud, as she sometimes did when she was alone in the car. It was the one time she felt able to speak her mind. "Maybe I'm just the kind of person people leave."

First her father, then Richard and then Nicole.

She'd assumed that was the end of it, and then the night before Nicole had finally called.

The call should have woken Milly up, but she had been lying awake stewing about Richard, having conversations in her head that she knew she'd never have in real life despite the assertiveness course because she was determined to keep things civil for her daughter.

She'd answered partly because it was Nicole and Milly had never not answered a call from Nicole, and partly because a small hurt part of her hoped that maybe Nicole was finally getting in touch to apologize or at least explain.

But there had been no apology or explanation, just a plea.

I need your help.

Nothing for eighteen months, not a squeak, and now she was expecting Milly to help.

During the conversation, admittedly short, not once had she asked how Milly was doing. She hadn't mentioned Richard's affair or the divorce or acknowledged how hard it must be for Milly to be going through exactly what her mother had gone through. She proffered neither explanation nor apology for not being there for Milly. It was all about her.

I wouldn't ask if it wasn't important. Please, Milly. I'm desperate.

Desperate? What did desperate look like when your life was pretty much perfect? Just how desperate could you be when you were rich, beautiful and the toast of the movie-going public?

Nicole didn't know the meaning of the word, but Milly did, although she worked hard not to show it. She'd been determined not to put that extra pressure on Zoe.

She was just about holding it together, which was another reason she should have said no to Nicole. She should have put into practice everything she'd learned from her assertiveness course. She should have said *No, sorry, I'm struggling enough with my own life as you'd know if you read your emails* or, better still (as she'd been taught that it wasn't necessary to give lengthy explanations), *Sorry, I can't help.*

But she hadn't said any of those things. She'd said yes.

Yes, she'd pick her up. Yes, she'd drive at night to lessen the chances of being seen. Yes, Nicole could stay with Milly. Yes, she'd find a way to hide her.

Which was why she was now, against her better judgment, sitting in the middle of nowhere waiting for a train that was late and a friend she wasn't sure she wanted to see.

The assertiveness course clearly hadn't worked. If she was more assertive, she'd demand a refund.

A sound cut through her thoughts, and she saw the train approaching. Finally.

She felt a slight stirring of dread. The fabric of their friendship had been stretched by their diversifying paths and was now torn in so many places it was barely holding together. Their relationship hadn't just changed, it was unrecognizable.

Usually the only emotion she felt before seeing Nicole was excitement, but tonight her stomach churned with an uncomfortable mix of hurt and resentment.

Where had Nicole been when Milly had needed her?

She was upset and a little bit angry but, most of all, deeply disappointed that their friendship had fallen short of what she'd believed it to be. Never before had she felt the need to protect herself in the friendship, but she did now. And it made her feel lonely.

Not lonely for company, because she had plenty of that, but lonely for that one person she could say anything to in the knowledge she'd be understood and not judged. Someone who knew what she was feeling without Milly having to spell it out.

The train slowed down and stopped, and Milly peered into the dimly lit station, but there were only two people visible. One was a man in his fifties, who immediately strode toward the parked car that Milly had noticed earlier, and the other was a woman of significantly advanced years wearing a coat that had seen better days and a hat that concealed most of her white hair. She was dragging a small suitcase and stooping badly, so bent over she was struggling to walk even with the help of a walking stick.

There was no sign of Nicole, which was confusing because it had been Nicole who had insisted Milly be poised for a quick getaway.

A quick getaway. Was that even possible in a small family hatchback? Milly hadn't been in the mood for drama. *We're not in a movie now, Nicole.*

And Nicole's response to her. *You have no idea what my life is like.*

Milly couldn't argue with that.

She had no idea what it was like to be one of the most in-demand actors of her generation, commanding millions for each movie.

And as if acting talent and looks (voted Most Beautiful Woman two years running) wasn't enough, Nicole's last blockbuster had required her to sing, and she'd stunned the world with her voice.

Milly sighed.

The last thing you should do when your life was a total mess was to spend time with someone whose life was perfect.

She glanced at the train again. Still no Nicole, and no sign of anyone else leaving the train. Maybe she was hiding in a dark corner, waiting for these other people to leave before emerging. Or maybe she'd changed her mind.

The old woman teetered slightly, almost losing her balance, and Milly shot out of the car, concern for the woman's safety overriding her promise to keep a low profile.

"Can I help you?" She put a hand on the woman's arm. "It's very late. Is someone meeting you?"

The woman lifted her head and looked directly at Milly and Milly stared into those unmistakable eyes and thought *I really am a fool.*

"You have to be kidding me. N—"

"Shh. Not until we're in the car."

Milly would have been impressed if she hadn't been so frustrated. Part of that frustration was directed at herself for being so easily duped. "We're in the middle of nowhere, and there is no one around."

"They're always around." Nicole slid her arm into Milly's and adopted her stoop again. "Help me into the car."

"Help you?"

How long was this charade supposed to continue?

But she wanted to get out of here as much as Nicole, so she dutifully put her arm around her friend and felt a flicker of shock as she registered how thin she was.

She guided her to the passenger side of the car, hoping no one was watching because she was pretty confident her acting abilities would fool no one.

Nicole handed her the walking stick and Milly tucked it into the back of the car along with the suitcase.

She took another quick glance around the station. "There is no one here." She slid into the driver's seat and closed the door. "You're going to bake inside that coat. Why the heavy disguise? Have you robbed a bank in real life or something? If I'm harboring a criminal, I'd like to know."

Nicole's eyes were closed. "I just need a short window of time when no one knows where I am. Can we talk about it later? I'm really not—" her voice shook a little "—I'm not feeling too good. And I'm freezing. I need the coat."

Freezing?

There was so much Milly had planned to say, but there was something about Nicole's fragility that sucked all the heat out of her emotions. But then she remembered her assertiveness course.

Her feelings mattered too. This wasn't only about Nicole.

"There is no one around, Nicole. This place is empty. We are the last people here. And before I drive anywhere, I want to know what this is all about. Why the sudden phone call and why the urgency?"

"You seriously don't know?"

"If I knew, I wouldn't be asking."

"Oh, Milly." Nicole gave a choked laugh and opened her eyes. "You haven't changed one bit, and I'm so happy about that."

"What's that supposed to mean?" Since Richard had walked out taking most of her confidence with him, she felt as if every part of her had changed. She could barely remember the person she used to be, but Nicole didn't know that because she hadn't asked.

She felt a pang of loss as she remembered how their friendship used to be. There had been no barriers between them, but now there was a barrier so big she couldn't see past it.

Nicole turned her head to look at her. "When we were young you always refused to read scandalous stories about celebrities. You thought it was distasteful that someone was making a career out of exploiting a person's misfortune, and you didn't want to be part of it. You were always kind, even to people you didn't know."

Was that how she'd ended up where she was, with everyone taking advantage of her?

"These days it's less about my principles and more about the fact I don't have a moment in the day to draw breath, let alone read gossip. I have a life, Nicole!" A life she was holding together by her fingernails. And suddenly the heat flared to life again. Maybe Nicole was hurting, but she was hurting too. "I don't have time to read much at all. I wish I did, but between raising my child alone and worrying what all this is doing to her, dealing with my selfish ex-husband, running a business at a time when everyone is watching what they're spending and wondering if life is going to be this tough forever, there's not a lot of spare time left for lounging around reading about people whose lives quite frankly seem pretty good from where I'm standing." She stopped, mortified. Why had she said all that? She'd blurted out far more than she'd intended. She'd told herself that she was going to be polite and give nothing of herself. She was going to show Nicole that this friendship didn't matter to her any more than it did to Nicole. That she'd moved on, just as Nicole had.

But that wasn't what she'd done. She'd had Nicole in her car for all of two minutes and already she'd been more honest with her than with anyone else in her life. She'd intended to be reserved and indifferent, and instead she'd shown that she was hurt. So much for protecting herself. So much for holding part of herself back. She might as well have ripped off a bandage and said *Look at these raw wounds*. Because that was how she felt. Like a giant wound. Any protective coating she might have had once had been eroded by Richard and now by Nicole. Love provided insulation from the cuts and bruises of life, and so did trust. Milly had lost both. She was a tortoise without its shell. A hedgehog with no spines.

She sat there, miserably embarrassed, and then Nicole reached out and touched her arm.

"I've missed you."

Milly felt something soften inside her, but she forced herself to ignore it. "Sure. You missed me so much you didn't get in touch for eighteen months."

She was so surprised to hear those words coming out of her mouth that she almost turned around to check there was no one else in the car.

Maybe the assertiveness course hadn't been such a waste of money after all.

Nicole removed her hand from Milly's arm. "Don't be angry. I know there are things we need to talk about, but the whole world is angry with me right now. I couldn't stand it if you were too."

"Why would *the whole world* be angry with you?"

"Perhaps *angry* is the wrong word. I should have said *the whole world hates me*." Nicole's voice shook a little. "I am currently the most hated woman on the planet."

She'd forgotten how all-or-nothing Nicole was. People either adored her or hated her. She was either devastated or ecstatic. There was nothing in between. No middle ground. To be friends with Nicole meant strapping in for a ride on a roller coaster with its steep ups and downs. She couldn't handle it. "Please, for once, can we leave the drama at the door?"

"For you it's drama, but for me it's my life."

Milly clamped her jaw shut to stop herself from saying something she might regret. "Nicole—"

"I want you to know that what they're saying isn't true. Well, some of it is—but not the way they've told it. It's all twisted." Her voice was barely a whisper. "I'm not sure which is worse—having people make up lies about you, or knowing that people believe those lies without question."

Milly was starting to wish she'd taken the time to do an internet search. She'd had a really bad night and hadn't had a moment to herself all day. Both her body and brain were tired, and she didn't have the energy for this. "What lies? What do people believe?"

There was a pause. "According to the press, I've broken up the happiest marriage in Hollywood. I'm a home-wrecker. The Other Woman."

Milly went cold. She thought of Richard. *There's someone else . . .* "You—what?"

"Go to any news site and you can read all about it. Two truths and a lie. Or is it two lies and a truth? I can't remember. And it doesn't really matter because no one is interested in the truth anyway. The people who write all that stuff about me just want clicks, and the people who read it want proof that my amazing-looking life isn't so amazing. Celebrity downfall is a great cure for envy, didn't you know? *Yes she's rich, but is she really happy?* Well, no, she isn't." Nicole slurred her words slightly, and Milly felt a growing wave of nausea.

I'm a home-wrecker.

Why did it have to be that? Nicole had a colorful dating history, with a reputation for falling for her costars, but to the best of Milly's knowledge she'd never been involved with anyone who was married. For Milly the topic was something of a trigger given recent circumstances. She had to force herself to remember that this wasn't about her.

"You are overthinking this, Nicole. Most people are too busy handling their own problems and making it through each day to worry about what is happening to you."

"That's where you're wrong. When people have problems they look around them for someone who has it worse so that they feel better about their own lives. They think *Well, at least I'm not her.* My problems are a source of entertainment. Remember when we used to play three wishes?"

And just like that she was right back in her childhood, curled up on her bed watching Nicole paint her nails.

If you could have three wishes, what would you wish for?

Milly frowned. "We haven't played that game for at least two decades."

"If I had one wish it would be to put the clock back and start again." Nicole's gaze was fixed on Milly's face. "How about you?"

One wish.

"I don't know. I don't waste time wishing for things anymore."

"Why not?" Nicole spoke softly. "Wishing tells you what you really want."

"Or else it just shows you what you don't have, and dwelling on that isn't helpful." Milly fastened her seat belt and started the engine. "We need to go. I have to be up early. My life doesn't go on hold just because you're here. How long are you planning to stay?"

"I don't know." Nicole's voice shook again. "Maybe forever."

Forever?

That was a joke, surely? Milly glanced quickly at her friend, but Nicole's eyes were closed again, and there was no hint of a smile on her face.

Forever.

Milly tightened her grip on the wheel. If she had to wish for one thing right now, it would be patience.

2

Nicole

She'd made a mess of things. How could she be so good at playing a part and so bad at real life? She needed a script. She needed to be told who to be.

She shivered and huddled deeper into her coat. Milly had the air-conditioning running in the car and Nicole was frozen, but she said nothing because she was pathetically grateful to Milly for picking her up and didn't dare ask for anything more.

She shouldn't even have asked her to do this. She didn't deserve it. She didn't deserve Milly. She'd been a terrible friend to her. She'd let her down, and the fact that Milly had still shown up for her made her feel even worse.

Her younger self had naively thought that fame and fortune would be the answer to everything. It had come as a shock and disappointment to discover that being a movie star insulated you from many things, but not human emotion. You could buy a big house with walls of glass and a view of the ocean, but that didn't ease the agony of heartbreak. A healthy savings account didn't protect you from mortifying shame or nerve-shredding fear. All it really did was make you even more alone because everyone around you thought you had no reason to feel anything but lucky and permanently joyful.

Her eyes stung, and she blinked several times and tried to focus on her surroundings.

"Where are we?" She'd been expecting to go directly to Milly's house in the village, but they'd driven straight through and were now heading toward the lake and Forest Nest, the exclusive resort owned and run by Milly and her family. The headlights picked out stone walls and fields, and she could just about make out the looming slope of the mountains to the right of her. It felt a long way from California, which was a relief, but still she felt a lurch of panic at the thought of being alone in one of the lakeside cabins. "I'm not staying with you in your home?"

"This is my home now." Milly slowed down as they reached a sharp bend in the road. "Richard insisted on selling the cottage." She didn't look at Nicole, not even a glance, which could have been because it was dark and she was concentrating on the driving or, more likely, because she didn't want to talk about it. It was a delivery of facts and no more.

Hurt hovered around Milly like an aura. Nicole could feel it, and she understood it.

Milly hadn't just lost her husband, she'd lost her home and Nicole hadn't been there to support her. That lapse, that total dereliction of her responsibilities as best friend, had formed a huge chasm between them. The only way of breaching that chasm was to tell the truth, try to explain, but given that there was a good chance the truth would make things worse, Nicole was delaying the moment. Did that make her a coward? Probably, but Milly had an idealistic view of relationships. Despite the fact her father had walked out when she was twelve, or maybe because of it, she expected a lot from people.

Nicole had let her down.

She wished she could put the clock back and do things differently, but it was too late for that. You made one bad decision and suddenly you were trapped on a path and there was no turning back. All she could do now was keep moving forward and make the best of things.

The divorce had shocked Nicole. She'd thought that Milly and Richard were the perfect couple. Yes, he was twelve years older than Milly, but he was handsome, charming and kind. He was also sure of himself, which was a draw to someone like Milly, who was rarely sure of anything. Being with Richard had given her more confidence. She'd blossomed. Richard had discovered what Nicole had always known: that Milly was one in a million. She was generous and genuine and had a quick sense of humor. Kindness shone from every pore in her body (although, the look she'd given Nicole when she'd described herself as a *home-wrecker* hadn't been *that* kind, so maybe the last eighteen months had knocked that out of her). Milly listened carefully when you talked and paid attention, rather than treating conversation as a game of tennis where someone was always trying to win a point.

If Nicole was casting her in a role (something she did without thinking when she met people), it would have been Girl Next Door. Freckles. Warm smile. Always there to offer a cup of tea and a hug in times of trouble.

She'd originally cast Richard in the role of Romantic Lead, but then he'd had an affair and left Milly, so now she had him placed firmly in Bad Guy territory. The one to avoid. The guy guaranteed to let you down.

And it turned out that not only had he left Milly but he'd forced her to sell her home. Nicole knew how much Milly had loved that cottage, and not for the first time in her life she felt a surge of fury toward Richard. She already had plenty of reasons to be angry with him, and now she had another one.

She hadn't intended to ask, but she couldn't help herself. "You couldn't have found a way to keep the cottage?"

"No. I couldn't afford it by myself, and we needed somewhere to live."

Guilt niggled. If she'd known, she would have given Milly the money. She would have found a way to make sure she could stay in her home. But it was too late for regrets.

It was too late for a lot of things. Her therapist had told her to remember that the past was gone, and that the future was ahead, and what she really needed to focus on was the present. Unfortunately, she'd had no advice on what to do if your present was crap and you didn't want to focus on that either.

"So where are you living now?"

Milly adjusted her grip on the wheel. "Remember the old boathouse? Our den?"

Their den. Scraped knees. Hide-and-seek. A buried time capsule. Childish promises.

Happy times.

"Of course. I also remember having to rush to the emergency department because you stood on a rotten plank and fell through the floor. So much blood." She remembered it as if it had happened yesterday. "Are you about to tell me you're living there?"

"Zoe and I moved in three months ago."

"I assume you swept the floor and did something about the spiders?" She was relieved to see Milly smile. It gave her hope that something might still be salvaged from the wreck of their friendship.

"We tried to make it a bit more comfortable, yes."

Nicole stared into the darkness, absorbing the changes in her friend's life. "So now you live by the lake. You always loved the place."

"I still do."

"Is it hard living where you work? Do people bother you?"

"No. We have a good team of staff. And the boathouse is a little way away from the rest of the cabins, so that helps. If guests have a problem, they contact the team at Reception. I don't advertise that this is my home."

Milly drove over the cattle grid and into a densely forested area that Nicole remembered well from their childhood. A carved wooden sign stood at the side of the narrow road.

Forest Nest.

Instantly she felt some of the tension drain away. Milly wasn't the only one who loved this place. She loved it too. It was geared toward outdoor life, and people staying here spent their time swimming, kayaking and having fun on the lake, hiking the fells, and cycling up steep mountain passes. Milly's mother believed in active holidays where you had fun and got muddy, and Forest Nest provided the perfect base for those experiences.

Nicole's mother, by contrast, had considered every holiday to be an opportunity for intellectual improvement, and Nicole had spent numerous sweaty summer weeks pounding the streets of Rome, Florence and Paris bored out of her mind as her mother lectured her on art and architecture. A talented vascular surgeon, Alexandra Walker (she'd drawn the line at taking her husband's name) had forgone a career in London in order to accommodate her husband's wish to live in rural Cumbria. A passionate conservationist, he was the one who had wanted children, and she'd agreed on the understanding that he would take responsibility for childcare. Unfortunately he'd reneged on that promise by dying two years after the move, leaving Alexandra with a lesser career and a parental role that was both unfamiliar and unwanted. Consigned to a life of disappointing compromise, she had spent her time trying to push her daughter to heights she herself had failed to achieve. She believed that every moment of the day should have a purpose and that time was wasted if it wasn't spent on self-improvement. Fortunately for Nicole that meant that her mother saw the long summer holidays as an inconvenience rather than an opportunity to spend time with her only daughter, so apart from their compulsory art appreciation week, Nicole had been allowed to stay with Milly for the rest of the time, providing she met certain study goals.

The summers she'd spent at Forest Nest were the happiest of her life. She and Milly had been expected to help out and do chores, but once they were done, their time was their own. She'd learned to swim and kayak. She'd headed into the fells with Milly and her mother and learned to rock climb, and she'd felt guilty for lying awake at night wishing she'd been born into a different family. A family where individuality was encouraged. Where you were loved for who you were rather than what you did.

Nicole had spent most of her life trying to make her mother proud, but so far it hadn't happened. Thanks to the lurid headlines of the last few days, she was resigned to the fact that it never would.

What must her mother be thinking now?

Nicole could almost hear her sigh of disappointment.

"Remember when my mother was encouraging me to be a doctor? She set up all those visits to medical schools."

Milly kept her eyes on the narrow track ahead. "You would have made a terrible doctor."

"I know. She arranged for me to watch her operating, and I passed out and bashed my skull on the floor." It seemed a strange thing to be talking about in the circumstances, but anything was better than focusing on the present.

There was a pause. "You're an incredible actor, so I think we can agree you made the right choice."

There was a time when praise like that from her closest friend would have given her a high. She'd been chasing validation for most of her life. Now she was numb.

"But I don't save lives, do I? No one *needs* what I do." Her mother had once asked her what she contributed to the world, and Nicole didn't have an answer. No matter how many awards she won or box office records her movies broke, her mother always made her feel like a spectacular failure.

"Not true," Milly said. "You enhance the lives of millions, and that's important. There are ways of making a contribution that don't involve being up to your elbows in someone else's blood."

"That's gross."

But the support, that tiny hint of their old relationship, made her feel a little better until she realized that their old relationship was dead and gone and that things would never be the same again because now Nicole had secrets. One particular secret that she wasn't sure she could ever tell Milly. And that secret was a

23

barrier to the intimacy that had made their friendship so rare and special.

They'd reached the end of the track, and Milly took a turn to the left, and there, perched on the water and surrounded by trees, was the boathouse. She pulled up outside and switched off the engine.

"We're here." Lights glowed on the deck, which stretched out over the lake.

Grateful for a distraction from her depressing thoughts, Nicole stared at the place that had been their forest hideout when they were young.

She hadn't anticipated such a transformation. The dilapidated building of her childhood had been replaced by an architectural dream of wood and local stone.

"This is incredible." She almost said that it was *romantic* and then realized that would be tactless. "Who did this?"

"Mostly Joel."

"Who is Joel?"

"Joel is our everything guy." Milly undid her seat belt. "By which I mean, he does a bit of everything. Plumbing, electrics, carpentry—whatever goes wrong in the cabins, Joel handles it. He's a miracle, to be honest. There's nothing Joel can't fix."

Maybe Joel could fix her life.

"He built this?" Nicole couldn't stop staring. "But you had an architect, surely?"

"Joel used to be an architect. A very successful one, I believe. Worked for a big firm. But then he had some family issues and turned up here looking for maintenance work, or anything really, and my mother gave him a job and let him use one of the older cabins that needed renovating. You know what she's like."

"Yes, I know what she's like." Generous. Warm. How many times had Nicole wished that Connie was her mother? She was the kindest person she'd ever met, with the exception of Milly herself.

Except that tonight, possibly for the first time ever, Milly had been impatient with her.

And Nicole had only herself to blame for that. She'd hurt Milly. And she hadn't wanted to do that, obviously, but Nicole had found herself in a hideous, horrible situation and hadn't known how to extract herself. When there were no good options, which one did you pick?

Milly was still talking. "Anyway, it turned out there was nothing Joel couldn't fix. Which is why I call him our everything guy. I think he only intended his move here to be temporary, but he has been here ever since. He bought one of the original stone cottages that we just drove past. He loves the outdoors. When he's not working he's usually climbing. I'm hoping that will keep him here, because if he left I'd be lost. It's great having him around. He's one of the good guys."

One of the good guys.

Were people that easily categorized? Nicole didn't think so. Good people could do bad things and often did in the world she inhabited. That world seemed far away.

Milly glanced at her. "There's no one to see you here. You can take the wig off. It must be uncomfortable."

"You get used to it." Nicole eased it off and ran her fingers through her flattened hair. "It did the job. You didn't recognize me. If my best friend didn't recognize me, then I'm doing okay."

She said *best friend* and held her breath, waiting for Milly to refute that claim, but Milly said nothing, and Nicole was grateful for that. Silence was better than a denial.

She gazed at the lake, saw moonlight flit across the surface and felt something close to peace for the first time in weeks. The sky was velvet black and studded with stars, a sight you rarely saw when you lived in a city. She turned to Milly, wanting to thank her, but her friend was already out of the car and heading toward the boathouse.

Nicole stuffed the wig into her bag and followed her. They walked along a path illuminated by small solar lights and then up a set of steps that led to the front door.

The door was on the far side of the property and not overlooked, but still Nicole found herself glancing over her shoulder. It was a hard habit to break, even here in the middle of nowhere. She'd been watched for so long she couldn't imagine not being watched.

She stepped inside the boathouse and waited while Milly touched a couple of switches.

Soft light flooded the space, and Nicole saw a comfortable living room with a vaulted ceiling and a wall of glass overlooking the lake.

"It's stunning."

"We wanted the structure to blend into the forest, and we made the most of the light. Wait until you see it in daylight. Uninterrupted views across the lake to the fells." Milly locked the front door behind them and dropped her keys into a bowl on the side. "But let's be honest, the entire place would fit into the living room of your house in LA."

Nicole didn't want to think about her house in LA. She didn't want to think about her life at all.

She envied Milly, but she knew her friend would never believe her, so she didn't say it.

People, even Milly she suspected, forgot that she was a real person. They saw her on the red carpet wearing a custom-made dress with her hair and makeup flawless, and they thought that was her life. But that part was no more real than the roles she played. Real was when she lay on the carpet in her bedroom having a panic attack. Real was having her heart broken with the whole world watching.

They thought her life was perfect, or maybe they just needed to believe that because the alternative was to accept that no one's life was really perfect, and that was too depressing to contemplate.

She smiled at Milly. "I think it's beautiful. Thank you for picking me up and for letting me stay with you." For a moment she thought that perhaps Milly hadn't heard her, but then her friend gave a brief nod as if acknowledging what they both knew: that it had been more than generous in the circumstances.

"Wait till you see the room where you'll be sleeping before you thank me," Milly said. "It's small. A study with a sofa bed, but I've done my best to make it comfortable for you. You didn't give me enough notice to do more than that." Milly headed to the kitchen area and poured two glasses of water. "Do you want something to eat?"

"No, thank you. I'm not hungry." She studied Milly closely. On the surface she hadn't changed at all: same shoulder-length dark hair, same light dusting of freckles on her nose and the same light blue eyes. But she seemed more wary than usual. Reserved. "Where's Zoe?"

"I arranged for her to sleep over with my mother."

Nicole felt a wave of shame. She adored Milly's mother, and the idea that she was reading all the negative press and probably thinking bad things about her made her feel slightly ill. Milly's mother was everything her own was not. She offered praise and encouragement and a listening ear without judgment. She built you up instead of knocking you down. When Nicole had won her first award, Milly's mother had sent flowers and a handwritten note. *You have always been a star to us, but now the whole world knows.*

"What did Connie say when you told her I was coming to stay?"

"She doesn't know. You told me not to tell anyone." Milly handed her a glass of water, and Nicole felt the emotion she'd been holding back almost overwhelm her.

Milly hadn't told anyone. Not even her mother. Who else in her life was that thoughtful and discreet? No one.

"You're an amazing friend, Milly."

Milly didn't respond to that. "This place isn't visible from anywhere. You should be safe enough, providing you don't leave the boathouse."

"That won't be an issue." Leave the boathouse? She felt like crawling under the bedcovers and staying there for the rest of her life. "Were you sad to move out of the cottage?"

"It was difficult at the time but hard to separate my feelings about that from everything else. A lot of things have changed."

Including their relationship.

Nicole felt a twinge of sadness and nostalgia for the days when friendship had seemed simple.

She knew she should be asking about Richard and about how Milly was coping, but she couldn't bring herself to do it. She wasn't brave enough to handle Milly's pain.

She couldn't deal with it. She couldn't deal with anything right now.

She felt injured and tired. She'd considered checking herself in to one of those exclusive health retreats, but then her presence would have been noted, because even when a place claimed to protect the confidentiality of their guests, people had a way of finding out, and then she would have been dealing with more headlines.

"I'll show you where you'll be sleeping." Milly walked through a door that led from the living room to the rear of the boathouse. Stairs curved upward, but Milly opened a door on the ground floor. "I've made up the bed."

An enormous ginger cat sprang off the chair, making them both jump.

"How did you get in here?" Milly scooped up the cat gently and stroked his soft fur.

"You have a cat? Since when?" Nicole reached out her hand, but the cat wriggled out of Milly's arms and stalked out of the room, affronted to have his rest disturbed.

Great. Even the cat was rejecting her.

"Since Richard left. He was a rescue. Zoe begged me to give him a home, and I couldn't say no to her. Fortunately, Tiger loves Zoe. He tolerates the rest of us. Don't expect affection."

Nicole had reached the point where she didn't expect anything from anyone, least of all affection.

She felt a pang of loneliness.

"I didn't know what you'd be bringing with you," Milly said, "so if there's anything you need, let me know."

What she needed was a hug, but she was afraid to ask. There had been a time when Milly would have held her, and she would have held Milly, and they would have taken comfort from the fact that no matter what happened they had each other, but that wasn't the case anymore. And it was her fault.

28

She missed the unquestioning affection that had always existed between them. She missed the insulating quality of their friendship, and the intimacy and luxury of being with someone who knew you well but loved you anyway.

Did Milly still love her?

And did she even deserve it?

She put her bag down and surveyed her refuge. Milly was right that it was small, but small didn't bother her. Small made her feel safer. At her home in LA with its walls of glass overlooking the sea, she made a point of never standing near the window because there was almost always a risk that someone was watching her. Inside these four walls, which she could almost reach out and touch, no threats could be lurking. And it was charming. Bookshelves covered one wall, and the stylish wooden desk tucked under the window overlooked the thickly wooded shoreline. There was a vase of fresh flowers on the table next to the sofa, which had been made up with fresh linens.

"I don't need anything, but thanks."

Milly opened the window a little wider. "There's a bathroom opposite. I put out clean towels and a new T-shirt you can wear to bed if you want it."

Nicole felt emotion thicken her throat. She hadn't been there in Milly's hour of need, but still Milly had shown up for her. More than that. She'd done everything she could to make Nicole comfortable.

"Thank you. Do I need to be careful walking around the boathouse at night? What if I need a glass of water? Do I need to turn off the alarm?"

"What alarm?"

"The intruder alarm." Nicole's palms felt sweaty. "You don't have one?"

"No. There's virtually no crime around here, so you can relax. And I don't have air-conditioning either, sorry. There are only about three weeks in the year when we need it. It's typical that you happen to be here during those three weeks, so I put a fan out. That's the best I can do." Milly walked to the door, and Nicole felt a sudden desperate need not to be left alone.

She didn't care about air-conditioning. What she wanted was company. Friendship. She'd often felt isolated in her life, but never like this. She wanted to talk. She wanted to put everything right between them. She wasn't willing or ready to accept that she'd killed what they had.

"Milly—"

"I hope you manage to sleep." Milly paused with her hand on the door. "If you need anything, call me."

Nicole knew that what she was offering was a glass of water, or an extra pillow. Not comfort. Not a hug.

Milly was shutting her down, which didn't surprise her because Milly always avoided difficult conversations and this definitely met that description.

She waited while Milly closed the door between them.

The gesture felt symbolic.

Exhausted, Nicole followed Milly's directions to the bathroom, scrubbed off her makeup, took a quick shower to remove the last of the persona she'd adopted to travel here safely and slipped on the T-shirt Milly had thoughtfully left out for her.

Then she headed back to the bedroom. She searched for a lock on the door, but there wasn't one, so she dragged a chair up to it and wedged it under the handle. Then she closed the window. She didn't care if it was stifling. She wasn't sleeping with the window open.

After a last check of the room, she slid between the fresh-smelling sheets and closed her eyes.

She had no expectation of sleeping, but she must have slept because when she woke the first fingers of light were sliding through the blinds.

For a few blissful seconds she couldn't remember where she was or why she was here, and then it all came back to her.

She sat up and checked the time. It was only four thirty. She'd been asleep for a few hours, no more. Still, that was more sleep than she'd had in a while.

She lay down and closed her eyes again but her mind, temporarily emptied during sleep, immediately refilled with the realities of her life. She knew she wouldn't be going back to sleep anytime soon.

She felt numb and exhausted and had no idea how to put her life back together again.

But at least for now she was safe, and she had Milly to thank for that.

Was Milly regretting her generosity?

The moment Nicole had described herself as *the other woman*, she'd seen the change in her friend. She wished now that she hadn't used those words because there was so much more to the story than that phrase suggested. She'd used flippancy to cover the depths of her pain, but she could see how it must have seemed to Milly. Why hadn't she just told the truth?

Her heart started to beat faster, and she took a few slow breaths and tried to push him out of her head. She wasn't going to think about Justin or the awful things he'd said to her. Not now. Not yet. She couldn't handle it.

She wasn't a bad person. Despite what everyone was saying about her, *she was not a bad person.*

And she definitely wasn't a destroyer of marriages.

Or was she?

To distract herself she stood up and flicked on the light. She saw that papers and a couple of files had been hastily stacked in a pile on the floor and felt a stab of guilt because Milly had given up this room for her. If she was really a good friend she probably would have gone somewhere else because once they found her—and they would eventually find her—it would make Milly's life difficult. But her plan was to leave before that happened. Just a few days, she'd told herself when she'd made her desperate call to Milly.

For now, she was where she needed to be. After everything that had happened she was emotionally and physically exhausted. It felt wrong that she was the one hiding while Justin was still living his life, his reputation apparently reinvigorated by the publicity, while hers had been trashed. Was he ashamed of himself? Did he feel at all guilty for what he'd done to her?

On the train she'd picked up an abandoned newspaper, and there he was on the front page.

We're More in Love than Ever screamed the headline above a photo of Justin hand-in-hand with his wife, who stared unflinchingly at the camera. The injured look in her blue eyes would have pricked Nicole's conscience had she not known it was fake.

The implication was that the affair was all Nicole's fault. That she'd led him astray.

She'd dropped the paper as if it was infected.

The man was a hypocrite and also a coward, and at some point she'd need to deal with that. Right now she was too bruised by everything. He'd broken her, something she wouldn't have thought possible because she never allowed people close enough to inflict that level of damage.

The press had some of it right, but most of it wrong. She could have told them the truth, but what good would it have done her? She'd been in the public eye for long enough to know that although some people were interested in the truth, most were more interested in a good story. Some people loved to gossip and judge, and they savored the misfortune of others.

She had to try to put Justin behind her, but in the circumstances that was almost impossible. The best she could do was make a plan, and maybe here, in this part of the world that was far removed from the one she normally occupied, she'd be able to do that.

Restless, she pulled a lightweight wrap from her suitcase and wrapped it around her shoulders before quietly moving the chair she'd wedged under the door handle.

She walked quietly to the kitchen, filled a glass with water and drank it quickly before venturing out onto the deck. The only access was from the house, so she felt relatively safe. As safe as she ever did these days.

The lake was still, patches of light shimmering on the surface and the trees casting dark shadows over the water.

She felt instantly calmer. The tightness in her spine eased, and her muscles relaxed.

Forest Nest had always had this effect on her.

She sat down on the porch swing and breathed. For now the heat wave had eased its relentless grip and allowed the air to cool.

The moment was all the more precious because she knew it would be short-lived. There were decisions to be made, and once they found out where she was she'd have to leave because it wasn't fair to inflict the goldfish bowl of her life onto Milly, who had enough problems of her own.

But for now, she could rest. There was no role to play. No character to inhabit and no need to look over her shoulder. Not yet.

At this precise moment in time no one knew where she was. And because it was barely dawn, she could enjoy being outdoors undetected.

Letting that feeling wash over her, she closed her eyes.

3

Milly

It still shocked her to wake up and find herself alone in the bed, even though she'd been doing exactly that for eighteen months.

It was her worst time of day, those early moments when she was alone with reality before she threw herself gratefully into the demands of life.

It was the stillness she noticed first, the almost unnatural silence that greeted her every morning. She still slept on the right side of the bed, her side, and the emptiness of the left side seemed to encapsulate everything that had happened to her. There was something about that stretch of smooth, untouched sheet that made her indescribably sad.

It might have been easier to cope with if she understood, but she didn't understand. She'd thought she and Richard were happy, and the fact that he'd been unhappy enough to have an affair and leave and she hadn't even known he'd felt that way left her with an even greater sense of failure.

He'd loved her once, she was sure of that. *You're everything to me, Milly. You're exactly what I need.*

Richard was twelve years older than her, which at times had

felt like a lot, and at other times like nothing at all. She'd met him when she was twenty-one, and he'd seemed so sophisticated compared to all the men of her own age whose idea of dressing for a date was to pull on a clean-ish T-shirt.

Richard worked in pharmaceutical sales and had just had a promotion. He wore suits and drove an expensive car that smelled of leather. He took her to dinner and sent her flowers. He made her feel safe.

Right from the beginning their relationship had been comfortable and easy and right. They weren't just lovers, they were friends. Good friends. He'd taken her for weekends away and proposed to her under the Eiffel Tower on a trip to Paris. For their honeymoon he'd whisked her off to Greece. They'd swum under a sky so blue it dazzled, in a sea so clear you could see right down to the bottom where shells nested in the sand. At night, her skin warmed by the sun, she'd worn strappy sundresses and sat across from him feeling beautiful and loved as they'd dined on plates of creamy tzatziki while watching the sun go down over the Aegean. The setting had been perfect, but they'd agreed that they didn't need a Greek beach or gourmet food to be happy. Their surroundings didn't matter. All that mattered was each other. In this crowded world, this massive sea of people who inhabited the planet, somehow they'd managed to find each other, and it felt like a miracle.

And it was true that their marriage hadn't been perfect every day, but whose was? Richard had been away for work so often that she frequently felt like a single mother. He never seemed to be available for the boring bits of parenthood, like doctor appointments or visits to the orthodontist, but she was mostly fine with that because her job was more flexible than his, and anyway she adored being with their daughter. There were times when Richard annoyed her, and she was sure she annoyed him, but that was part of marriage, wasn't it? It wasn't just showing up for the candlelit dinners and laughs, it was weathering the tough stuff. The parts that weren't dreamy.

Her conviction that their relationship was solid made it all the harder when it ended. She hadn't seen it coming. Just as she hadn't seen it with her father.

She'd been twelve years old when her father had walked out, taking her sense of security with him.

Her mother hadn't seen that coming either, and for months she'd operated in a daze, convinced that he'd return once he realized what he was missing.

He loves you, Milly. Even if he wanted to leave me, he'd never leave you.

Milly had clung to that, feeling a weight of responsibility that she didn't entirely understand. When he hadn't returned, Milly had taken it to mean that even if he did love her, then he didn't love her *enough*.

She'd been looking for someone who would love her enough ever since, and she thought she'd found that in Richard.

With a sigh she sat up in bed. She had to stop dwelling on it. Churning. She hadn't wanted this to happen but it had, and now she had to find a way to live with it. What she needed was a clean break from him, but when you had a child together, that was not an option. How was she supposed to move on when she was forced to talk to him and see him in person and bite her tongue when he was unreliable?

This new version of Richard was nothing like the Richard she'd married, but she was determined to keep things calm and civilized for Zoe, so she'd been careful to avoid conflict. The result was that she stewed and boiled inside.

Not having Nicole there to talk to had been one of the hardest things about the past eighteen months, and seeing her in person the night before had made it even harder because Milly had been reminded of what they'd lost.

After that tense car journey she'd felt so exhausted and vulnerable she'd almost thrown her arms around Nicole and forgiven her for not being there for her, but something had stopped her. Self-preservation? A desire to be less of a pushover? Maybe it was fear of rejection, although she should be used to rejection by now. She'd experienced enough of it.

And she still didn't really understand why Nicole was here.

She reached for her phone and did the one thing she'd resisted doing up until this point. She looked at the news reports that Nicole had mentioned. They weren't really news reports of course, because the sex life of an actor, even a Hollywood star, wasn't news, it was gossip. It had no relevance to the public beyond morbid fascination, but that didn't stop the story dominating, probably because it provided light relief from the flood of grim stories that populated the headlines.

All the versions of the story seemed to be saying the same thing. That Nicole had tried to destroy one of the longest and most enduring marriages in Hollywood. There were pictures of her and Justin Fisher looking loved-up on a beach somewhere, and then a short blurry video presumably shot by a fellow diner showing Justin Fisher's wife storming into a restaurant in Malibu where Nicole and Justin were dining together. After a few minutes of shouting (excruciating to watch!), Justin's wife had picked up the water jug and poured the contents over Nicole's head.

Milly winced. She watched the video five times, pausing it in some places, and what she noticed was that in the few seconds before Justin Fisher's furious wife interrupted them, Nicole had looked happy. Genuinely happy, not acting happy. She was smiling at Justin as if they'd just shared a joke that only the two of them could possibly understand. There was an energy between them, a chemistry that even a wobbly camera had captured.

Was Nicole in love with him? The idea of it threw Milly because it had never occurred to her that Nicole might lower her guard sufficiently to let anyone that close.

Was that why she seemed so fragile? There was a time when she would have known because Nicole would have shared it with her in one of their late-night email sessions or video catch-ups.

But now she didn't have a clue. She had no idea what was going on in her friend's life.

She closed the video and flicked through the rest of the coverage. Almost every piece she read included old photos of Nicole with other men, those images presumably provided to prove that she had *form*, a history of seducing other women's husbands.

She switched off her phone. She knew that plenty of those rumors weren't true. How true was this one?

Something about this situation wasn't making sense to her.

Nicole had been the subject of lurid headlines before and never tried to hide from it. She'd shrugged it off as part of the job.

What was different about this? Why the urgent need to hide away?

There was something Nicole wasn't telling her, but that might have been Milly's fault because she hadn't exactly encouraged conversation.

With a sigh she forced herself out of bed.

She knew what Nicole was like. She went from man to man, searching for something that she couldn't find inside herself. Some sort of validation. And because no one could give her what she needed, the relationships inevitably ended leaving hearts scattered underfoot like pieces of broken glass.

She didn't want to think about that now. Whatever had happened was done. Justin Fisher was reunited with his wife, who was clearly willing to forgive his transgressions. Would Milly have taken Richard back if he'd knocked on her door and said he'd made a mistake?

No way.

She turned on the shower and waited for the water to heat. The only way she might consider taking him back would be if it felt like the right thing for Zoe. But since he was showing no signs of regret, it wasn't a dilemma she was likely to have to face.

She stepped into the shower and started her routine for the day. It felt like an effort, but she knew that once she got going she'd be fine. The day would be busy because every day was busy. She had a staff meeting at ten o'clock, and before that she was going to head to her mother's house so that she could take Zoe to school. That was one part of the day she refused to miss, a routine she'd been following since Zoe's first day at school.

She worried endlessly about Zoe, about what impact the divorce would have on her, about what was going on in her head. Remembering how she'd felt when her father had walked out, Milly had been determined that her daughter wasn't going to suffer those same feelings of worthlessness. She'd been careful to emphasize that Richard's decision was his own and had nothing to do with Zoe. That Zoe bore no responsibility for his choices. And Zoe always insisted that she was fine, and oddly enough in the beginning she did seem fine—better than Milly—but over the past few weeks something had changed. Milly had noticed her shoulders were a little more slumped, her eyes a little more tired and the little frown between her eyes more prominent.

All she could do was make sure she gave Zoe the opportunity to talk if she wanted to. She couldn't make her confide. She wished she could have a conversation with Richard about it, but she knew he'd tell her she was fussing and that she worried too much. He didn't seem to worry at all, and she wasn't sure whether that was because he'd totally abdicated responsibility for anything other than the so-called fun aspects of childcare *(Why does Zoe need an asthma review? Hasn't she grown out of it?)* or because he was afraid of being forced to acknowledge that his actions might be having a negative impact on their daughter.

She was basically alone with the problem. And now she had Nicole in the mix.

But she'd figure out the whole Nicole problem later. For now, her friend was going to have to stay in the cabin out of sight.

She dressed quickly in what she now thought of as her hot-weather uniform: cropped linen trousers with a loose shirt. She fastened the trousers and grimaced as the button strained against her waistline. Some people lost weight when they were unhappy. Not Milly. Misery didn't put her off her food, it made her hungry, although it was more complicated than that.

Cooking was her favorite form of relaxation. Some people smoked or reached for a glass of wine to relieve the tension of a long day. Some went for a long run. Milly's sanctuary was the kitchen.

There was an almost ritualistic quality to preparing food, and she found it soothing. She loved the process, from the selection of the freshest ingredients to the presentation on the plate. It used all the senses, took her mind off her problems and left her with a sense of well-being. She loved the sound of mushrooms sizzling in hot oil, the scent of garlic, the sweetness of strawberries, the feel of a ripe mango as it gave a little under the pressure of her fingers.

It took her back to her childhood and cooking with her mother and Nanna Peg, her grandmother, who had lived with them for a while after Milly's father had left.

Her love of baking had started with them. Some women dreamed of spa days, but for Milly nothing surpassed the soothing quality of beating butter with sugar until it turned into a soft, creamy fluff.

She'd known from an early age that food was about more than simple nutrients. The way food tasted, the whole dining experience, the way it made you *feel*, was the reason some people would spend a small fortune on a meal out in a top restaurant.

Milly knew all about feelings. Sometimes she wished she didn't know quite so much. She pictured her emotions as powdered sugar sprinkled over the surface of a cake, vulnerable to the elements instead of being buried deep where they might have been harder to reach. But over the years she'd learned to handle those feelings, and cooking helped. It calmed her and conjured up happy memories of those days in her grandmother's kitchen when they'd stirred and sifted and she'd been bathed in a warm conviction that life, while unstable and frightening a lot of the time, was ultimately going to be okay.

Since Richard had walked out she'd cooked more than ever before, and once she'd baked something it was impossible not to sample it.

She started every day full of good intentions, and then gradually the stress mounted and those intentions evaporated. One upsetting phone call from Richard (and there had been far too many of those lately) was all it took to have her reaching for her mixing bowl. Word had spread, and now she often made cakes for special celebrations, and she'd even done a couple of weddings. That would all have been fine if she could only stop eating what she cooked.

Was that why Richard had left? Because of the extra inches around her middle?

The woman he'd left her for (her name was Avery, but Milly usually thought of her as *the woman* because it made it easier to cope with somehow) was a yoga instructor with perfectly toned abs and smooth long hair that never seemed to curl however humid the weather. She was twenty-five, more than two decades younger than Richard, and Milly wondered if he was trying to rewind time, as if being with someone that young might somehow hold back his own aging process. And in a way the whole thing was Milly's fault because she was the one who had suggested yoga when Richard had complained he had backache from spending too long sitting at his desk and in the car.

Now she wished she'd simply poured him a large gin.

Dispirited, she chose a pair of bold silver earrings that would hopefully draw attention away from her waistline and headed downstairs to the kitchen.

She made herself a cup of strong black coffee and took it out onto the deck.

At this time of day, the only sound came from the birds and the soft lapping of water against the shoreline.

A sense of calm wafted over her, and she felt the tension in her shoulders ease. Plenty of things in her life were difficult, but not living here. She loved it here. Who would have thought it?

When Richard had forced the sale of the family home, she'd felt bereft and also angry because the house was Zoe's one piece of stability in the earthquake of parental separation. Milly had felt like a failure for not being able to afford to keep the house. It was another loss for both of them. Another major change in which Milly had been given no choice.

It was her mother who had suggested they move into the boat-house, and Milly had known from the day they moved in that it was the right decision.

In their old house, memories had lurked in every corner, many of them painful. She'd walk into the kitchen and be reminded of the moment Richard had told her about the affair. In the small garden she'd be hijacked by a memory of seeing him taking phone calls from his lover while trying to hide behind the hedge. Instead of being a safe haven, the house felt like a stage where a dramatic ending had played out.

But the boathouse was a haven, and it was *hers*. Richard had no presence here. He'd never set foot inside the place, and on the rare occasion he remembered to come and pick up Zoe, Milly was careful not to invite him in.

This was her space, and she protected it fiercely. She'd learned over the past few months how important it was to have something that was hers and not a leftover of what had been theirs.

She leaned on the balcony rail and stared across the water.

She rarely had a chance to savor the view from her new home because she was always in a rush to make breakfast and get ready for the day, but with Zoe staying at her mother's, she had a little time, and she allowed herself a rare moment of indulgence.

The surface of the lake was still, the reflection of the trees that surrounded it stretching across the water. Behind were the fells that she loved so much, their contours accentuated by the bright morning sunlight.

Her eyes were gritty from lack of sleep, and she took a sip of coffee.

It took a moment, and a prickle of instinct, to tell her that she wasn't alone.

She turned and saw Nicole curled up asleep on the porch swing that had been a housewarming gift from her mother.

Her face was scrubbed clean of makeup, her hair loose around her shoulders.

She looked young and vulnerable and not so far from the girl Milly had befriended on her first day at school.

Milly still remembered the intensity of that connection and the bond that had only deepened over time. The strength of their friendship had felt like a superpower, an invisible layer of protection from everything life might throw at them. They'd been invincible, and yet here they were behaving like two polite strangers.

How had they reached this point?

They'd both had hopes and dreams, and some of those had come true. Milly had gained the family and stability she'd wanted, and Nicole had achieved fame and success. But neither of them had expected things to turn out the way they had.

A divorced woman and a fugitive.

Was it possible to get back what they'd lost?

And how was she supposed to conceal the fact that Nicole was staying with her?

No matter how careful they were, eventually someone would discover she was here, and then what?

With a sigh, Milly went indoors to fetch a blanket for her friend.

4

Connie

"So who did she go on a date with? Is he good enough for her?"

"I don't know, and you're not to ask." Connie put a cup of coffee in front of her mother. "When she walks through that door, you're not to say a thing."

"Why not? I want to know. As her grandmother, I'm entitled to be worried about her."

"You think I'm not worried about her? I'm her mother. It's worse for me." Connie glanced at the door to check there was no sign of Zoe and dropped into the chair. She'd been awake half the night thinking about Milly, desperately hoping that this might be the start of a new phase for her daughter. The last eighteen months had been incredibly tough on everyone. Milly had been crushed by Richard's affair and flattened by the divorce, and Connie, witnessing her daughter's distress, had been crushed and flattened too. It was like going through it all over again, only this time it was worse because this was Milly, and she knew and understood every morsel of her pain. All she wanted was for her child to be happy again. Didn't every parent want that?

Every day she relived the moment Milly had burst into the house, sobbing. *He's left us. He's gone.* Seeing her kind, competent daughter reduced to a wounded, insecure husk of herself had been more painful than Connie could have anticipated.

And it took her back. It took her right back to when the same thing had happened to her.

She still remembered the feeling of helplessness.

Never again.

"Seeing her in pain is worse than being in pain myself. Do you have any idea how hard it is to watch your child suffer?"

Her mother raised an eyebrow. "I may have a small idea."

Connie flushed, mortified that only now was she truly understanding how her mother might have been affected by her own ups and downs over the years. "Was it like this for you when I went through it?" It seemed so long ago now, and the memory of all those raw feelings had softened and blurred with time.

"Yes. But you're a parent so you just have to get on with it. When your child suffers, you suffer too. It's part of the deal, but you don't show it. You want your child to know you have confidence in their ability to handle whatever comes their way. You raised Milly to be strong and capable, and she is."

"I know all that. And I know she can handle it. But I don't want her to have to, if that makes sense." Connie stood up and selected a couple of oranges from the bowl on the table. "I want to see her smile again. Really smile, not a forced don't-worry-about-me smile."

She sliced the oranges in half and reached for the juicer.

"I understand. But all we can do is offer support." Peggy paused. "And for the record, I still worry about you, so don't think that ever goes away."

"You worry about *me*? Why? I'm not the one whose life has been blown apart."

"No catastrophizing!" Her mother waggled a finger. "And I worry about you for the same reasons you worry about Milly. Because you're hurting. Also, I worry that you've put your own life on hold."

Connie stopped juicing oranges. "I haven't exactly—" She broke off. Had she put it on hold? Yes, in a way she had.

From the moment Richard had walked out, she'd stepped up to be there for her daughter. She'd made Milly and Zoe her priority. She'd offered childcare whenever it was needed, and she'd done her best to bolster Milly's confidence. She'd hidden her own distress behind a mask of calm confidence, but there had been nights when she'd fallen into her own bed exhausted by the stress of holding everything together for her daughter.

"I'm fine." Connie poured the juice into a glass. "And I'll be even better when Milly starts moving on with her life again. I just want to fix it, and I can't."

"No, you can't," Peggy said. "It's the hardest thing about being a parent. You can't fix everything. And you shouldn't. It isn't your job to fix things when they're adults. It's your job to support them while *they* fix things."

Connie knew the theory, but she wished she knew how to do that and not worry herself sick in the process.

She made herself a strong coffee. Zoe would be down any moment, and she needed to pull herself together, but after a bad night she was feeling particularly vulnerable. "I used to think of myself as a pretty relaxed mother. Competent. I ran a successful business and raised a child. Even when Milly was bullied by those awful girls in the year above her, I didn't lose as much sleep as I'm losing now. And she's an adult." She looked at her mother in despair. "How can this feel worse?"

"Because once they're adults you have no control. You have to let them make their own decisions and mistakes, and all you can do is watch and support. Also, when the same thing happened to you, you were too busy holding everything together to spend too much time worrying. You just got on with things."

Connie frowned. "I'm still busy."

"You spend your time supporting Milly and Zoe and helping out at Forest Nest. It's time to think about yourself, Connie. Do something that distracts you. Something that needs your full attention. Switch your phone off! You need to detach yourself from their problems for a while. Rediscover *you*. That way perhaps you won't spend your whole time worrying about Milly and Zoe. And I'll worry a little less about you."

Connie couldn't imagine switching her phone off. What if Milly or Zoe needed her in an emergency? "Is this a good time to say I'm sorry for all the worry I ever caused you?"

"All part of life." Her mother waved a hand dismissively. "And look at you. You came through it. You can't get rid of all the bumps. All you can do is hope for good people around you who will be there for you while you crawl over those bumps. And if you think you have it bad, you should put yourself in my position. I'm worried about you, my daughter *and* my granddaughter, so that makes my burden twice as heavy as yours and gives me the right to ask about her date."

Connie wondered how it was that her mother always managed to make her smile. "Maybe, but I still think we need to be careful when we ask her about last night."

"You have to be careful, but I get a pass because of my mature years." Peggy spooned sugar into her coffee. "My role is to interfere and give her the benefit of my many decades of wisdom. How did she meet him?"

"I don't know. I don't know anything about him. And we're not going to know unless she chooses to tell us. Should you be using that much sugar?"

"I'm eighty-two," her mother said. "I'll eat as much sugar as I like. And just because you've been kind enough to let me stay with you while they fix my roof doesn't give you the right to nag me."

"I like having you here. You're an easy guest, apart from your sugar habit. And your tendency to speak your mind. And talking of your roof, how is it coming along? Are they making progress?"

"We had all that rain last month so they think it will take another few weeks. I'm going over to take a look later."

Connie frowned. "You're worried they're not doing a good job?"

"They're doing a great job. No, in this hot weather they'll have their shirts off, and that's the closest to action a woman of my age gets. I don't want to miss it."

Connie laughed. "You do know you're not allowed to say that kind of thing anymore?"

"I can say what I like in my own home. And speaking of action, Milly probably met him through one of those dating apps. I've been reading about those. I wondered if I might try it myself. I'll ask Zoe to take a good photograph of me. I can pass for seventy-five on a good day with the light behind me."

"Why do you need a photograph, Nanna Peg?" Zoe appeared in the doorway yawning, her chestnut curls tangled from sleep and her eyes still bleary.

At that moment she looked so much like Milly at the same age that Connie felt her breath catch. It was the freckles and the blue eyes and also the ready smile. Milly had always been a smiler. She'd been gentle and good-natured and an all-around daddy's girl. Until her daddy had walked out. After that, part of her had closed off, and for a while Connie had been afraid that her daughter might be too wary of love to ever allow herself to fall for anyone, but then she'd met Richard.

Connie had liked Richard. Connie had *loved* Richard. Not anymore.

Every time she thought about him she wanted to break something.

"Nanna Peg doesn't need a photograph. She was joking." She opened the fridge. "What can I make you for breakfast, sweetheart? Eggs? Fruit and yogurt? I've squeezed you a fresh juice."

"Whatever happened to heaped bowls of sugary cereal or a big fat bacon sandwich?" Peggy took a sip of coffee. "The problem with your generation is that all the joy has been stripped out of life. No additives, no alcohol, no red meat—the list is endless, and you take it to extremes. A little of everything was my motto. And here I am at eighty-two in a hiking group."

"I'm thirteen," Zoe reminded her with a grin. "I don't drink alcohol."

"Ignore Nanna Peg," Connie advised. "Most people grow out of their rebellious phase in their teens, but your great-grandmother is getting worse with age. Your mum messaged to say she's on her way."

"Yes, she messaged me too." Zoe dropped her schoolbag by the door and sat down at the table. "Eggs would be great, thanks, Gramma."

"At least make them into pancakes," Nanna Peg said and Connie sighed as she put the glass of orange juice in front of Zoe. "Pancakes or omelet?"

Zoe wrestled with herself. "I love pancakes, but I don't want to get fat."

"Fat?" Peggy peered through her glasses. "You're skin and bone, and not surprising given the amount of energy you burn. Whoever said you were getting fat?"

"No one." Zoe flushed scarlet. "Pancakes, then. And I won't add much sugar. Sugar is on the banned list too, Nanna Peg, in case you didn't know. So how did the date go? Do we know?"

Connie sifted flour into a bowl and added eggs and milk. Where had that *fat* comment come from? Maybe it was just an age thing. She was growing up and changing. "The date? We do not know, and we are not going to ask."

"What your grandmother means is that *she* isn't going to ask. But I intend to," Peggy said, "but if in the meantime you find out anything, you're to text me. Anything. Do you hear me?"

Zoe saluted. "I hear you, Nanna Peg, but she won't tell me, you know she won't. She tries to protect me from everything. Like last Saturday when Dad was supposed to take me to my drama class. I heard Mum pleading with him on the phone, but when she came to tell me she pretended he had car problems. I suppose she thought that was less hurtful than telling me the truth—that Avery had booked a table for both of them and he was going for a romantic dinner."

"You heard that?" Connie was appalled, not only because Zoe had overheard but because Richard had been thoughtless enough to say it to Milly, who was already hurting. She'd felt angry toward him for a while, but now she wanted to kill him.

"Dad has a loud voice. Don't worry. I get it. He'd rather hang out with Avery than a thirteen-year-old. It's not exactly news. He made that clear when he moved out." Zoe gave an awkward shrug and took a sip of juice. "I'm not that interesting."

Was that what she was taking away from all this? That she wasn't interesting?

"Not true. You're one of the most interesting people I know." Connie beat the pancake mixture so vigorously that some of the mixture spattered the countertop. What she really wanted to do was wring Richard's neck for what he was doing to his family, but that wasn't an option. And it wasn't about her. She had to keep reminding herself of that. Her feelings weren't important here. Milly was adamant that they were never to say a bad word about Richard in front of Zoe, and although it pushed her self-control to the limits, Connie was trying hard to respect that request. "I'm sorry you heard that. It must be very difficult for you, honey. It's okay to feel upset or angry or any of the things you're probably feeling." Maybe she should take up boxing or jujitsu. Something that would allow her to punch something without getting arrested.

"It's worse for Mum than me. She's so hurt, although she pretends she's fine." Zoe paused with her hands around the glass. "I heard her crying a few nights ago. I almost went into her room, but it was late and she thought I was asleep, so I don't think she wanted me to know. Do you think I should have gone in?"

Connie stopped mixing. She ached at the thought of Milly lying alone in the dark crying and of Zoe hovering outside trying to work out what to do.

Her mother was right. She needed to try and detach instead of feeling every blow as if it was aimed at her personally.

Peggy cleared her throat. "I think you were right to leave her alone with her feelings on that occasion. Good decision."

"It didn't feel good. For a moment I really—" Zoe stopped herself in mid-sentence. "I'm worried about her, that's all. I just want her to be okay."

So that made three of them, Connie thought, returning her attention to the bowl in front of her. Grandmother, mother and child. It was funny how life's traumas rippled through generations, affecting all of them in different ways.

"Your mother is going to be fine," Peggy said finally. "She can handle anything that comes her way, and so can you. She will be happy again, trust me. These things just take a while. No one can be happy all the time, especially if they're not eating sugar, bacon or anything with additives. It's a wonder anyone manages to raise a smile these days."

Zoe giggled. "I love you, Nanna Peg."

"Of course you do. I'm a very lovable person. Full of sugar, of course, so you don't want too much of me. But I'm here for you, pet. And so is Gramma. You can talk to us about anything. One of the advantages of being my age is that there's not much I haven't seen in life. I think that mixture has taken enough punishment, Connie."

Connie flushed and spooned mixture onto the hot pan, watching as bubbles formed.

Zoe stood up and fetched maple syrup from the fridge. "I don't understand why Dad and Avery bother going out to dinner. Avery doesn't eat anything, and she doesn't let Dad eat either. Why pay all that money to gaze at each other over a lettuce leaf? Last time I stayed over, Avery's lunch was three almonds and a single slice of apple."

Peggy's eyes widened. "Goodness. Does she eat a large breakfast?"

"She doesn't eat breakfast. She's following all those rules you disapprove of, Nanna Peg. She won't touch meat, and she's obsessed with not consuming anything that has additives. She insisted on seeing a full ingredient list last time we went for a pizza. In the end all she ordered was a salad with no dressing."

Connie flipped the pancakes.

Was that where the sudden concern about her weight had come from? Was it in response to something Avery had said? Or was it that Zoe was being influenced by watching her?

"I can't imagine your dad not eating meat." Connie slid a couple of pancakes onto a plate and put them in front of Zoe. "No additives in this, and the eggs are organic from our own hens, so enjoy."

"Dad is trying, but he has lapses. Never in front of her, though. He's vegetarian now, and he has given up alcohol, but when he drove me home we stopped for a burger. We ate it standing outside so that the car didn't smell." Zoe looked guilty. "He made me promise not to tell anyone, and I just told you."

"We're not *anyone*," Peggy said. "And there is nothing you can't say to us."

Connie felt a flicker of concern. Were there things that Zoe was keeping from them? Things her father had made her promise not to say? Her anger with Richard was growing by the minute. "Is it all right when you stay over, honey? Do you like it?"

Richard had moved in with Avery, who lived in a glass-fronted apartment in a city about an hour away. Every few weeks he picked up Zoe and she spent the weekend with them. Connie knew how hard Milly found those weekends.

"It's okay." Zoe shrugged. "It feels a bit weird. I worry about Mum. And I miss the lake and the mountains when I'm there. I don't think I'm a city person. All that noise and traffic and so many people all squashed in one place. It's all concrete. Even the trees look as if they'd rather be somewhere else. And Avery has a lot of rules that I keep forgetting." She poured maple syrup onto her pancakes. "But I don't want to hurt Dad's feelings, and sometimes you have to do things you don't really want to do, don't you?"

"Yes," Connie said. "You do."

Zoe's maturity humbled her. Connie sometimes thought her granddaughter was the most grown-up of all of them, but really shouldn't Zoe just be hanging out with her friends and not worrying about the adults in her life?

She made a few more pancakes and put them in the middle of the table.

"How are rehearsals for the play going?" It would probably be better for her blood pressure to move the subject away from Richard and the saintly Avery. "Are you having fun?"

Zoe swallowed her bite of pancake. "Yeah, it's fine."

That wasn't the reaction Connie had expected.

Zoe had wanted to be an actor from the moment she understood that such a thing existed. For years Connie had been a willing audience as Zoe had staged plays in the living room, clapping madly when her granddaughter had emerged from behind the curtains to take a bow.

They'd wondered if it might be a phase, but then Zoe had joined the drama club, and since then it was almost all she thought about.

Connie remembered how excited Zoe was when she'd auditioned and got the part in *A Midsummer Night's Dream*. "How are you finding learning your lines?"

"Okay." Zoe shrugged. "We're doing the play in English at school, so I'm reading it all the time."

"You're not looking like someone who is having fun." Peggy finished her coffee. "Tell us."

"It's nothing." Zoe kept her eyes on her plate, which told Connie that whatever it was, it definitely wasn't nothing.

"Are you struggling, honey? I thought Hermia was exactly the part you wanted."

Zoe poked at her pancake with her fork. "It's exactly the part Cally wanted too. We've kind of had a falling-out. I wish I hadn't auditioned now."

Cally and Zoe were as close as Milly and Nicole had been, so Connie understood how upsetting that would be.

"Didn't Cally get a part?"

"She's Hippolyta, but she doesn't get to say very much. So now she hates me." Zoe said it lightly, but there was a thickening in her voice that made Connie want to hug her.

"I'm sure she doesn't hate you, darling."

"Well, it feels that way." Zoe finished her pancake. "Anyway, whatever. Don't mention it to Mum, will you? She has enough to think about. I'll figure it out."

"Everything you say to us stays with us," Peggy said briskly. "Including everything you tell us about your mother's date."

They heard the sound of the front door opening, and all froze.

"That's her now." Connie made a fresh cup of coffee and raised her voice. "We're in the kitchen, Milly."

Milly appeared in the doorway, and Connie felt a rush of love closely followed by concern.

She looked so tired. As if she hadn't slept at all.

"You look tired," said Peggy, who didn't believe in holding back. "I hope that means you had fun last night. If you'd like to share, we're here to listen."

Milly gave her daughter a hug before sitting down at the table. "Nothing to tell. Thank you for having Zoe at such short notice."

"You don't have to thank me for having my own granddaughter to stay," Connie said. "It's a treat for me."

"And for me," Peggy added. "I learn a lot from her. Last night she gave me a lesson on emojis. I messaged my hiking group this morning and added two flowers and a cupcake and received some very confused responses. I should have joined a younger group. The conversation would be more interesting. More about sex and less about varicose veins and hip replacements."

Peggy had always been an active part of the local community, but still Connie couldn't believe her eighty-two-year-old mother had joined a hiking group.

Milly smiled at Zoe. "Are you ready for school?"

"Almost." Zoe finished her breakfast and stood up. "Give me two minutes to brush my teeth and grab my stuff." She vanished from the room, and Connie put a mug of coffee in front of her daughter.

"Have you had breakfast?"

"No. I'm trying to be good."

What was good about starving yourself? Was that because of

Avery? Connie was acutely aware of how humiliated Milly felt that her husband had left her for a much younger woman.

"You can't head into a busy day with an empty stomach." Connie slid one of the pancakes onto a plate, added some fresh blueberries and put it in front of her daughter. "Eat."

"How was your evening?" Peggy caught Connie's glare. "What? At my age you can't blame me for wanting to hear about other people's sex lives."

"Talking of sex lives, I see poor Nicole has been hitting the headlines again." Connie made a desperate attempt to change the subject, and Milly paused with her fork halfway to her mouth.

"Nicole?"

"You didn't see it? The story is everywhere. She's been having an affair with that actor. Oh, what's he called? He played the young King Henry VIII in that movie where everyone seemed to be naked the whole time, at least the women were." Connie rubbed her forehead. "I'm terrible with actors' names."

"Justin," Peggy said. "His name is Justin."

"That's right! Justin Fisher."

Peggy helped herself to the last pancake. "I never liked him. He's too smooth, and his eyes are close together. I never trust a man whose eyes are close together. He looks shifty."

"He's won plenty of awards." Connie watched as her daughter toyed with the food on her plate. "He was described by one critic as *a national treasure*."

Peggy sprinkled sugar on the pancake. "Apparently Nicole has been treasuring him a bit too much, and his wife wasn't happy about it. The media was full of images of him holding hands with his wife saying they'd never been happier, although it was obviously a lie because the words didn't match the facial expressions. You would have thought an actor would have managed a more convincing performance."

"Poor Nicole." Connie felt a flash of sympathy. "She doesn't have a good track record with relationships."

"I blame her mother." Peggy finished the pancake. "She was a cold fish. She operated on my varicose veins, and there was more empathy in the scalpel. That kind of upbringing has to have an impact. And it can't be easy having no privacy. The girl can't get away from scrutiny. It's hard to have a proper relationship when everything you do happens in public."

Connie noticed that Milly still hadn't touched her food. "Have you talked to Nicole lately?"

"I—" Milly glanced at the clock on the wall and put her fork down. "Is that the time? I really need to go. Zoe!"

"I'm here." Zoe appeared in the doorway, and Milly almost knocked the chair over in her haste to leave the kitchen.

"Thanks again. See you later. I love you."

Connie glanced at the food on Milly's plate. "But you haven't eaten your—"

The front door slammed, and they heard the sound of the car pulling away.

Connie looked at her mother.

"Well, that was weird."

"It was weird. She changed when you mentioned Nicole. Did you notice that?"

"I only mentioned Nicole because you asked her about her date, and I was trying to change the subject."

"Judging from her reaction, I'd say it wasn't a good change of subject. Maybe it was sensitive for her, all those headlines about Nicole having an affair with a married man. Not that I believe headlines. They make everything up these days. It's all about clicks. And I'm sure she and Nicole are fine. Those two were inseparable as children."

"I know. But talking about friendships, how worried should we be about Zoe and Cally?"

"Friendship issues are part of life. They'll sort it out."

"I hope you're right." Connie sank onto the nearest chair. "Milly didn't eat breakfast. This is all Richard's fault. I want to hurt him. I never thought I'd say a thing like that out loud." Her voice shook. "I didn't know I could feel this way, but I do."

"If that woman he ran off with has made him turn vegetarian, he's probably already being punished, so I wouldn't worry too much." Peggy chuckled. "The thought of Richard having to choke down a chickpea burger or a tofu stir-fry cheers me up."

It didn't cheer Connie up. "How can he be so unkind to Milly? Telling her that he's choosing to go for a romantic dinner instead of taking his child to her drama class as planned?"

"He's a man-child, with no sense of responsibility."

"But it's as if he is *trying* to hurt her. And why? He's already left her. He doesn't need to keep making it worse. What has she ever done except be loyal to him? He never used to be like this. I don't understand what has happened to him. It's almost as if he wants her to hate him." She realized that her hands were shaking. "I'm scared of seeing him face-to-face because at the moment I truly want to kill him."

Peggy stood up and patted her shoulder before clearing the table. "I know, and I understand why you would feel that way, but don't kill him. You have your whole life ahead of you. If anyone is going to do it, I will."

"You?" Picturing her mother as a murderer took some of the heat out of Connie's emotions. "How? You're going to stab him with your knitting needle? Impale him with your walking pole?"

"Maybe. I've always been clumsy, as you know. Or maybe it will be a car accident. My driving isn't as good as it was, so maybe I might not see him if he happens to be crossing the road." Peggy loaded the breakfast dishes into the dishwasher. "I haven't decided, and when I do decide I won't be sharing it with you, or that will make you an accomplice, and Milly and Zoe need you. I might get away with it. I'll plead diminished capacity. If they saw me trying to remember where I parked my car in the supermarket they wouldn't have any trouble believing it. On a bad day I don't even have to fake confusion. And anyway, what can they do to me? Send me to prison for life? At my age I'll croak on them before they've turned the key in the door."

Connie gave a hysterical laugh. "I never thought we'd be sitting around plotting a murder."

"I know. It's all rather exciting. Is it too late to consider a career change, do you think? Maybe I could recruit my hiking group." Peggy closed the dishwasher. "We could call ourselves the Wrinkled Assassins. Our calling card could be a set of false teeth."

But this time Connie was too upset to laugh. She knew she wasn't handling this situation well, and she also knew she had to do better, for Milly's sake but also for her own. She reached for her phone.

"I can't carry on like this."

Peggy looked alarmed. "You're not planning to confront Richard, are you? We mustn't alert him to our animosity. It might be a good idea to make sure we both have strong alibis."

"I'm not planning murder. I'm trying to work out the best way to handle this situation. I'm searching the internet for tips on how to stop worrying about your adult child."

"Good luck with that." Her mother sat down next to her, and this time her expression was serious. "You've been a wonderful mother to Milly, particularly over the past eighteen months, but it's time to put other things in your life. When did you last go to choir practice?"

Connie looked at her. "The week before Richard walked out. I couldn't commit to rehearsals in case I was needed to look after Zoe."

"Your book club?"

"I haven't been reading much, so there wasn't any point in going. Also I didn't really want people asking me about Milly." And although the group had carried on emailing her in the beginning and sending her the book choices, those emails had tailed off.

She squirmed a little as she faced the truth. Her mother was right. In her efforts to support Milly, she had stopped doing things that she used to enjoy.

She'd let friendships dwindle because everyone else's children seemed to be soaring through life with no problems and she'd found the conversations difficult. And it wasn't that she wished problems on other people—far from it—but somehow hearing how smoothly everything was going for someone else's child made her ache even more for her own.

Peggy was watching her. "You need to put something in your life that doesn't have anything to do with Milly and Zoe. Something that's just for you."

Connie looked at her blankly. She was too tired and stressed to even think about herself. "What?"

"I don't know. Yoga?"

"Yoga? Is that a joke?"

"Bad suggestion. I'd forgotten about Avery, although you could always take her class and launch an attack while she is in downward dog. Very difficult to defend yourself in that position. It really doesn't matter what you do. Learn to pole dance. Take up skydiving. Anything. I'm not supposed to fix your problems, remember?" Peggy patted her hand. "I'm supposed to support you while you fix them, and that's what I'm doing."

Maybe she should take up yoga, Connie thought, then she could show up at one of Avery's classes and tell her exactly what she thought of her.

5

Milly

Zoe settled into the passenger seat and looked at her expectantly. "How was the date? Was it fun? Did you like him? Tell me everything."

Milly felt a stab of guilt. "Zoe—"

"I'm okay with it, honestly. You deserve to be happy. Can I meet him?" She broke off, uncertain. "If you don't want to talk about it, I get it."

How had she ever got herself in this tangled mess? She tried never to tell lies, and she hadn't lied. She just hadn't told them what she was doing, and when they'd made assumptions she hadn't corrected them because she knew that if she'd corrected them, then they would have wanted to know the truth, and that would have meant violating her promise to Nicole.

Also she didn't want to talk about Nicole. She'd told no one that her friend had ghosted her. It had been too painful, so she'd kept that to herself. It felt like another failure on her part. She imagined people looking at her and thinking *First her husband, and then her best friend.*

It was at times like this she wished she wasn't so close to her family. Normally she was grateful for it, but it made things complicated when you had something to hide.

"Zoe, there's something I need to tell you, and I need to tell you before you get home tonight."

"What? Is he at the boathouse? Are you about to tell me that your date went so well he's moving in?"

"No! Why would you—" Milly took a deep breath. "It wasn't a date, Zoe. I never said it was a date."

"But Gramma and Nanna Peg said—"

"I know what they said. When I told them I needed you to stay with them for the night, they jumped to conclusions, and I didn't correct them."

"Why not?"

"Because they needed to think something, and I couldn't tell them the truth. I made a promise to someone." And now she was about to break that promise, but she couldn't see any other way. Zoe lived in the boathouse. What was Milly supposed to do? Arrange for her daughter to stay with her grandmother for the duration of Nicole's visit however long that turned out to be? That wasn't going to happen. After all the upheaval Zoe had endured in the past eighteen months, Milly was determined to minimize any change in her life. No, Zoe was staying in her own home. Sleeping in her own room.

All the same she felt uncomfortable because she prided herself on being one hundred percent discreet and dependable as a friend, and that wasn't going to change just because Nicole's own behavior had fallen short. If someone told her a secret, she guarded it fiercely. And Nicole's presence was a secret.

She wished she'd thought to discuss this part with Nicole so at least she was warned.

"I'm going to tell you something, and you can't repeat it to anyone. Not to Dad, not to your friends at school—especially not your friends at school. I'm trusting you with this because I know you won't gossip."

Did she know that? Zoe was thirteen and had a close group of friends. Granted, they spent far more time outdoors on their bikes than they did curled up indoors painting their nails, but they were still teenagers, and they still giggled and talked. Milly didn't know what they talked about, but remembering herself at the same age she was pretty sure there weren't many topics that would be out of bounds. Zoe probably talked about things she wouldn't discuss with her mother, which was exactly how it should be, of course. But gossip? The sharing of secrets? That was different. Having Nicole Raven staying in your house would be enough to make the average teenager burst with excitement, but hopefully Zoe would be able to contain herself.

Milly drove out of the village and eased into the traffic on the main road.

Zoe was virtually vibrating with expectation. "What?"

"Do you promise not to say anything?"

"I promise! Am I supposed to swear a blood oath or something? This is pretty intense. What's going on?"

"Last night I had to go out, that's true, but I wasn't on a date."

"I know! You just said that, but where were you, then? Mum, you're killing me. Just say it!"

But once she said it she wouldn't be able to unsay it. She wished she'd never been put in this position. "Nicole called me a couple of days ago."

"Nicole?" There was a pause as Zoe absorbed that. "You mean *our* Nicole? Aunt Nicole?"

"Yes, our Nicole." She felt a pang of loss because there had been a time when she had indeed thought of her friend that way. When they were young she'd thought of Nicole as family. *Sister.* She'd had such a shiny view of their friendship. "She called and asked me for help. She's in some trouble."

"Is this anything to do with that story a few days ago? The one with Justin Fisher pulling stupid faces next to his wife? Awkward. You could tell he *so* didn't want to be there. She had her hand locked around his wrist, like literally trapping him in place so he couldn't run."

It probably shouldn't have surprised her that her daughter knew more about it than she did, but what did surprise her was that Zoe hadn't mentioned it.

"You've seen those stories?"

"Everyone has seen those stories."

"You didn't mention it."

"Because you hate that stuff. You always have."

That was true. "I'm guessing it's linked. She's being hounded by the press. She asked for my help, and I agreed. I picked her up from the station last night. We got in late and both went straight to sleep. We haven't talked about it properly yet." That conversation was still to come, and she wasn't looking forward to it. Even though Nicole had hinted that there was more to the story than the headlines suggested, technically she was Avery in this situation. Milly wasn't confident she'd be able to offer nonjudgmental support. She wanted to be worldly and broad-minded, but she wasn't feeling either of those things. She was feeling disillusioned and disappointed, and she didn't understand why people couldn't exercise more self-restraint. There were plenty of men in the world, plenty of single men, so why did Avery have to target Richard?

She realized that Avery and Nicole had somehow merged together in her mind. She needed to separate them.

"You're saying Aunt Nicole is staying in our house?" Zoe's voice was an excited squeak. "Like hiding?"

"Yes, I suppose you could say she is hiding." Milly felt a sudden flash of panic. What if someone knocked on her door before she got home? It was unlikely, but not impossible.

Hopefully Nicole would have the sense not to open the door.

"This is amazing!" Zoe virtually bounced on her seat. "Aunt Nicole in my house. Unbelievable."

It was a good thing that one of them was excited.

"You've known her since you were a baby, and we've stayed with her before."

"I know we have, and that was amazing too, but this is different. Nicole Raven is *in my house*! It's a very big deal." Zoe was transformed by the news. There was no slump in her shoulders, and her face was one big smile. "Can she share my room?"

"I've made up the sofa in the study for now."

"I can't believe she's staying with us. How long for?"

"I don't know." *Forever.* No, surely Nicole had been kidding about that. On the other hand if her presence was going to make Zoe this happy, then as far as Milly was concerned Nicole could move in for good. "You can't say anything to anyone."

"I won't. But why is she hiding? She shouldn't be the one hiding. He should be hiding. He's so fake. And weak." Zoe injected the last word with all the disdain of her thirteen years. "Also a cheat. Nicole can do so much better."

Milly hadn't expected that reaction. She hadn't expected her daughter to have an opinion on the subject at all. She still thought of her as a child most of the time. "The news reports are calling her a *home-wrecker.*"

"Ugh," Zoe said disparagingly. "They always blame the woman. Have you noticed that? Cally says it's a sign the patriarchy is alive and well. Aunt Nicole is single," she said. "She didn't cheat, lie or break promises did she? *He's* the one who is married. He made a choice, and now he's been caught out he's like making out he's some sort of victim because he's too much of a coward to own his decision."

This conversation wasn't going the way Milly had expected it to. "You've talked about it with your friends?"

"Aunt Nicole is our favorite actor. She's Amara, Mum. She saved the world, remember? You saw the movie."

One minute they were grown-up and talking about the patriarchy and the next they were children talking about a character as if they were real.

"Right. Well, Nicole/Amara is staying with us, and we can't tell anyone. I probably should have checked you were okay with it before agreeing, but it all happened quickly, and she was desperate, and I felt I should offer support." And she still didn't know if that made her a good friend or a total pushover.

"Of course you had to help. She's your closest friend."

64

And for Zoe that was all it took. It seemed simple to her, just as it would have seemed simple to Milly at the same age. You helped your closest friend. You dropped everything for your closest friend. Sisterhood was real.

Until it wasn't.

"So you won't mind her being there?"

"Mind? Are you kidding?" Zoe grinned. "I mean, she's like the biggest actor in the world. So hot right now. I really liked her as that archaeologist in the dinosaur movie, but Amara was her best part. I have seen that movie at least nine times. She doesn't take any crap from anyone."

"Language."

"Sorry, but it's true. She's so strong. She meets every obstacle head-on."

Milly wished she was more like Amara. If she was, she'd talk to Richard face-to-face about his bad behavior instead of calling when she knew he wasn't going to answer his phone and leaving an insipid message.

Although, he did the same to her. He'd left a message on her phone an hour ago telling her he wasn't going to be able to have Zoe to stay at the weekend after all.

As usual he'd left her to break the news to his daughter. She was expected to reframe the message in a way that was more palatable. But now wasn't the moment. She was too upset with him to keep her tone neutral.

This was one of those times when she missed her old friendship with Nicole. She could have vented and maybe laughed, but now there was no chance of that.

She forced her mind back to the current problem. "I'm glad you're excited, but keep it to yourself."

"Got it. It's a secret. But you're going to have to tell Gramma and Nanna Peg, otherwise they will keep asking about your date. Also they're always popping into the boathouse on their way past, so unless Nicole is going to be hiding under the bed the whole time they're going to find her."

She wasn't wrong about that.

"I am going to tell them, but I wanted to discuss it with Nicole first."

Zoe grabbed her schoolbag from the floor of the car. "And how exactly are you going to hide her? Is she going to wear a disguise or something?"

"I haven't figured that part out yet. For the moment she is staying indoors, and hopefully that will be enough." Milly pulled up outside the school. Her head was throbbing. "Have a good day. I'll be back here at four to pick you up."

"Five. I have an extra drama session because the play is coming up."

"Five it is." Was it her imagination, or did Zoe seem less enthusiastic about that than she should have been? "How's that going?"

"Great." Zoe smiled brightly. "I'll see you later, unless you want to send Nicole, and if she could come dressed as Amara, that would be even better. At least it would make me popular."

"She's keeping a low profile, so she won't be coming dressed as Amara. Oh, there's Cally—" Milly spotted Zoe's best friend heading toward school. She gave a little beep of her horn, and Cally glanced briefly at the car but then carried on walking. "She didn't see us. If you sprint, you can catch her."

"Sure. See you later." Zoe opened the car door and headed toward school, but she didn't sprint or yell for Cally to wait.

Milly watched her go and only then did Zoe's words penetrate her busy brain.

At least it would make me popular.

What did she mean by that? To the best of her knowledge Zoe had never had any trouble making friends, but her best friend had always been Cally. They had the same special bond that Milly and Nicole had once had. *As close as blades of grass*, as her mother used to say.

So why the comment about being popular? Was she being flippant, or did it mean something?

Exhausted at the thought that she now had something else to worry about, she drove home, thinking instead of what her daughter had said about Nicole.

She didn't cheat, lie or break promises did she? He's the one who is married.

The same could be said of Richard, but Milly had directed most of her anger toward Avery. She'd been angry and upset that Avery had chosen to have an affair with a married man when she could have picked anyone. But Richard could have chosen not to, couldn't he?

He could have chosen Milly. But he'd chosen Avery.

Milly's eyes stung. She hated feeling this way. Richard was getting on with his life, and she was still stuck in the same place, her confidence stripped away.

That was why she preferred to blame Avery. It was easier to handle emotionally than acknowledging that Richard had made a choice not to be with her.

But he had made that choice, and it was time he took responsibility for it. And it was time he took responsibility for his daughter.

She pulled over and dialed his number. It went straight to voice mail, which was a relief, and she almost left her usual civilized polite response acknowledging that she'd received his message and would pass it on, but then she stopped herself. *Be more Amara.*

"You know what, Richard?" Her voice was strong and clear. "If you can't keep your promises to your daughter, then don't make them in the first place. Every time you don't show up, you're telling her she's not important, that she doesn't matter, and I'm damned if you're going to make her feel as if she doesn't matter. So don't do it. Just don't."

She was shaking as she ended the call, but she also felt vaguely satisfied. Okay, so she hadn't actually said the words to his face, but at least she'd made it clear that his behavior was unacceptable. It was a start.

Maybe she wouldn't ask for a refund on her assertiveness course after all.

Feeling a little more in control than usual, she headed back to Forest Nest and parked outside the building that housed the reception area for the resort and their offices.

"Hi, Milly!" Anna was working behind the reception desk. "Everyone is already in the meeting. There's a coffee waiting for you."

"Thanks, Anna. Any problems?"

"Not so far. There was a leak in the bathroom in Aspen Lodge, but the new guests aren't due to arrive until five, and Joel thinks he will have it sorted by then. He sent his regrets. He's prioritizing plumbing over the meeting. He says he needs to talk to you later about doing some maintenance on the deck."

"No problem. I'll find him when we're done here. Thanks, Anna." She walked through to the private staff offices that were behind the desk.

The buzz of conversation eased as she walked into the room. "Hi, everyone. I know you're all busy, so let's make this quick." She sat down, took a sip of coffee and glanced at her team. Most of them had worked at Forest Nest for years, first for her mother and now for her. The people here felt more like family than colleagues. "Sofia? Why don't you start?"

Sofia was head of Guest Relations. She made it her business to know as much as she possibly could about each person checking in so that they could deliver a bespoke service.

"The guests in Hazel, Blackthorn, Elder, Hawthorn and Aspen have all checked out this morning, and those cabins are booked out next week so we have a busy turnaround day. Mark and Philip Tyrell are in Hazel, and this is their honeymoon, so we need to add a bottle of fizz to their welcome pack, Lorna."

"Got it." Lorna was head of Housekeeping and prided herself in keeping the mud and all evidence of the lake and forest outside the cabins.

"Blackthorn Lodge is booked out to a young couple from Australia who have visited before," Sofia said. "They'd like mountain bikes for the whole week. Geoff?"

"Already waiting for them outside the lodge."

"He's six foot three—"

"I know. It's in the notes. We didn't have the right bike, so I had to do a fast negotiation with my opposite number at a certain hotel we will not name, but it's all sorted."

Not for the first time Milly was grateful for the excellent relationship they maintained with all the local businesses. It was something her mother had started, and Milly had been careful to continue that approach.

This area was blessed with more than its fair share of upmarket hotels, which meant they couldn't afford to let their standards drop even for a moment.

Milly was confident that what they provided was every bit as luxurious as the five-star hotels close by, but with more flexibility and a personal touch. They kept meticulous records on every guest and offered a degree of privacy that was rare these days. The cabins had views across the lake and forest, and there was a wildness to the surroundings that guests found restorative.

"Elder is booked by a family who are new to us. It's a seventieth-birthday celebration, so we have three generations in that lodge . . ." Sofia carried on, running them quickly through the names and details of the new arrivals so that everyone had all the necessary details.

Milly checked her notes. "Brendan Scott has booked Beech for the whole summer to finish writing his novel, so we just need to get in there at some point this week and make sure the place is clean for him." There was silence around the table, and she glanced up. "What? Did I miss something?" She saw Sofia glance at Lorna, but Lorna kept her eyes down.

Trouble, Milly thought, but decided it was probably best dealt with privately.

"Leo is going to start opening the coffee shop at seven from tomorrow, and he'll be serving the usual cakes and light lunches, with help from Tilly, who started two weeks ago and is doing brilliantly." Maybe she should volunteer to help out. A commercial kitchen, even a small one, might cure her of her urge to bake in her own home. "Lorna, we're going to start including some of their homemade brownies in the welcome packs."

"The woman staying in Aspen is gluten-free," Sofia said, and Lorna made a note.

"Tilly makes a perfect gluten-free cupcake, so I'll substitute with that."

Geoff smiled at her across the table. "How do you know it's perfect? You've already tried it?"

"I've tried everything we offer to the guests," Lorna said. "I ordered the cupcakes for my birthday along with a massive bunch of flowers."

Sofia raised her eyebrows. "You ordered your own cake and flowers?"

"Yes, because I knew that if I waited for Duncan to do it, then it wouldn't happen. Romantic gestures aren't really his thing."

Duncan was Lorna's long-term boyfriend, although she'd recently confided to Milly that she wasn't sure if he was the one or not. *How do you know if you want to marry someone or not? It seems a big step.*

Milly, who had been questioning everything about her relationship since Richard had cheated on her and then walked out, had no advice to impart. In the end she'd suggested Lorna follow her heart, and she'd tried not to think about the fact that she'd done exactly that and look where it had got her.

Conscious that she'd left Nicole on her own for far too long, Milly tried to move the meeting along. "I'm replenishing the reading nook this week, and remember that Leo and Tilly can also do packed lunches, so if any of the guests are planning a long hike and need that, they can order with him the night before and pick it up after seven. And if they need any equipment, they can talk to Geoff. Okay. We're done. Onward, team."

Everyone stood up, and Milly reached out a hand to Lorna. "Can I have a minute, Lorna?"

She waited for the others to leave the room and then sat down again.

"Problems?"

"It's nothing. I can handle it. You've got enough going on, Milly."

That was true, but she'd have even more to handle if she lost Lorna to one of the local hotels, which was always her nightmare scenario. Good staff were in high demand.

"What are you handling? Or should I ask *who*?"

Lorna looked at her for a moment, torn. "Brendan Scott," she said finally. "I knocked on his door this morning to check when would be convenient to change bedding and towels and clean the place and there was no answer, so I assumed he wasn't in, and I opened the door."

Milly sensed that whatever was coming wasn't going to be good. "And?"

"Turned out he was in, but he hadn't heard me knock. He said he was writing and he never wants to be disturbed when he's writing. His exact words were 'I checked in to this place precisely so that I wouldn't be disturbed, so why are you disturbing me?' He looked furious. Like he was going to commit one of those murders he writes about." Lorna shuddered. "I'm sorry, Milly. I know he's famous and important and he pays a lot of money to book that cabin for the whole summer. I hope he doesn't complain."

Milly wondered why people couldn't just be kind and polite to each other. It would make life so much easier. She'd never been rude to anyone in her life, not even the horrible woman at the doctor's who had told her that she should be grateful to be given an appointment at all, even though it was in a month's time and Zoe's leg was clearly infected. She always tried to be civil, not because she was some sort of saint but because having worked in a service industry all her life, she knew how hard it was and how people were usually doing their best, and yelling at them just made it even less likely that they'd help you.

But yell people did, and she knew what it was like to be on the receiving end.

"You have nothing to be sorry for. If there any apologies owing around here, it sounds as if they should be coming from him." But she had no expectations of that happening. Brendan Scott was a repeat guest, and a long-stay guest at that, which was valuable to them. She couldn't afford to lose his business, so it was a delicate situation. "When does he want us to clean the cabin?"

"I don't know. He flustered me so much I just wanted to get out of there." Lorna gathered up the empty mugs from the table. "I'll go back later and ask, but I need to make sure my last will and testament is up to date first, because I swear he looked as if he was going to kill me. He's a moody monster."

That decided it. "Don't go back. I'll handle it."

"You? But you can't—"

"Yes, I can. This isn't the first time he has stayed here. I've dealt with him before." And she remembered that the last time he'd stayed with them, a few years before, Richard had asked him to sign a book and had stammered with gratitude when Brendan Scott had signed with a flourish and handed him a copy of his next book as a gift.

Richard had been starstruck. *He's a superstar, Milly.*

Milly already had one superstar staying at Forest Nest. She didn't have the energy for another one, and she didn't think success should excuse you from displaying good manners.

"I'll take charge of the housekeeping for that cabin for the rest of his stay. Strike it from your list."

"Are you sure?" Lorna breathed out. "I feel as if I should argue with you, but honestly it would be a relief."

"I'm sure." Not that she was looking forward to the conversation, but she valued Lorna too much to delegate it. "Anything else on your mind?"

"No. That's it."

"Great. You're doing a fantastic job, Lorna." *Please don't leave.*

Lorna left the room with her head held high, and Milly followed her out of the building.

The sun warmed her face, peeping through the trees that shaded the reception building and the offices, and for a moment she pushed the problem of Brendan Scott and his black moods to the back of her mind. She'd work out the best way to deal with him later.

Instead of getting back into her car, she took a shortcut through the trees to the coffee shop where guests often gathered first thing in the morning.

It occupied a prime position overlooking the lake, and already a couple with their two children were sitting outside on the deck sipping cappuccinos and milkshakes in the sunshine.

She knew it was their first time here. They were staying in Cherry Lodge and would be checking out in the morning. Which made this their last day. Her mother had always insisted that guests were treated like friends, and Milly had continued that tradition. She was responsible for her mother's legacy, and she took that responsibility seriously. "Everything okay here? How has your week been?"

"Perfect, thanks, Milly. Bliss in fact. We've already booked for next year. And now we're killing time until horse riding at eleven." The man smiled at his daughter. "Highlight of the week."

"Horse riding?" She took a minute with them, chatting to the children and mentally filing away information that the team could use to enhance their next visit.

Then she walked into the café to talk to Leo.

"Hey, Milly." He was adding marshmallows to the most indulgent hot chocolate she'd ever seen. "Can I get you something?"

Would Nicole be hungry? What did she eat? Probably not carbs.

"Nothing, thanks, Leo. Just wanted to say hi and check everything was okay." She scanned the blackboard. "Today's specials look good."

"The roasted veg and mozzarella ciabatta is Tilly's creation, and it's a winner. Come back later and sample it, if you like." He put the hot chocolate on a tray along with a cappuccino.

"I might do that." It would be nice to bring Nicole here and sit on the deck so she could enjoy the view, but she knew she couldn't

73

risk that. It would be safer, much safer, to make her food at home. "Any problems?"

"Apart from me trying to resist Tilly's double chocolate cookie? No, all good."

Satisfied that everything seemed to be running smoothly, she took the path that led from the café to the lake and then followed it around the water and past the sign that said *Private—nesting birds*.

Nesting birds and fugitive actors, she thought as she carried on walking.

She was proud of this place, and the part she played in keeping it running. Her grandparents had built it, her mother had expanded the business, and Milly had added all the extra luxury touches from the waterside café that buzzed with activity all day to the tubs that overflowed with colorful blooms on every terrace and deck. She'd planted pots of fresh herbs for each cabin and added locally sourced food to the welcome baskets. She'd built a sauna and a games room, which had proved a hit in wet weather.

The boathouse was tucked into an inlet in the lake, hidden behind the trees, visible only at the last minute.

There was no sign of Nicole, but she could hear the shower running, so she headed for the kitchen and selected four of the eggs her mother had given her when she'd dropped Zoe off the day before.

She cracked them one by one into a large bowl and whisked them with a fork until the mixture lost its streaks and turned golden.

Then she took a pair of scissors and snipped a thick bunch of chives from one of the herb pots she kept on her windowsill. She chopped them finely, sprinkled them over the mixture and then turned on the heat under the pan.

She waited until it was exactly the right temperature and then poured in the eggs, letting them cook for a moment before coaxing the sides inward, tilting the pan so that it cooked evenly. When it was starting to set she crumbled on some soft goat cheese, added a few young spinach leaves and then folded it in half, allowing the heat to slowly melt the cheese and wilt the spinach.

"Hi." Nicole wandered into the kitchen, her hair still damp from the shower. She was wearing a pair of cutoff shorts and a T-shirt, and her face glowed pink from the heat of the shower.

She poured herself a glass of water and drank the whole thing.

Milly watched her for a moment, wondering what it must be like to be that beautiful.

If she looked like Nicole, maybe Richard wouldn't have left.

She turned the heat off under the pan. She had to stop thinking like that. It wasn't helpful or healthy.

"I made breakfast. Sorry it's so late. I had a meeting. We'll eat this out on the deck. There's no one around." Milly divided the omelet and slid each half onto a fresh plate. Then she sprinkled the top with finely chopped parsley and handed one of the plates to Nicole, who lifted it to her nose and sighed.

"It smells incredible, but I don't normally eat breakfast."

Tiger appeared in the kitchen, alerted by the smell of cooking.

"You had a long journey, and you didn't eat last night. I don't want to have to take you to the emergency department because you've fainted. The eggs are fresh and organic, so is the cheese, which comes from the goats down the road. And don't tell me you're not hungry because that isn't possible."

"I'm hungry, but I'm always hungry. It's part of the job." But Nicole lifted the plate again and breathed deeply. "Okay. Let's do this. I don't suppose one plate of eggs is going to do much harm. And my acting days may be over anyway." She said it lightly, an almost throwaway comment, but Milly knew Nicole. Whatever gulf there might be between them, she knew her. And she knew the comment wasn't made lightly.

"That's the way you feel?" Milly handed her a fork. "You love acting."

"Maybe. But I don't love all the things that go with it. And things are complicated at the moment." She paused, and Milly had the feeling that she was going to confess something momentous, but then she shook her head. "I'll figure it out."

Figure what out?

In the old days they'd had no secrets from each other, but that was then and this was now.

And how complicated could Nicole's life be, really?

Milly had a job to do, a child to care for, a life to live, and she had an A-list movie star hiding away in her home. It didn't get much more complicated than that.

Was Nicole afraid to do another movie because of the adverse publicity? No, surely not. She was used to that.

She wanted to ask what this was all about really, what Nicole was doing here, but she was conscious of all the jobs stacking up waiting for her attention. She didn't have time for a long conversation. Later, she thought. It would have to wait until later.

"What are you going to do all day? I'm worried you'll be bored."

"I never have time to myself. This is going to be a treat."

They settled themselves at the table by the water and Nicole sampled a mouthful of her food.

"Oh—" she said and closed her eyes, lost in a dream state as she chewed "—this might be the best thing I've ever tasted."

"It's just eggs and cheese."

Nicole shook her head and opened her eyes. "No, it's—" She sliced another piece with the edge of her fork. "I don't know what you've done here, but you should open a restaurant."

"When? In my spare time? Also, I'd just comfort-eat more than I do already, which wouldn't be good." But she was warmed by the compliment. And the biggest compliment was that Nicole had devoured every mouthful and was looking sadly at her empty plate as if she could have eaten exactly the same again had it been on offer.

"What did you do to that food? I feel a thousand times better. It's like magic."

"Good." Milly put her fork down. "I told Zoe about you. I couldn't see a way to avoid that."

"It's fine. I understand."

"She won't say anything." She hoped to goodness that was true and that Zoe wasn't currently huddled by the lockers with her friends telling them her new and shiny secret.

"You should tell Connie too. And Nanna Peg." Nicole put her fork down. "Unless they're shocked by my latest scandal, of course." She sounded flippant, as if she didn't care, but Milly knew she cared a lot. Nicole was desperate for approval. Desperate for a place in the sun.

"Nothing shocks them. And they love you, you know that."

"Do they? Even though I've been a useless friend lately?"

Was she expecting Milly to deny it? Because that wasn't happening.

"I haven't told them about that. They don't know we haven't been in touch." They would have been upset for her. Angry with Nicole. And Milly didn't want that. She'd kept hoping it would come right, and by the time she'd realized that wasn't going to happen, there didn't seem any point in telling them. "Are you sure you're comfortable with me telling them you're here? It would make things easier."

"Yes. Having me here is an imposition. I don't want to make this harder for you." Nicole sounded almost humble, and Milly stood up and cleared the plates.

"I have to get to work."

"Now? I thought we could talk. Like we used to."

Like we used to.

There was a wistful, apologetic note in Nicole's voice, and for a moment Milly felt a yearning so strong that she almost flung her arms around her friend just for the comfort.

She was tempted to blurt out how frustrated she was with Richard, how tough life was and how much she was struggling. That's what she would have done in the past, and somehow just sharing it with Nicole would have made it all the more bearable. The old Nicole would have hugged her tightly, shared her disgust at Richard's behavior and then somehow managed to say something that made her laugh, despite everything that was happening. She'd often thought that a really true friend beat comfort-eating, drugs or alcohol every time. But that was then and this was now.

Nicole hadn't been there for Milly at her lowest point. She hadn't cared enough, and Milly couldn't get past the hurt she felt about that. Her pride and her sense of self-preservation wouldn't let her get past it. The trust between them had been damaged. If Nicole didn't need her, then she'd make sure she didn't need Nicole. She'd offer sanctuary and whatever practical help was needed because she liked to think she was the sort of person who would help anyone who was desperate, but that was all she was offering.

And she needed to accept that in life people disappointed you and let you down. That was a fact. But she'd be fine. She'd been forced to manage without Nicole in the wings cheering her on, and she'd survived, hadn't she?

Maybe it hadn't been fun, but she'd survived. And she was proud of that.

"There will be plenty of time to talk later. I need to get to work. We're fully booked and short-staffed. I need to talk to Joel about maintenance, and then I'm rolling up my sleeves and cleaning a few cabins." Not a few. Just the one currently inhabited by Brendan Scott, but Nicole didn't need the detail. "You should probably stay here, out of sight. Is there anything you need before I go?"

"A new identity? A do-over of my whole life?" Nicole gave a tired smile. "Just kidding. No, there's nothing I need. And I'll be fine. I'll have a quiet day. Thank you."

Milly thought of Nicole having an entire day to herself and felt a twinge of envy. She would have given a lot for a quiet day.

6

Nicole

The last thing she wanted was a quiet day.

Nicole watched as Milly hurried away from the boathouse. She wanted to stop her. She wanted to grab her and say *I'm so sorry for everything*, but she didn't recognize this version of Milly. The Milly she knew was open and friendly and held nothing back, but this Milly was reserved and contained as if she'd retreated somewhere that Nicole couldn't reach.

It was Nicole's fault, and she badly wanted to fix it. She'd never needed Milly's listening ear and wise advice more than she did now, but how could she expect her friend to give her the support she craved when Nicole hadn't done the same for her?

She didn't know how to make things right between them, and anyway Milly was now out of sight, her mind on her own challenges.

Her life had changed irrevocably, and there was no going back.

Nicole felt a twinge of envy. Things were obviously difficult for Milly, but she had a job she loved and was surrounded by people she trusted. She had her mother, grandmother and Zoe, and she was part of a community that cared about her. She had a normal life, and she lived in this gorgeous boathouse with no intruder alarm and no need for security cameras, and she didn't have to wake up and read lies about herself in the media. She could go where she liked when she liked without worrying about who might be watching. She liked her life and knew exactly what she wanted to do. She had a direction.

Nicole had no direction. She had major decisions to make, but she was too overwhelmed by everything to make them. She was terrified. For years she'd planned every move she'd made, every part she'd taken, but she hadn't planned for this to happen.

She needed to talk it all through, but with Milly unavailable, there was no one she could trust. Justin had been the first person she'd allowed herself to trust in a long while, and that had turned out to be a mistake.

In the past, even when surrounded by people who wanted things from her, she'd never felt lonely because in the back of her mind she knew that whatever happened she had Milly and their friendship had felt like a security blanket, but that had been yanked away. Now she really was alone. Completely alone at a time in her life when she desperately needed a true friend.

She had to figure things out on her own. Make decisions on her own.

For once she had to focus on herself and not a part she was playing, but thinking about herself took her right back to the beginning.

Nicole had been ten years old when she'd realized that she needed to change. Being herself just wasn't enough for her mother. It was impossible not to notice that the other children's parents always seemed proud. They clapped loudly at school plays and concerts, they cheered from the sidelines during sports matches, they beamed with delight at the artwork displayed on classroom walls. Amy Clayton's mother had actually clapped her hands when she'd seen Amy's self-portrait as if her daughter had painted the *Mona Lisa*, which she most definitely hadn't (Nicole had actually seen the *Mona Lisa* on a trip to Paris with her mother, and Amy's random splodges didn't come close). All of which proved to Nicole that there was something wrong with her.

She was determined to be the child her mother wanted, some-one her mother would be proud of, but how was she going to achieve that?

She envied her friend Milly, who never had to earn praise or affection. Both seemed to be in unlimited supply in her house-hold, her loving relationship with her mother and grandmother so different from Nicole's own experience that sitting in their cozy kitchen was like landing on an alien planet.

The only thing her own mother seemed to appreciate was aca-demic attainment, so Nicole threw herself into that, but she knew that no matter how hard she worked she was never going to gain straight A's, so that was unlikely to yield the approval she craved.

Her gift seemed to be entertaining people. Making the other children laugh. She was a wickedly good mimic, imitating teachers when they were out of the classroom and once calling the school office pretending to be someone's parent so that they could be ex-cused from sports.

In their English class when they all took turns to read aloud from whichever book the teacher had chosen, Nicole threw her-self into the task with voices and actions. It was after one of those lessons where the whole class had insisted she read for the entire time, because Nicole actually brought a boring book to life, that the teacher had taken her to see the head of drama.

As they'd walked into the room the teacher had pushed Nicole ahead and said, "I've found you a star."

Nicole had glanced over her shoulder to see who the star was, and it had taken several moments to absorb the fact that the teacher had been talking about her. She'd soaked up the praise like a thirsty plant absorbs water, and she'd never forgotten those words or that encounter because it had been the start of everything.

The drama teacher had given Nicole several parts to read and then immediately offered her the lead in the school play.

Nicole had all but floated home on a tide of praise and ap-proval. Finally, she'd found the thing she was good at. This was her gift.

She couldn't wait to tell her mother and see her clap her hands as Amy's mother had, or beam with pride like Tina Pearson's mother had when Tina had stumbled onto the stage to receive a prize for her short story.

But Nicole's mother hadn't done either of those things. Instead she'd banned drama class. *You won't get your grades up by prancing around being an exhibitionist.*

Nicole had understood then that she would never make her mother proud.

I'm not enough, she'd thought, I'll never be enough.

But for the drama teacher she'd been enough, and that was all the encouragement Nicole needed. She'd discovered something she excelled at, and it gave her an alternative to being herself. She could pretend to be someone else. She could step into another person's life, which seemed infinitely better than her own. There was no way she was giving it up.

And having made that decision, it worked to her advantage that her mother's interest in her was limited. Thanks to the demands of her job as a surgeon, she was rarely home.

Nicole had forged her mother's signature on the permission slip for drama classes and told her mother she was having extra tuition at school.

And that had been the beginning.

She worked hard enough at her academic classes to make sure she didn't draw attention to herself, but the best few hours of the week were her drama classes. She paid more attention in that one class than she did in all the others put together. She absorbed every instruction.

When you're playing a part, you don't just pretend to be someone else, you become someone else. You are that person.

To a young girl who hated the life she was living and was struggling to find her place in the world, it was an invitation. If she could be someone else when she was acting, what was stopping her being someone else in real life?

She thought about that moment often, and she was thinking of it now as she sat on the porch swing on Milly's deck, safely out of view.

She wasn't used to doing nothing. When she wasn't on set, she was reading scripts, memorizing lines and letting herself sink into the character she was to become. There was no time to be herself.

She'd had her first big break at nineteen while she was still in college and an agent had seen her performance on stage. Since then, she'd worked nonstop. She'd spent so much of her life playing other people she no longer knew who she was. Acting roles had brought her accolades and adulation. Being herself was unlikely to have the same effect.

Who was she when she wasn't acting? And would anyone really like that person?

Unsettled by her own thoughts she stood up and headed to the kitchen to make herself a coffee.

Maybe she'd delve through Milly's books and find something to read. She had decisions to make. She needed to work out what to do, but she didn't feel ready to confront her reality.

She picked up her mug and was halfway across the room when she heard a rap on the door.

"Milly?"

Nicole froze as she heard the male voice. Milly had said that no one came to her cabin, but apparently today someone had decided to do just that. That was unlikely to be a coincidence, surely?

Panic closed in on her, and she tried to reason with herself. No one had seen her arrive. It wasn't possible. Or was it? No, this wasn't someone looking for her. It was someone looking for Milly. And when they didn't get an answer, they were going to leave.

She heard the sound of the door opening and the voice came again, louder and closer.

"Milly? Are you there?"

He was inside the boathouse. Actually inside.

She hadn't locked the door. How could she not have locked the door?

The mug slid from her shaking hands, sloshing boiling water over sensitive skin. She registered the scald, but only dimly because right now she was far more afraid of something else.

He was in the house. *In the house*. And she couldn't breathe. She couldn't suck air into her lungs. Desperate, she grabbed a knife from the block on the kitchen counter, but her hand was shaking too much to do anything with it.

The crash of the mug on the slate floor brought the man striding into the kitchen, and he stopped when he saw her, his expression cycling through shock, surprise and then recognition.

Nicole clocked the exact moment it dawned on him who she was. She'd been through this scenario a thousand times in her life. It happened in restaurants or when she was walking down the street. People would glance at her, and then the glance would turn into a stare, and there was a moment of doubt: *Is it her?* Curiosity was usually followed by either a request for a selfie or an autograph or both.

She should tell him that Milly wasn't here. She should tell him to go, but she couldn't get her breathing steady enough to talk, and she saw his gaze go from her face to the knife.

"Okay." He raised a hand. "I can see I scared you badly. I'm sorry. I was looking for Milly. You're fine. Everything is fine. You should put the knife down."

Her heart was beating frantically, and she felt a swirl of dizziness engulf her.

"I'm Joel." His voice was calm and quiet. "I work here. I came to see Milly, that's all. I'm a friend of Milly's. I didn't know you were here. Everything is fine."

The words penetrated the cloud of panic in her head.

Joel. Milly had mentioned a Joel. The guy who built this place?

He wasn't a stranger who had broken into her house. He wasn't a photographer or a crazed fan.

He was Joel the *everything guy*.

She repeated his name in her head, trying to calm herself, but she felt as if she was having a heart attack, her breathing coming in frantic gulps no matter how hard she tried to slow it.

She looked at him, terrified, and he nodded.

"You're having a panic attack. And given that I'm the cause of it, I should probably leave, but I can't leave you like this so I'll call Milly—"

"No." She pushed the word out and shook her head. "No."

She closed her eyes and forced herself to breathe slowly, as she'd been taught.

"You're safe." Joel's voice was slow and steady. "You're completely safe. I'm going to take that knife from you, and then we're going to get that burn under cold water."

She felt him ease the knife from her trembling fingers, talking the whole time.

"That's good. You're going to be fine. My sister had panic attacks for a while, and she told me it's helpful when someone reminds her that it's going to pass, so I'm telling you this is going to pass. Try and slow your breathing." His voice was hypnotic, soothing, and she listened while he told her how he'd restored this place from its original dilapidated state. He talked her through each stage in detail and as she focused on his words, the pain in her chest eased and the dizziness faded.

Her legs were shaking badly, and she leaned against the counter for support. "I'm okay." She whispered the words. "I'm sorry."

"You're sorry? I'm the one who scared you half to death, and I feel terrible about that. You're pale and you don't look great, to be honest." He frowned. "I really think I should just call Milly."

"No." She was miserably embarrassed that he'd witnessed her reaction. She didn't want Milly to know. There was so much she hadn't told Milly. "Just go."

"I'm not leaving you like this. And also your hand is turning red. We really need to get that under cool water." His gaze slid from her face to the mess on the floor. "I terrified you."

"I wasn't expecting—"

"Anyone to just walk in." His voice was rough and apologetic. "My bad. I don't normally barge into people's homes uninvited, but Milly and I have been trying to catch up all morning. It's changeover day, so it's always hectic. The café said she was over here, so I thought I'd see her before she headed off to her next task."

Her mouth was dry, and now that the panic had faded she could feel the burn on her hand throbbing. "You just missed her."

"Right." He walked to the sink and turned on the water, adjusted the flow of water until it was the correct temperature and then stood a little to one side, careful not to crowd her.

Deciding that the quickest way to get rid of him was to comply, she stuck her hand under it and winced as the cool water ran over the burn.

"Hold it there," he said. "I'm going to clean up the mess, as I'm responsible for it."

She didn't want him to clean it up. She just wanted him to leave, but he was already sweeping up the jagged shards with a brush and dustpan he'd retrieved from the cupboard.

She told herself that Milly trusted Joel, so that was a little reassuring, although Milly trusted almost everyone, so maybe not. Milly lived in a place where she didn't bother with an alarm and didn't lock the doors.

Joel disposed of the broken shards, mopped the floor and then joined her at the sink.

"Can I look at your hand?"

"It's fine. You can catch up with Milly if you leave now." *Go, go!* She started to pull her hand away, but he caught her arm and held her fingers under the water.

"You need to keep it there for a while longer, otherwise you'll have a nasty burn. I know it feels like overkill, but it's worth it, believe me. I'm talking from experience. When I'm not burning myself, I'm hammering pieces out of myself." His smile was so warm and genuine she almost responded, but then she remembered that people could fake warm and genuine. She did it all the time.

Was he expecting her to introduce herself? This was so awkward. And she had no wish to prolong the encounter.

She wondered if he and Milly were involved. The fact that he'd walked in without waiting for an invitation suggested a level of familiarity that went beyond work colleagues. She remembered Milly's words from the night before. *If he left I'd be lost.*

If they were together, then Nicole would be relieved because it would prove that Milly had moved on from Richard. And Joel was undeniably attractive. If she was casting him in a role it would be the Sexy Carpenter. His hair was mussed, and he had paint spatters on his jeans. The hand holding hers under the running water had roughened skin and a dark bruise that suggested he'd trapped a finger recently. He was the type of guy who rolled up his sleeves and fixed things himself rather than calling someone else to fix them. And then there was the fact that he had muscles in all the right places and a smile that crinkled the corners of his eyes.

Was he interested in her friend?

If that was the case, then Nicole didn't want to blow it for her by being frosty or rude.

"This place used to be a splintered spider trap."

"Yes. I had to rehome a few as I worked." Still holding her hand under the water, he glanced up at the slope of the ceiling with affection. It was obvious that he loved the building, and she felt a flash kinship.

"Milly and I used to play here as children. It was our den." She volunteered that information without thinking and then wished she could snatch it back because she never gave out personal information. Not to anyone.

He shifted his gaze to hers. "I didn't know the two of you were friends."

Were they? She tugged her hand away from his. "Thanks for your help. I'll tell Milly you were looking for her."

A wave of despair washed over her as she faced reality. She'd been here for less than ten hours and already her cover was blown. It was bad for her and bad for Milly. In her head she'd imagined having a week or maybe two to recover a little and decide on what she was going to do before needing to leave the sanctuary of Milly's home. Instead she hadn't managed a day. She was going to have to leave right away. But go where?

Joel turned off the water.

She expected him to leave but he didn't. He dried his hands carefully and then looked directly at her.

"I'm not much good at subterfuge and games, so I'm not going to pretend I don't know who you are. I scared you, and I'm sorry for that because I'm guessing in your position you have to be pretty careful around people you don't know."

And equally careful around the people she did know, which was worse in some ways. In her experience the people who could hurt you the most were the ones who were closest to you because they knew all your vulnerabilities.

She held his gaze. "People aren't always what they seem."

He nodded. "I'm sure that's true, particularly for someone in your position. I'm guessing that you don't want anyone to know you're here, otherwise Milly would have mentioned it. So I just want to say that you don't have to worry about me. I shouldn't have just walked in, but I did, and I can't change that. But no one is going to hear about you from me."

She was sure he believed that, and she wanted to believe him too, but she also knew from experience that all it would take was a few pints in the local pub for him to start trying to impress his friends. *You'll never guess who I met.*

He was still watching her, his gaze steady. "You don't believe me, so I'll say it again. No one is going to hear about you from me."

She was startled by how easily he'd read her, and now she was wondering what he was thinking, really.

Had he seen the latest stories about her? Of course he had. And he probably believed every word, because far too many people thought that what they read in the press and online was fact. It shamed her to think what he might have seen. The assumptions he would have made about her.

He gave her a brief nod and walked to the door, but instead of leaving he paused.

"This place is quiet on the whole. Just guests and a few extras who come here to walk and take advantage of the café. It's pretty easy to spot someone who doesn't fit. If you notice anyone you don't like the look of, call me and I'll come right away. I live close by. And if you need to be smuggled out, I have a van."

She froze. Maybe not a Sexy Carpenter, she thought. Maybe someone less wholesome who gave his victims a sense of security before he finished them off. A man you would never suspect.

Joel muttered something under his breath and gave her a mortified look. "I can't believe I just said that. I sounded like a serial killer, didn't I? Just to clarify, the van is for my climbing gear. In my spare time, I climb."

"Right."

"It's true. It's the reason I chose to live here. Well, not the only reason, but one of them. The van's a mess. Full of ropes, and—ropes for climbing, obviously." He broke off and shook his head. "I'm going to stop talking now because every time I open my mouth, I'm making it worse." His apologetic smile was so attractive that she found herself smiling back. Or maybe she was smiling because he was so adorably flustered.

"Don't worry. Most serial killers don't announce themselves before they invite you to step into their van."

"I'll remember that." He pulled a card from the pocket of his jeans and put it on the side table. "That's my number. If I can help, use it."

Another person would have been touched by the offer, and it made Nicole sad that she couldn't be like that. Unfortunately she'd learned to be wary of everyone. "Thank you."

There were times when she wished her brain didn't work the way it did. Times when she wished she could meet someone and not question their agenda.

But this was who she was now, and there was no changing it. Which was why she waited until he left before carefully locking the door behind him.

7

Milly

Milly headed along the path to Beech Lodge, rehearsing her script in her head, partly because that way she didn't have to think about Nicole and partly because she was very bad at difficult conversations and the only way for her to get through them was to practice until she was word-perfect. If she didn't do that, she stuttered and said things she didn't mean like *It doesn't matter, don't worry about it.*

Thanks to her newfound assertiveness skills, she was confident (more or less) that she could handle the situation with Brendan Scott.

She'd be polite but firm. Professional. She'd assure him that the whole team was keen to accommodate his wishes. All they required was that he express those wishes in a calm, civilized manner and not scare the staff.

Good morning, Mr. Scott. I'm the owner and manager, and I wanted to have a quick word—

No, that was too much waffle. She needed to keep it brief and direct. A man like him would appreciate that.

Mr. Scott, I'm Milly, the owner and manager. We'd be grateful if you could tell us when you'd like us to service the cabin so that we do so without intruding on your personal space.

She reached the steps that led to his cabin. Her heart was hammering, and she felt a little sick.

Honestly, what was wrong with her? The worst thing that could happen was that he'd be defensive and angry and then check out immediately in protest. But that would be pretty bad because Brendan Scott was a long-stay guest making a significant contribution to her bottom line.

Maybe this was a bad idea. Maybe she wouldn't say anything at all.

She was about to back away and retrace her steps when the door opened. Brendan Scott stood there, a look of frustration on his face. His wide shoulders filled the doorway, and all the words she'd been rehearsing flew from her head.

"Yes?"

She resisted the urge to take a step back.

He looked tired, she thought. Stressed, with shadows under his eyes. His hair looked as if he'd dragged his fingers through it a thousand times in the last hour.

She felt a stab of sympathy because although she hadn't had a chance to look in the mirror since she'd hauled herself out of bed that morning, she was pretty sure she didn't look much better than he did.

"I'm sorry to disturb you—" Her voice came out as a croak. "It's not important. I'm—"

"You're Milly. I remember you from last time." He paused, and his expression shifted into a look of apology. "And you're here to take me to task for being rude to Lorna."

"Oh . . . you know her name?"

"She wore a badge. It said *Lorna*." There was a hint of laughter in his eyes. "I assume that's her name, although as a crime novelist it did cross my mind that the woman at the door could have in fact murdered Lorna and was impersonating her in order to gain entrance to my cabin. It would be a good twist, don't you think?"

Milly, who generally preferred her fiction a little less dark, recoiled. "That's the way your mind works?"

"On a good day. Sometimes it's just blank, as it has been for the past few days and nights, which is why I took it out on poor Lorna." He opened the door wider. "Come in. If you're going to yell at me, I'd rather you did it in private." He stood to one side, and she hesitated and then walked into his cabin.

"For the record, I don't yell. I'm very conflict-averse." She paused in the doorway, taken aback by what she saw. Every available surface, including the floor, was covered in sheets of paper, and each sheet was covered in scrawling handwriting. There were papers on the sofa and on the chairs and sticky notes on the walls.

Beech was one of their most in-demand cabins, partly because of its secluded position but also because of the wide deck that reached over the water. She could see that Brendan had set up his desk on the side of the deck that was shaded by trees. A laptop sat open, and next to it was a notepad and several pens. She counted at least six mugs on the table.

"It's a mess, I know." He crouched down and moved a few sheets of paper on the floor so that she had somewhere to put her feet. "I wasn't expecting visitors. I've reached a crucial part of my book, and I needed to visualize each chapter and see the flow of the story. There's no lasting damage to the cabin, I can assure you."

"I didn't think there was." She glanced around her in fascination, slightly awed. "This is how you write a book? How do you keep it all straight in your head?" It looked like a nightmare to her, but she didn't consider herself to be a particularly creative person. Except in the kitchen.

"This is how I keep it all straight. This and muttering to myself. And this isn't how I write every book. They're all different. Some days it doesn't go as well as other days, and then I'm not at my most sweet-natured." He ran his hand over the back of his neck. "I'd offer you a cup of tea, but I seem to have run out of mugs."

She eyed the mugs lined up on the table. "That happens if you don't load the dishwasher."

"I guess. Now, tell me how I can make it up to Lorna. Flowers? Chocolates? A signed book by her favorite author—I might be able to pull some strings with my contacts?"

"There's no need for that, but thank you for offering. Lorna is fine, but I'll clean your cabin from now on, so maybe we can agree on a schedule that works for you?"

"I scared her away. Damn. So why did you draw the short straw?"

"I'm brave as a lion."

He raised an eyebrow. "Really?"

"No." She smiled. "I'm a total coward, but I'm the boss. The buck stops with me."

He studied her face. "I don't suppose you'd agree to do it at the end of my stay?"

"Two months?" She laughed and glanced around her. "You'd be buried under your own detritus, Mr. Scott."

"Call me Brendan. And yes, you're probably right. Okay, then. Clean sheets and towels would be great, but until I get past this stage—" he gestured to the papers "—I'd appreciate it if we could hold off on cleaning floors and surfaces."

"I promise not to move a single piece of paper." She looked at the deck. "Can I load those mugs into the dishwasher, or are you doing a firsthand exploration on the growth of toxins in cold, long-abandoned tea?"

"It's coffee. I'm a coffee guy." He looked embarrassed. "And I don't expect you to wash up after me."

She decided he was really very attractive when he wasn't glowering, and it surprised her that she'd even noticed because she'd thought she was still too bruised by Richard to care about things like that.

"I want your stay to be perfect." She looked at the mugs again and then at the kitchen, which was pristine. "There are no dirty plates. You don't eat?"

"When I'm deep in the book, no. At least, not what you'd call a meal. I snack. Biscuits. Those incredible croissants they sell in your café. The occasional takeout, which I dispose of afterward because I'm not a total animal."

No vitamins, she thought. Nothing healthy. No wonder he looked tired.

"I'll deal with the laundry, clear the kitchen and leave the rest until you ask me." She handed him a card. "My number is on there. Call if you need anything."

"Thanks." He took the card from her and followed her to the door. "You run this place with your husband? I remember signing a book for him last time I was here."

She paused on the steps. "My grandfather purchased the land and built the first cabins. It was my mother who turned it into what it is now. She's still involved from the sidelines, but she handed over the reins to me a couple of years ago. My now-ex-husband—" she stumbled over the words because she still wasn't used to saying them "—works for a pharma company and was never involved in the business. We're divorced. He found someone else."

He leaned against the doorframe, still watching her. "Then, he's a fool."

Was he flirting with her?

No, of course he wasn't.

Richard *was* a fool. You only had to look at the way he behaved toward his daughter to know that.

"He is a fool, you're right about that. Maybe you could recommend a way for me to kill him?" She couldn't believe she'd just said that, but Brendan Scott frowned and seemed to be giving it serious consideration.

"I'd suggest staging an accident. That way suspicion wouldn't fall on you. I'll put together some ideas for you, and you can pick one. A good drowning might be the answer." He glanced toward the lake. "It's the perfect spot for it."

"He doesn't swim, so he wouldn't be in the water."

"Better and better. Makes drowning more plausible. Also easier." He rubbed his hand over his jaw, thinking. "Maybe a small boating accident?"

She laughed, which was something she rarely did when thinking about her ex-husband. "That would be terrible publicity for Forest Nest. And just so that we're clear, I'm not asking you to do away with him."

"I know. But occasionally it takes some of the heat out of the emotions to think about it."

"Do you do that a lot? Plan the fate of people you don't like?"

"Sure. It's one of the perks of being a writer. Sometimes I give people a really grisly end."

And now she was intrigued. "You actually put people you know in your books?"

"All the time. But they're heavily disguised so no one but me would know who they are." He gestured to the books on the table. "My last book has a character who may or may not bear a slight resemblance to one of my law professors from college. A truly miserable excuse for a human being."

"You were a lawyer?"

"Yes, although I only practiced for a short time because by some stroke of luck my first book was accepted by a publisher. Which rarely happens, by the way. I got lucky. That part of my life was more fairy tale than horror story."

"I can't imagine writing a book."

"At this moment, neither can I—hence the mess and my less-than-friendly approach with Lorna. But it helps to be here. You live in a great place."

"I think so, but not everyone agrees." She thought of Richard, who had moved to a city. "No bright lights. The nearest nightclub is an hour and a half away. In winter the roads are often impassable because of the weather, and in summer they're impassable because of the tourists. To a lot of people, it's not exciting. Which is probably why I like it."

Maybe that was her problem. She wasn't a very exciting person. She loved her family and her home and enjoyed baking and hiking. Was that wrong?

He studied her for a moment. "I live in New York, and trust me when I say city excitement can be overrated."

She was flustered by the way he was looking at her.

"Why the Lakes? It seems like a long way to come for peace and quiet. Do you have a connection with the place?"

"My grandmother was born in Carlisle, although she moved to the US when she married my grandfather. And to answer your question, the book is set here so that as well as availing myself of the peace and quiet, I'm using it for inspiration."

"Are you telling me you've drowned someone in our lake?"

"Not literally, but in my book? Yes. But I've changed the name of the lake, so don't be concerned about it having an adverse effect on tourism."

She was about to say that fewer tourists on the roads in the peak summer months wouldn't be a bad thing, when she spotted Joel striding along the path.

"Ah—there's Joel, and I need to talk to him about boring plumbing issues. What time can I come back and clean the cabin?"

"Does after two work for you? I plan on going for a walk then."

She calculated that she could freshen the place and still be in time to pick up Zoe from school. "That's fine."

"Great. And if there's anyone you would like me to turn into a victim just let me know. Always happy to help."

"Your generosity is noted."

She was just thinking that he was surprisingly easy to talk to when he gave her a smile of such breathtaking charm that her heart gave a couple of extra beats.

Unsettled by her own reaction, she returned the smile and hurried to meet Joel.

At least her conversation with Brendan Scott had been positive. He wasn't leaving, and she was relieved about that. It would have been hard on their bottom line if he'd left at this stage of his booking. She ignored the little voice in her head that was telling her there were other, more personal, reasons that she was pleased he was staying.

It was a little bizarre that she had a famous author and a famous actor hiding out at Forest Nest at the same time. What next? Royalty?

She jogged the last few steps to Joel. "Hi. I was just on my way to find you." She paused to catch her breath and saw his expression. "What's wrong? You couldn't fix the leak in Aspen? We're going to have to rehouse the guests?"

"No." He put down the box of tools he was carrying. "Nothing like that. I went looking for you—"

"You were my next priority after Brendan Scott. Has something happened?" She'd never seen him so serious, and now she was worried because the last thing she needed was for things to go wrong in peak summer season when they were fully booked.

"I went to the boathouse to give you an update. I assumed you were there, and I thought I'd save us both the trouble of chasing each other round the resort, so I went inside."

"Well, we've found each other now, so—" And then she realized what he was saying. "You went inside?"

"Yes. The door was ajar. And I met your—" he turned his head quickly, checking who was nearby "—I met your friend."

"Ah." And remembering the lengths Nicole had gone to in order to avoid being recognized, Milly immediately saw the problem. "And I'm guessing she was a little freaked out."

"That's an understatement. I wanted to call you, but she insisted I didn't bother you. But I thought you should know." He shook his head in apology. "I feel terrible about it. She obviously didn't want anyone to know she was there, and I tried telling her that no one was going to hear it from me, but I could tell she didn't believe me."

"I'll reassure her. Don't worry, Joel."

"How long is she going to be staying with you? Because we could consider ramping up security around the place."

"That would probably just draw attention to the fact that she's here. But it's worth thinking about." Except that she didn't really want to have to think about it. People came here to relax. Extra security wouldn't look good, and people would start asking questions. "I'll talk to her. Thanks, Joel."

"The plumbing is a simple job, by the way. It will be fixed by the time the guests check in," he said. "I need to get a part, and then I'm going to do it right away. That's what I came to tell you."

"You're a star." She hurried back along the path toward the boathouse. She wasn't worried. Joel was completely trustworthy, and once she assured Nicole of that, she'd be fine.

The boathouse door was locked and bolted from the inside, which meant Milly had no access. She tapped lightly on the glass, but there was no response, so she took out her phone and messaged Nicole.

I'm at the door. Are you there?

Nicole appeared a moment later, almost unrecognizable in a blond wig and a pair of glasses with purple frames that dominated her face.

She opened the door.

"Sorry. I was being careful."

"I understand. Joel told me what happened. It's my fault for not closing the door properly when I left. I don't always bother locking it, but I probably should." And with Nicole Raven hiding out in the boathouse, she definitely should.

And she saw now that underneath the wig and the glasses, Nicole looked ill.

"If you're worried about him telling people you're here, then don't. I've known Joel a long time. He won't mention it. But maybe we should talk about increasing security, just in case."

"No need. I won't be here." Nicole headed back into the boathouse toward Milly's study that she'd used as a bedroom.

Confused, Milly followed her and saw Nicole push the last of her things into her small suitcase.

"You're leaving?"

"I have to. Coming here was a mistake. I've made things difficult for you and also for me, and it isn't going to work." She zipped the case. "I have a cab picking me up in thirty minutes. I used the name Silvia Coates by the way, in case he goes to Reception."

"Wait. Slow down." Milly's head was spinning. She hadn't wanted Nicole to come, had she? So why was she feeling so upset at the thought of her leaving? "Are you leaving because Joel knows you're here? He—"

"It's not just that, although I don't trust people as easily as you do so I'm not going to pretend it doesn't play a part. I'm leaving because being here isn't helping. I was running away from my life, and I ran to the only person I've ever been able to trust. You. My best friend. My only real friend. It was a reflex action. When I'm in trouble I reach out to you." Her voice cracked, and she cleared her throat. "But things are awkward. And it's my fault. When you were in trouble, I wasn't there for you. I blew the most precious thing in my life. And I'm sorry for that. Sorrier than you'll ever know. If I could turn the clock back I'd do everything differently, but that only ever happens in movies. So we'll both just move on, and I don't expect you to forgive me or believe me when I say that if you ever need me in the future, then reach out and I'll be there for you. Whenever it is, whatever you need, I'll be there."

Milly wasn't sure she did believe her because once a person had let you down once they could let you down again, couldn't they? But she sounded sincere, and underneath the blond wig and the purple glasses Milly saw vulnerability and a sheen of tears.

She could see that Nicole was suffering. And just like that all the hurt and defensiveness that had been making her boil inside vanished. She'd been determined to keep her distance, but now she realized that however strained things were, however difficult, the bond between them was still there and probably always would be.

"I don't want you to leave."

"I have to, and not just because things are difficult between us. I'm a mess, Milly. My life is a mess. You have no idea." Nicole's voice was thickened with emotion. "I thought by coming here I'd have space to figure things out, but it's more complicated than that. I had a panic attack when Joel walked into the kitchen. Did he tell you that?"

"Of course you did. There was a strange man in the house. Anyone would have—" She stopped, seeing Nicole's expression change. "You mean you had a real panic attack? Not a figure of speech? No, he didn't tell me that."

How long had Nicole been having panic attacks, and why didn't she know about it?

And in what way was Nicole's life a mess? Was this just about her affair with Justin, or was there something else?

She felt a mix of frustration and sadness as she compared how their relationship used to be with how it was now. A few years ago she wouldn't have been asking herself these questions because she would have already known all the answers.

Nicole folded the T-shirt Milly had lent her. "I asked him not to, so I suppose it's a point in his favor that he respected that. And to be fair, the poor man handled it well, particularly given that he couldn't possibly understand. And I overreacted, of course, because of everything that has happened."

"What has happened? You haven't actually told me any of it. We haven't talked."

"You were busy," Nicole muttered, and Milly squirmed a little inside.

She had been busy. She was always busy, but that wasn't it, was it? Not really.

Nicole had tried to talk to her several times. Last night when they'd walked into the boathouse. This morning when Milly was rushing off to work.

Milly had brushed her off not because she was busy but because she was hurt. Also the conversation with Nicole would have been uncomfortable, and she avoided uncomfortable conversations.

If she was a different type of person, a better person, she would have sat down and talked right away. She would have told Nicole how upset she was, and they would have discussed it in a mature fashion, but instead Milly had held everything inside and nurtured the hurt.

"How long have you been having panic attacks?"

"It really doesn't—"

"How long?"

"Just over a year. Ever since that man broke into my house."

Milly went cold. "Someone broke into your house? Oh, Nic—"

"Hazard of being famous." Nicole gave a careless lift of her shoulders. "They do tours past movie stars' homes, did you know that? *Hey, you know that actor you're fixated on? That's where she sleeps every night.* I try not to think about it."

A man broke into her house.

Milly felt a flush of shame. She'd made the mistake of judging from the outside. Of thinking that everything in Nicole's life was pretty perfect and that she could buy whatever wasn't. But that wasn't true, was it? You couldn't buy anonymity.

And while she'd been wallowing in her problems, Nicole had been battling her own. And she hadn't known or even suspected.

"You didn't call me. You didn't even tell me."

"Well, by then we weren't really talking, and I hadn't responded to all your trauma with Richard, so I didn't feel particularly deserving of your sympathy. It's fine. Everything was fine. I have a panic button. The police came quickly. I was lucky. It's in the past." Nicole grabbed her phone from the bed and dropped it into her bag.

Not so lucky, Milly thought, and not in the past if her reaction to Joel was anything to go by.

"How did he get in? You have massive walls and gates and security."

"Yeah, well, it turns out that my security guy wasn't as loyal as I'd thought. He took a bribe. The plan was to kidnap me and demand a ransom. Can we talk about something else?"

Milly was flooded with horror. "I can't believe you didn't tell me.

I should have been there for you. I would have been there for you." Emotion filled her chest and rose to her throat. "How did we reach this point, Nic? We used to tell each other everything."

Nicole gave a tired smile. "We were kids, Milly. What we had to tell each other wasn't exactly life-changing, was it?"

"It shouldn't matter. Maybe the conversations get tougher, but when have we ever not been able to talk to each other? If anything, it's even more important that we talk about the life-changing stuff. Isn't that what friendship is?"

"In theory." Nicole paused, as if she was about to say something else, but then she shook her head. "Maybe we just expected too much."

"I refuse to believe that." Milly felt as if she was holding tightly to something that was slipping through her fingers.

"I let you down," Nicole said softly. "I wasn't there for you, and we'll never get past that."

"Yes, we will. We can fix this. The blame isn't all yours. It's mine too." She could see that now. "I was upset. You'd shown that you didn't need me, and I was determined to show you that I didn't need you either. It was easier to keep my distance than have a frank conversation. I'm not good at difficult conversations, you know that. Ask Richard if you don't believe me. I let him leave messages so that I don't have to actually talk to him. I'm pathetic."

Nicole gave a faint smile. "Not pathetic. I get it with Richard. But us? If there was one thing you and I did well, it was talk."

"And that's still the case." Milly felt terrible. She'd been unforgiving and unyielding. It hadn't occurred to her that something bad might be happening in Nicole's life. In trying to protect herself from more hurt and be more assertive, she'd kept herself at a distance, but was she really going to let pride and fear of rejection stop her from trying to fix what they'd broken?

"Don't go. We'll talk. Right now. I want to hear about everything that has happened to you. I want you to tell me about Justin."

Her phone started to ring, but she ignored it.

"You have a job," Nicole said. "People relying on you. You should answer it."

"No, I can—" Her phone rang again, and this time she checked it and saw a message from Lorna marked urgent. She sighed. "You're right, I do need to answer this. But promise me you won't go anywhere. Lock the door behind me, and this evening, after Zoe has gone to bed, we'll talk. Please?"

Nicole looked at her for a long moment and then nodded.

"If that's what you want."

"It is." And it didn't matter how uncomfortable the conversation made her, they were going to have it. "Cancel that cab."

8

Connie

Connie spent the morning cleaning the house and doing laundry. It crossed her mind that she could wander over to Forest Nest and see what was happening, but since she'd handed over the reins to Milly two years ago she'd been careful to limit her presence around the place. She was conscious that appearing too often might make it seem as if she didn't trust her daughter. But it had been hard to relinquish something that had been such a big part of her life for so long. She made herself available for busy times, but they had a good, strong team supporting them, and she was rarely needed. Which had turned out to be both good and bad.

There were days when she wondered if she'd done the right thing by passing over responsibility. Having devoted the best part of her life to nurturing and growing the business, it felt strange that it was no longer a priority. Forest Nest featured in her earliest memories. She remembered sitting at the desk in her mother's office with a coloring book, aged seven, waiting for Peggy to finish work for the day so that they could do their "walk around" together. When school had demanded more of her time during the week, she'd helped in all her spare moments. She'd done whatever needed doing, from sweeping floors to making up beds with fresh sheets.

She'd started working at Forest Nest full-time when she'd left school, and when her mother had decided it was time for Connie to run the place, she'd given free rein to her ideas. It was Connie who had seen the potential of tapping into the luxury end of the market. She'd watched what was happening around her and knew there were people who wanted to enjoy the wildness of nature while maintaining all their creature comforts. Connie had upgraded the cabins and built new ones. She'd offered creature comforts and more. Bookings had soared.

And now it was Milly's turn. The café had been Milly's idea, and Connie had to admit that it had been a good one. The place was always buzzing with people, and being able to enjoy breakfast and lunch on the deck overlooking the water had proved to be a popular option for those who didn't want to cook.

Watching her daughter grow into the role had been satisfying, and Connie had been ready to take a step back and do more with her life, but then Richard had walked out and her life had been given over to supporting her daughter and granddaughter.

She sighed as she folded the clean laundry into a neat pile.

She couldn't believe history had repeated itself. Not for the world would she have wanted Milly to go through what she had gone through. When David had walked out of their marriage with no warning, it had been the lowest point of her life. The business had sustained her. Forest Nest had given her a reason to get out of bed and keep moving, and not just because she needed to provide for Milly.

And now here they were, back in a similar position.

Was that why she found the whole thing so stressful? Was a small part of her reliving that time of her life alongside Milly? Or was it simply that seeing your child suffer was the ultimate parental challenge?

She frowned as she stared out the window.

She kept telling herself that Milly's emotions weren't her emotions, but knowing that in theory didn't help in practice. She didn't just sympathize, she *felt* the emotions along with her daughter as if they were somehow invisibly connected.

But she couldn't carry on like this, could she?

Her mother was right. She needed to put more focus on her own life instead of constantly being on alert in case Milly needed something. She needed to do more for herself.

If she found a new purpose, maybe she'd stop worrying about Milly for five minutes. It wasn't as if Connie's worrying was helping anyone.

But what exactly was she going to do? Two years ago she'd been planning to travel and see the world, but then Richard had left and she'd known that there was no way she'd be comfortable leaving her daughter with no support. Milly was running a business and had a child, and Connie knew exactly how challenging that could be, particularly during the teenage years. She'd decided that she needed to be there for all the small things that made such a difference. School pickups, the occasional meal, moral support. All the things her own mother had done for her.

And even though it was eighteen months since Richard had walked out, she knew she still wasn't ready to do an ambitious trip. She'd worry too much to enjoy it.

No, she needed to start small.

Still thinking about it, she grabbed her bag, locked the front door and walked into the village.

It was another glorious day. She was tempted to make herself a picnic and head up to her favorite place near the lake. She could even take a book.

The village was small, little more than a hamlet, but it felt like home to Connie. She loved the stone cottages, the slow pace of life and the proximity of nature. A stream bubbled alongside the road, spanned by a pretty stone bridge that dated back several centuries. In winter smoke curled from the chimneys of those houses but now, in summer, flowers bloomed in borders and spilled from pots, bringing vibrant color to an already bright summer's day.

Feeling more upbeat, she walked into the bakery to buy fresh bread.

She was trying to decide between a sourdough loaf and a rye bread when someone tapped on her shoulder.

It was Paula, from the choir. Connie hadn't seen her in months, and coming so soon after the conversation with her mother she wondered if this was the last nudge she needed.

"Connie! It's good to see you." Paula's warmth flowed over her. "We were talking about you just this week because we're short of sopranos. When are you coming back?"

She'd always enjoyed singing, and she knew the choir members well. And would being unavailable for one evening a week really make much difference to Milly at this point?

She opened her mouth to say that yes, she would come back, when Paula gave her shoulder a sympathetic squeeze.

"No pressure. I can imagine things must have been very hard. How is poor Milly doing? I thought about you the other day when I was over at my Tanya's for her twentieth wedding anniversary. I swear those two are as much in love now as they were on the day they married, and the kids are doing well."

Connie wondered how it was people could be so unthinkingly tactless.

"I'm pleased." She said it firmly. She didn't want to become the sort of person who couldn't be happy for someone else, but still she found herself wanting to head for the door. "I need to go, Paula. Great to see you."

"How is Zoe doing? A breakup like that has a terrible and long-lasting impact on a child."

And just like that Connie's moment of optimism passed and she was thinking of Milly again. Worrying about Milly. And Zoe.

Long-lasting impact.

Zoe seemed to be handling everything well, but what if she

wasn't? Was there something more Connie could be doing to make her feel loved and secure?

"Milly and Zoe are both doing well." Her lips felt stiff and dry as she responded. "My daughter is a wonderful mother." Did she sound snappy and defensive? Yes, probably, but at this point she didn't care.

"But having to sell their home—perfectly awful."

Connie's heart was pounding. "Not awful at all. They've moved into the boathouse, and it's a wonderful place to live. It's right on the water. They couldn't be happier."

She said the words but couldn't stop thinking about what Zoe had said about Milly crying herself to sleep.

And now she just wanted to get home before the anxiety could tighten its grip. She didn't have the emotional energy for a picnic, and she knew she wouldn't be able to concentrate enough to read a book.

"Anyway, back to the subject of the choir," Paula said and smiled at her. "When are you coming back?"

"I'm not." The words left Connie's mouth without her even having to think about it. What she needed wasn't sympathy, or reminders of everyone else's perfect lives, or dire prophesies about how Richard's actions might have wrecked Zoe's future, and that was what she'd get if she went back to the choir. This was a small community. Everyone not only knew everyone else's business but they had an opinion on it and didn't hesitate to voice it.

There would be no escape or distraction because everyone would be asking about Milly.

Most people were well-meaning and genuinely caring (although she was starting to wonder about Paula), but if her objective was to fill her head with something else for a few hours, then choir wasn't going to be the answer. Nor was book group or any of the other hobbies she'd enjoyed before Richard had walked out. She'd joined those groups because they were local. The convenience of proximity.

But that wasn't what she needed or wanted.

Paula frowned. "But if Milly is doing well, why can't you come back?"

"Because I have some exciting things going on at the moment, and I can't make the commitment to rehearsals." Eager to extract herself from the conversation as swiftly as possible, she chose a sourdough loaf and handed over her credit card. "But do give my love to everyone."

Feeling a little sick, she left the bakery and walked along the street, her mind clouded by the past. There had been times early on when she'd worried about the impact of her own divorce on Milly, of course, but she'd been too busy holding everything together to dwell on it. She couldn't change the fact that David had chosen to abandon his daughter, but was there something she could have done differently? Better?

Part of motherhood seemed to be adjusting to living in a permanent state of guilt.

She was frustrated with herself for letting Paula's comments affect her so deeply. Just because another person said something didn't mean it was true.

But now the niggle of worry was there, and she couldn't remove it.

Her mother was right to be concerned that Connie had put everything on hold so that she could help Milly, and she needed to do something about that. But it was obvious to her now that she couldn't go back to the things she'd been doing before. People knew too much about her and her situation.

She paused outside the library, scanning the notices in the window. Some of them had been there for so long they'd been faded by the sun.

Babysitter needed.

Gardener for hire.

Dog walker available.

It was all the usual things, including an ad for the hiking group her mother enjoyed so much.

Connie loved the fells and enjoyed being outdoors, but as much as she loved her mother the last thing she needed was to go hiking with her too. They'd end up talking about Milly and Zoe. They wouldn't be able to help themselves. And anyway, she needed something different.

She was about to turn away when a small poster caught her eye.

Waterside Trekking—enjoy the beautiful Lake District scenery from horseback.

She felt a rush of nostalgia. As a child she'd loved horse riding, and for a short time she'd even dreamed of having her own pony, but it hadn't been practical and eventually that hobby had drifted into the past along with so many other things.

She stared at the picture of the horse and rider trekking along the side of the lake with mountains stretching beyond. It looked so tranquil.

She shook herself. She was sixty. Far too old to take up riding again. Ridiculous. And anyway if she wanted to try riding, she could simply go to the local stables. Given the number of guests from Forest Nest that were sent their way, they'd probably give her a friendly rate. But again, that was too close to home. And she didn't want to mix business with pleasure, even though her role in the business was much smaller than it once had been.

No, whatever she ended up doing as a distraction, she was going to do it away from her home turf.

She stared at the ad again and on impulse she pulled out her phone and dialed the number.

"Is that Waterside Trekking? I'd like to book a ride please— yes, a two-hour trek sounds perfect." Did it? Would she survive two hours when she hadn't been on a horse in years? She wouldn't be able to walk afterward. "I'm not exactly a beginner, but it has been a while since I've ridden . . . How long? Oh, about forty-five years." She cringed as she said it, but the woman on the other end of the phone didn't seem alarmed or at all put-out by the fact that Connie wasn't in the first flush of youth.

Nor did she recognize her name when Connie gave it. She didn't ask how Milly was coping or whether it looked as if Zoe was going to be scarred for life.

Maybe this had been a good idea after all.

The woman was still talking, asking when Connie wanted to come.

"When?" Connie hadn't thought that far, but now that she'd made the call she decided that the sooner she did it, the better. Otherwise she might change her mind. "As soon as possible. When do you have availability?"

When she heard the woman telling her that they'd had a cancellation that afternoon if she was interested, she almost refused. She'd expected to have time to think about it. To change her mind and cancel if she wanted to.

But before she could stop herself she was promising to be there and getting directions.

She ended the call and stared at her reflection in the shop window.

She was going horse riding.

And for now she wasn't going to mention it to anyone. This would be something just for her.

9

Nicole

Zoe arrived home like a whirlwind. She dropped her school-bag in the living room and flung her arms around Nicole without a moment of hesitation.

"I can't believe you're here."

At least someone was pleased to see her, Nicole thought as she hugged her back.

The hug felt so good she was glad she'd given in to Milly's entreaties to stay.

She'd spent the rest of the day worried that she should have gone through with her plan, but now that Zoe and Milly were home she was pleased she hadn't left.

"I can't believe how you've grown." She eased away and studied Zoe, taking in her smooth skin and clear, direct gaze. "Look at you."

She felt a pang. Milly's child. She remembered holding Zoe as a baby and wondering how anyone could handle being responsible for something so helpless. But Milly hadn't seemed at all worried by that side of things.

Milly adored motherhood. Right from the beginning that much had been obvious.

"I haven't told anyone you're staying, I promise." Zoe smiled awkwardly. "My friends would freak out if they knew, though. They all love you."

"They love the roles she plays on the screen." Milly retrieved Zoe's bag and put it on a chair so that they didn't trip over it. "They don't love *her*. They don't know her."

"You know what I mean." Zoe grabbed a banana from the bowl on the table and peeled it. "I'm starving. What's for dinner?"

"Caesar salad. And I think it's important to make the distinction, that's all," Milly said. "Nicole isn't the characters she plays."

"I know that! I'm not ten years old." Zoe rolled her eyes, in that moment looking every bit the teenager. She finished the banana and disposed of the skin.

"Zoe still wants to follow in your footsteps and be an actor," Milly said to Nicole. "All advice welcome, I'm sure. Apologies in advance if she bombards you with questions."

Zoe gave a small shrug. "Actually, I'm not sure I do want to be an actor anymore. I might do something else."

Milly looked confused. "Like what?"

"I don't know. Computer engineering maybe?"

"But you love drama," Milly said. "It's your favorite thing. She's playing the part of Hermia in *A Midsummer Night's Dream*, Nicole. I noticed that it's streaming at the moment. You and Nicole could watch it together, and she could talk to you about the part."

"Nicole won't want to do that, Mum. It's boring. I'm going to change, then I'll help you cook."

"But—" Milly started, but Zoe had already left the room, the sound of her feet on the stairs echoing through the boathouse. Milly stared after her, a worried frown on her face. "That was strange. I assumed she'd be talking nonstop about the play. She was so excited when she got the part. She auditioned for it because she watched you play the role so many times."

"Maybe she just felt awkward talking about it."

"Maybe."

Nicole gazed at the door Zoe had just sprinted through. She

was relieved Zoe hadn't asked for advice on acting because her advice at the moment would be *Don't do it*. "I can't believe how grown-up she seems. I remember giving her dress-up clothes when she was four."

"I know. It's unsettling how fast time passes." Milly grabbed a loaf of sourdough, cut a few thick slices and then hacked it into rough chunks. "One minute she's lining up her soft toys on the bed, and the next she's talking about the patriarchy. It gives me whiplash."

"She's wonderful, Milly. So bright and confident. I don't remember us being so sure of ourselves. Were we?"

"I don't know. I can't remember that far back. Come and talk to me while I cook. One of the advantages of this heat wave is that we can eat on the deck." Milly paused. "Unless you'd rather not sit outside?"

The urge to hide away was powerful, but she fought it hard.

"It's not overlooked. It will be nice to eat with a view of the lake. I love your deck. I particularly love your porch swing." She watched as Milly removed a stack of ingredients from the fridge. "What can I do?"

"Nothing. Just sit there and talk to me while I prepare. Glass of wine?"

Nicole shook her head. "I don't drink."

"Since when? You were drinking when we visited you last."

Nicole remembered precisely when. "I decided I wanted to be healthier." It wasn't the truth, but it could have been, and fortunately Milly didn't question it.

She walked back to the fridge and pulled out a jug. "Homemade lemonade? It's beautifully refreshing in this weather." Milly added ice to three glasses and poured the lemonade.

"Delicious." Nicole decided not to think about the sugar content for once. At this point, did it even matter? "How has Zoe been about Richard?" Just saying the words made her heart hammer her chest, but she knew she had to ask, even though she wasn't sure she wanted to hear the answer. It was a question she should have asked a long time ago.

"Hard to say." Milly tossed the chunks of bread in olive oil and herbs and tipped them onto a baking sheet. "Mostly she seems to be handling it, but you never know what is going on underneath. I think she protects me, and I protect her. Which means we don't have too many honest conversations about it. But she has good friends, which makes me feel better about the whole thing. If there's something she feels she can't talk to me about, hopefully she'll be talking to them."

"Like we did."

Milly added a few more herbs. "Like we did. This reminds me of that time we stayed with you in LA and you didn't want to go out to eat because someone always recognized you, so I cooked in your kitchen. You didn't know where anything was kept, and most of your pans were unused."

Nicole laughed. "I remember that time too. You complained that my knives weren't sharp enough." But what she really remembered wasn't Milly creating magic in her kitchen with its ocean view but what happened afterward. On the terrace. She pushed that memory aside and leaned in to take a closer look at the sourdough. "That looks amazing. Is that from the local bakery?"

"Only if you count me as the local bakery. I make it. Which I shouldn't, because baking isn't doing anything for my waistline. But it does a lot for my stress levels, and that's my priority." Milly slid the chunks of bread into the oven. "You probably don't want carbs, and that's fine. I can serve yours without."

Nicole's stomach rumbled for the first time in weeks. "I'll eat whatever you're having. And I know it will be better than anything I'd have in a top restaurant."

Milly removed chicken breasts from the fridge and heated some oil in a pan. "Do you really never cook for yourself?"

"Mostly I order room service."

"I mean when you're at home."

Nicole watched as Milly rubbed the chicken with oil and herbs.

"I haven't spent a single night in my home since the intruder.

I've been living in hotels." She'd expected Milly to look shocked, but she hadn't expected to see the sympathy.

"That must have been hard."

Nicole shrugged. "They were pretty nice hotels, and I was on location most of the time anyway, so it's not as dramatic as it sounds."

"But you should feel safe in your own home. I'm starting to understand why you're so jumpy."

"That's me. Jumpy. Does Zoe cook with you?"

"Yes, when she is around. There's something about preparing food side by side that is conducive to conversation."

"You were the same with your mother and Nanna Peg. Remember when we used to make cupcakes?" Nicole felt a rush of warm memories. "How is Nanna Peg?"

"She's great. She's staying with my mother at the moment while her roof is fixed, but she's hardly ever there. She hikes with a group four times a week." Milly adjusted the heat under the pan and added the chicken. "We could do that if you like?"

"You're suggesting we hike with eighty-year-olds?" Nicole smiled at the thought and Milly laughed too.

"That wasn't what I had in mind, but it would be interesting. Alternatively we could pick a quiet trail where no one will see you."

Nicole was tempted, but she knew that this brief thaw in their friendship might not last once she'd said everything that needed to be said. "Let's see how things go." She watched as Milly fried chicken breasts, rinsed salad leaves and mixed a dressing.

"So are you and Joel . . ." She let the sentence hang, and Milly glanced at her.

"What?"

"Together. You obviously know each other well. You don't have to answer that if you don't want to."

"Together? You mean romantically?" Milly laughed and turned her attention back to the chicken. "No. There's nothing romantic between us. I mean, he's great. I'm fond of him. But he's more like a brother. And honestly, the last thing I want or need is more emotional complication. I can't handle any more rejection."

Nicole could sympathize with that sentiment, but it made her want to strangle Richard.

She wanted to find out more about how Milly was coping, but at that moment Zoe reappeared.

"Something smells good. Is it nearly ready? I'm starving."

"You're always starving," Milly said. "Can you check the croutons for me?"

Zoe opened the oven and sniffed. "Mm. They smell delicious."

"Give them a shake and check they're not burning."

Zoe grabbed an oven glove, pulled out the tray and shook it. "They look fine. Five more minutes."

"Enough time for you to lay the table. We're eating outside. Do you have homework?"

"Yes, but I can do it after we've eaten. How about you? How was work?" Zoe grabbed cutlery and plates from the cupboard. "How did the interviews go? Did you find anyone good?"

"One person. It all helps. You know how short-staffed we are."

"I can help on the weekend if you like."

"That's thoughtful of you, but I'm sure we'll manage. Won't you be seeing Cally?"

"Not sure if she's around."

Nicole watched the two of them together, envying the ease of their interaction and their close bond. She'd never had that sort of relationship with her mother. The only person she'd ever felt that close to was Milly.

Her life was so busy, so demanding, that it was only in the past few weeks that she'd realized how lonely she was.

She had no one. And being part of this family, even if it was only for a short time, made her question her life.

They sat round the table on the deck, enjoying the food and conversation. The breeze created ripples on the surface of the water, and the air was fresh and clean.

It was all very relaxed and easy until Zoe asked Nicole what role she was playing next.

That question was difficult to answer, so Nicole simply smiled, grateful for her acting ability.

"I'm taking a short break. Still weighing up my options. How about you? Congratulations on getting that part in *A Midsummer Night's Dream*. You're going to be brilliant! How's it going?"

"Okay, thanks." Zoe ate quickly and then put her fork down. "I need to do my homework. I'll leave you two to catch up, and I'll see you later."

Milly frowned. "But you haven't seen Nicole in ages and—"

"It's fine," Nicole said. "We'll have plenty of time to catch up, I'm sure."

Zoe carried her empty plate into the kitchen, leaving the two of them alone.

Nicole finished her drink. "Why are you looking so worried?"

"Because that's not like her. Normally she'd be firing questions at you about Hollywood and acting. Usually it's all she talks about." Milly topped up Nicole's glass. "Sorry. Ignore me. It's just that something isn't quite right with her at the moment, and I can't work out what it is."

"Have you asked Richard if he knows?"

"No. I should probably do that. Anyway, enough of my anxieties. If you want to tell me why your next project is a sensitive subject, then I'm listening."

Nicole finished her salad. "You don't miss a thing, do you?"

"I've known you a long time." Milly pushed her plate away. "Maybe this is the part where you tell me why you're here. A few bad news headlines have never made you run before."

"It's complicated." How much should she say? "I've been dropped from my next movie because they didn't appreciate the negative publicity. Which feels unjust, given that none of it is my fault and that Justin is about to film his biggest role ever. His reputation is fine, of course. If anything, it has been enhanced."

Milly looked irritated. "But you're a huge star! How can they do that?"

"Justin's wife is close to the head of the studio, so I assume she has influence. Whatever. It doesn't matter. The way I feel now, I'm relieved that I'm on hiatus."

"That's unfair. You don't deserve it."

Nicole laughed. "Since when has life been fair? We all get good and bad, and just because you don't deserve something doesn't mean you don't get dumped with it."

"But why didn't he stand up for you?" Milly took a sip of water. "I suppose that wouldn't have endeared him to his wife."

"Exactly. Also, he didn't care enough." She watched as a heron glided past and landed gracefully on a branch at the edge of the lake.

"Tell me about Justin." Milly put the glass down. "Were you in love with him?"

Justin. She'd been trying not to think about it, but maybe now was the time. And she owed Milly some sort of explanation.

"I thought I was. For the first time ever. But now I'm wondering if I just wanted to be in love. If I wanted something more permanent. Something that had meaning." Loneliness had caused her to lower her guard. "I didn't break up his marriage, whatever the papers may say." She added that because she was aware this was a sensitive topic in the circumstances, but when she looked at Milly she saw no judgment.

"What happened?"

There was no reason not to tell the whole truth, about this part at least.

And maybe it would be good to talk about it instead of keeping it all inside.

"Justin and I have known each other for a while. We've done a couple of movies together over the years. Always got on well. He's smart and funny. A nice guy." Nicole paused. She'd thought he was a nice guy, but was he really? "The chemistry was there right from the start, but we never did anything about it because he was married.

119

But then there was one night when we were filming and he just wasn't himself. We couldn't get the scene right. And it was a tough one because it was raining and we were freezing, so in the end we took a break and went back to the trailer to warm up. I asked him if something was wrong, and he told me he'd just found out his wife was having an affair. I was shocked because they were supposed to have one of the most solid and envied marriages in Hollywood, but it turns out that was a sham. She'd had at least two affairs that he knew about, but each time he'd forgiven her and taken her back because he cared about her. But she killed that. He told me that there was no way he was taking her back this time. It was over."

Milly listened closely. "But no one suspected?"

"They're both actors. They made sure they were seen together all the time and were appropriately loving."

"So you—"

"No, not then. Through the whole shoot, we were just friends. I provided a listening ear. And I'd never really been friends with a guy before. Not like that. I'm not that great at trusting, as you know."

Milly nodded. "When did it turn into more than friends?"

"Filming took about six months, and it was intense and claustrophobic. By the end of it we were sharing every meal together and hanging out whenever we weren't on set. And then one night it became something more. I don't know who made the first move—" Nicole frowned as she thought back "—Yes, I do. It was him. We were in his trailer, talking and sharing a bottle of wine when he leaned in and kissed me. And the weird thing was we'd kissed before on set, plenty of times, but this was different."

"So that was it? That was the moment?"

Nicole shook her head. "I was wary. I don't have a great track record, as you know, and I could feel myself falling for him. I liked him. And I was scared that he'd go back to his wife. But he said there was no way. That it was over. He'd never had an affair before. Despite everything, he'd stayed faithful. And when he told me that it made what we had seem all the more special. And the more he told me about his marriage, the more I believed that it really was over. They hadn't had sex for over a year." She flushed. "Promise me you won't sell that juicy fact to the press."

Milly sighed. "Nic—"

"I know, I know—you would never do a thing like that. Why isn't everyone in the world like you? It would be a better place." She finished her lemonade, wishing in that moment that it was wine. "Anyway, I believed him. More fool me, as it turned out. But we were together for almost a year, and it was blissful. Not together the whole time of course, because by then I was working on something different and so was he, but we used to fly to meet each other and have these amazing weekends. We had a trip to Rome and had a midnight trip around the Colosseum wearing wigs and glasses and pretending to be Spanish tourists. I thought he was the one. I thought I'd finally found someone who was going to be in my life forever." Saying it aloud sounded so stupid now.

Milly reached across the table and took her hand. "What happened?"

"There were photographs. His wife saw them. Turned out that he really had been faithful up until that point—he was honest about that—but seeing him with someone else shook her up. I think it made her realize that she was going to lose him. She didn't want to lose him. She decided she wanted him back." She felt Milly's hand tighten on hers, and the comfort of knowing that someone cared, that she wasn't alone with everything, was almost overwhelming. She'd missed their connection so much. "She confronted me in the restaurant as if I was some sort of evil seducer and she was the wronged wife. It was truly awful. And of course someone filmed it, because everyone films everything these days." She often relived that moment, the deep humiliation and the devastation.

"And Justin decided he wanted to stay with her? After two affairs?"

"It was more than two." Nicole rubbed tears from her cheeks. She hadn't even known she was crying. "But yes, he decided he wanted to stay with her. So that was that."

It wasn't quite all of it, but it was enough for now.

"You poor thing. No wonder you're feeling raw." Milly was still holding her hand, offering comfort as generously as she would have done when they were children.

"You probably think I deserve it because he was married."

"No one deserves to get their heart broken, Nic. Life is complicated. He led you to believe his marriage was over, and you believed him."

Nicole felt a rush of love for her friend. And although a part of her knew that Milly wouldn't have been so warm and accepting if she'd known what Nicole wasn't telling her, she ignored it. "It's over now, anyway. Done."

"When you called me you said you were desperate. What tipped you over the edge?"

"The press wouldn't leave me alone. Everywhere I went, I had a camera pointed at me. That incident in my home shook me up. I was scared in hotels. I didn't trust anyone. I needed somewhere quiet and safe to think, and I couldn't think of anywhere else. I called you."

"I'm glad you called me. And I'm glad you're here."

"Really?" Nicole put her free hand on top of Milly's so that they were joined across the table. "You mean that?"

Something softened in Milly's eyes. "Yes, I do."

The relief was indescribable, but it was threaded with guilt. "I wasn't there for you when you needed me, and I thought—"

"Why weren't you? Tell me why. Help me understand."

The question caught her off guard.

Nicole felt the breath trap in her throat. From the moment Milly had picked her up from the railway station she'd known this moment would come, but now it was here and she wasn't ready.

She should simply tell the truth, but their relationship was still tender and vulnerable, and she was afraid that if she did that, what they had might be destroyed forever. She couldn't take that risk. Their friendship meant too much to her. If the last few months had taught her anything, it was that.

"I was in a bad place." That much was true. "Things were difficult."

"But then, why didn't you reach out to me?" There was a small furrow of confusion between Milly's brows. "Since when haven't we done that?"

"You had enough problems. And I was barely holding it together. I sort of retreated. It was a survival thing." There was more. So much more, but she wasn't ready to divulge that. "But you've heard my sad story. Now I want to hear yours."

For a moment she thought Milly might linger on the topic of their estrangement, but her friend sighed and eased her hands away.

"Mine is nowhere near as glamorous as yours. But if you think you were a fool, you should try being me. When Richard said he was working late and traveling, I believed him."

There was so much she wanted to say, but Nicole forced herself to just listen.

Milly glanced toward the house to check there was no sign of Zoe. "It had been going on for six months before he told me. Six months. And I didn't know. Can you believe that? I felt like such an idiot."

"Milly—"

"No, don't say anything. There's nothing to be said. I should have guessed, but I was busy getting on with what I thought was our shared life, and I didn't notice that my husband was contorting himself into various positions with Avery that clearly had nothing to do with yoga."

"Do you still love him?" Nicole held her breath as she waited for the answer.

"I don't think so, although it's complicated because of Zoe. You can't completely sever a relationship when you have a child. I remember how broken up I was after my dad walked out, and I don't want Zoe to feel that. I want her to know we both love her, and just because we've decided that we can't continue being married, our relationship with her will never change."

Nicole felt an ache in her chest because she knew it wasn't Milly who had decided that, it was Richard. "You're a wonderful mother. Zoe is lucky to have you."

"It's not all roses, I can tell you. Being a single mother can be lonely and a bit scary. Like just now when she suddenly announces she wants to be a computer engineer when all she's wanted to do since she was four years old is act. I know something's wrong, but I'll just have to wait until she's ready to talk to me. And in the meantime I barely recognize Richard. He's—" Milly stopped in mid-sentence. "Never mind."

Nicole nodded. "You're afraid that if you say what you really think, Zoe might hear you. You can tell me another time, when Zoe is at school."

"Good idea. We'll go to the top of a mountain and yell loudly."

"That sounds therapeutic." It really did, but best of all was the promise of spending time together. Of trying to find their way back to the friendship they'd both taken for granted for so many years.

"I need to put Richard behind me, and you need to put Justin behind you." Milly raised her glass in the air. "To moving on."

Nicole toyed with her glass but didn't raise it. After everything that had happened, she couldn't bring herself to toast anything. "That's an admirable sentiment."

"But?" Milly put her glass down, her gaze fixed on Nicole's face. "You're not still hoping the relationship will work out, are you? Because he's already—"

"No." It was a shock to realize just how much she hated thinking about Justin when only a couple of months ago thinking about him had been her favorite pastime. "I'm not hoping for that. It's over. Done."

"Then, why can't you forget about him? Why can't you just move on?"

Nicole stared across the lake and swallowed hard. "Because I'm pregnant. You asked me what tipped me over the edge. Why I called you. That's the main reason. I'm having his baby. By myself. And yes, it's lonely and scary, and also more than a little complicated."

10

Milly

Milly loved being a mother but there were times when it would have been nice to know you could have a conversation without being interrupted or overheard. The night before had been a prime example. Nicole made her shock confession (Pregnant! Milly was still reeling from that unexpected news), but before Milly could delve into the details, Zoe had reappeared, homework finished and clearly keen to make up for her earlier disappearing act.

Her presence had effectively shut down the one topic Milly had wanted to talk about.

But even then the conversation hadn't gone the way she'd anticipated because every time she mentioned Zoe's drama group, or the play, her daughter changed the subject.

And it was worrying her.

For as long as she could remember, Zoe had wanted to be an actress. When she was little she'd dressed up and performed in front of an audience of stuffed animals. Milly had been roped in to play various parts alongside her, and when Zoe was old enough to join the local drama club, Milly had patiently provided a taxi service. When she'd been given the part of Hermia in *A Midsummer*

Night's Dream, they'd celebrated by going for ice cream sundaes at the café. For weeks Zoe had talked about nothing else, but suddenly she was avoiding the subject.

Milly knew something wasn't right, but Zoe clearly wasn't ready to talk about it.

Instead she'd asked Nicole about her life in Hollywood and what it was like to wear so many great clothes. Nicole had seemed relaxed, showing no sign of the fact that just a few moments earlier she'd announced a major life change. But she was an excellent actress, of course. She could portray one thing while feeling something entirely different. Milly, on the other hand, couldn't act at all, and she'd sat tense and anxious, worrying about her daughter and also about her friend. Pregnant? It would change everything.

And now she understood why Nicole had used the word *desperate* when she'd called asking for sanctuary.

She'd never pictured Nicole in a long-term relationship or settled with children. She knew from previous conversations that it wasn't something Nicole had pictured for herself either.

How did she feel about it? And did Justin know?

She had so many questions and so far hadn't been able to ask any of them.

She'd hoped Zoe might decide to have an early night for once, but in the end it was Nicole who had gone to bed first, claiming exhaustion and jet lag, and she still hadn't emerged from her room when Milly had made breakfast and driven Zoe to school.

On her way back to Forest Nest she'd called her mother to tell her that Nicole was staying and ask her if she had any idea what was wrong with Zoe, but the phone had gone to voice mail, which was puzzling because Milly couldn't remember a time when her mother hadn't answered her phone. She'd been Milly's rock, and she felt a little ashamed for not making more of a fuss of how supportive and present her mother had been. She was going to remedy that next time she saw her.

Back home there was still no sign of Nicole, so Milly had left a note on the countertop.

I'll be back at lunchtime, and we'll talk. Call if you need me.

And then she'd gone to work, this time remembering to lock the door of the boathouse behind her.

She tried to push Nicole and Zoe out of her head as she dealt with the problems of the day. An irate guest who had tried to cancel their booking for the following week and had been outraged to discover that they would lose the money they'd paid. A woman who wanted to book two adjacent cabins for a Christmas celebration. As well as troubleshooting, she interviewed three people for two positions on the team (finding good staff was a never-ending nightmare) and had a meeting with a local outdoor-pursuits company who were interested in collaborating. Halfway through her morning Lorna burst into the room, staggering under the weight of an extravagant bouquet of flowers.

"Look! Aren't they amazing?"

Milly was impressed. "Incredible. And it proves Duncan is capable of romantic gestures after all. Good for him."

"They're not from Duncan. They're from Brendan Scott. Isn't he a sweetie?"

Milly chose not to remind Lorna that just the day before she'd described him as a *moody monster*. "That's a thoughtful gesture."

"I can't wait to see Duncan's face when he sees them."

Milly felt sorry for Duncan, who had always seemed to her to be solid and kind if maybe a little unimaginative.

Thinking of how brutal Richard had been—*Life with you just isn't that exciting, Milly*—she was currently of the opinion that kindness in a man was underrated.

"The card says *With apologies from a grumpy author.*" Lorna's cheeks were flushed. "I'm going to use it as a bookmark and keep it forever. I love his books."

"You read crime?" Milly thought she knew her team pretty well, but still she was surprised. She'd had Lorna pegged as a lover of happy endings.

"Yes, and he's the best. Keeps the reader guessing the whole time. You know sometimes books claim you'll never see the twist coming, and then you see the twist on page two? Well, that's not him. I don't let myself buy one of his books until I have a full day off because I know that once I start, I won't be able to stop. Nothing will get done. Duncan knows that once I have a new Brendan Scott, all I want from him is mugs of tea and finger food so that I don't have to stop reading to eat."

"What kind of finger food?"

"He makes me these little rolls of ham, and cubes of cheese. Baby tomatoes. Tiny wedges of cucumber. And he doesn't try and engage me in conversation until the book is finished. Bliss."

Milly tried to think of a single time Richard had done something similar for her. Not in the months before he'd walked out, certainly. Before that? She let her mind slip further back but still couldn't think of a time when he'd done something that thoughtful. About once a month he'd bring her a cup of tea in the morning, but he always made it so milky she usually left it untouched.

Why hadn't she told him how she liked it? Why hadn't she said *I hate my tea milky*?

He'd never made her food. If she suggested they eat out, his response was always that her food was better than anything you could order in a restaurant, and while that was flattering, it also meant that there was rarely a night when she didn't cook.

It crossed Milly's mind that if Lorna didn't want to hang on to Duncan, then maybe she'd snap him up herself. "Buying flowers is easy. But delivering a plate of food you can eat without a break in your reading is a wonderful gift. It's personal."

"Personal?"

"It shows he knows you and wants to make you happy. That's romantic." She felt a pang of envy. "Lucky you."

Lorna frowned. "A few nibbles on a plate aren't that special."

"They are when someone has put them together because they know it will please you. Anyway, back to Brendan Scott—" Milly changed the subject before she could feel even more morose about the state of her own love life. "Does this mean you want to go back to cleaning his cabin?"

Lorna's face was a picture of horror. "I still find him daunting. Also knowing what goes on in his head is a bit freaky, if you know what I mean. Although I'm not suggesting writers act on the stuff they put in their books. At least I hope they don't, or you should be taking a look under his floorboards before he checks out. Was there a funny smell in there? Any signs that something might be decomposing?"

Only the food in his fridge. "No. All occupants appeared to be alive. But can I assume from that comment that you don't want to clean his cabin?"

Lorna flushed. "If that's okay. I feel guilty giving you more to do."

"I'm happy to do it." She decided that perhaps she wouldn't look too closely at why that might be. He definitely hadn't been flirting with her. She was embarrassed that it had crossed her mind that he might be. "I'm glad he sent you the flowers. It was a nice touch, although he shouldn't have glared at you in the first place."

"He's a creative genius." Barely able to see past the volume of blooms, Lorna was in a forgiving mood. "I should have made allowances. Was it okay when you went yesterday?"

"Yes." As promised, she'd returned in the afternoon when he was out and had been careful not to touch the sheets of paper that were carpeting the floor. She'd piled all the dirty mugs and plates into the dishwasher and set it to run while she'd changed sheets and towels and freshened up the rooms. A quick look inside the fridge had revealed that he clearly had no plans to cook a nutritious dinner for himself. She'd removed the single piece of ancient, dried out cheese hiding away at the back and on impulse paid a swift visit to the café. She'd picked up a light summer salad and a slice of lemon tart, which she'd left in his fridge along with a note.

At least she wouldn't have to worry about him starving or poisoning himself.

"Anyway," Lorna said as she adjusted her grip on the flowers, "I wanted to show you these and make sure you were fine with everything."

"I'm fine." She wondered what Brendan was doing right at that moment. Tapping away at his laptop? Staring across the lake waiting for inspiration? Letting another mug of coffee go cold?

Maybe she'd drop off another meal later, just in case he was hungry. This time she'd make it herself.

Lorna left the room, and Milly checked her phone. There was nothing from Nicole. Which meant what? Had she left? Was she regretting telling Milly everything?

It was funny how friendships work, Milly mused. She'd been so upset, so determined to keep Nicole at a distance, but then the moment Nicole had opened up, the resentment and hurt inside her had retreated. In the moments before Zoe had turned up, it had almost felt as if they were back in the old days, before the foundations of their friendship had been shaken.

She went back to work and was in the middle of signing off invoices when her phone rang. It was Richard.

Her heart rate increased, her body already anticipating trouble. Richard only ever called when there was a problem. He'd be canceling or postponing something, all the time delivering the message that his new life was full and busy and *fun* and that he didn't really have time for her.

She considered letting it go to voice mail but then remembered that she'd vowed not to keep doing that, so she forced herself to answer.

"Hi, Richard." She stared at the photo of Zoe that she kept on her desk. No matter what he said, she was going to be polite and civilized for Zoe's sake. For their daughter.

"I got your message. And I have to say I did not appreciate the tone."

"The tone?" She felt something tighten inside her, the usual warning from her body that conflict was coming and she'd better duck and take cover.

"Yes. Normally you're a mild person. Gentle and kind. You're accommodating."

Mild? What sort of word was that? What sort of person did *mild* describe?

The sort of person who made excuses for a man who was behaving badly.

She thought back to the message she'd left. Be more Amara. "I simply pointed out that if you're making plans with your daughter, you should stick to them. And you should."

"Obviously I'm doing my best. I don't need to be lectured by you."

Her palms felt sweaty, and her pulse was sprinting so fast she wondered if a conversation with Richard might count as a workout. They told you to get your heart rate up. They weren't specific about how you were supposed to do it.

It embarrassed and annoyed her that she had this extreme reaction to conflict.

She was no longer ten years old. This wasn't her father shouting at her mother and then walking out. Richard had already left her. What more could he do?

She rubbed her fingers across her forehead to relieve the ache. Sadly there was plenty he could do, the worst of which would be to make things more difficult for their daughter.

What had happened to the man she'd loved for so many years? The man who had promised to love her forever. The man who had swung Zoe round in his arms when she was four years old and taught her to swim and ride a bike. *Go for it. Daddy will catch you.*

She felt a pang of sadness as she thought back to those happy times. Her life had felt so right. As if things had worked out exactly as they should. She hadn't anticipated ever finding herself in this position.

"All I'm asking is that you think of Zoe's feelings. She's particularly vulnerable at the moment. Speaking of which, I think something is bothering her." It was playing on her mind. "I don't suppose you have any ideas what might be wrong?"

"She seemed fine to me."

"She mentioned that she might give up drama. Has she said anything like that to you?"

"No, but she's a teenager. They change their minds about things all the time. Don't fuss."

Was she fussing? She was never sure if she was being anxious or astute. "I just think we should make sure she has the chance to talk if she wants to. This has been a difficult time for her."

"And you're saying that's my fault."

Milly bit her lip, determined not to let things escalate. "It's not about fault. It's about making sure we're putting her needs first in all this."

"I'm doing my best. Plans change, Milly. Life happens." He was snippy and irritable. "You have no idea how tough it is for me trying to juggle everything and keep everyone happy. It's a nightmare, frankly."

What exactly was he juggling? She was the one trying to keep all the balls in the air while he led the life he wanted to lead and occasionally saw his daughter when he could fit her in.

"By 'everyone,' I assume you mean Avery." Was it wrong to feel a twinge of satisfaction that everything might not be as smooth as she'd assumed? Did that make her a bad person?

"It's tough for Avery too. She has to share me with you and Zoe."

The hand that wasn't holding the phone curled into a fist.

"What did she expect? That's what happens when you get involved with a married man who has a child."

"I've never known you to talk like this before. What has happened to you?"

Milly stared into the distance. What had happened to her? The man she'd loved and trusted had left her, that was what had happened. And for months she'd grieved and blamed herself and wondered what she could have done differently. She'd busted a gut trying to make a bad situation as good as possible for her daughter. She'd moved out of the home she loved because that was what Richard had demanded. She'd turned up to work every day even when all she wanted to do was to curl up under the covers.

"Your comment about Avery was a little insensitive, that's all." She fixed her gaze on the photo of Zoe and kept her tone soft. "We're all doing our best in difficult circumstances."

"I'm just trying to be happy. To live a happy life. It's not a crime, Milly. Not that I expect you to understand that."

"What's that supposed to mean?"

"Nothing. Forget it."

The window of her office overlooked one of the forest paths, and she watched as a family of three made their way along the trail, loaded up for the day with backpacks and a huge picnic bag. The man carried the little girl on his shoulders, and Milly felt an ache of envy and sadness. Seeing a happy family enjoying their time together made her realize what a mess her own was.

"I don't want to forget it." So much for trying not to escalate things. "What is it that I don't understand, Richard?"

"You don't understand about enjoying life. Your whole focus is on duty and responsibility. All you think about is boring chores. Doctor's appointments, and parent–teacher meetings and acting as a taxi service for Zoe. You've turned your life into a never-ending to-do list."

"Because these things have to be done!" The injustice of it was like a knife to the heart. Something hot started to simmer inside her. "Doctor's appointments, parent–teacher meetings—they all have to be done, and someone has to do them. And that someone is never you, so it has to be me."

"I know you like to think you're doing it all, but I helped out plenty of times."

"Helped out?" The slow simmer became a dangerous boil of anger. "The responsibilities of life and parenthood are not mine for you to 'help' with. They're ours, to be shared equally. It's called being an adult, Richard. If I spent too much time doing 'boring chores,' then it's because you weren't doing your share."

If she didn't calm down she'd have a heart attack, and she could not leave Zoe in the care of this overgrown child. Zoe's teeth would fall out, she'd have no clean clothes, and she'd never make it to school on time. Also, she'd give up drama, and Richard wouldn't even think to ask her why.

"It's not my fault that you've forgotten how to enjoy yourself. I should probably call you Martyr Milly."

His words were so wounding, so deeply unfair, that for a moment Milly was robbed of breath.

"This conversation started because I was asking you to stick to the plans you make with Zoe. Or is she one of your 'chores' too? I'd hate to think that seeing your daughter deprives you of your precious fun."

She was glad she was alone in the office. There was no chance of Zoe overhearing.

What had happened to him? Since when had he been this selfish?

"I'm going to ignore that because it seems you're determined to be difficult. And as for Zoe, I can't pick her up from drama this weekend because it's Avery's mother's birthday, and we're taking her for a champagne afternoon tea at a manor house near here, but she can come and stay with us next weekend. I'll pick her up Friday after school and drop her back Sunday night."

"And Avery is okay with that?" She was going to stay calm. She was going to overlook the fact that Avery's mother's birthday was taking precedence over his commitment to his daughter. "It isn't going to get canceled?"

"Avery suggested it. She put it in the calendar."

And Milly was expected to flex because that was what she did. And if she didn't do it, Zoe suffered and Milly was labeled *difficult*.

Milly felt the familiar pain deep inside her. The truth was she hated the weekends that Zoe stayed with Richard. She usually worked because that was a better alternative to mooching around aimlessly, trying not to wonder if Zoe was going to end up liking Avery more than her own mother. Was she more fun? Did Zoe think her mother was boring?

She dragged her mind back to the present.

"I'll let Zoe know. But don't forget her drama club. She can't miss it because it's not long until the performance."

"You just said she's thinking of giving it up."

His comment reawakened her anxiety.

"Even if that's true, she can't give it up at the moment. She has made a commitment. It's not fair on everyone else for her to drop out at this late stage."

"Lighten up, Milly. If you want to make her carry on going to drama, that's up to you, but she's going to have to miss next week either way. If I bring her back for drama, I'll be spending the whole day in traffic. Zoe will be fine. Avery has a friend who works at the theater in the city, and she's got us front-row seats for *A Midsummer Night's Dream* on Saturday night. Zoe is going to love it."

Zoe would love it. Milly had tried to get tickets herself, even though going there would be a massive trek, but it had been sold out.

But Avery had contacts.

The wave of insecurity almost knocked her off her feet.

She tried to ignore it. In the end all she wanted was for Zoe to be happy, and this was going to make her happy.

"That's kind and thoughtful of Avery."

"She's a kind and thoughtful person."

The implication was that Milly was anything but kind and thoughtful.

She opened her mouth to say that Avery hadn't exactly been kind and thoughtful when she'd taken a hatchet to Milly's marriage but managed to stop herself.

She ended the call, so upset that she didn't know what to do with all the emotion swirling inside her. She picked up her half-empty mug, tempted to throw it hard at the wall, but then she put it down again. If she did that she'd have to clear up the mess. Another job.

Martyr Milly.

For the first time in eighteen months she felt relieved she was no longer married to him.

11

Connie

I can't believe you're back again this morning. I thought you'd be aching from head to toe." Janice, who owned Waterside Trekking, led Harley out of his box and handed the reins to Connie.

"I can hardly move, but yesterday's ride was the happiest two hours I've spent in as long as I can remember. I can't wait to do it again." She stroked Harley's neck. "Can you stand taking me out again? Did I bore you yesterday?"

Janice tightened the girth and pulled down the stirrups. "That's the great thing about horses. They're perfect listeners. There are just two of you on the ride this morning. Hello, Brian! We were just talking about you. Pepper is all ready and waiting in her stall."

A man about Connie's age walked into the yard carrying a riding hat.

Connie felt a thud of disappointment. Not that she'd expected to be the only person on the ride. Far from it. Yesterday she'd been one of eight, and it had been perfect. She'd blended in and, apart from friendly small talk when they'd been gathering in the yard before leaving, had spoken to no one. No one had asked about her life. No one had sympathized with her about Milly's situation. No one had asked how Connie was coping.

She'd felt delightfully anonymous as part of a group.

But riding with Janice and one other person?

She'd be expected to make conversation.

Resigned to it, she smiled politely. "I'm Connie."

"Brian." Unsmiling, he gave her a brisk nod and let himself into Pepper's stall. He clearly knew what he was doing, because what seemed like only moments later he was mounted and talking quietly to the lively mare, his hands light on the reins as he calmed her.

Connie, who could barely move after her ride the day before, was rethinking her decision to ride again so quickly. Harley was nowhere near as boisterous as Pepper (thank goodness!), but still Connie was wishing she'd waited until her muscles had recovered.

Gritting her teeth and forcing her legs to move, she mounted Harley and waited while Janice led her own horse out of the stable.

There was a slightly awkward moment as Harley took a few side steps, and Connie found herself side-by-side with Brian.

"It's a beautiful day," Connie said politely, and Brian frowned and glanced briefly at the sky, as if he hadn't noticed the weather before Connie had mentioned it.

He said nothing in response, and Connie was briefly offended that he'd made no effort in response to her show of good manners, but then decided it gave her the excuse to ride in silence, which was exactly what she wanted.

He obviously wasn't the chatty sort, and that was a good thing. She didn't want chat. She wasn't here to chat.

And at least now no one could accuse her of being rude.

He was probably the type who thought every woman of a certain age was on the lookout for love, and in her case nothing could be further from the truth. It was a casual assumption so often made by society, that you needed to be with someone in order to be happy (in much the same way as people assumed that everyone of childbearing age would be having children if they could). She'd experienced it after Milly's father had walked out. Within months of him leaving, people had tried to match her with single men, until she'd announced that she was happier by herself. And it was true. It wasn't an excuse or a way of fending people off.

What most people didn't understand was that she wasn't looking for love. She didn't want, or need, to be in love because she was entirely content with her life just the way it was, and she had no wish to risk destabilizing what she'd built with such care.

Brian, whatever might be going on in his head, had nothing to fear from her.

They set off along the trail and straight onto the fells, winding their way upward along a track with views across the lake. The mountains rose, the lower slopes overgrown with ferns, the upper ones rocky as the terrain grew steeper.

Connie felt herself relax. People said you got used to a place if you lived there, that you no longer appreciated the charms that drew people from around the world, but that wasn't true for her. She loved this place. She loved the vast skies, the shimmering lakes and the craggy horizons, and there was no better place to appreciate the scenery than from the back of a horse.

They rode in silence, and after a while Janice, who was in the lead, turned in her saddle. "Ready to canter?"

They took off along the track, and Connie forgot that she was still aching from the day before, and she forgot that she was annoyed to be sharing the ride with one other person.

Her only focus was the rhythmic thud of hooves and the sheer exhilaration of being on a horse while enjoying exquisite views. Far beneath her the lake sparkled in the sunshine, stretching along the valley floor like a silver ribbon. A smile spread across her face.

She experienced the same sense of elation and happiness that she'd felt the day before. Here, on Harley's back, there was no past or future. There was only this moment.

Eventually they slowed to a walk, and Connie reached forward and patted him gently, watching as his ears moved in response to her soft words of praise and appreciation.

They reached a viewpoint on the trail and stopped to take in the vista and give the horses a brief rest.

Janice was responding to a message on her phone, and Connie felt the usual powerful urge to check hers in case her mother, Milly or Zoe needed her. But she resisted. They were all more than capable of managing by themselves for a few hours.

Instead she stared across the lake, surprised to discover that she hadn't given them a thought when she'd been cantering along the trail. It was only now, when she was still again, that her thoughts settled back on her family and her anxieties. Her mind was a boomerang, programmed to return to family.

Why did she find it so hard to switch off? Why did she feel guilty when she took a little time for herself? They really *were* more than capable of managing by themselves, so why did she worry so much?

It was love, of course, but she sensed that it was more than that. Habit? She'd handled everything alone for so long it was hard to give herself permission to loosen her grip.

Did she need them to need her? Was that it?

Who was she when she wasn't being a mother, a grandmother or a daughter?

Who was Connie?

Unsettled by the question, she glanced at Brian and saw that he was also gazing across the lake, a distant look in his eyes. She had no idea if he was contemplating the meaning of life or thinking about what he'd eaten for breakfast.

Some instinct made her want to ask if he was okay, but she suppressed it.

He'd made it more than clear that he didn't want to chat, and she understood that.

And she was grateful for it, because she wasn't looking for a heart-to-heart or a confession session on all the challenges they were handling in life (because did anyone get to their age without navigating something big?). Sometimes it was good to talk, but other times it was good to try and forget. To enjoy the moment.

To step outside the worry or the sadness or whatever weight life was pressing onto you and throw it all off for a brief time.

But still she wondered, and when Janice asked if the two of them would like to do a full-day ride the following week, Connie found herself saying yes. And so did Brian.

Silence didn't seem to matter when you were on a horse, particularly as they mostly rode nose to tail, which rather limited opportunities for conversation.

She could have spent the whole day riding.

It was like pressing Pause on her life, and she was surprised by how good that made her feel.

12

Milly

Milly knew there was no way she'd get any more work done after that conversation. It felt as if someone had thrown her emotions in a blender.

While she was stewing and trying to handle all the change in her life, none of which had been of her choosing, Richard was living his best life.

And it wasn't as if she wanted him to be unhappy exactly—although the way she was feeling at the moment she might have wished the occasional bad day on him—but she didn't see why his happiness should come at her and Zoe's expense.

Something needed to change.

Grabbing her bag, Milly stalked out of her office.

She resisted the urge to vent her frustration by slamming the door, and instead she walked briskly along the path and even managed to offer a polite greeting to a couple of guests who were passing.

The sun was beating down, but here in the shade of the tall trees the heat was less intense. She heard birdsong and the soft lap of the water against the shore. Normally it calmed her, but today it didn't seem to be working.

She unlocked the door of the boathouse, yelled "It's only me," and then slammed the door hard.

Tiger leaped up from his favorite position on the rug in a patch of sunlight, his back arched and his fur vertical as he prepared to defend his territory.

Nicole was sitting cross-legged on Milly's yoga mat in the living room, her hand pressed to her chest and her eyes wide. She was wearing yoga pants and a bright blue tank top.

"You made me jump."

"Sorry. I shouldn't have slammed the door. I might need anger management classes." Milly kicked off her shoes and sent them skittering across the floor.

"You?" Nicole watched her. "You're the calmest person I know. I've never seen you truly angry."

"Well, take a good look, because you're seeing it now." Milly dropped her keys and bag onto the table. She could feel her heart racing.

"Do you want to talk about it?"

"Honestly? No, I want to break something." She paced across the living room and back again. "But I don't want to clean up the mess after, so I'm internalizing my fury."

"That doesn't sound healthy." Nicole stood up in a single graceful movement. "I borrowed your mat. I hope you don't mind. I always stretch in the mornings or I stiffen up. I should never have insisted on doing my own stunts in that superhero movie. I've been paying the price ever since."

"No problem. I don't use it anyway. I bought it the week Richard walked out because I was determined to get lean and toned, but every time I saw the mat I thought of Avery and it upset me, so it mostly lives in that spot by the cupboard."

Just thinking of Avery sent her blood pressure soaring again.

Avery, who was struggling with the fact that Richard had responsibilities.

Avery, who was responsible for upending Milly's entire life.

No, that wasn't true. She forced herself to breathe. Richard had done that.

Nicole eyed her and bent down to roll up the mat. "By the look on your face, you should have bought a punching bag."

Clearly feeling at risk from Milly's pacing, Tiger sprang from the floor to the sofa.

"He said my whole focus was on duty and responsibility!" The words exploded out of Milly. "He said that all I think about is boring chores. He said I've turned my life into a never-ending to-do list!"

Nicole was still holding the mat. "I assume the *he* is Richard?"

"Yes. And it's true I have a to-do list—who doesn't?—but that's because there are things that need to be done and he doesn't do them, so that leaves me! And whenever he does do something, which is so rare I can't even quote you a time when he did, apparently he is 'helping' me."

Nicole's eyes widened. "He said that?"

Milly forced herself to breathe. "You'd be angry too?"

"I'd be steaming."

Milly felt a little better. "I'm sorry. Here I am ranting, and we should be talking about you." She felt a stab of guilt. "All morning I've been waiting for you to call so that we can carry on the conversation Zoe interrupted last night, and then Richard called me, and now I want to kill him."

"I want to kill him too. And forget about me—there's plenty of time to talk about that. First we need to calm you down."

"I don't know how. I've never been this angry before." She felt as if she was boiling inside.

"You need to vent your excess anger somehow. Exercise?" Nicole tucked the mat away. "You could go for a run?"

"I'm horribly unfit. That would kill me, not calm me." Milly rubbed her fingers across her forehead.

"Cook something, then. Chop an innocent vegetable into tiny pieces and fry it in hot oil. That always works for you."

"That's true. It does." Milly wondered why she hadn't thought of it herself.

She stalked to the kitchen and pulled open the fridge with such force that all the bottles stacked in the door rattled together. She grabbed leeks and mushrooms, and Nicole leaned against the countertop, keeping a safe distance.

"Tell me about Avery. She's a yoga teacher?"

"Yes. But not just that." Milly grabbed a sharp knife and slit the leeks down the middle in a single decisive move.

Nicole flinched. "Careful! If you slice your finger off, you won't be able to make rude gestures."

"Avery has her own studio and a huge social media following." She felt a wave of insecurity, which seemed to be happening more frequently.

"You stalk her on social media?"

"No. I'm not a masochist." She washed the leeks, and then the mushrooms, splashing water everywhere. "I looked a couple of times at the beginning and it made me feel bad about myself, so I stopped."

"Why did it make you feel bad?"

"All the usual reasons. She's twenty-five. Successful. Skinny. Blonde. Your average nightmare. And she runs her own business. And she's fun, apparently." She heard the hurt in her own voice. "A whole lot of fun. Unlike me, who is officially boring and also a *martyr*, according to Richard." She lined up the leeks and chopped them so quickly that Nicole drew breath.

"I'm not sure if this is helping your stress levels, but it's definitely not helping mine. You know I'm not good with blood."

"I have excellent knife skills. I may be no fun, but I can chop a leek."

"Okay." Nicole was calm. "Am I allowed to point out that you're also fun and run your own business?"

"I inherited my business."

"Which you have successfully grown into an aspirational destination through a mixture of extreme hard work and ingenuity."

It was true, so why didn't hearing it said aloud lift her mood?

"Maybe. But holding it all together requires a poise that eludes me." She sloshed olive oil into a pan and started to fry the leeks. "In every one of Avery's social media posts she looks calm and together, as if an anxious thought has never entered her head. The sky behind her is always blue. It has been raining nonstop here for months, but somehow the sun shows up for her. Her life looked so perfect, and mine was—is—such an imperfect mess." She pushed the leeks around the pan, waiting for them to soften. "Ignore me. I'm angry, upset and worried about Zoe. Let's talk about you. I want to talk about you and Justin and the baby."

"Later," Nicole said. "First let's address the whole social media thing. You do know it's all fake? That's the whole point of social media, at least for someone like Avery. She's trying to persuade the people watching that she has a perfect life and if they subscribe to her app or show up at her classes, then they too can have a life like hers. It's not about truth, it's about building an audience. She is showing them a life they can aspire to. It's no more real than a movie."

"You don't know that."

"I'm uniquely qualified to know it. Let me show you something." Nicole grabbed her phone from the pocket of her yoga pants and started to scroll. "Look. Tell me what you see."

Wondering what this had to do with Avery, Milly stopped stirring the leeks and took the phone from her friend. She saw a photograph of Nicole posing for photographers on a red carpet. She was wearing a figure-hugging dress that plunged almost to her navel and was slit to the thigh. Jewels sparkled at her throat, and her makeup was immaculate. But what really caught the attention was her famous, full-wattage smile.

"That dress is spectacular. You look happy." Milly felt a twinge of envy as she handed the phone back. "As if you really are living your best life."

"Right. This was taken three weeks ago at a time when I'd never felt more miserable. It took a team of people five hours to get me looking like that, and I wanted to cry the whole time." Nicole's voice was husky. "That photo tells you nothing about what was really going on. And those blue-sky yoga photos? She probably waited for that one blue-sky day and took a whole bunch of them together and changed her outfits. It's not real, Milly. You should know that."

"Maybe I do deep down, but being left in such a brutal fashion distorts your vision and hammers your confidence. Not just because I'm not a svelte yoga teacher, although that doesn't help, but because Richard chose her." The conversation with Zoe in the car had been playing on her mind. "He wasn't seduced or tempted or led astray, he made a choice. And he could have chosen me. He could have chosen Zoe. His family. The life we'd built together. But he chose Avery."

Tiger padded warily into the kitchen, lured by the smells of cooking.

"You're saying that as if it's something you only just realized," Nicole said.

"It is. I wasted so much time being angry with Avery, blaming Avery. But she didn't take anything he didn't want to give. He made a choice." Admitting that hurt. "It's humiliating."

"Why? This isn't about you, Milly. It's about him. He must have had some sort of midlife crisis. Blew something in his brain." Nicole bent down to stroke Tiger, who was rubbing himself against her legs as if he sensed she was the only calm one in the room. "Would you take him back?"

Something in her tone made Milly wonder if there was something more behind that question. Was Nicole thinking of Justin's wife?

"No. I don't even like him at the moment. He has changed."

Nicole glanced up. "What has changed?"

"He's acting strangely. Recently I've seen a side of him I really don't like." Milly turned back to the pan and added the mushrooms. "Not just the fact that he had an affair, but the way he shirks responsibility. He does what suits him, and the rest of us have to fit round him and just be grateful when he shows up. And I hate how that must make Zoe feel. I want him to show her that she is more important to him than anything else."

"You're always thinking about Zoe."

"I don't want her to be hurt. I would lie down in front of a bus for her." Milly turned down the heat and headed back to the fridge. "I'm sure every mother feels the same way."

The moment the words left her mouth she wanted to pull them back, but it was too late for that.

"Not every mother." Nicole scooped up Tiger and held him close. "Zoe is lucky to have you."

"That was tactless. Forgive me." She waited for Tiger to object to being held and wriggle away, but he sat still, tolerating the affection, as if he sensed that Nicole needed the comfort more than he needed to escape.

"Nothing to forgive. It's the truth. Most mothers would put their child first. Just not mine." She hugged Tiger. "But maybe in the end all this will make Zoe tougher. She'll learn an important lesson. That sometimes the people you love can hurt you and disappoint you. They can make bad choices that you don't understand. And you will probably still love them anyway. But however they choose to behave, you can choose to be okay."

Milly mixed together eggs and cream.

"Are we talking about Zoe or you now?"

Nicole laughed. "Definitely Zoe. I'm not okay. I'm as messed up as they come. Look at me, thirty-six years old and still trying to get my mother's approval. Pathetic, right?"

"Not pathetic." She couldn't imagine where she'd be without her mother's and grandmother's support. It was something she took for granted. Something everyone should be able to take for granted. "Has your mother messaged you?"

"What do you think?" Nicole kissed Tiger on the head, and he wriggled out of her arms, clearly deciding that kissing was more than one independent cat could reasonably be expected to tolerate.

Milly sprinkled flour on the work surface and rolled out a circle of pastry. "As you just said to me, you do know it's not you?"

"Ah, but in this case it *is* me. I'm a big disappointment."

"Because your career has been *such* a failure." Milly flashed her a smile. "You really should have done better. Tried harder."

Nicole didn't return the smile. "But what's it all been for? What was the point of it? The irony is that at the beginning I did it for her, you know? To prove to her that I was good at something. The first big role I landed, I thought, this is it. She'll be proud of me now. But she wasn't. So I thought, maybe that isn't enough. I need bigger roles. I need to win awards and be noticed and then maybe she'll notice me too. So I did that, and it still wasn't enough. And then I gave up on approval and just wanted to show her."

Milly was upset for her friend all over again. All Nicole had wanted was for her mother to act the way any other mother would. She'd wanted to feel valued. She'd wanted to make her mother proud. And no child should have to work at that.

"And you did show her."

"Yes, and suddenly my career is soaring, people are looking at me with envy, and I'm asking myself what the heck I'm doing. Why I'm doing it, because my mother doesn't seem to care what I do or what I achieve. I've shown her, and she just doesn't care. Lately I've been questioning my life. My choices."

Milly assembled everything and slid it into the oven. Her own emotions had settled as she'd listened to Nicole. Whatever her difficulties with Richard, she was loved and supported by her family, and she always had been. She didn't win awards, and few people outside the village knew her name, but she felt valued. And she knew how much that was worth.

"You're successful, Nicole. Beyond successful."

"But what is success? Because if you're not enjoying the life you're living, if you're hating almost every moment, then that doesn't feel like success to me. I've come to the conclusion that fame can be dangerous because it distorts reality. And it's so easy to get sucked into it." Nicole paused. "Do you know how it feels to be adored? To have crowds calling your name and people wanting to take a photo with you? Everyone thinking you're great. It's intoxicating. You feel validated, important, secure—and I'd never had that before. Maybe if I'd had those things earlier in life, I wouldn't have been so naive." She shrugged. "I'm not blaming anyone. I'm just stating a fact. I once got ninety-eight percent in an English exam and I rushed home to tell her thinking that finally I would have made her proud, and do you know what she said? 'What went wrong, Nicolette? What happened to that two percent?'"

She remembered that conversation: she'd been there when Nicole's mother had said those words.

Milly wiped her hands and stepped toward her friend. "Nic—"

"I grew up feeling like a failure. I was desperate for her approval." She took a glass from the cupboard and filled it with water. "Desperate for any evidence that I was worth loving and not a total failure as a human being. When I didn't get that validation from her, I looked for it elsewhere. To begin with, it was men. Men who paid me attention. My self-esteem was so low I wanted to believe those things they said about me. And then I realized that they weren't giving, they were using me. Their opinion of me wasn't any higher than my mother's. I stopped dating." She took a sip of water and Milly nodded.

"I know. I remember that time."

"But the public—" Nicole's eyes filled, and she blinked rapidly. "I was hungry to be loved, and they loved me. And it was easier to bathe in the approval of an amorphous crowd than to try to seek the approval of one person. I felt special. I felt good about myself for the first time ever." She took another sip of water. "It's embarrassing to admit that."

This felt like the conversations they used to have when they were growing up. They'd never been afraid to bare their feelings.

"Why is it embarrassing?"

"Because it was no more real than those social media posts you were looking at. All the attention I've been given in my life—it's an illusion. Smoke and mirrors. The biggest deception of all." Nicole put the glass down. "For a short time I thought what I had with Justin was real. I thought he loved me."

And the betrayal would have hurt all the more for that. Milly could understand that.

"Are you sure he didn't?"

Nicole shrugged. "In the end he loved his career and his image more. Did he use me to raise his profile? I don't know, but that's what happened. I can't believe I actually suggested that we both just walk away from it all, buy a plot of land and grow vegetables."

Milly tried to picture it, and doing so made her smile. "Do you know anything about growing vegetables?"

"No, but I thought it would be fun to learn. Particularly if we were doing it together."

Together. And that was what this was of course: Nicole's attempt to create something that resembled a family.

Imagining her excitement and then her devastation wiped the smile from Milly's face.

"I assume he didn't grab the chance."

"No. Probably a good thing, because we both know I wouldn't have known how to cook the vegetables even if I'd grown them." Nicole shrugged. "Anyway, that's my sorry story. And this is a heavy conversation to have in the middle of the day."

In the past they would have talked about whatever they wanted to talk about, whenever it felt right to do so. They wouldn't have cared what time of day it was.

Milly felt a pang of nostalgia. "It's a heavy conversation for someone who hasn't had lunch and probably didn't eat breakfast. And don't tell me you never eat breakfast, because you're pregnant now, so things have to change." Suddenly she felt protective. "That baby needs you to eat something."

Nicole raised an eyebrow. "Are you mothering me?"

Someone needs to.

"I'm not mothering you as much as caring for you and encouraging you to care for yourself." Milly grabbed salad items from the fridge. "You're going to have a slice of mushroom and leek tart, with a large salad. You can help make the salad."

And she intended to take some of the food to Brendan Scott. In case he was hungry. Because it was her job to care for her guests, and he didn't seem to consider nutrition when he was busy writing.

Not for any other reason.

Nicole looked at her doubtfully. "If cooking is what it takes to be a good mother, I'm doomed."

"Anyone can make a salad." Milly checked the tart and adjusted the oven temperature. "And you're not doomed. You're going to be an amazing mother."

"You don't know that." Nicole rinsed salad leaves. "It's not as if I had a great role model. I'm scared I'm like my mother. What if I've inherited her inability to connect with my child?" She tipped the leaves into the bowl. "I'm her daughter after all. I have her genes."

Milly saw the doubt and fear in her friend's eyes and felt a rush of compassion because she understood where the insecurity came from. "You are not your mother."

"I know, but—" Nicole looked at her helplessly. "He told me I'd make a terrible mother, and I can't help wondering if he's right. I can't stop thinking about it."

"Who told you that?" Milly was appalled. "Justin?"

She didn't know the man, but she was starting to form an impression, and it wasn't good.

"He said I'm selfish and that my lifestyle just isn't compatible with having a child."

The heat inside her, newly calmed, blazed to life again.

Milly grabbed the olive oil and a bottle of vinegar. "It's not true, Nicole, and you know it."

"Do I? My schedule has been manic. I've taken one job after another."

"That doesn't make you selfish. It makes you a successful working woman, and working women have babies all the time. He clearly doesn't understand how capable you are." She mixed a dressing in a jar and shook it vigorously.

It should be possible to ignore the things people said, shouldn't it? But she knew from her own experience that wasn't always possible, and it was clear that for Nicole, Justin's words had sunk into her like a splinter.

"What if he is right?" Nicole was desperate for reassurance. "What if I do it all wrong? Make mistakes?"

Milly put the jar down. There was plenty she could have said, but Nicole didn't need platitudes, she needed honesty, and she needed to believe in herself.

"You probably will make mistakes. Everyone does. When it comes to parenthood, we're all making it up as we go along. But history does not have to repeat itself. You can choose what type of mother you want to be."

She'd never even thought about it before, but as she did now she could see that in many ways she'd done all the things her own mother had done. Maintained many of the same traditions. Followed her example of offering unconditional love, free of judgment.

And she acknowledged now that her mother's belief in her had given her a belief in herself. She'd coped with difficult times because it hadn't occurred to her not to. Her mother had taught her that when you were knocked down, you got back up. Did she sometimes find life hard? Yes, but she still got herself out of bed and did what needed to be done. Just as her mother had.

"I already know what sort of mother I'd like to be." Nicole said without hesitation, "I'd like to be exactly like you."

Emotion hit Milly like a thump in her chest.

All morning she'd been feeling like a failure, and with those few words Nicole made her feel better.

She swallowed. "That's possibly the best thing anyone has ever said to me."

"It's the truth. If I'm half as good a mother as you, I'll be doing okay. But that doesn't mean I'm not still scared. I didn't plan any of this."

How much of life did any of them really plan? You thought you were in control, and then out of nowhere something happened and you realized that control was an illusion.

"Can I ask you something?" The food was forgotten as they both focused on the conversation. "When Justin said he didn't want anything to do with the baby, did that make you reconsider?"

"You mean did it make me consider not keeping my baby? No." Nicole rested a protective hand on her lower abdomen. "I decided I'd do it without him. But I'm scared."

"Of course you are. I think most women feel that way whether they're alone or with someone. It's a big change. And a big responsibility. But that doesn't mean you won't be great at it. And you will. And I will only ever be a phone call away."

Nicole looked at her, the turmoil of the past eighteen months present in the room with them. "Do you mean that?"

How had she ever thought she could keep her distance? Whatever happened, the bond between them ran too deep to be easily destroyed.

"I'll be with you every step of the way. I can lend you the books I used and recommend websites. But in the end you'll do it your own way." To hide the emotion she was feeling, she grabbed cutlery from the drawer. "Take this out to the deck, and I'll bring the rest."

She lifted the quiche onto a board, sliced it and plated it.

Then she covered the rest so that the flies wouldn't descend on it while it was cooling and joined Nicole on the deck.

"This looks delicious," Nicole said, and Milly took a sip of water and picked up her fork.

"I wish food didn't make me feel better about life, but it does. What does that say about me?"

"It says you're a good cook," Nicole said as she savored a mouthful of food. "Honestly, who wouldn't be comforted by this? It's ambrosial. Although, if you really don't want to comfort-eat, let me cook next time. There's no way you'll be soothed by anything I put on your plate."

Milly smiled. "Maybe that's what we need to do. The Nicole Diet. Then I wouldn't feel so bad about myself."

Nicole stabbed at her salad. "Why do you feel bad about yourself?"

"Uh . . . because I'm unfit and flabby, and looking in the mirror depresses me."

"I think you look great. Do you work out?"

"There are never enough hours in the day." She squirmed, because she wasn't only lying to Nicole, she was lying to herself. "It's an excuse, I know. But I hate the gym. All those mirrors and skinny people around you, most of them filming themselves on their phones. I'm terrified my flab might go viral."

"You don't need a gym to work out. You're surrounded by hills and trails. You can run and climb."

"I think you might be overestimating my basic fitness level," Milly said. "I don't run anywhere."

Nicole put her fork down. "Okay, so it's time for a review of our current situation. You're unfit and feeling generally bad about yourself. I'm terrified to leave the house and am also terrified about the future. How are we going to fix this?" She leaned forward. "Strategy time."

"You have a strategy that can fix all that?" She remembered all the times they'd done this when they were young. Boys. School-work. Scary parties. Becoming a movie star. Whatever the goal was, Nicole would come up with a strategy. "You've got that look on your face."

"Which look?"

"The one that scares me because it usually means you're going to make me do something I don't want to do."

Nicole didn't deny it. "What are you like at five in the morning?"

Milly burst out laughing. "Comatose. Unless I'm lying there fuming about Richard."

"Not anymore. Starting tomorrow you're going to be down here at five wearing your running shoes. You are going to start by running for fifteen minutes. You can walk the rest and gradually increase the time. How does that sound?"

It sounded awful.

"I won't be doing any of that because there is no way I'm getting up at five. Also, I hate to break this to you, but I can't run

154

for five minutes. I'd be doubled over and panting for breath after three. And anyway, I don't want to get thin for Richard."

"You're not getting thin for Richard. This isn't about losing weight. This is about getting fitter and stronger because you want to. I guarantee it will change the way you feel about yourself. You will feel healthier and more energetic, and you will start to love the feel of the early morning."

"Again, no." But she knew that once Nicole had an idea about something, it was hard to shift her.

"I'm going to walk into your bedroom tomorrow and haul those covers from you so that you don't have a choice. It's tough love."

Tough love.

An idea came into her head. Nicole wasn't the only one who could come up with a strategy. "I'll do it if we do it together."

Nicole shook her head. "No way. I'll be staying here at base, making you a delicious cup of coffee for your return. And anyway, someone has to stay with Zoe."

"No, they don't. I don't like leaving her overnight, but she's fine for twenty minutes in the morning, and we can lock the door." She saw the panic in Nicole's eyes and almost relented, but then she thought about the reality of it. "You can't shut yourself away forever, Nic. You have a life to live. You *deserve* to have a life. You can't let other people stop that."

"You don't get it."

"That's probably true. I can't begin to imagine what it must be like to not be able to walk down a street without being recognized. To be afraid in your own home. But I do know you're scared, and I know about being scared. I've been scared for most of my life. Scared about people leaving. Scared about Zoe growing up with daddy issues. Scared that I might be on my own for the rest of my life." She gave a short laugh. "Which makes no sense because the last thing I want at this point is a man. Ironic, isn't it? Most days I feel invisible, and you feel far too visible. What a pair we are. But we're going to do this."

"I can't." Nicole's voice was a whisper, and Milly realized that when her friend had called her saying that she needed somewhere to hide, she had meant it literally. She'd worried about how Nicole would be able to keep a low profile, and only now was she seeing that given the choice Nicole wouldn't set foot outside the boathouse.

And she felt guilty as she remembered how readily she'd dismissed Nicole's problems as trivial. There was nothing trivial about it. How must it feel to not be able to live life normally? To not be able to drop into a coffee shop when you liked or even arrive at a remote railway station in the middle of the night without wearing a disguise?

She felt grateful for her life. Compared to Nicole's existence, it was simple and unglamorous, and most of the time it was relentless hard work, but she had a freedom that she took for granted. A freedom she wouldn't swap for fame and fortune.

"Remember that party we both went to when we were fifteen?" Milly gently coaxed a wasp away from the food. "I was too scared to go, but you said you'd be right there by my side, and you were, and that's what I'm going to do for you. We are going to leave this house, and I am going to be right by your side."

Nicole didn't smile. "You think you can defend me from an overenthusiastic fan or worse?"

"I don't think we'll meet anyone, and if we do, I will say a bright, cheerful *Good morning* and draw their attention to something on the lake while you power past. You're pregnant, Nicole. You need to stay healthy, and that includes fresh air and exercise."

Nicole hesitated. "People want to do me actual harm!"

Sensing a weakening of resolve, Milly lifted her chin.

"They're going to have to go through me first."

13

Nicole

They ran every day at five o'clock in the morning, and as Milly had predicted they saw no one.

The first time they left the boathouse Nicole wore a wig, dark glasses and a hat pulled down over her eyes, but after she almost broke her neck tripping over an exposed root of a tree, she agreed to remove the glasses.

"I will be watching," Milly had promised, "and if I see anyone I will warn you, and you can put your glasses on. Although honestly, I think sunglasses make you look more like a movie star. It's movie-star uniform, isn't it? Just behave like a normal person."

"I am a normal person. But everyone forgets that."

"If anyone should be hiding, it should be me." Milly tugged her baggy T-shirt down over her hips. "Workout gear isn't very forgiving."

"You look great."

It shocked Nicole that Milly had so little confidence in herself, and then she realized that in an entirely different way she had no confidence in herself either, so she was hardly in a position to judge.

She couldn't get Justin's words out of her head. *You'd be a terrible mother.*

Not because she thought he was right—talking to Milly about it had made her feel better on that score—but because it was a truly awful thing to say to someone, particularly when that someone was a person you'd professed to love.

Milly scooped her hair into a ponytail. "If I really look great, why are you putting me through this torture?"

"Because it's not enough to look great. You also have to feel great. And by the time I've finished with you, you're going to be feeling like you've never felt before."

"Like I'm going to die, you mean?"

As predicted, Milly had only managed ten minutes of slow jogging on the first and second days. By day five she was managing fifteen minutes and at the end of the first week she hit twenty minutes, although by the time they completed that last run, she was breathing so hard Nicole was worried she'd have to resuscitate her.

Exercise was something she took for granted as being part of her job. Most days she did it without thinking, but she thought about it now as she constructed a doable workout for her friend.

Nicole taught Milly how to warm up and stretch, and halfway round the lake she found the stump of a tree that was exactly the right height to do step-ups.

"This is perfect. Go for it. Twelve reps, minute off, then another twelve reps."

"You're inhuman," Milly had panted as Nicole had made her step onto the tree trunk so many times she eventually collapsed onto it for a rest. "Enough."

"It's great for your quads."

"My quads disagree."

Being outside like this had been terrifying at first, but she discovered that the more she focused on Milly, the less she thought about herself. The exercise was easy for her. She could have run around the lake eight times without having to pause for air, but even though she knew the training schedule she followed probably wasn't practical for most people, still she was shocked by how generally unfit her friend was. And she was appalled by how little attention Milly paid to herself. Zoe was her first priority, then her mother and Nanna Peg, the business, Richard, and then, if there was any time left, which there never was, herself. She worried constantly about Zoe and claimed that was part of being a mother, and Nicole in turn worried that she simply wouldn't be good enough and that her baby deserved better.

Fortunately helping Milly took her mind off her own problems.

The forest was their friend, shielding them from prying eyes and offering no end of opportunities for varying the workout. The joy of being outdoors was indescribable, and she appreciated every moment. The scent of the trees, the crunch of leaves and twigs under her feet, the birdsong, a shaft of sunlight breaking through the branches.

For the first time in as long as she could remember, Nicole felt free. The early-morning runs gave her a tiny, delicious taste of what life would be like if she was anonymous, and she found herself starving for more of it. To be able to leave the house at any time of day. To be able to step outside her front door without cameras being pointed at her. To walk down a street without being stopped. To be able to sleep at night without worrying about who might be trying to break into her house.

And they were back home every day before Zoe was even awake. That quiet hour where they relaxed in the kitchen or took their coffee onto the deck was fast becoming Nicole's favorite time of day.

She banned croissants and pancakes and instead encouraged Milly to chop fresh fruit and nuts onto plain yogurt. When her friend tried to sneak in a spoonful of honey, Nicole positioned herself by the cupboard like a sentry.

"You don't need it."

"I do need it. Local bees. Organic."

"It's still sugar. You don't need it."

Milly had sighed and eaten the yogurt without the honey, a martyrish expression on her face.

Nicole ate the same thing, even though it had been at least a decade since she'd eaten breakfast. And it tasted so good. The creaminess of the yogurt and the delicious bite of the nuts. Berries she ate all the time (low in calories), but somehow these berries tasted better.

Everything tasted better. The eggs Milly used to make their omelets on the days they didn't eat yogurt. The vegetables, many of which were fresh from Connie's garden.

And that had been a highlight for Nicole. Seeing Connie and Nanna Peg again.

They'd accepted her presence without question, welcoming her as they always had, with warmth and total acceptance. To them she was Milly's best friend, and the trajectory of her career hadn't changed that.

"In the end it's just a job," Nanna Peg had said, waving a dismissive hand when Milly had explained that Nicole was taking a break. "Whether you're a librarian or movie star, when you close your front door, you're just you."

If she'd wanted to step out of her life, then this was the place to do it.

Nicole didn't mention her pregnancy. She wasn't ready to talk about it. The only person who knew about that was Milly, and she knew Milly would never betray that trust.

Their friendship seemed to have settled back into a comfortable place, but Nicole was constantly aware of the things she hadn't told Milly, things that could bring their friendship crashing down again. And that knowledge niggled, like a stone in her shoe. She tried to ignore it. She told herself that there was no reason for Milly to find out and no reason to tell her. What good would it do now? They were becoming close again. That was the important thing. There was no rule that said you had to share absolutely everything with another person, was there? Even if that person was your oldest and dearest friend.

She comforted herself that it was all in the past, not even relevant now, and gradually she found herself relaxing.

And relaxing was easier than she would have imagined because she loved it here. There was a sense of being cut off from everything that existed beyond the lake and the trees, and she felt more secure and at ease than she had for a long time.

At first she'd assumed it was the idyllic surroundings that were making her feel better, but then she realized it was being with Milly, who, despite Nicole's undoubted deficiencies as a friend, bathed her in kindness.

It made her understand how many of her relationships were transactional. Most of her team were there because she paid them. No one was with her because they cared. Not even Justin, as it turned out.

But Milly cared. She had always cared, and the fact that her love for Nicole stretched back way before she was famous to a time when she'd worn braces and cried because her mother hadn't bothered to show up to watch her in the school play made their relationship all the more special. It was special because it was real, and so little in her life was real.

Nicole spent most of her time pretending to be someone else, but with Milly she didn't have to pretend.

Her whole world became the boathouse, the lake, the forest, Milly and her family. Everything else had ceased to exist.

When she thought about her old life—and she tried not to— she pushed it aside like crumbs under a rug, hiding it from sight.

"Won't your agent be wondering where you are?" Milly asked her one morning after they'd managed to jog for a full thirty minutes. They were two weeks into their running routine, and this time Milly was barely out of breath.

"I told her I needed a break. I probably did her a favor. I'm not exactly hot stuff, thanks to Justin trashing my reputation."

"Does she know you're pregnant?"

"My agent?" Nicole felt the same little lurch of panic that she felt every time she thought about the baby. And thinking about the baby meant thinking about Justin, and she didn't want to think about him. It also meant thinking about her future, and she had no idea what that was going to look like. She knew she had decisions to make, but she wasn't ready to make them. She kept telling herself that there was plenty of time. "I've worked without a break since I was nineteen, one project after another and sometimes several at the same time. I've earned a rest."

She ignored the fact that the supposed rest had been forced on her by circumstances. That if it hadn't been for Justin, and the pregnancy, she'd probably still be working every waking hour and most of the sleeping ones too. It was her life.

And now her life was on hold.

Milly checked the fitness tracker Nicole had bought her as a gift. "Time to head home."

"Not yet. Ten more minutes of running."

She'd made a point of pushing her friend a little harder each day, and this time Milly didn't try to fight her on it. Nicole tried not to feel smug as Milly took off down the forest track, her movements strong and sure.

"Look at you!"

Nicole lengthened her stride so that she could catch her, and then Milly stopped dead and Nicole almost crashed into her.

"What the—"

"There's a man up ahead." Milly turned and tugged the brim of Nicole's hat farther over her eyes. "Stay behind me. I will say a bright and happy *Hello* as we jog past. You keep running."

Nicole's limbs felt shaky. "You're sure I shouldn't hide behind a tree?"

"I'm sure." And a moment later Milly said, "Oh, panic over. It's Joel. Phew."

"Joel?" Nicole groaned. Wasn't that just typical? "In that case I'm definitely hiding behind a tree. I made such a fool of myself last time he saw me."

"You're overreacting."

"No, overreacting is what I did when he walked into the kitchen." Nicole wished she'd never agreed to run with Milly, but it was too late to hide or turn back or do any of the other things that entered her head because she heard the sound of feet hitting the trail and then Milly's cheerful greeting.

"Hi, Joel!"

"Hey there. You two are up early." He flexed his shoulders and scanned Milly's gear with interest. "Never seen you running before, Milly."

"This is the new me. I'm going to dazzle everyone with my fitness." Milly took advantage of the rest to take a mouthful of water from her bottle. "Also, it was the only way I could tempt Nicole out of the house."

"Is that right?" He smiled at Nicole. "It's good to see you out and about. I've been concerned that you were trapped indoors."

He made her sound like a butterfly who kept smashing itself against the window in a bid for freedom.

"It's nice to be out." She noticed that he was barely out of breath despite the fact he'd been running fast when they'd spotted him. "We haven't seen you running here before."

"I run every day, but usually in the evenings."

Milly glanced along the trail. "Did you see anyone else on your run?"

"You mean, are you likely to see another human?" He shook his head and glanced back the way he'd just come. "No. Gets busier at six thirty. Most people are here to relax and enjoy themselves, remember."

Nicole wondered how that must feel. To wake up in a cabin by the lake and be able to do anything you wanted with the day. "Lucky them." The moment she said it she was embarrassed because she knew that she'd had a great deal of good fortune. And she was grateful for it. But people felt that her success somehow made her immune to all of life's blows, and of course that wasn't the case.

But Joel was looking at her with concern, not judgment. "So you leave the boathouse once a day at dawn? I suppose it's better than nothing. But just in case you find that a little limiting, my offer stands."

Milly put the cap back on her water. "What offer?"

"I offered to sneak Nicole out of here in the back of my van. I thought if I took her somewhere the tourists avoid, she could have a proper walk. Get out and enjoy the scenery. Nature. Forget about things for a while."

"In the back of your van?" Milly gave him a look. "That sounds super creepy, Joel. I'm not surprised she didn't accept."

"I accept." The words rushed out of her before she could change her mind.

Every day Milly left for work and every day Nicole watched the time pass minute by minute, waiting for the moment when her friend came home again. She had far too much time on her hands. Too much time to think. She'd started to write a script for something to do, but her heart wasn't in it. And sooner or later she was going to have to expand her world again. Good mothers didn't hide away in the house, did they? She needed to start carving some sort of new life for herself.

"If you're sure," she said, "then, I accept."

And now she was wondering if perhaps he hadn't meant it. If he'd only said it because he knew she'd say no.

But Joel smiled. "I'm sure."

"But not in the back of your van, please!" Milly rolled her eyes. "Just sit in the front and wear a hat."

"We can decide that part later." Joel checked his watch. "I need to go. The fridge in Aspen needs some attention, and it's my first job of the day. Enjoy the rest of your run."

He took off down the path, and Milly and Nicole finished their loop of the lake and headed back to the boathouse.

"Are you really planning to go with him?" Milly paused for breath at the bottom of the steps. "You surprised me when you said yes."

"I surprised myself. But I've been enjoying our runs, and I need to get out more. We both know I can't carry on like this." She paused, second-guessing herself. "Do you think it's a stupid idea?"

"No. Joel is completely trustworthy. Also, he knows this area well. He'll take you somewhere off grid where you're unlikely to see anyone except serious climbers."

But now she was regretting her decision. What had possessed her to even say yes? She'd been disappointed and betrayed by the people closest to her, so what was she doing trusting a stranger?

She didn't trust strangers, but she did trust her instincts, and they were telling her that Joel was everything he seemed to be. A decent human being. And if a small part of her was reminding her that she'd trusted her instincts about Justin too, then she ignored it.

Still, the doubt niggled. "Would you come too?"

"If you want me to, then of course." Milly didn't hesitate. "But you'll be fine with Joel. It will do you good to have a conversation with someone who isn't me."

"I love talking to you."

After so long apart having her friend back was a comfort she knew she never wanted to do without again.

They headed indoors and found Zoe already up and in the kitchen, earphones in place, listening to something as she made coffee and scrambled eggs. A bowl of fresh berries sat on the countertop.

She was unaware that they were in the house until Milly tapped her on the shoulder and she turned.

"Sorry. I didn't hear you." She removed her earbuds. "How was your run?"

Oh, to have the confidence to wear earphones, Nicole thought. There was never a time when she wasn't aware of her surroundings, and if someone tapped her on the shoulder like that she would have kicked them, jabbed her fingers into their eye sockets and asked questions later.

"It was great, thanks. What are you listening to?" Nicole stole a berry and popped it in her mouth.

Zoe shrugged. *"A Midsummer Night's Dream."*

"Right." She remembered how worried Milly was about Zoe and wondered if she might be able to help. After all, acting was the one thing she knew a great deal about. "You're playing Hermia?"

"Yeah." Zoe turned away. Her tone and body language said that the subject was closed, but Nicole refused to be deflected that easily.

She banked on the fact that Zoe was too polite to shut her down the way she might her mother.

"Hermia is a great part. She's a strong character, able to stand up for herself. A little feisty." She felt a pang of nostalgia for the days when she'd played the same part. It had been the performance that had changed her life because the woman who had become her agent had been in the audience on opening night. "Are you having fun with it?"

"Yeah, I guess." It was said with such a lack of enthusiasm that Nicole finally understood why Milly might be worried. Something wasn't right.

The more she watched Milly in action, the more respect she had for her. It seemed to her that being a good mother involved far more than offering unconditional love and practical support where necessary. You had to be a mind reader.

"Do you want to talk about it?"

Zoe paused and then turned to look at her. "Not really."

Nicole ate another berry. "It's just that I'm pretty sure that whatever you're feeling playing this part, I will have felt it at some point."

"I doubt it."

"Try me."

"It's not the part itself." Zoe stirred the eggs and then sighed. "Cally went for the same part, and I got it." She muttered the words. "And now she's not speaking to me."

"Oh, Zoe." Milly made a distressed sound. "Why didn't you tell me?"

"Because I knew you'd worry. You have enough to think about with Dad." Zoe turned the heat off under the pan. "It will be fine. And don't give me sympathy or I'll cry, and if I go into school with red eyes I'll be toast."

Nicole sent Milly a silencing look and handed Zoe a plate. "Cally is your best friend?"

Zoe nodded and put a slice of toast on the plate. "We've been friends forever, and if I'd known she was going to react like this I never would have auditioned. It's not worth it." She tipped the eggs onto the toast. "You probably think that's stupid."

"It isn't stupid at all. Envy is something that all actors have to learn to deal with. It's hard." Nicole paused, choosing her words carefully. "But you can't let other people's envy stop you doing what you are desperate to do."

Zoe stared at the eggs, which were slowly congealing on the plate. She looked utterly miserable. "But she's my best friend. We've never fought before. Not like this. And the hardest part is that when something is wrong she's the one I talk to, but now she's the thing that's wrong." Her voice cracked a little, and she paused to take a breath. "And I don't have anyone to talk it through with."

Milly's fists were clenched, her distress almost as great as Zoe's.

Nicole handed Zoe a knife and fork. "What do you think would have happened if she'd got the part and you hadn't?"

"I don't know." Zoe poked her breakfast without enthusiasm. "I would have been happy for her, I hope. Disappointed too, obviously. But I wouldn't have let it get in the way of our friendship. No way."

She sounded so sure. There had been a time when Nicole might have said the same thing and believed it, but she knew better now.

"In every friendship there comes a point where you're tested. You go in different directions. Things change. That can shake the firmest of relationships." She could feel Milly looking at her, but she kept her attention on Zoe.

Zoe shrugged and ate a mouthful of breakfast, not even bothering to take the plate to the table. "You and Mum have gone in different directions, and you're just fine."

Nicole's mouth was dry. "We've had our moments."

"But my mum is still the first person you call when you're in trouble, so whatever moments you've had, you've figured them out. And I have to do the same with Cally, but that's hard when she's not speaking to me. That's why I've been thinking I might just give the whole thing up. Maybe then things will go back to how they were."

"But they won't, will they? Because you will have given up something you really wanted because she couldn't handle her own emotions. Because she couldn't be pleased that something good was happening to you. And at first you'll be relieved that things seem fine again, but a tiny part of you will always remember that you gave it up for her, and that resentment will niggle like a splinter. A friend who expects you to give up what you love isn't that good a friend."

Zoe put her knife and fork down, her food only half-finished. "I guess."

"Have you told her how you feel? Have you been honest?" Nicole felt like a fraud and a hypocrite saying the words because she hadn't talked honestly to Milly, had she? The secret she was carrying sat inside her, a hard, calcified lump of deception. And there was a very good reason why she hadn't followed her own advice and talked honestly to Milly. She was terrified their friendship might not survive it.

Why had she started this conversation? She wasn't in a position to advise anyone on friendship.

"Maybe I should do that. If I can even get her to listen to me." Zoe scraped away the last of her food and put her plate into the dishwasher. "But I still think I might rethink the whole acting thing."

"Why don't you give yourself time before deciding that?"

Zoe poured herself a glass of water, and Nicole helped herself to another couple of berries.

"I find it helps to keep my eye on the work itself. When you're home tonight, do you want to rehearse with me?"

Zoe was wide-eyed, her cheeks suddenly flushed. "I don't know. It's a bit nerve-wracking. You're Amara—I mean, I know you're not really Amara, but you're so brilliant I think I'd feel

self-conscious. It would be like stripping naked in front of a su-
permodel, you know?"

Nicole laughed. "Please don't strip naked. And I'm just an actor,
like you."

"Um—nothing at all like me," Zoe muttered, but she looked
happier. "I don't suppose—no, of course you wouldn't."

"Wouldn't what?"

"Would you come to my drama group? Watch us? Maybe give
us some tips?"

Nicole hesitated, and it was Milly who intervened.

"You know she can't do that, Zoe. Nicole has to keep a low
profile, and if she turns up at your drama group everyone will
know she's staying here."

Zoe looked embarrassed. "Yeah, I get that. Stupid idea. Sorry
for asking."

"Don't be sorry." For a wild moment Nicole almost said that
yes, of course she'd do it, but she couldn't bring herself to say
those words. She couldn't face subjecting herself to public scrutiny and judgment again. She was loving this quiet life more than
she could possibly have imagined.

Milly poured herself a coffee. "Thespian or not, Zoe, you need
to hurry up or we'll be late for school."

"Maybe I'll join you for your run on the weekend," Zoe said.
"Oh wait, I can't. It's my weekend to go to Dad's."

Nicole glanced at her friend. She knew how difficult she found
those weekends, but nothing showed in Milly's face as she reached
into the fridge and pulled out more berries.

"You can join us the weekend after. If you can keep up."

Nicole felt admiration and the same pang of envy she often felt
when she watched Milly with Zoe. In her opinion, they had the
perfect mother–daughter relationship.

Zoe vanished to get ready for school, and Milly handed Nicole
a bowl of berries.

"Well, you can definitely stop worrying about whether you'll
be a good mother or not. You're going to be brilliant. Thank you."

"For what?"

"For getting her to talk about it. For handling it all so well. I told you that you'd be an amazing mother, and you just proved it."

"She's a teenager, not a baby. It's different."

Milly laughed. "Babies are much easier than teenagers. Or perhaps I should say it's a different type of stress. One is physically exhausting, and the other is mentally exhausting. As you will discover. Anyway, thanks."

Nicole felt a little better. Maybe she wasn't going to be such an awful mother. Maybe there was hope. "You're welcome."

Milly added yogurt to her berries, but this time she didn't bother reaching for honey. "I can't believe Zoe and Cally aren't talking to each other. I feel sick for her."

Nicole had only recently learned that was a thing: feeling your child's emotions as if they were your own. If Zoe was worried, Milly worried. If Zoe was in pain, Milly was in pain. It was as if the two of them were invisibly connected.

She wondered sometimes why that connection had been missing for her mother. There had been so many times during her childhood when she'd been in pain and she was sure her mother hadn't felt a thing.

But it was obvious to her that Milly felt everything.

Over the past couple of weeks Nicole had watched Milly and Zoe together and studied their interactions.

She liked the way they chatted together so naturally, each one tossing a line of conversation that the other one caught and ran with. She liked the way Zoe talked so openly to Milly, and although she hadn't told her about Cally, it was because she was trying to protect Milly. And she admired the way Milly listened carefully to everything her daughter said, never interrupting, and never judging. She bestowed hugs and comfort when needed and calm good humor when things were tense. It was obvious from the conversation they'd had on their morning runs that Milly had bitten her lip again and again rather than allow herself to say bad things about Richard in front of their daughter.

Nicole wasn't sure she would have been able to display the same restraint.

And she couldn't help wondering how different things would have been if her mother had been more like Milly.

Nicole's entire inner world had been a secret from her mother, and she hadn't had to work hard to keep it private because her mother had never been interested enough to look.

It had been years since she'd seen her. She didn't know exactly how many years because she was afraid to count them. Every year that passed was yet more evidence of her lack of importance in her mother's life.

The last time she'd been in touch with her mother was when Nicole had been in London for the premiere of one of her movies. Ironically she'd been playing the part of a daughter estranged from her mother, an emotional role that she'd found so true to life that she hadn't had to dig that deep for inspiration.

On impulse she'd called her mother and asked if she'd like to meet up, but her mother had told her that she was at the airport about to fly to Australia where she had a new job as the head of vascular surgery in a major hospital.

Nicole had listened in disbelief.

Her mother was moving to Australia and hadn't even mentioned it. If Nicole hadn't called at that exact moment, would she even have known?

Nicole had wished her luck, as if she was nothing more than an acquaintance from the past, and had never called her mother again.

It was too humiliating. In her lowest moments she'd actually wondered if her mother had chosen Australia on purpose because it was a country Nicole rarely visited.

She'd been upset all over again, but that final move of her mother's had confirmed what she'd always known: that their relationship would never be what Nicole wanted it to be. Gradually she'd accepted the situation for what it was.

She'd wondered briefly if she should reach out and tell her that she was pregnant, but she'd dismissed the thought right away.

What was the point? And in the unlikely event that her mother was interested, would Nicole want her anywhere near her child? No, she would not.

She thought of Milly's words.

You can choose what type of mother you want to be.

When Nicole had said she wanted to be like Milly, it was true.

She wanted to be the sort of mother who sat down and listened and laughed with her child no matter how busy she was. The sort of mother who was hands-on, who didn't ration hugs, who loved unconditionally.

She wasn't going to think about her relationship with her own mother. She was going to think about Milly's relationship with Zoe, and Connie's relationship with Milly. She was surrounded by good role models. There was no reason why she should emulate the bad one, even if it was the one closest to home.

And she was going to prove Justin wrong.

14

Milly

Milly tapped on the door of Brendan's cabin, and when there was no answer she let herself in.

She dropped the bag of fresh linen in the hallway and took the bag of food straight through to the kitchen, noticing as she did so that most of the sheets of paper had been cleared from the floor.

She was unloading food into the fridge when she heard a noise behind her.

Heart thumping she turned, a fresh melon in her hand.

Brendan Scott stood in the doorway, his hair wet from the shower, a towel looped around his neck. He wore a pair of shorts and had a clean shirt in his hand. His chest was bare, water still clinging to his shoulders and his bare legs.

He raised an eyebrow. "Death by melon? That's a new one."

She lowered the melon. "You scared me."

"Sorry. I should have called out from the bathroom, but you didn't strike me as the jumpy type."

She'd never been the jumpy type, but that was before Nicole had come to stay with her. Now she was suffering from hyper-vigilance. Yesterday she'd found herself checking the bushes for photographers when she left the house, and she'd insisted that Zoe walk to the main entrance of Forest Nest to meet her dad so that there was no chance Richard might catch sight of Nicole.

The fewer people who knew she was there, the better.

"I had no idea you were here." And now she was flustered. "Did I get the time wrong? I thought you told me you'd be out this morning."

"That was the plan, but my book was going well so I ended up working for most of the night." He rubbed the edges of his hair with the towel. "I wanted to get it done while I was in the flow of it."

"So you've finished?"

"Just a draft, but a draft is good." His smile told her just how good.

She couldn't imagine it, being able to create something from nothing like that. "You probably want to go right back to bed and catch up on sleep. I'll finish off here and then leave you alone. I can come back later to clean the cabin and change the sheets and towels. I apologize for disturbing you." She carried on unloading the food from the bag. She felt self-conscious, which was ridiculous because she was just doing her job. Of course, she didn't usually do her job with a shirtless man hovering. But she wasn't a teenager. She was past feeling flustered, surely?

"Why are you apologizing? We had an arrangement. I'm the one who changed it. No need to leave, unless it bothers you working around me."

"It doesn't bother me." Although it might have been easier if he put his shirt on.

Perhaps he read her mind because he tugged on his shirt and strolled into the room. "What delicious treats are you bringing me today? That dish you left a few days ago—what was it? Roasted peppers and goat cheese. Sublime."

She wasn't a teenager but discovered she was still capable of blushing like one. "Good. You need to eat."

"I appreciate it. It's kind of you. Catering isn't exactly part of my package here."

"I'm bringing you leftovers, that's all." She didn't say that these days she planned a portion for him into every meal she prepared. "I love to cook, and I always make too much. Ask Zoe."

"Zoe is your daughter?"

"Yes." Close up she could see how tired he looked. She imagined him in the early hours, hunched over his laptop on the deck, losing track of time. "Have you had breakfast? Coffee? I could make you something."

"I'm sure you have things you need to do. It's the weekend, after all."

"I don't have anywhere else I need to be. Zoe is with her dad this weekend." And she was trying to fill her time and not to think too much about it, because dwelling on what might be happening was a quick way to make herself feel horrible. She'd been awake half the night worrying that Richard might say bad things about her in front of Zoe. She'd managed to upset herself over conversations that had only happened in her mind, but in her defense Richard didn't seem to be exercising much restraint at the moment. Milly didn't want Zoe to find herself in the middle of it all.

She loaded the last of the food into the fridge, trying hard not to think about Richard. Trying not to wonder how you could go from smiling together at your new baby to dividing up weekends and holidays. "I made lemon chicken, which you can heat up and eat with rice. I noticed you had some in the cupboard. Also a roasted vegetable tart that you can have with salad. I made some poppy seed bread rolls this morning, so I've put a couple on the side for you. At least you won't starve for the next couple of days."

"Where have you been all my life?" He fastened the buttons on his shirt. He didn't seem in any hurry to get back to his work. "Is it hard for you when she's away?"

Milly closed the fridge door. She was tempted to spill out the truth, but the last thing he needed was to hear about her problems and worries. Overthinking was one thing, but oversharing was something she tried to avoid. "It's fine. I get time to myself, and that's a treat."

"Time you spend waiting on other people and staying busy." He watched her for a moment. "Will that delicious-sounding chicken keep until tomorrow?"

"Yes. I made it fresh this morning." She pulled a box out of the other bag. "And I brought you a slice of my chocolate fudge cake."

"I think I might be falling in love with you."

She knew he was joking, but still his comment made her heart pound a little harder. "You should probably taste it before you make the final decision."

He put the towel over the back of the chair. "What's your favorite food? Does anyone ever cook for you?"

"Cook for *me*? No. I mean, Zoe helps. She loves cooking too. It's something we do together."

"Have dinner with me tonight."

Dinner? She was so surprised she almost dropped the box containing the thick wedge of chocolate cake.

Why was he asking her? Because he felt guilty that she was cleaning his cabin at a weekend? Because he felt he needed to pay her back for the food? Her mind spiraled through the options.

"What did you have in mind?"

"Well, having tasted the quality of your food I'm not offering to cook for you. I'd be too nervous of scaring you away." He gave a wry smile. "I was thinking a restaurant. A good one, so that you're not sitting there thinking you can make something better at home. You have more than your fair share of fine dining establishments around here."

"That's a kind offer, but you don't have to do that." She was embarrassed that he thought he should. Maybe she shouldn't have brought him food. In trying to make his life a little easier, she'd overstepped.

He frowned. "I'm not inviting you out of some sense of obligation, Milly. You're good company. I'd like to take you for dinner. If you'd like to join me."

Was she good company?

She stared at him, trying to read his mind, wishing she was

better at this. She'd let Richard crush her confidence so badly that when a man asked her to dinner she assumed he was being polite.

But Brendan thought she was good company. Not boring or a martyr.

And now she was tempted. More than tempted.

Dinner would mean dressing up and eating in a restaurant where someone else had prepared the food.

When had she last done that?

Richard's voice echoed in her head. *You don't know how to enjoy yourself.*

Brendan was watching her. "If you have other plans, it's not a problem."

Plans?

She thought about Nicole but knew her friend well enough to know that Nicole would want her to go. More than that, if she turned him down and Nicole found out, then she'd probably kill her.

"I don't have other plans." She said the words before she could think her way to saying no. Her plan had been to get through the weekend as best she could, filling every moment with work. But now he was offering her an alternative. And she was going to take it. She'd prove to Richard, and to herself, that she was more than capable of enjoying herself. "Thank you. I'd like that. Where did you have in mind?"

He mentioned a restaurant that was so well-known she knew right away there was no chance of them being able to get a reservation.

"You wouldn't get a table at this short notice. People travel from everywhere just to eat there."

"Have you eaten there?"

"No, but it's the place I recommend to guests when they have a special celebration." She didn't add that it was outside her price range and that there was no way Richard would ever have paid that much for a plate of food Milly could cook him at home. "You have to book at least three months in advance."

"I'll give them a call. They might have a cancellation."

She thought he was being overly optimistic, but then she remembered that he was famous and probably had contacts. "Would you like me to call them?"

"No. You do far too much as it is. I've got this."

I've got this.

The three (or was it technically four?) words that no one ever said to her. She was always the one taking charge. In control. It felt good not to be for a short time.

"Great. If you manage to get a table, then message me a time. And if not, let me know if you need me to suggest somewhere else."

"Why don't I pick you up from the boathouse around seven?"

She didn't want him near the boathouse in case he spotted Nicole. "I'll meet you here. It's probably easier."

"Sure, if that's what you prefer."

And now that it was all planned, the doubts started.

"Are you sure you'll have the energy for dinner? If you worked all night, you must be exhausted."

"I'm energized because finally the book is going well. You have no idea how good that feels. I have a draft. Once I have a full draft, I can relax. I have major work ahead on it, but it's work that I know I can do." He was more relaxed than she'd ever seen him. There was warmth in his eyes and something else that she couldn't quite interpret. Something that made her deliciously jittery.

"Is the fact that you've finished your draft the reason I could finally walk across your floor without stepping on sheets of paper?"

His smile widened. "It's connected. I should probably thank you because you were the one who finally gave me the idea that fixed it."

"Me?"

"Yes. I changed the killer. Instead of it being the estranged younger brother, it's the dutiful ex-wife. It's brilliant. No one is going to predict that."

She remembered Lorna saying that she was never able to predict the ending of his books. "I'm trying to figure out how I inspired this. Are you saying I look like a murderer?"

"You look nothing like a murderer. And neither does the murderer in my book. Which is why no one is going to suspect it."

"So how did I give you the idea?"

"Because you were talking about your ex-husband."

"I wasn't the one suggesting different ways of murdering him. That was you."

He laughed. "You'll have to forgive the way my mind works. And now I've given you a major spoiler, so I'm hoping you don't read my work."

These days she wasn't reading much at all. She was usually asleep before her head hit the pillow. But if she did read a few pages she made sure it wasn't something that would keep her awake or give her bad dreams. "Will I offend you if I admit that I don't?"

"Not at all. Given that I've just ruined the next book for you, I'm relieved. Although, obviously, you could ruin everything for me by going online and spilling the ending of my next book." He leaned a little closer. "Are you good at keeping secrets, Milly? Because if you're not, I'm going to have to keep you trapped here until the book comes out. Which would be a good plot for a story, come to think of it."

It was hard to focus on the conversation when he was looking at her with that gleam in his eyes.

"When does this book come out?"

"Late next year."

"Then, it's lucky for both of us that I'm excellent at keeping secrets." Milly thought about Nicole. "You can trust me. Just tell me that the victim in your book isn't called Richard."

"His name is Callum, but I can change it to Richard if you prefer?"

"Definitely not." She imagined Richard picking the book up and discovering himself dead by her hand. "Stick with Callum. So now you've cleared up all the paper, does this mean I can finally clean your floor?"

"If you're sure that's okay."

She laughed. "It's my job."

"But not really," he said and rubbed his hand across his jaw. "It's only your job because I scared Lorna away."

"Forest Nest is my business, and I do whatever is needed. Sometimes it's taking bookings. Sometimes it's arranging a celebration cake. Sometimes it's cleaning a floor."

"And you don't mind it?"

"Not at all. I love my job. Does that surprise you? It probably seems very boring to you."

"Boring?" He let his hand drop. "Living here? Working here? Not boring at all. It's a great life choice."

Everything he said made her feel better about herself. She could have talked to him all day, but she had work to do and presumably so did he, so she scooped up her empty bags and his damp towel and got to work.

She changed sheets, put fresh fluffy towels in the bathroom and emptied the bins. She flung open windows and did some basic tidying, careful not to touch any of the remaining notes or stray pieces of paper.

As she mopped the kitchen floor she could see him standing on the terrace, staring out over the lake, deep in thought.

His job probably required a great deal of thinking and mental stamina, she decided, whereas hers needed physical stamina.

Her back was aching from too much bending over, and she scooped up the bags of dirty laundry and was on her way to the door when he stopped her.

"I have one question before you go."

She dropped the laundry bag, aware that her face was probably unattractively hot and sweaty. "What?"

"Is your chocolate fudge cake as good as the key lime pie you brought me the other day?"

She laughed. "That's for you to decide."

She was still smiling as she closed the door behind her and headed up the track toward the café to check on the team.

She was halfway there when it occurred to her that for the past hour she hadn't thought about Richard or what he might or might not be saying to Zoe. She'd been laughing and happy and distracted. And tonight she was going for dinner with Brendan Scott. She was going to wear a dress and put on makeup and do her best to wipe Richard's words from her memory.

Feeling more positive, she reached for her phone and sent a message to Zoe.

Love you. Hope you're doing okay there xx

15

Zoe

Zoe was lying on her bed in the spare room in Avery's flat when the message pinged on her phone.

She knew it would be from her mother (Cally still wasn't speaking to her, which actually made her feel a hundred times worse than her parents' divorce did), but she didn't look at it right away because she knew her mum hated the weekends she spent with her dad and Avery, and looking at the message would make her imagine her mother all lonely and upset at home. But then she realized that if she didn't reply she'd worry her mother, and everyone was already worrying far too much, so she picked up her phone, read the message and composed a reply.

Love you too. All good here. X

She stared at it and then deleted the second sentence. It wasn't exactly good, was it? If she sounded as if she was enjoying herself, she might upset her mother. If she sounded miserable, she'd upset her mother. She had to sound neutral.

Love you too. Learning my lines! X

There. That was better. And her mum would be relieved she hadn't given up on the play. Yet. She pressed Send, lay back down on the pillow and went back to staring up at the ceiling.

She didn't hate being here, but she didn't love it either.

The one good thing about being with her dad was that he wasn't as emotionally intuitive as her mother, so she didn't have to try so hard to hide her feelings. He didn't seem to notice if she was happy or sad or quiet. Or maybe he just felt guilty and didn't want to confront the consequences of his actions so instead chose to ignore them.

There had been that one excruciating moment early on when her dad tried to explain that he hadn't meant to fall in love with Avery, and that the passion had taken him by surprise and over-whelmed him, and Zoe had wanted to cover her ears and eyes and tell him that if there was one thing a thirteen-year-old did *not* want to talk about it was her father's passions.

Fortunately, he'd seemed to find the conversation as awkward as she did and had never mentioned it again.

Now on the weekends they were together they focused on doing things in the moment and didn't talk about the *situation*. Some-times it seemed odd to Zoe that he never asked how her mother was, but presumably if he really cared about her feelings he never would have left in the first place.

And although the first few times she'd met Avery had been stiff and awkward, it was getting easier.

On the weekends when she stayed with them Avery mostly left her alone to do "teenage things" (Zoe wasn't sure what those were exactly, but if it bought her the right to alone time, then she was happy to sign up for it), apart from that one time she'd of-fered to teach Zoe some yoga moves that might ease the slump in her shoulders. Zoe had wanted to point out that her shoulders had been just fine until her dad had run off with Avery, but she didn't want to create even more tension, so she'd simply nodded politely and said she'd think about it.

To be fair, Avery was mostly okay. It could have been worse. She'd done her best to make Zoe feel comfortable in the apartment, which wasn't easy because the place reminded Zoe of a showroom. At home she snuggled on the sofa with Tiger and everything was worn and familiar and comfortable, but in Avery's place there was lots of glass and white furniture and a large modern rug with a weird squiggly design and paintings that were probably considered works of art but to Zoe looked as if someone had tripped while holding a paintbrush.

She missed the lake and the trees and the birds. She missed home.

The first time she'd stayed she'd wanted to ask if next time she could bring Tiger for company, but one look at Avery's white sofas made her realize that this place was not animal-friendly, so instead she'd compromised and brought a photo of Tiger sitting on her mother's lap.

On the positive side she had her own bathroom, and there was a small TV in her room. Avery never cared what time she turned her light out, so she often read until far too late and then felt exhausted the next morning.

And Avery could be funny, but every time Zoe laughed she felt a little bit guilty because it felt like a betrayal of her mother.

Not that any of this was her fault. She didn't think that for a moment.

She hadn't wanted her parents to split up, of course she hadn't. But she was old enough to know bad things happened, and at least her mother hadn't died like Mina's, so she was grateful for that. And right now, the worst thing in her life was Cally not speaking to her because she talked to Cally about everything, and now she had no one she could be truly honest with. Also, Cally knew a ton of things about her, which made her feel vulnerable. Fortunately she hadn't told her about Nicole, even though keeping that secret had almost made her burst.

She hadn't told her dad either. Her mother had told her not to tell anyone at all, so she'd kept her mouth shut.

She had a weird feeling that something had happened between her dad and Nicole. Last time they'd stayed with her, Zoe had seen them talking to each other on the terrace of Nicole's house in LA, and she hadn't been able to hear what they were saying, but they'd been standing really close together talking intently, and her dad's expression had been weird, and for a wild moment Zoe had been scared that they were having an affair and that this conversation was something she should tell her mother about, but then they'd flown back home, and a few days later her dad had left and moved in with Avery. Which didn't explain the conversation between her dad and Nicole but did explain another conversation she'd overheard a few weeks earlier.

And that was another thing she hadn't shared with her mother. She felt bad keeping a secret, but she knew she'd feel worse if she shared it. So she was trying to accept that she was just doomed to feel bad.

One thing she knew for sure: adult relationships were so complicated she wasn't sure she wanted one.

16

Milly

I can't believe he got a table! That restaurant is booked out for months." Milly riffled through her clothes and pulled out a pair of freshly ironed linen trousers. "These will do."

"He probably has contacts. He's a major author. And those will not do. You are not leaving this house wearing those." Nicole sat cross-legged on Milly's bed, watching her get ready.

"What's wrong with them?"

"Oh please!" Nicole sprang from the bed. "Move aside."

She proceeded to go through every item in Milly's wardrobe. Everything she held up, Milly rejected.

"I can't wear that, it won't fit." And later. "That's ancient. I've had it since I was eighteen."

Nicole looked at her in disbelief. "Don't you ever clear out your wardrobe?"

"No. I hate throwing things away. I always tell myself that one day I might fit into it again."

Nicole turned her attention back to the Milly's clothes. "How many things in here do you actually wear?"

"Uh . . . two pairs of linen trousers and the shirts," Milly

said. "There's a black dress that fits. I suppose I could wear that."
Who would have thought that picking something to wear could
be such a trial? She was beginning to wish she hadn't agreed to go
to dinner.

"No, not black," Nicole said dismissively. "Black is too safe."

Milly sighed. "*Safe* sounds perfect. You're making me nervous.
This whole evening is starting to feel like a mistake."

What had she been thinking? Chatting to Brendan in the comfort of his cabin was one thing, but sitting across from him at a
romantic restaurant with candles flickering was something else
altogether.

"It's not a mistake. It's exactly what you need." Nicole pulled
out the black dress. "Is this the one you mean?"

"Yes. But is it too dressy?"

"It doesn't matter what you wear as long as you wear it with
confidence."

"Says the woman who could wear a sack and still look good. I
don't have any confidence, which is why I stick to my linen trousers and shirt. Honestly, I'm fine in that. I feel comfortable."

"Comfortable is for when you're ninety." Nicole studied the
dress. "Does this make you feel good?"

"Not particularly. Clothes never make me feel good."

Nicole added the dress to the growing pile of rejects. "You're
going on a date. It's important that you feel good."

"It's not a date. It's just dinner." Milly was growing more uneasy by the minute. She chewed the edge of her fingernail. "Do
you really think it's a date? Do you think *he* thinks it's a date?
You're worrying me."

Nicole raised an eyebrow. "Well, what did you think it was?"

"I don't know. Dinner with a friend."

"Right. That's what it is, then. And stop biting your nails.
You're not twelve. I'm going to give you a manicure in a minute,
so I'm going to need something to paint." Nicole went back to
the wardrobe. She emerged moments later with a summer dress
in shades of blue and green. "This is pretty."

She'd worn it on a trip to Greece with Richard, early in their relationship. "It won't fit."

But looking at it reminded her that she hadn't always chosen to wear safe black or navy. Who had she been back then? Who was the woman who had chosen that happy swirl of blue and green?

Nicole removed it from the hanger. "Try it."

"I will look like a sack of potatoes in that." And whoever she'd been back then, she wasn't that person now.

Nicole thrust it toward her, and Milly took it with a sigh.

She knew Nicole well enough to know that there was only one way to deal with this situation.

"Fine, I'll put it on. And I'll look completely crappy, and then maybe you'll shut up and let me wear my linen trousers." Deciding that the sooner she proved her point, the sooner they could get this whole clothing issue out of the way, Milly stripped off and pulled on the dress. She was astonished to discover it slid easily over her hips.

"Wow." Nicole grinned. "Yes, you're right, you look awful. Let's hope they have a power outage in the restaurant so no one can see you."

Milly walked toward the mirror. She stared at herself and then turned sideways. "I can't believe it fits." She pressed a hand to her now-flat stomach. "I must have lost weight."

"A side benefit of all that running. And not pouring an entire hive of honey over your yogurt. You look gorgeous. Right. That's what you're wearing tonight."

Milly tugged slightly at the hem.

"You don't think it's too short? If it's breezy, the skirt part blows up. I don't want my fat thighs on show."

"I'm not dignifying that with an answer." Nicole went back to the wardrobe and pulled out a cashmere cardigan in the same shade of blue. "This is pretty. You can take it as an extra layer in case you're cold. Now we need to think about jewelry, and then hair and makeup."

By the time they'd finished, Milly almost didn't recognize herself.

She felt a twinge of nostalgia. "This reminds me of when we were teenagers getting ready to go to a party. You always chose what we wore."

"Only because left to your own devices you would have worn jeans everywhere." Nicole hung the cardigan on the door alongside the dress. "Do you have a bag that would look good with this? Let's put all your bags on the bed, and then we can choose one."

"We don't need to put them on the bed," Milly said. "I only own two bags. I'll just take the one I use every day."

"That massive, battered tote bag you haul around everywhere? You are not using that."

"My everyday bag is brilliant. Very roomy. Holds everything. I actually have a clean T-shirt in there in case of accidents and a couple of spare light bulbs for the cabins."

"Will you listen to yourself?" Nicole rolled her eyes. "You are not going to an expensive restaurant with a hot guy carrying spare light bulbs in your purse."

"How do you know he's hot?"

Nicole pulled out Milly's drawers one by one, checking the contents. "I know him. I met him a couple of times on set. I was in one of his movies."

"What?" It took Milly a moment to absorb the full implications of that. It hadn't occurred to her, even for a moment, that Nicole and Brendan might know each other. "Why didn't you mention this before?"

"Because I didn't know he was staying here until you mentioned that you were going to dinner." Nicole opened another drawer. "Do you own sexy underwear?"

"No. And it doesn't matter because he is not going to see my underwear unless a breeze catches that dress you're making me wear." It unsettled her that they knew each other. "Which movie? Were you a murder victim or something?"

Nicole riffled through the contents of the drawer. "You know I never take that type of role. I was the hardened New York cop investigating a serial killer. It was the type of movie you would have watched from behind the sofa."

"It sounds like the type of movie I would never watch at all, even if you were in it."

"That too."

A horrible thought occurred to her, and she gulped. "Did you—?"

"Sleep with him? No. Not even a flirtation." Nicole turned her head and gave Milly a slow smile. "But he's definitely hot. You go, girl."

"I'm not going anywhere except the restaurant," Milly said hastily. "I think I might cancel. I wish I'd never said yes."

Nicole looked at her curiously. "Why did you?"

She was asking herself the same question. "Because he makes me smile. And because Richard said I didn't know how to have fun and I wanted to prove him wrong. But this doesn't feel like fun anymore." She sat down hard on the edge of the bed and breathed. "It feels stressful."

"Well, you've had sex with the same man for a long time, so the prospect of moving to someone new is bound to be a little unnerving, but it will be great."

"Sex? Who said anything about sex? Do you think that's what this is?" Her sense of panic grew. Had she mixed up the signals? She had a feeling she was way over her head with this. "I thought we were just going to eat a plate of food together. Now you're telling me this is about sex?"

"Calm down." Nicole grinned at her. "Start with the plate of food and see where it goes from there."

"It's not going anywhere from there! I'm not ready to take my clothes off in front of a stranger." The thought made her grow cold. "I can't do it. I can't do any of this."

"Yes, you can." Nicole delved into the final drawer and pulled out a set of silk underwear Milly had forgotten she'd owned. "I bought you this, and it still has the tags on it."

Milly was embarrassed. "I know. But it was too pretty to wear. And it cost a fortune. I was afraid I'd ruin it. Also, it's handwash-only and I don't live a handwash kind of life."

Nicole carefully removed the tags. "You're wearing it tonight. So now all we have to sort out is the bag issue. You are not taking that abomination you cart everywhere during your working day. You're going to an expensive restaurant, not the supermarket."

"Then, that leaves the little black clutch. It's in the back of the cupboard. Probably buried under a decade of dust."

Nicole pulled a face. "Black isn't great. Are you sure you don't have anything else? What do you usually use when you go to restaurants?"

"I don't really go to restaurants. I take my normal bag, or sometimes I just put my keys and credit cards in my coat pocket."

Nicole flopped onto the edge of the bed and pressed her hand to her chest. "I feel faint. Are you serious? You put your keys and credit card in your coat pocket? Why don't you treat yourself to a bag?"

"Because I'm never going to use it. And I'm not good at spending money on myself. I have Zoe to think about."

Nicole frowned. "Are you worried about money? Is the business okay?"

"Yes, it's fine, but you never know what's coming down the road, do you?" She hadn't anticipated Richard leaving her. It had reminded her of something she already knew: that the unpredictable happened. "I can't rest on my laurels and assume the business will continue to do well."

"With you at the helm I think it will." Nicole reached across and gave her hand a squeeze. "Okay, I am going to stop thinking of all the bags I have at home that would be perfect with that outfit. I don't have anything suitable either, so in this emergency situation we are going to make do with what we have, and in the fullness of time I am going to teach you how to spoil yourself. You need to treat yourself to a few nice things."

"Things don't really make me happy." She'd never understood

how buying something could fix a low moment. "Not for long, anyway."

She sat down on the bed next to Nicole, who shifted to give her room.

"What makes you happy?"

That was easy to answer. "My family. Cooking with Zoe. Making popcorn and watching a movie together. Spending time with my mother and Nanna Peg. Having you as a friend. This place." She glanced out the floor-to-ceiling window that looked over the lake. "The mountains and the forest. Just being here. I think I get more feelings of contentment from breathing in the scent of the forest on our morning runs than I ever would from a pretty bag, even if it does match my dress. You probably think I'm crazy."

Many people would think it was a small life, she knew that, but it was a life she loved. It was the only life she wanted.

"Not crazy at all." Nicole sounded wistful. "I've always envied what you have."

Milly turned to look at her, surprised. "You envied *me*? Why?"

"Because you're loved. You've always been loved. And I have no idea how that feels because no one has ever loved me, not even my own mother." There was a pause, and then Nicole cleared her throat. "And now this is getting maudlin. Sorry."

Milly was so overwhelmed by emotion it took her a moment to respond.

She swallowed hard. "Well, that's just not true, is it? And you know it isn't. Because I love you." She put her arms round her friend. "I've always loved you. You're my best friend." She felt the pressure of her friend's arms as Nicole hugged her back.

"Still? Despite everything?"

"Always, no matter what."

There was a long pause, and Nicole drew breath as if she was about to say something else.

"Milly—"

"What?"

There was another pause. A moment when she could hear Nicole breathing.

"Nothing. But if you smudge that makeup I spent hours on, I will kill you."

Milly pulled away. She had a feeling that wasn't what Nicole had intended to say. Was she worrying about being pregnant, was that it? "Perhaps I should cancel tonight. We could stay in together and have toast and cereal in our pajamas."

"Sounds tempting, but you are not canceling tonight. You always do this. You've always been the same. I had to drag you to parties." Nicole stood up briskly and headed back to Milly's wardrobe. Whatever she'd been about to say obviously hadn't been important.

"And then you'd abandon me the moment we arrived and vanish into a dark corner with Mark Wilson."

Nicole laughed. "Mark Wilson. I haven't thought about him for years. I wonder what he's doing?" She knelt down and started rummaging around in the bottom of the wardrobe. She emerged triumphant with a pair of strappy sandals that Milly had worn to a wedding about five years before and hadn't touched since.

"I can't wear those. And last thing I heard, Mark Wilson was married to Trisha Day."

Nicole sneezed as dust found its way up her nose. "The same Trisha Day who blew up the physics lab?"

"That's the one, although I'd forgotten about that. I think she has changed since then. She works for an insurance company. Probably persuading people to insure against explosions." Grinning, Milly reached for her flat shoes, but Nicole snatched them out of her hand.

"You are not leaving the house in those." She thrust the sandals at Milly. "You're wearing these."

"I will be in pain all evening. They hurt my feet."

"It will be worth it because they are going to look great. And you only have to walk from the car to the restaurant. The pain will be brief."

There was no point in arguing, but it occurred to her, as she crammed her feet into the sandals that had been one of her purchasing mistakes, that if Nicole went to these lengths every time she left the house, then it was no wonder she was hiding from her life.

17

Nicole

She waved Milly off, watching nervously as her friend wobbled her way down the path in the shoes. On reflection maybe the shoes had been a mistake—or maybe they'd turn out to be an icebreaker when she lost her balance and landed in Brendan Scott's arms.

Once Milly was out of sight, Nicole turned the key in the lock. She took a deep breath.

She'd so nearly told her. In that moment when Milly had assured her that they'd always be friends, a small part of her had wanted to test that. She'd wanted to say *There's something I have to tell you*, but she hadn't been able to bring herself to say the words, and now she was relieved that she hadn't. If she'd said them, she probably would have ruined the friendship, and she definitely would have ruined Milly's evening. She didn't want to do that. This was a huge step for Milly, and Nicole was delighted she was going out, and not just because it made her feel a tiny bit less guilty about everything.

The silence enveloped her, and she glanced around, feeling a little lost.

If she was honest, she would have loved an evening in her pajamas watching movies together, but having been the worst friend possible she was determined not to put a foot wrong from now on.

And having helped Milly get ready, she felt as if she was part of it. She was invested. She wanted it to go well. She felt nervous thinking about it and hoped Brendan was as nice as she remembered and didn't do anything to make Milly back off.

It had felt good sorting through clothes and searching for things to wear. Like old times.

Not knowing what to do with herself now she was alone, she went back to Milly's bedroom, tidied all the clothes away and then wandered into the kitchen and made herself a cup of herbal tea.

Despite the breeze it was a warm evening, so she took her tea onto the balcony and settled herself on the porch swing overlooking the water.

A family of ducks bobbed into the reeds close to the water's edge, and she watched as they dipped under the water and emerged with a shake of feathers.

She felt comfortable and relaxed, which was surprising. What was also surprising was how quickly the place had started to feel like home.

When she'd arrived at the railway station in the middle of the night, it had been because she'd seen no other option for herself. She'd expected Milly to refuse to help (and she wouldn't have blamed her), and even when it had become clear that Milly did intend to help, she'd been convinced that their friendship would never return to the way it had once been. But now here they were giggling like children and arguing over which shoes Milly should wear.

Nicole took a sip of tea, feeling relief and gratitude, ignoring the ever-present niggle of guilt. A few weeks ago she hadn't been able to even imagine what her future might look like, but now she'd been given a glimpse of what might be possible.

It wasn't only Milly's friendship that had changed things, it was the fact that she had remained anonymous here. Every morning she woke and expected to find a horde of photographers camped in the bushes, but so far all she saw when she peeped cautiously out the window were birds and red squirrels.

She'd started the morning runs as a way of helping Milly, but now they were the best part of her day.

But deep down she couldn't forget the fact that she had decisions to make, big decisions, and for the first time in her life she had someone else to consider.

She rested her hand on her abdomen and thought about the baby. She felt ridiculously protective.

Yes, she was scared—*terrified* might be a better word—but she was also excited. Her panicked thoughts about how she'd cope, and what sort of mother she'd be, were interspersed with tantalizing images of a different life. Family life. She'd never really had that and had never been able to picture it for herself, but she could picture it now. She would have it now. And she was determined to give her baby all the things she hadn't had. She imagined being there when her child took their first steps, getting up in the night to soothe them after a bad dream, reading together, playing. She imagined being there for every parent–teacher meeting, for every school performance, however small. She was going to do everything differently from her own mother. She was going to create a stable and loving home for her child.

But she was all too conscious that those ambitions didn't fit well with her present life.

She couldn't be present for a child while she was taking one project after another. When work sucked up all of her time. Equally importantly, she didn't want to expose her child to the circus that was her life.

Something had to change, and she was still figuring that part out.

Milly had been encouraging her to make an appointment with the local doctor, but Nicole had been putting it off. She'd told herself that it was still early days, that there would be plenty of time for that when she'd decided what she was going to do next and where she was going to live. The way she felt at the moment, she would happily have stayed here forever and not moved anywhere.

Despite the obvious challenges (almost all of them related to Richard!), Milly's life seemed idyllic to her. Could she have something similar?

Was that even possible?

She stared across the water, watching as the ducks emerged from the reeds and swam along the edge of the lake, staying close together.

It hadn't occurred to her at any point that she might one day be thinking of giving up what she'd spent her entire life striving to attain.

But that was what she was thinking now.

She wanted a simple, low-key life where she could enjoy the things other people enjoyed. She imagined bringing the baby over and going for a walk with Milly. Sitting at the kitchen table with Connie and Nanna Peg, talking about sleep patterns and teething and weaning.

She imagined signing the baby up for the local play group and music group and meeting new people. Normal, everyday people who didn't spend hours in hair and makeup every day before emerging to play a person that wasn't them.

Was that sort of life even possible for someone like her?

And would she miss her old life?

She definitely wouldn't miss the movie industry. People only saw the glamour, but there was another side. A darker side. She wouldn't miss the politics, the pressure, the endless publicity machine, the people who lied and took advantage. People who used her. But the acting? She'd miss that. She still loved acting.

She needed to find a way to indulge her creative self, while avoiding all the ruthless, cutthroat parts of the business. She didn't need accolades or red carpets. Talking to Zoe had made her wonder if she should teach acting. Get involved with local groups. Children would be more fun than adults. Was that even a possibility?

Maybe, but first she needed to expand the life she was living. Push her boundaries. It wasn't enough just to run in the early mornings. She needed to get out during the day and start to live life instead of avoiding it. She needed to take baby steps into a new future.

On impulse she reached for her phone and sent a message to Joel.

If you're free tomorrow, I'm ready to climb into the back of
your van.

No. She couldn't say that. It sounded awful.
She deleted it and started again.

Needed: one getaway driver. Tomorrow?

She sent it before she could change her mind and then waited
a few breathless seconds before the reply came.

Sorry, but who is this?

She froze, and then another message came immediately.

Just kidding. Tomorrow works. 6:30 a.m.?

She felt a rush of relief and elation, and also a flicker of frustration with herself. She was so jumpy and on edge the whole time
she no longer recognized a joke when she saw one.

But it was done now. She was going to leave Forest Nest for the
first time since she'd arrived. And she was going to have to hope
it didn't go horribly wrong.

18

Milly

Milly stepped out of Brendan's sports car and grabbed the skirt of her dress before the breeze could catch it and expose the underwear Nicole had insisted that she wear. (Why? There was no way she was ready to show another person her underwear.) It had been years since she'd worn this dress, and she'd forgotten how flimsy it was. Still, it had given her a quiet confidence boost, and she was grateful to Nicole for insisting she try it on. Less grateful for her friend's insistence that she wear the shoes.

All she'd done so far was walk to the car, but already they were biting into her feet. What had possessed her to buy them in the first place? They'd been purchased for a wedding, and she recalled dancing barefoot at that same wedding, which presumably meant she'd found them unwearable after the first few hours.

She silently cursed Nicole as she walked with Brendan to the restaurant, trying not to twist her ankle. She wore flats or trainers when she was working and walking in heels felt strange and unsafe. If this was what Nicole had to endure each time she appeared on a red carpet, then she felt sorry for her.

Fortunately, she made it inside without drama or mishap, and they were shown to a table on the terrace. It had an uninterrupted view of the lake and beyond to the craggy fells in the distance.

And when she glanced around her at the other diners, she was glad Nicole had made her wear the dress. It had been the right choice.

And Brendan looked good too, although it crossed her very undisciplined mind that he'd looked equally good fresh out of the shower, wearing just shorts.

Tonight he was wearing a pair of chinos and a pale blue shirt the same shade as his eyes. Of course, deciding what to wear was easier for men, particularly when it came to shoes.

She was willing to bet his footwear wasn't testing the level of his pain threshold.

She was looking forward to sitting down so that she could give her feet a break.

"This is incredible. I had no idea this terrace existed." In her opinion the restaurant had earned its reputation, and that was before she sampled the food. "How on earth did you get a table here at such short notice? Who did you bribe?"

"No one. I called and told them I needed a table for a special celebration. Turns out the chef is a fan. This table cost me an entire set of signed copies, and the promise that his name will appear in my next book."

She laughed. "So does that mean that the murder victim is no longer called Callum?"

"He's still Callum. But somewhere in there I have to introduce a chef. This table is okay for you? You're happy being outdoors?"

"It's perfect." She settled herself in her seat, slid off her shoes with a quiet sigh of relief and gazed at the view. The surface of the lake sparkled in the late evening sunshine and a few sheep were grazing close to the shoreline. "I've read brilliant things about this place."

She glanced around her, taking a proper look at their fellow diners. Their table was surely the best in the restaurant, tucked into a corner away from the rest of the guests. The terrace was strung with miniature lanterns, and candles flickered in the center of each table. It was the sort of place that stayed in the memory of the people who were lucky enough to eat here.

She had a feeling she wouldn't be forgetting it in a hurry either.

She'd been worried she wouldn't know what to say or what to do because it had been so long since she'd had dinner with a man who wasn't Richard, but Brendan seemed so comfortable and relaxed she found herself relaxing too.

"You and Richard didn't eat out much?"

"Generally I cooked." He always said he preferred her food, but now she wondered if he was just saving money that he'd then spent on Avery.

She shut down that thought. She was not letting Richard or Avery intrude on this evening.

Tonight was special, and she intended to enjoy every moment.

A burst of laughter from a table close by made her turn her head, and she noticed a woman casting surreptitious glances in Brendan's direction.

She seemed to be making a decision about something, and then she stood up and approached the table.

"I know this is an intrusion, but I just had to say I love your books." Her face was scarlet. "Would you sign my menu? I'll use it as a bookmark."

To his credit Brendan was gracious and charming and signed the menu, and the woman returned to her seat flourishing her prize.

Brendan gave Milly a look of apology. "Sorry about that."

"Don't worry." She almost confessed that she was used to it because her best friend was Nicole Raven, but she stopped herself in time. Even if Brendan and Nicole had worked together, there was no way she'd reveal her friend's presence. "Do you get hounded by the press a lot?"

"The press? No." He shook his head. "More that I'm hounding

them because a certain amount of publicity is useful when a book comes out. But I don't get followed down the street or anything. Occasionally a reader recognizes me, but when they do, I'm grateful. Without readers I wouldn't have this job."

She'd looked him up and read a couple of detailed features on him, so she knew the public were interested in the man behind the books.

And in that moment the reality of the situation hit her. She was here, on a date, with Brendan Scott. And she felt like an impostor. In her head she could hear Richard's voice telling her she was no fun. She tried to block it out, but the words were imprinted on her memory. The pressure to be entertaining company almost had her walking out of the restaurant.

When Brendan had suggested dinner it had sounded like a good idea, but now she was here, sitting across from him it felt intimate and awkward and totally different from the encounters they'd had when he'd been wearing cutoff shorts and four days of stubble.

Flustered, she studied the menu without seeing anything on the page.

What was she going to talk about? The weather? She was going to bore him to death before the main course was served.

Brendan put his menu down. "I probably ought to warn you that there is every chance I've actually forgotten how to do this."

"This?" She looked up and tried to look natural and not as if she was close to having a panic attack. "You mean eating dinner?"

"No. I never forget how to eat. That's a talent I was born with." He smiled. "I mean being sociable. I've been trapped indoors focused on the book for so long I may have forgotten how to talk to an actual person. Most of the people I've been relating to over the past couple of months have been fictional. I'm not sure I can remember how to converse with a real human being, so you'll have to be patient and forgive me if I'm less than scintillating company."

He was worried that *he* might not be good company?

She almost laughed. "It's a new experience for me too, but for different reasons."

"You haven't been out much since your divorce?"

"No. When you're a single working mother, life has a tendency to get in the way." She didn't tell him that she'd had no wish to go on a date with anyone until he'd invited her.

And she was still wondering why she'd said yes.

"Well, that's good, because now that we've both admitted we're very out of practice neither of us has to try and impress the other."

Really? It couldn't possibly be that easy, could it?

The waiter arrived at their table, and they both placed their orders.

"Do you always work that intensely when you're writing?" Milly thought about all the notes stuck around the cabin and the fact that the fridge was usually empty. "It must be exhausting. Not very healthy."

"It's not healthy at all, but over the years I've discovered what works best for me. If I keep walking away from the book and taking time out, it's harder to get started again when I sit down at my laptop. I prefer to immerse myself, work so hard I forget to eat and tidy up—" his brief look of apology was an acknowledgment of the fact that she'd witnessed the state of his cabin "—and finish a draft. Then I can relax and take my time over the revision process. I've learned that if I live with those characters day in, day out for a few months I stay locked in the story. Creativity doesn't always respect office hours."

"So you emerge at the end of your few months and discover that the world has ended and your bins are overflowing."

"Something like that."

It fascinated her to hear about a life that was so different from hers. "Still, it must be very satisfying writing a book that people love to read."

"It is. Just as it must be satisfying cooking something that people can't wait to eat, or running a place like Forest Nest where people go to escape and make happy memories. Different skill set, but still a skill. You're good at what you do."

She wondered if he was making fun of her. Not the cooking, she could see the validity in that comparison, but the rest? "Making beds and cleaning bathrooms?"

"I was thinking more about how you make people feel relaxed and welcome. I saw you the other day with that little girl. She was giving you a picture she'd drawn for you. I bumped into them later in the café. Her parents told me she'd been in hospital and that you'd sent her a note and a gift."

"Katy? The family have been coming here since before she was born. They spent their honeymoon at Forest Nest. They rang to say they might not be able to use their week because poor Katy was in hospital and they thought they should cancel so that we could rebook it."

"But you wouldn't let them. You held the week for them anyway and said you'd absorb the cost if necessary." He nodded. "They told me. And they also told me that looking forward to being here kept Katy going when she was sick. What would have happened if they hadn't been able to come?"

"I either would have tried to rent it at the last minute or I would have lost money." She shrugged. "Probably not the best business decision, but I can't think of anything more stressful than having a child in hospital. I didn't want them to worry about the holiday on top of everything else."

They paused the conversation as their appetizers were placed on the table.

He picked up his fork. "I don't think it was a bad business decision. You have guaranteed that they'll be returning here every year for the foreseeable future, I should imagine. But I know you didn't do it for that reason. You're the warmest, kindest person I've ever met." His voice was gruff. "Also your cooking skills are off the scale. I'm convinced you're the reason I finished the book. It's the first time I've reached this stage and felt fresh and clearheaded. Normally I'm existing on a diet of junk food and sugar, and it takes me a while to recover. The other night I dreamed about your lemon chicken. I'd ask for the recipe, but I know I wouldn't be able to reproduce it."

She made a mental note to make him her lemon chicken again soon.

"Did you always want to be a writer?"

"I always loved telling stories and reading, but I assumed everyone was like that," he said. "I didn't know that most people don't walk around with stories and characters in their heads. And it didn't cross my mind that it could be a career until I began working as a lawyer. I realized how complex people are. Everyone around me was interested in the *what*. The facts of the case. I was more interested in the *why*. What makes good people do bad things?"

She was interested in the *why* too. Why Richard had behaved the way he had. Why he was always so moody with her now.

"Thinking about the *why* sounds more like psychology than law."

"An interest in psychology helps when you're a writer. I've always been curious about people."

"But you write about bad people."

"Sometimes, but the most interesting villains are the ones who start out as good people but get driven to do bad things by circumstances. Maybe they make a decision that seems right at the time and turns out to be a mistake. Then they have to cover up the mistake, so they make another decision and that's worse."

"So you're saying that the chef that needs to be in your book was a really good person until someone stole his fish knife? Then when he found out, he gutted them."

The smile spread across his face. "You're better at this than you think."

Despite her anxiety, the conversation flowed, and over the best meal she'd ever eaten they traded life histories. She discovered that he'd spent the first five years of his life in Cumbria, and then his parents had separated and he'd gone to live with his mother in Boston.

"You're not in touch with your father?"

"No. My mother always said that parenthood didn't suit him. I have no memories of him. He died shortly after they separated. How about you?"

"My dad left when I was twelve. And it was hard." She didn't need to elaborate. Brendan was a writer. She knew instinctively that he'd sense all the things she was leaving unsaid. "He said he loved me and would always love me, but all I kept thinking was that however much he loved me it wasn't enough for him to want to stick around. I think that's why I married Richard so young. I was looking for stability, and he seemed to offer that." She'd never said it aloud before. Never really acknowledged it. "I was looking for some sort of guarantee, and of course, that doesn't exist."

"No," he said. "But that early experience shaped you. And it must have made it extra tough when Richard left because you were dealing with parts of the past as well as the present."

"Yes." It was true, and she wondered how he could see instantly what it had taken her ages to work out. "But mostly I was worried about Zoe. About the impact on her."

"She's lucky to have a mother like you. I think you're incredible. And resilient. You're running a business and raising a child, and you still find time to make delicious lemon chicken and nurture your guests."

He thought she was incredible. Not boring or a martyr. Incredible.

She flushed. "I'm just getting on with life."

"That's the very definition of resilience. Did your mother marry again?"

"No. Her friends were always trying to match her with people, but she wasn't interested. And we never talked about it until last year when Richard left, and she told me then that she'd grown to love her life exactly the way it was and that she had no intention of disrupting it. I think she liked the idea of being in control of all aspects of her life. But it was difficult for her when Richard left me because it brought it all back for her too."

He nodded. "It must be hard watching your child go through tough times. You're lucky to have such close family."

"I know." And she felt guilty for all the worry she'd caused her mother. She was going to make sure that from now on she would be a bundle of sunny positivity whenever she visited. "How about you? Never married?"

Their main course was delivered at that moment and he waited until they were alone again to answer.

"I married straight out of law school, and it lasted a year. So I think we can both agree it was something I wasn't good at. But it was an experience, and all experiences teach you something."

"I think relationships are just hard. People change, and they want different things."

He studied her for a moment. "What do you want?"

In that moment he reminded her of Nicole. *If you could have three wishes . . .*

It was something she rarely thought about because she was so focused on making it through each day, but she thought about it now and realized that she'd been stuck in the present since Richard had left, and that was entirely her fault.

She hadn't wanted Richard to walk out. She hadn't wanted him to leave her. She hadn't wanted any of it to happen, and because of that she'd refused to let herself move on. And by not moving on, by not accepting things as they were, by looking for areas of blame both in herself and him, she'd kept things the same. But they weren't the same, and all she was really doing was denying the truth. And denying herself a future. She'd spent her whole time looking back, wanting to somehow find the place where she'd dropped the ball so that she could undo everything that had happened, but now she realized that there was no going back. There never had been. There was only what lay ahead, and instead of seeing a bleak future she saw possibilities.

What *did* she want?

"I want what I have," she said finally. "Is that boring? Maybe it is to someone else, but I love Forest Nest and the people who stay with us. I love this part of the world, and it feels like a privilege to be able to live and work here."

"You love the people who stay with you, with the exception of the moody thriller writer."

"He's appalling," she agreed. "Nightmare guest."

"You could do away with him."

"Generally we find that murdering our guests doesn't have a positive impact on customer reviews, but I suppose we might risk it if it was truly warranted." She stared at him. "Why are you laughing?"

"Because you're funny. You're good company. Here, try this." He speared a piece of meat and handed it to her. "But brace yourself. Because it's going to be the best thing you've ever tasted."

"This whole meal is the best thing I've ever tasted." She ate the meat and made an appreciative sound. "You're right. That's good."

"Isn't it? Have another piece."

"I'd better not. I don't want to think about how many calories are in that."

"Why would you even care? We're eating out somewhere special. We can worry about calories tomorrow. Or not."

And it was such a change from Richard, who on more than one occasion had said, "Are you sure you want that slice of toast, Milly?" that she took another bite of his food and offered him some of hers, and in that moment she didn't feel like someone's wife or even their ex-wife. She didn't feel like Zoe's mother or the boss of Forest Nest. She felt like herself. Milly.

They ate and talked, and talked some more until eventually the people around them melted away, and they were the last people left on the candlelit terrace.

When they finally walked back to his car she had a powerful urge to take his hand, but she resisted, afraid that she might do or say something she'd later regret, but then he pulled her into his arms and kissed her, and she kissed him back, feeling the hard pressure of his body against hers, the flat of his hand on the small of her back urging her closer, and the warmth and skill of his mouth on hers. The kiss came with a promise of something more, something she hadn't imagined for herself, hadn't even known she needed. She wanted the moment to last forever, and when she finally eased away from him, dizzy and happy, she discovered that she regretted nothing.

They drove home, and he had one hand on the wheel and the other on her leg.

She covered his hand with hers.

Neither of them said anything until they pulled up outside the boathouse, and then he turned to her, cupped her face in his hands and kissed her again.

"Milly, Milly," he murmured the words against her mouth, "I don't want tonight to end."

"Neither do I."

His lips traced a path from her mouth to her jaw. "My cabin is just down the track."

She closed her eyes, transported by his touch. She was tempted, oh so tempted, but another part of her knew she wasn't ready. She had so much to think about. So much to process. And she was glad that she had Nicole staying because she knew it would help to talk it through. "Tonight was a big step for me. I've been with Richard since I was twenty-one."

He drew back. "So we'll take it slowly." He stroked her cheek with his thumb. "How would you feel about a second date?"

He made it all sound so easy and natural. She smiled at him. "I'd like that. When?"

"Tomorrow?"

She was ridiculously flattered that he wanted to see her again so soon. "Zoe is back tomorrow evening."

"Does that matter?"

She thought about it. "I'm not sure I'm ready to introduce another change into her life at the moment."

But something had changed in her own life.

This was the first time since Richard had left her that she hadn't spent the whole weekend thinking about Zoe with Richard and Avery and feeling slightly sick. The first time that the focus had been on herself. And it made her realize that she needed to stop wasting her weekends worrying and start living her life.

He let his hand drop. "You're a good mother. So how about lunch during your working day? She'd be at school?"

"Yes, I could do that."

"Good, let me know when."

"I wouldn't be disturbing you?"

"Some things are worth being disturbed for."

He waited until she was safely inside the boathouse, and she watched from the door as the lights from his car gradually vanished into the distance.

She felt a brief moment of regret that she hadn't gone back to his cabin with him, then she turned and saw Nicole standing there.

Her arms were folded, her foot was tapping, and she had a big expectant grin on her face. "Well?"

"Well, what?"

"Details! I want details."

Milly walked through to the kitchen, the smile she was wearing on the inside almost as big as the one on the outside. "Nothing to tell."

"You're lying. I can tell by the happy expression on your face that you're lying." Nicole followed her, determined not to let it drop.

"The food was wonderful."

"I'm not asking about the food."

Milly poured herself a glass of water. Took her time. "The terrace of the restaurant was pretty. Great views."

"Not asking about that either, although I'm glad obviously."

Milly drank the water. "I had a lovely evening. Brendan was very good company."

"Of course he was. So why didn't you go back to his cabin?"

"Because I have a guest staying."

Nicole looked appalled. "Please tell me you're joking. You came back for me?"

"No. And I am joking. I came back for me." She put the glass down. "Because although I was tempted, very tempted, I'm not ready to take it further yet."

"What?" Nicole's shoulders slumped. "Why not?"

"Do you have any idea what a step forward tonight was for me? I went on a date. That is the first time I've dated anyone since Richard. It felt strange and a bit scary."

"But he obviously put you at ease."

"He was easy to talk to. A good listener. And—"

"And?" Nicole's eyes lit up with anticipation, and Milly laughed.

"And he's a very good kisser."

"I knew it." Nicole gave a sigh of satisfaction and grabbed a couple of mugs from the cupboard. "This calls for hot chocolate and a girly heart-to-heart in bed, like we used to."

"I've just eaten a meal."

"You'll be fine. Hot chocolate is an essential part of a midnight confession session. Also it's one of the few things I can make without consulting the internet." Nicole prepared it, and together they carried the mugs up to Milly's bedroom.

And as they curled up on Milly's bed, talking about everything and nothing until the early hours, Milly felt truly happy for the first time in ages. It wasn't just the kiss, or the delicious anticipation of her next meeting with Brendan, it was the knowledge that finally, after all the ups and downs and heartbreak, she had her best friend back. And if anything it felt as if they were even closer than before.

And no matter what happened in the future she was sure this time, absolutely positive, that nothing would ever come between them again.

19

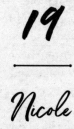

Nicole

Nicole waited until the van appeared on the track and then sprinted toward it.

Joel pulled up, leaned across and opened the door for her. "I've never driven a getaway vehicle before. I might need some tips. Do you want to sit in the front or the back?"

If she was being sensible she'd probably hide away in the back, but she was tired of living her life that way.

"Front is fine."

He waited while she settled herself and fastened her seat belt. "No one will recognize you, anyway. I see you're a blonde today."

She didn't tell him that no matter what her disguise, someone usually recognized her. She didn't want to burst the bubble. "Let's go."

He reversed the van in the turning space and set off down the track. "As a matter of interest, what made you decide to trust me?"

"Who said I trust you?"

"Ouch." He looked so wounded that she smiled.

"The answer to your question is that Milly trusts you, and I trust Milly."

"She's a good person."

"Yes, she is." She noticed that his eyes crinkled at the corners when he smiled. "She deserves better than Richard, that's for sure."

"That, we can agree on. So where do you want to go, or are you going to let me decide?"

"You decide. Somewhere remote. Somewhere we're not likely to meet people. I'm guessing that's a tough ask for the Lakes in the summer."

"Not necessarily. Summer tourists have a pattern. They mostly get up late, enjoy a slow breakfast and then congregate in all the most popular areas. We won't be going there. I'm not saying we won't meet anyone, but they'll be hikers or climbers, and you can stay behind me and keep your head down. Also, we have Buster."

"Buster?" She heard a whine from behind her and turned to see a beautiful spaniel, tail wagging, legs braced as he swayed with the movement of the van.

"Are you okay with dogs? I probably should have asked."

"I love dogs." She would have had one, but she'd decided it wasn't fair with her lifestyle. But her lifestyle was about to change, wasn't it? Maybe there would be room for a dog in this new family she was dreaming about. She almost smiled at herself. She needed to figure out how to care for a baby before she added in a lively puppy. "How long have you had him?"

"He's not mine. He belongs to my sister, but I'm dog-sitting while she's away. You don't have a dog?"

"Up until now I've never been in one place for long enough."

"Up until now?" He turned off the main road and followed a winding road that led into a valley. "Does that mean you're thinking of hanging around?"

"I don't know. My life is complicated. So complicated it makes my brain hurt to think about it." She hoped he wouldn't ask in what way it was complicated because she didn't want to talk about it. She wouldn't have known where to start. It wasn't clear in her own head, so she certainly wouldn't have been able to share it.

Fortunately he was one of those rare people who knew when to let a subject drop.

"In that case you were right to get out in the mountains. It's the perfect cure for an overheated brain." He drove out of Forest Nest, past the sign and toward the village.

It was early, and there was little traffic.

He took narrow roads that snaked along the valley, past another lake and then gradually started to climb.

She gazed out the window, loving the wildness of it and appreciating the fact that right at this moment no one knew where she was.

She was as close to being invisible as she'd ever been, and it was a good feeling. She felt free and normal and happy.

"I'd forgotten how stunning it is here. The scenery is like nowhere else."

"Milly says you spent your childhood here."

They crossed a stone bridge, and she glanced down at the river rushing beneath it.

"Yes. That seems like a lifetime ago. And do you know the weird thing? All I wanted was what I have now. I had such a clear goal in my head."

He slowed down to allow a couple of sheep to cross the road. "And now you have it, you're not sure if you want it anymore."

She turned her head to look at him, wondering how he could read her so clearly. "I'd be mad not to want it, wouldn't I?"

"No. People change. I'm not the same person I was at eighteen, and I don't suppose you are either."

She thought back to the excitement of that time. It had felt like a nonstop adrenaline rush.

"I've been lucky."

"Luck plays a part, sure, but there's always more to it than that. Talent. Hard work. Resilience. Focus. Sacrifice. Do you miss LA? Are you homesick?"

She should be, shouldn't she?

At night she slept on Milly's spare bed, and if occasionally she thought of her giant custom-made bed in her house with its expensive mattress, it wasn't because she missed it but because she was relieved she wasn't there.

"I don't miss it. I'm not homesick." Saying those words aloud cleared her head. She should sell the house. She hadn't spent a single night there since the incident with the intruder. "Have you ever just wanted to start fresh?"

"Yes." He slowed down as they approached a hairpin bend. "And I did. Five years ago. I was living in London. Worked for a big international firm. Spent half my life in airports or doing site visits. It was relentless."

"How did you end up here?"

"My brother-in-law died suddenly. My sister was struggling on her own with two little girls. My nieces." His smile was soft. "I wanted to be closer to her so I could help when needed. I was willing to take any job that gave me flexibility and some control over my time. Connie had a job for a maintenance person with carpentry experience, and it seemed ideal to me. I assume you know Connie."

"Yes." Nicole felt a rush of affection. "I always wished she was my mother."

"I know what you mean. She's been great to me. Gave me time off whenever I needed to take the kids for Suzie. Let me leave early. I made sure the jobs got done, and she didn't care how I managed it all." He eased the van closer to the edge of the road to allow a car to pass. "After a decade of working for a corporation that felt as if it was full of machines, not people, she restored my faith in human nature."

"I can believe that."

The road climbed up through the valley, and she gazed at the wild beauty around them, reflecting on the ups and downs of life.

"How is your sister doing?"

"She's doing well, thanks. Tough couple of years, and then she met someone. Pete's a doctor. They got married last year."

"You like him?"

"Very much. He's a great guy. And the girls adore him."

"So Uncle Joel is no longer so much in demand."

"I see quite a bit of them, but it's usually planned rather than an emergency." He turned into a small parking area with just one other car. "We can walk from here. It's steep, but it should be quiet, and the views from the top are incredible. I packed water and a snack into my backpack. And I have a spare layer if you need it, but I doubt you will because it's hot."

It was more than hot. It was sweltering, but she didn't care. She was just so happy and grateful to be outdoors.

"I'll be fine, but thank you."

She stepped out of the car and felt the sun warm her face. The fells rose up around her, cocooning them from the outside world. She heard the soft rush of water from the nearby stream and the occasional bleating of sheep. Fuchsia-pink foxgloves speared through dense ferns, adding a splash of bright color to the landscape.

"It's peaceful."

"It's a magical spot." He changed into hiking boots, hauled a large backpack onto his back and snapped a lead onto Buster's collar. "He's good, but I don't take any chances around sheep."

She laced up the hiking boots Milly had given her and rammed a hat onto her head, tugging down the brim.

He watched her. "Is that for disguise? Because we're pretty much the only people here."

"Reflex action."

He nodded. "Well, Buster and I have your back, so hopefully you can relax. I'm guessing that's something you don't do very often."

"Hardly ever." But she felt relaxed now. The landscape was wild and beautiful, and it made her feel so small and insignificant that her problems shrank to nothing, and she wished she could just stay here, in this moment, and never go back to her life.

She'd never been able to get into mindfulness (although she did yoga for her backache), but as she followed him up the narrow trail, picking her way between rocks and scrambling up the steeper parts, the repetitive action of putting one foot in front of the other was oddly calming.

They climbed steadily toward the ridge in the distance, occasionally stopping to drink water. And during those pauses Joel did most of the talking. He didn't ask about her life. He didn't question her about anything, but he spoke freely about himself.

She learned that he'd been born and raised in a small town about half an hour from Forest Nest and that his sister still lived in the same town. His mother had died when he was five, and he'd been very close to his dad.

"My dad first brought me up here when I was seven. He gave me a book with all the Lakeland fells listed, and we ticked them off as we did them. I climbed a hundred and eighty with him. After he died my sister and I did his favorite climb together in his memory."

She learned that he'd always liked building things and that one of the reasons he'd taken the job in London was that, after his father died, he couldn't bear to be in the Lakes because it was so full of memories that every walk was painful.

So he'd moved away, and while his sister was getting married and raising a family, Joel had been building a life and a career in London, flying round the world working on big prestigious projects.

She learned that he'd had two long-term relationships, neither of which had worked out, mostly because he was always working and couldn't find a way to be more available to a partner while still doing his job.

And then there was the day when he'd been staying in an anonymous hotel room in Toronto and he'd had a call from his sister to say that his brother-in-law had died suddenly. He'd flown home right away.

"And that was it." They paused on a ridge, and he delved into the backpack and pulled out a couple of chocolate bars. "I resigned from my job, moved in with my sister for six months and kept things going until she was able to function again."

"You're a good brother."

"She would have done the same for me." He held out a chocolate bar, and she almost took it but then shook her head.

"I don't eat chocolate."

"What, never?" He tore the wrapper off his and ate a piece.

"Not for years."

"Allergies? You don't like chocolate?"

"I love chocolate."

He studied her face for a moment and then glanced over her shoulder to the path they'd taken. "Look at how far we've walked. You don't think you could safely eat a square of chocolate?"

"Do you know one of the things you need to be a successful actress? Self-discipline. You learn lines, no matter how tired you are, you show up on time, you play nice, you train for whatever part you're playing, you say no to chocolate."

He nodded and snapped off a piece of chocolate for himself.

"Makes sense. In a way it's no different from how you succeed in any field. But today you're not an actress. Today you're just Nicole. You're off duty, so if you want to change your mind about that chocolate at any point, let me know."

Today you're just Nicole.

"I spend my whole life pretending to be other people. I'm not sure I know how to be just Nicole."

He smiled. "You start by doing all the things your movie-star self wouldn't do. Anyway, you don't really want this chocolate, so I'm putting it away now." He reached for the backpack, but she grabbed his arm and then the chocolate and the resultant tussle made them both laugh.

She ate the first piece of chocolate and closed her eyes, savoring the smooth sweetness. "Oh my—"

"You'd forgotten how good it is." Still laughing, he watched as she broke off another piece.

"You've corrupted me. This is a slippery slope. Temptation."

"I would have called it *having fun*." He waited while she ate the last of the chocolate and then swung the backpack on. "This is so much lighter now you've eaten the chocolate. At least now you'll have the energy to finish the walk. We're about halfway."

"Are you going to give me more chocolate at the top?"

He set off up the path again. "You don't eat chocolate. Why would I give you chocolate?"

"Because—" She cannoned into him, and he shot out a hand to steady her. "What? Next time warn me before you stop."

And then she saw the couple approaching them down the path.

"It's fine." Joel's voice was calm. "We're in the middle of no-where. Even if they think you look a bit familiar, they're not going to recognize you here out of context."

Nicole sighed. She had a feeling he was about to have a rude awakening.

They drew closer, and the man lifted his hand by way of a greet-ing. "I'm relieved to see you. We're not sure if we're on the right path. How far to the road? If we can find the road, we can just fol-low it back to our car."

Joel turned and pointed the way they'd just come, but the woman wasn't paying attention. She was staring at Nicole.

"Oh my God. You're . . ." she was almost stammering ". . . she's that actress. You're that actress. Ted? You know who I mean—the famous one—I can't remember her name—"

Nicole froze, but Joel laughed.

"She gets that a lot, don't you, Wendy?"

Wendy?

He was looking at her, so she assumed he was talking to her.

"I—uh, yes, I do. I'm always being told I look like that actress. I can't remember her name either."

"I keep telling her she should make a career of it," Joel said, "that whole look-alike thing. She could open village fetes or cut ribbons and things. Make herself a fortune. I think there's a web-site where you can book people. Do you want her to autograph something for you? That would be funny."

The woman was staring at Nicole. "It's uncanny. You could *be* her."

"Well, not really," Joel said, "because then she'd have to act, and Wendy can't act to save her life, can you, Wend?"

"No. Acting isn't really my thing." But it seemed to be Joel's thing. If she hadn't been feeling so exposed and vulnerable, she would have been in awe of him.

"Also you'd have to be able to wear high heels and walk on a red carpet." Joel winked at her. "Remember that time you wore heels to my cousin's wedding? You turned your ankle. We spent the whole afternoon in hospital getting X-rays."

"It was a painful experience. I haven't worn heels since."

"I don't care, though." He grabbed her hand and pulled her closer. "Some men love a woman in heels, but I think you look sexy in hiking boots, Wend."

"Hiking boots rule." She felt the warm pressure of his fingers on hers, and she held on tightly.

"You really do look like her." The woman gave her a bemused smile. "Your husband is right. You could make good money as a look-alike."

"We'll keep that in mind. It was nice bumping into you." Joel kept hold of Nicole's hand and used the other to gesture down the path. "Keep going straight down. It will take you about an hour to reach the road. Enjoy." With that he gave her hand a tug, and they carried on trudging up the path.

Nicole kept walking, waiting for him to let go of her hand, but he didn't.

She was afraid to turn around in case she drew attention to herself.

"Have they gone? Are they still walking, or are they taking photos? Or maybe they're calling the tabloids."

Joel glanced over his shoulder. "They're still walking. Not looking back. I think you're okay, Wend. You need to work on those acting skills, though. You were terrible back there."

She laughed. "You, however, were brilliant. I had no idea you had so much talent. It was genius. Thank you."

"Anytime, Wendy."

"Do you think we fooled them?"

"Maybe, or maybe they were just too polite to argue with me. But it got rid of them." He shook his head and continued up the path. "I assume from your resigned expression this happens a lot."

"Yes. But it doesn't usually make me laugh like that."

"We should be grateful."

"For what?"

"That they didn't arrive five minutes earlier and see you with chocolate smeared around your mouth. Now, shift yourself, Wend, or we won't make it to the top before dark."

It took another couple of hours to make it to the top, but it turned out to be worth every breathless stride.

She had a three-hundred-and-sixty-degree view across mountaintops and valleys, lakes and streams.

"My niece always says that coming up here is like a geography lesson. Hanging valley, glacial spur," he said and gestured and then handed her more chocolate from the backpack. "Here—you've earned it."

"This is fantastic." She settled herself on a large rock and gazed at the view. It seemed to stretch forever. "Thank you. It has been the best day ever."

"You're welcome." He ate another piece of chocolate himself. "I've done most of the talking. Tell me a little about you. I don't mean the movie stuff, I mean other things. Do you have family? I never see your family mentioned."

She kept her eyes on the view. "I prefer to keep that part of my life away from the public eye."

"Understandable. Are your parents alive?"

"My dad died when I was two, so I have no memory of him at all. My mother . . . We're not in touch. She doesn't like me. And now you're going to say all the usual things about how you're sure that isn't true et cetera, so let me save you the bother. She really doesn't like me. It's not a feeling, it's a fact."

There was a long silence. "So no family, then."

"Milly is my family. She has always been my family."

222

He nodded. "You're lucky, both of you, having a friendship like that."

She almost told him then. She almost told him how she'd messed it up, and how she woke up in the night sweating in case Milly somehow found out about the stuff she hadn't told her, and how she was terrified that if she found out it would be the end of their friendship and Nicole would lose the only relationship that had ever really mattered to her.

But she didn't tell him, partly because there were some things you kept to yourself, and this was definitely one of those, and partly because today had been the most perfect day she'd had in as long as she could remember, and she didn't want to taint it by worrying what might be coming down the line.

With luck it wouldn't happen, and everything would be fine.

"I meant it when I said this has been the best day ever." She turned to look at him. "If I had just one wish—" She broke off, embarrassed when she saw his quizzical look. "Ignore me. It's a game Milly and I used to play when we were kids."

"And if you had one wish?"

She stared across the landscape. "That I could do this every day. That this was my life." The moment she said it she felt foolish. There was no way he'd understand. He'd think she was crazy.

He took so long to respond she thought that maybe he wasn't going to, that he really didn't have a clue what to say to her, but then he gave a shrug and passed her the last of the chocolate.

"It could be real life, Wend. All you have to do is stop messing around with that pathetic career of yours and get yourself a proper job as a look-alike. You'd be sorted."

He scrunched up the wrapper and stowed it safely back in the backpack, and she laughed and ate the chocolate and realized that even when you took into account the high points of the last few years—the awards, the accolades, even the beginning of her relationship with Justin when she'd thought she was in love—this was still the best day she'd had in a long time.

She couldn't wait to get home and tell Milly all about it.

She smiled on the journey back and was still smiling when he dropped her back at the boathouse.

"Thank you for a perfect day." On impulse she leaned across to kiss his cheek.

"You're welcome, Wendy. Anytime you want to climb into the back of my van, just call me."

She was going to do that. And that in itself felt like progress. A new step in her life.

She all but danced her way up the path and opened the door. "Hey, Milly, where are you? You will never believe what happened. I never thought I could laugh about it, but—" She broke off as a man emerged from the kitchen.

Richard.

Her stomach dropped.

Oh no. No, no, *no*!

All the happiness, the joy, the optimism she'd felt only moments earlier drained out of her.

Shock flickered across his face as he recognized her. "You! You're here."

Milly emerged from behind him. "Yes, and you need to make sure you don't say anything to anyone, Richard. Thanks for dropping Zoe home. Have a good journey back."

Richard didn't budge.

"This certainly answers some of the questions I've been asking myself."

Milly sighed. "What questions?"

Nicole was shaking.

She wanted him to leave. She wanted him to stop talking.

"You've changed over the past few weeks, Milly, and I was wondering what had happened. What was different. And now I know." He didn't shift his attention from Nicole. "You're the reason she's started being difficult and confrontational."

Milly's eyebrows rose. "Richard—"

"And I don't need to ask what you're doing here. You're hiding out, keeping a low profile because you've been playing your

224

games again. Ruining other people's relationships instead of trying to find one of your own. How many marriages are you going to destroy before you find yourself a new hobby?"

"Richard!" Milly was aghast. "What is *wrong* with you?"

"Wrong with *me*?" Finally, he turned his head to look at her. He stared at Milly for a long moment and then gave a short laugh. "You don't know, do you? She hasn't told you."

Nicole's heart was pounding so hard she thought her chest might explode.

They'd been friends once, she and Richard. He'd sneaked her into the hospital when Milly had just given birth to Zoe. He'd once challenged a photographer who had stuck a camera in her face during a private dinner. And yet somehow they'd reached this point.

She wanted to turn back the clock. She wanted to have another chance. She wanted to make different decisions, different choices, anything that might have prevented her from finding herself where she was now.

Milly was staring at him in exasperation. "Told me what? You're making no sense, and I think you should leave now. I won't have you being rude to my friends, especially as you arrived here uninvited."

"You wouldn't be protecting her if you knew the truth."

Milly stepped past him and opened the door. "Good-bye, Richard."

"She's the reason we're no longer together. If it weren't for her, there's a good chance we'd still be married." Ignoring the open door, Richard turned back to Nicole and took a step toward her. "Time to tell her the truth."

"That's enough!" Milly grabbed his arm and pulled him back. "The reason we're not together is because you had an affair and left me. Remember that tiny detail?"

"I had an affair, that's true, and I'm not proud of it. I take full responsibility for that, but I never intended to leave you." Two red blotches appeared on his cheekbones. "It was—I don't know what it was. A moment of wild stupidity. It probably would have blown over, and you never would have known about it if it hadn't been for her."

Milly let go of his arm. "What are you talking about? I have no idea what's going on."

Nicole curled her fingers into her palms. Unfortunately she knew exactly what was going on. This was the moment she'd dreaded. Why, oh why hadn't she just said something before now?

She should have told the truth and explained everything to Milly, but she'd been afraid.

She'd been a coward.

And now she was paying the price because Richard showed no signs of holding back.

"Remember that time we were staying with her in LA? She overheard me talking to Avery, and she gave me an ultimatum. Leave Avery, or leave you. She forced me to choose."

It shouldn't have been so difficult to hear it because she'd replayed that conversation in her head so many times.

She knew it was bad, but somehow it sounded even worse when he said it.

The guilt was so intense she almost doubled over.

Richard was watching her. "And she threatened to tell you if I didn't. And I knew she wasn't bluffing, because you and she have always had an unnaturally close relationship."

Milly's breathing was shallow. "It's called *friendship*, Richard. There's nothing unnatural about it."

"The two of you were closer than sisters. From the first moment you introduced us I could tell she didn't want me around."

Nicole felt the ground shift.

"That isn't true." She somehow managed to find her voice. "That is *not* true."

"Isn't it? Why don't you just admit it, Nicole? Milly is the only person in your life who has stuck by you. None of your relationships last. Your own mother didn't want anything to do with you. Milly was all you had, and you didn't want to share her with anyone. You were jealous of me. Of my relationship with her. Of what we had together. You have always been jealous because you

226

thought I came between the two of you. You wanted me to leave her so that you could have her all to yourself."

His words made her shrink.

"That's not what happened." Outrage drove her to defend herself. "You were betraying her trust. I wanted you to be honest with her, that's all. To make a choice. Is that so wrong? I didn't want you lying to Milly. I wanted the best for her."

His words rang in her head. *Your own mother didn't want anything to do with you.*

She wanted to cover her ears with her hands to block it out. It was as if he'd jabbed a knife deep into the most vulnerable parts of her and then twisted it.

"But it wasn't your decision, was it?" Richard's tone was flat. "It wasn't your place to intervene in our relationship. But you did it anyway, and this is where we are now." He turned to Milly. "You've known her forever, and you think she's your best friend, but would a true friend really do that? She destroyed our marriage, Milly. You might want to think about that when you're protecting her from the fallout of having done exactly the same thing to someone else."

Without giving them a chance to respond he left the boathouse, slamming the door behind him.

Silence descended. Nicole couldn't breathe. Her vision was blurred by tears.

She needed to say something, do something, but what?

Where should she start? How could she possibly make this right?

She couldn't find the words. Maybe there weren't any words that would fix this because some of what he'd said was true.

20

Milly

Milly stared at the door that Richard had just slammed behind him.

She felt shocked and shaken. What did that all mean? What had just happened here?

She was struggling to make sense of it, to turn the words and the looks into something she could comprehend.

Nicole had known about Richard's affair. Nicole had confronted him. And she'd never mentioned it to Milly. Not then, and not in response to any one of the desperate emails and messages Milly had sent in her direction after Richard had left her.

She'd ignored her.

Milly walked to the nearest chair and sat down before her legs gave way.

She'd thought that Richard's affair had been the lowest point, but now she was discovering it was possible to go lower.

And there was no point in asking whether what Richard had said was true, because she could see from Nicole's face that it was.

The fact that Nicole had known intimate details about the state of Milly's marriage even before Milly had was so deeply uncomfortable and humiliating that she wanted to curl up in a ball and hide. She felt like a fool, as if she'd missed something obvious that everyone else had known about. Being the last to know something was never a good place to be, especially when the topic in question was your marriage.

"Why didn't you tell me? When you overheard Richard's conversation on the terrace that day, why didn't you come straight to me?" She couldn't believe her friend had known all this time and hadn't said a word. And there had been so many opportunities.

Eighteen months of opportunities.

And the last few weeks when they'd gradually healed their relationship, or so Milly had thought, Nicole still hadn't said anything despite multiple opportunities.

The sense of betrayal was painful.

Nicole stood still, arms wrapped around herself. She hadn't moved since Richard had walked out. "I didn't know what to do." Her voice was a whisper. "I didn't know how to handle it. You were so happy on that vacation. You had so many plans for the future. You talked about Richard the whole time. It was obvious that you had no idea what was going on. Not even the vaguest suspicion."

And she felt like a prize idiot. She'd trusted her husband, and she'd also trusted her best friend.

"And it didn't occur to you that it might have been a good idea to tell me? Or was it fun to watch me humiliated?"

"Fun?" Nicole's voice rose. "It was a nightmare, Milly. I didn't know what to do. I didn't want to be the one to drop that bombshell and shatter your world. I didn't want to come between the two of you and be the one who wrecked your marriage."

There was a knot in her stomach. She tried to think back to that time, to work out what she'd been doing when Nicole had overheard that conversation. Had she been swimming in the pool with Zoe? Changing for dinner? Afterward there must have been tension between Nicole and Richard. Why hadn't she spotted the shift in the mood?

Or had she simply not been looking, living her life in her own happy bubble, blinkered to the truth, trusting those around her because if you couldn't trust your own family, who could you trust?

"So you gave him an ultimatum. You made him choose."

She imagined Richard's reaction, the panic of a cornered animal as he realized he'd been caught out.

How had he reacted to that ultimatum? Had there been any hesitation on his part? Had it crossed his mind, even for a second, to choose her?

How long would he have continued the affair if Nicole hadn't confronted him?

The thought of it made her nauseous.

"I was trying to make him do what was right. Trying to make him see what he was risking. I didn't think for one minute he would choose her. Why would I?" Nicole pressed her fingers to her forehead. Slim fingers with perfectly shaped nails. "You adored each other. You finished each other's sentences. You were always touching. You'd been together forever. I envied your relationship. You had the perfect marriage."

The perfect marriage. What a joke. "You mean apart from the fact he was having an affair."

Nicole gave her a look of despair. "I thought maybe it was just a stupid midlife crisis moment. A mistake that he was already regretting. When I overheard him on the phone he and Avery were fighting. He was telling her not to call him while he was away with you. It didn't exactly sound loving."

"And if he'd chosen me? Stayed with me, what then? Would you ever have told me, or would you have let me carry on believing my marriage was fine? Would you have sat back and watched me humiliate myself?" Milly stood up and paced to the other side of the room. Her head was throbbing. She couldn't think straight.

She thought back to the night before, her evening with Brendan. She'd been so hopeful. She'd felt calm and happy, as if she'd taken a real step forward. And now she was being dragged back.

"I don't know what I would have done." Nicole was crying now. "It was a horrible position to be in. I didn't want this to happen to you, and I didn't want to be part of it. I didn't know what to do or say."

She hadn't imagined, even for a moment, that Nicole had known about the affair, but it explained so much.

"This is why you ghosted me, isn't it?" She turned to face her friend. "At the time I didn't understand—I've never understood. I couldn't work out why you would do such an awful thing to me, but this is why."

Nicole's eyes filled, and Milly felt as if her heart was being crushed.

"You felt guilty that you'd made him choose, and he chose Avery. You felt too guilty to tell me. Too guilty to talk to me even though I needed your support more than at any other point in my life. You basically abandoned me."

And that had been the worst thing.

She remembered how lonely she'd felt. How desperate. And how losing her best friend at the same time as losing her husband had been the most bitter blow. Their friendship would have given her strength, and the absence of it had weakened her at a time when she was at her most vulnerable.

Every problem she'd had in life, she'd navigated it with Nicole by her side. But not this time.

"I felt terrible," Nicole whispered. "And every message and email you sent telling me how devastated you were made me feel worse because I was the cause. You sounded broken. Raw. I was worried that if I confessed my part in it, you'd never forgive me."

She regretted those emails now. The honesty of them. She'd written them to her closest friend, never suspecting that her friend already knew what was happening or that she wouldn't reply.

She'd bared her soul. Held nothing back. And all she'd had in return was silence.

And that hurt more than anything.

"It was cruel to ignore me."

"I didn't intend to ignore you." Agony was visible in Nicole's eyes. "I didn't know what to do! I didn't know how to tell you in a way that wouldn't destroy our friendship. And I did try. I sat there for hours, literally staring at the screen. I typed a million emails to you and then deleted them."

"You ignored my phone calls."

"What was I going to say? *Hey, I told him to choose, and he chose the other woman?*" Nicole took a deep breath. "I wanted to answer your calls, but I thought if I told you the truth I'd make it worse. It would be like punching you when you were already on the floor. I'd been a terrible friend. And the more time that passed, the harder it became to know what to say because then I'd also have to explain why it had taken me so long. I told myself I'd think about it a little longer and then do it. And I keep putting it off and putting it off, another hour, another day, and then you stopped emailing, and it was too late. I'm sorry. I really am sorry. I never should have given him that ultimatum. It's all my fault. I don't blame you for being upset."

How could Nicole not understand? After all their years of friendship, and the fact that she knew Milly better than anyone, she still didn't understand?

"I don't blame you for that," Milly said. "I can see how awkward and difficult that situation was. I have no idea what I would have done if I'd been in your position, but I do know I wouldn't have ignored you. You knew how upset I was, how devastating the whole thing was to me, and you weren't there for me. You were my best friend, and you weren't there for me." Emotion rose and broke, cracking her voice. "Not an email. Not a phone call. Not a single kind or supportive word."

That was the thing she found hardest to deal with.

Nicole wiped the tears from her cheeks with her fingers. "I thought you'd blame me—"

"Of course I wouldn't have blamed you. Would I have been upset? Yes, of course, but not with you. That wasn't your fault.

He didn't leave me because you made him choose, he left because that was what he wanted to do."

"But just now he said—"

"I heard what he said, and I have no idea why he said it—perhaps he was trying to transfer blame, I don't know—but you weren't the reason he had an affair, and you weren't the reason he left me. He's an adult, and the responsibility for both those actions belong with him. But ignoring me—" Milly almost choked on the emotion wedged in her throat, emotion that she didn't want to be feeling "—*that* was your fault. Your choice. You were my best and dearest friend, and you weren't there for me when I needed you. And I get that you felt awkward and guilty and embarrassed, but I was desperate! I opened myself up to you, and still you didn't respond. I emailed you when I was hyperventilating at three in the morning, terrified and alone, and you didn't respond to that either. I had never needed you more, and you weren't there for me."

Nicole stared at her, her breathing shallow. "Milly—"

"All our lives our friendship has been the one unshakable, dependable thing. And it's not as if it's something you think about every day or anything, but it was always there, and that was the luxury of it. Our friendship was a lifeboat in rough seas, a warm blanket in cold weather. Knowing you would always be there for me made me feel secure and safe, and I think it was the same for you. And when I realized that you weren't there for me—" she swallowed "—you knew everything about me, so you must have known how ghosting would hurt me, and yet you still did it. And losing you was as bad as losing Richard." Milly saw the devastation on Nicole's face and felt herself start to unravel. She needed to end the conversation. She needed space to process what had happened. There was no point in going round and round with both of them too upset to resolve anything. "I have to—I can't do this. I can't stay here."

"What do you mean?" There was a note of panic in Nicole's voice. "You're leaving? Where are you going?"

Good question. And there was only one answer. One place. The place she always went when she was hurt or upset.

Family.

"I'm taking Zoe, and we're going to stay with my mother tonight."

"No!" Nicole shot out a hand and then withdrew it as quickly. "You shouldn't have to leave your own house. If you want to be on your own, then I should be the one to go."

"Go where?" Milly grabbed her bag and her jacket. She might be wounded, but she was still practical. "We both know you can't leave this place." Even now, after such a betrayal, she couldn't put her friend in a position that would expose her.

Nicole looked anguished. "But—"

"I can't talk about this now." She knew that if she stayed, she'd start worrying about Nicole and Nicole's feelings, and she needed to focus on herself. She needed to work out how she was going to deal with this. What she was going to do. What it all meant. "I'm going to get Zoe, and we're leaving. Lock the door behind me."

21

Zoe

Zoe sat on the edge of her bed, listening to every word of the conversation going on in the room beneath her. It wasn't as if she had a choice but to listen. The wood used in the construction of the boathouse ensured excellent acoustics. Sound traveled easily, and her mother and Nicole weren't exactly using indoor voices.

She'd heard what her father had said (and it was a weird feeling suddenly discovering that your father could behave so badly: she'd preferred it when she thought he was a perfect human being, although admittedly she'd have to go back a few years for that), and she'd heard every word her mother had said.

She'd sympathized with Nicole because overhearing something like that was major and seriously heavy, and the fact that her mother was upset because Nicole hadn't told her what she'd seen made Zoe's skin prickle with guilt.

And it was no good telling herself that unlike Nicole she hadn't actually overheard the conversation. Maybe she hadn't known exactly what was going on, but she'd had a strong suspicion. Because she'd overheard a conversation between her father and Avery too. Weeks before they'd visited LA. Weeks before her father had walked out.

And she hadn't told her mother either.

22

Connie

"I don't know how to thank you for your kindness. Bringing me home. I'm not used to being a burden on anyone." Connie poured wine into a glass and handed it to Brian. Her whole body ached. She felt like a walking bruise.

"You're far from a burden. And I would rather have taken you straight to the hospital." Brian took the glass from her and settled himself at the kitchen table. "Are you sure I can't change your mind and take you to have a checkup? It would put my mind at rest."

"Definitely not. I don't want to waste precious hospital resources. It's just a few scratches and a little bump on the head, that's all. Fortunately I was wearing a helmet, so no real harm done."

Brian gave her a long look. "It was a nasty fall, Connie. Helmet or not, you hit that rock with force."

And didn't she know it. Her head hitting that rock had sounded as bad as it had felt.

"The poor rock. Was it hurt? We should have checked." Connie made a joke of it. "Not the horse's fault. The dog ran out from the bracken and made me jump too. And I'm sure I'll ache from head to toe tomorrow, but nothing that won't mend by itself. If you can put up with looking at my bruised lip and my messy hair, then we're fine."

"You're a stubborn woman, Connie."

"I think you mean I'm *independent*." She wasn't the sort who needed care and sympathy. She looked after herself, and she preferred it that way.

"Call it what you like, but everyone needs a little help now and then." His gaze was fixed on her face, which she was sure looked as bad as it felt. "Can I at least persuade you to call your daughter?"

"Milly? Goodness no. I don't want to bother her with this. But talking of daughters, tell me about Annie. Any news?" She poured herself a glass of ice water from the fridge. Her head was throbbing too badly to even think about wine. She felt a little sick, but presumably that was the shock of it all. "You must be so worried, you poor thing."

"I spoke to her first thing this morning. She's recovering from the surgery, and they're saying that she should be discharged in the next couple of days."

"That's good."

"I wish I wasn't so far away, that's all. I can't exactly pop over to Australia. It's not easy when your children decide to settle in faraway places."

"Particularly when that child is your only one." She felt relieved that Milly had never expressed any desire to live anywhere but the Lakes and that she'd been as enthusiastic to work in the family business as Connie had been to have her there. Not that she would have stood in her way if Milly had chosen to move somewhere distant. She believed strongly that people should live the life that felt right for them. "I admire you for being so encouraging and endlessly supportive of her, particularly when you were dealing with your own loss. You have great courage."

"I'm not sure it's courage. I wanted her to be happy, that's all. Isn't that what every parent wants for their child? Would part of me have liked her to stay here and move in next door? Yes. But that wasn't how things worked out, and I learned to make the best of it. Sometimes that's all you can do, isn't it? You keep busy and build your own life." He took a mouthful of wine and set the glass down. "But thank you for listening. You've been a good friend, Connie. I don't know what I would have done without you over the past week. It makes me even more embarrassed to remember how rude I was the first time we met a few weeks ago."

Her laugh turned into a gasp as pain jabbed her ribs. Wincing, she sat down opposite him. Who would have thought that falling off a horse could be so painful? "No need to be embarrassed. I understand. People in our position are always being encouraged to look for romance. I'm sure you're quite the catch for a woman who is interested in catching someone. Fortunately for you, that's not me."

He toyed with his glass. "After Paula died, everyone kept saying to me, 'You need to get back on the horse.'"

"We did get back on the horse," Connie pointed out, "but we did it literally, rather than figuratively. And then fell off it, in my case."

They'd been riding daily, and she couldn't remember precisely when their polite greetings had turned to conversation. One day they'd exchanged a few words, and the next they'd gone for lunch in a pub garden. During their many conversations since then she'd discovered that he'd worked in construction for many years, been a widower for twelve years, that he had a thirty-year-old daughter in Australia (currently suffering from appendicitis) who was married with a five-year-old, and that he had no interest in finding anyone else.

Assuming that he was sharing that detail to ensure she didn't harbor fantasies about a romantic future, Connie had assured him that she had no interest in giving up her lovely independent life.

Neither of them was looking for love, but they both agreed that their new friendship was something to be treasured.

She raised her water glass. "To being happily single. And to getting back up when we fall off the horse. Preferably without broken bones." Had she broken a rib? No, she was sure it was simply bruised. Like the rest of her. Nothing that time wouldn't heal.

Brian lifted his glass in response. "You're an extraordinary woman, Connie." He broke off. "Did you hear something? Footsteps?"

The sound of the doorbell echoed through the house, and Connie turned her head.

"Now, who can that be on a Sunday evening?"

She didn't feel up to visitors. Maybe Brian was right. She should have gone to the hospital for a checkup. She was going to have an early night. But first a hot bath to ease the aches and pains.

"It could be Prince Charming." Brian put his glass down. "I can hide under the table if you like so that I don't ruin your chances."

"I'd be more interested in his horse. You know that about me by now."

Brian laughed. "I do."

"It's probably someone selling something. Hopefully if we ignore it, they'll go away."

But they didn't go away. The bell went again, and then Connie heard the sound of a key in the lock.

"That must be my daughter." She stood up and immediately wished she hadn't as pain tore through her skull. Once Brian had gone she was going to put an ice pack on her head.

Seconds later, Milly appeared in the doorway.

Connie automatically pulled her hair forward over her face to try and hide the bruise that was fast developing. She angled her body so that Milly wouldn't notice the rip in her shirt. Fortunately for her, Milly was distracted.

Her eyes were bloodshot, her eyelids red and puffy. Connie felt her stress levels soar.

Now what?

Zoe had been with Richard this weekend, and Milly always found it hard. Was that what this was?

And then she saw Zoe hovering behind Milly.

Her emotions started to churn, and she took a slow breath. Whatever had happened (no doubt something thoughtless Richard had said or done), whatever the problem, nothing would be solved by her getting in a state. If there was one thing her conversations with Brian had reinforced, it was that you were of much more use to your child when you were calm and supportive. An emotional response simply escalated everything.

"What a lovely surprise," she said. "Come in, both of you. This is Brian, a friend."

"And I was just leaving." Brian stood up. "Good to meet you, Milly. I've heard a lot about you. All good things, in case you were wondering."

Milly produced something close to a smile and shook hands with him.

Brian reached for his jacket. "I'll see you next week, Connie. And please take care of yourself."

"I will." She was grateful that he didn't mention her accident in front of Milly. "Keep me updated on news of Annie."

He gave her a nod and a warm smile, and a few seconds later she heard the front door close behind him.

She felt an immediate sense of loss and wished he hadn't rushed off.

"I'm sorry." Milly dropped the bag she was carrying. "I should have called first, but—" She stopped and stared at her mother in horror. "What happened? There's blood on your lip and on your shirt. Your elbow is scraped. Did you fall?"

So much for hoping Milly wouldn't find out.

"I had a little tumble from the horse, and Brian kindly brought me home. I'm fine."

"But—"

"Don't fuss, Milly. I really am fine." She didn't feel at all fine, but she had to hope it would settle in time.

"I interrupted you. I didn't realize you had company."

"It's not a problem. Brian was about to leave when you arrived." It wasn't exactly the truth, but she didn't want Milly to feel worse than she evidently already did. "He teaches a wilderness-survival course first thing on Monday, so he doesn't like to stay out too late."

"How long have you—"

"Been friends? A few weeks. We met horse riding." *And bonded over the stresses of parenting adult children.* "Tell me what has happened. You don't arrive at my door with Zoe and an overnight bag unless something is wrong."

The room started to spin, and Connie sat back down at the kitchen table.

Something was very wrong.

Milly turned to Zoe. "It's getting late. You should probably get to bed. Is it okay if we stay here tonight, Mum?"

Stay? She'd been hoping to crawl into bed via a hot bath, but that wouldn't happen now. She resolutely ignored how bad she felt and focused on her daughter.

"You know you're always welcome. Have you eaten? Can I make you anything?"

Zoe shook her head. "I'm okay, thanks. Dad and I stopped for burgers on the way home. I'll go straight to bed. But, Mum—"

"I'm fine, honey, honestly." Milly reached out and hugged her. "Just a bit tired. It has been a long week. Don't worry about me."

"Right." Zoe hesitated, as if she had something more to say, but then seemed to change her mind and instead headed upstairs to the bedroom she used whenever she stayed, her feet clomping heavily on the stairs.

That is someone carrying a heavy burden, Connie thought.

"She was with Richard this weekend." She poured Milly a glass of ice water. "Did something happen?"

Milly sat down at the table, and her face crumpled. "Sorry. I promised myself I wasn't going to cry."

"Oh, sweetheart." Connie put the glass on the table and sat down next to her daughter. Milly's anguish transferred itself to her like an electric current. She grabbed the box of tissues from the end of the table and handed one to Milly.

Milly blew her nose. "Richard insisted on bringing Zoe right to the door, and he came into the house with her bag. I couldn't stop him."

Connie had always thought that Milly's desire to keep the boat-house a Richard-free zone was understandable but impractical in the long term. "Does it matter that he has seen the boathouse?"

"Unfortunately the boathouse wasn't the only thing he saw. Nicole arrived back while he was still there."

"Oh dear. So now he knows she is here. Well, presumably you asked him not to say anything to anyone. Is that what is wrong? You're worried he might tell someone Nicole is hiding out with you?" She didn't see how that worry could have caused Milly to look as if her world had ended.

"That's not what's wrong." Milly blew her nose again. "There's something I haven't told you. About Nicole." She scrunched the tissue into a ball. "We had a sort of blip in our friendship. We lost touch for eighteen months."

Whatever Connie had been expecting to hear, it wasn't that.

The two girls had always been such good friends. Inseparable, she'd thought. She'd honestly believed that nothing would ever come between them. There had even been occasions when she'd envied their friendship and wished she could have found something simi-lar in her own life. She had friends, of course, plenty of friends, but nothing that came close to the bond that Milly and Nicole shared.

"When I say we lost touch, what I really mean is she ghosted me." Milly slumped over the table, the misery rolling off her in waves. "She didn't answer my calls or messages. From the moment I mentioned that Richard had walked out and that he was having an affair, she stopped responding. We have been there for each other through thick and thin, and then I hit the lowest point of my life and she wasn't there for me."

And Connie knew how that would have made Milly feel.

She put her arm around her daughter.

"I had no idea. I assumed the two of you were talking all the time." And she couldn't begin to imagine why Nicole would have done that. It didn't make sense to her. But it helped to explain why Milly had leaned on her so heavily since Richard had left. She hadn't had her friend supporting her. "Why didn't you tell me?"

"I don't know. I didn't want you to worry. And I didn't under-stand it. I didn't know what I'd done wrong. And then out of the blue she called and begged me to let her stay for a while so I said yes—" Milly sniffed and pulled another tissue from the box.

"Because you have a long and wonderful friendship that is worth hanging on to."

"Maybe. Or maybe I'm just an idiot." She took a shuddering breath. "But tonight, finally, I found out why she'd ghosted me. It wasn't that she was too busy or just wrapped up in her own life. It was all to do with Richard. The moment he saw her he went bal-listic." Milly related what had happened, and Connie listened, try-ing to mask her own reaction.

"So Nicole overheard his conversation with Avery?"

"Yes, and it's worse than that." Milly told her the rest of it, and it took Connie a moment to digest what she was hearing.

Nicole had known about the affair. Nicole had confronted Richard and told him to choose.

Being a good friend, Connie thought. Trying to protect Milly.

"That's terrible."

"I know!" Milly's eyes filled again. "It really is terrible. I still can't quite believe it. It's all such a shock."

Connie was grateful she'd never been in the position Nicole had found herself in. What a dilemma.

"I've always thought that must be the very worst situation to find yourself in as a friend. Knowing something big that could hurt someone you love. How do you handle it? Do you tell or do you keep it quiet? She was brave to confront him, but for him to then leave you afterward—just timing, of course, but I can see how that must have made her feel. Presumably that's why she found it difficult to talk to you. She must have felt awful. Poor Nicole."

There was a tense silence, and then Milly pulled away from Connie and looked at her with hurt in her eyes.

"Poor Nicole? You think it's terrible for *Nicole*?"

"Of course." And only then did Connie realize that Milly didn't see it the same way.

She looked so wounded by her mother's unexpected defense of Nicole that Connie almost snatched the words back.

"Milly, honey—"

"You're feeling sorry for *Nicole*?"

Should she lie? No. Milly was evidently too upset to see things clearly. Her job here was to present a balanced view. Sometimes being the best parent to a child meant helping them accept difficult truths.

She cleared her throat and tried to do that. "I feel bad for both of you. You've been through so much, and I hate to see you suffer. But this has to have been hard for Nicole too. She found out information she would much rather not have known and had to make some hard decisions. I think that's a horrible position to find yourself in, don't you?"

It was obvious from Milly's expression that she hadn't given any real thought to that question.

"I can see it was difficult, but she should have told me. I never would have blamed her for something that was so obviously not her fault. And then she should have been there for me, but she basically dropped me, and I don't understand how she could have done that because I would *never* have done that to her. There were no circumstances in which I wouldn't have been there for her."

Connie was hit by a wave of dizziness, and she took a sip of water, hoping it would pass.

She was feeling increasingly unwell.

She would have liked to have suggested they both go to bed and pick up the discussion in the morning, but she could see Milly was too upset, and she didn't want to worry her daughter by admitting how bad she felt.

"I'm sure she did it because she was afraid, honey. She blamed herself. I expect she thought she'd been a bad friend. She was afraid she was the reason Richard left."

"Obviously she wasn't."

"Nothing is obvious when emotions are heightened, Milly.

Thoughts are just that—thoughts—but they're all too easy to believe when you're in a spiral."

Milly sniffed. "So, you're saying it was fine for her to ghost me?"

"None of this is fine. But I think, sometimes, it's good to try and understand why a person might have done what they did. The way she saw it, she'd let you down. Been a bad friend."

"That wasn't the part that made her a bad friend. It was ignoring me. Not being there for me. She should have known that. We'd been friends for long enough."

Connie was starting to feel distinctly odd. Everything seemed far away, and objects in the kitchen seemed blurry. "Think about it from Nicole's point of view. She grew up feeling as if she had to earn affection. She didn't trust that love could be unconditional because that wasn't her experience." And she'd worried about Nicole. Unlike many, she'd always seen Nicole's fragility and vulnerability. She'd felt it in her hugs and seen the longing in her eyes when she'd talked about her mother.

Remembering it made Connie angry. Alexandra Walker had a great deal to answer for in her opinion.

Milly took a sip of water. "It wasn't her experience at home, but I've always loved her unconditionally. She knows that."

"Maybe. But I'm guessing her childhood made her feel she had to earn that love, and that it wasn't unconditional. We all bring the past into the present, whether we are aware of it or not. Your friendship was all fine when things were going well, but this was something different, and she knew it. Perhaps she felt that bond between you had never been tested."

Milly frowned. "But when she called me asking for help I was there for her, despite the fact she hadn't been there for me. I showed up, even though I was hurt. She's been living in my house, and there have been plenty of occasions over the past few weeks when she could have told me the truth, but she didn't. I've been a good friend to her—" She broke off and stared at the table for a moment. Then she gave her mother an agonized look.

"What's wrong?"

"I picked her up and I gave her sanctuary, but I wasn't warm. I didn't—" Milly shredded the tissue with her fingers "—I didn't hug her or anything. I couldn't. I was so hurt. I wanted her to know I was upset. Or maybe I was just afraid of being rejected again. I don't know. But I wasn't approachable."

Connie felt sorry for both of them. "And she knew you were upset, and knowing that—"

"She wasn't going to risk making things worse by telling me the truth." Milly finished her sentence, and her body seemed to droop. "I did punish her. I didn't mean to. At least, I did mean to, but I didn't really think through the impact it might have on her."

"You were hurt. Nicole ghosting you felt like a rejection. And that probably reminded you of your father." And Milly's father was someone she definitely didn't want to think about right now.

"Bringing the past into the present again." Milly blew her nose. "Since when have you been a psychologist?"

"It's called age, dear. It brings wrinkles and aching joints but also a degree of wisdom." The throb in her head was worse, and Connie took another sip of water. Should she take some head-ache tablets?

"Do you think I have unrealistic views of friendship? Do I expect too much?"

That was a difficult question to answer even without a head-ache. "I think all relationships are complicated. People aren't mind readers, and no one can always do or say the right thing in every situation. And no friend, however good, can be everything to you."

Milly reached for another tissue. "I know, but I suppose I would have liked her to show up even if she said the wrong thing. Saying the wrong thing is better than saying nothing. It would have been a comfort just to know she was there for me."

"You have a long and loyal friendship. I'm sure you two will sort this out. Where is Nicole now?"

"Back at the boathouse." Milly glanced at her phone. "Maybe I should call her. But I don't really know what to say."

"Why don't you both sleep on it and talk about it tomorrow?"

Milly swallowed. "That's good advice. Thanks for listening. You always make so much sense." She glanced gratefully at Connie and then frowned. "Mum?"

"What?"

"You looked a little strange, that's all. Unfocused. Are you sure you're all right?"

"Oh, it's nothing. I have a bit of a headache, that's all." Connie waved a hand dismissively. "I managed to hit a rock when I landed."

"What?" Milly looked appalled. "Why didn't you call me? Did you go to the hospital? What did they say?"

"I didn't need the hospital. Brian very kindly brought me home."

"He should have taken you to the hospital." Milly stood up and gently angled her mother's face so that she could take a closer look. "You have bruising around your eye. How did I not notice that before now?"

"It's probably only just appeared. Or maybe it's the light. Don't fuss, Milly. I'm fine. I was wearing a helmet."

"You should have said something and not let me go on and on about my problems. I'm going to drive you to the hospital."

"I'm not going to the hospital. But I think I will have an early night." Connie stood up, and the room started to spin. She reached out to grab the table.

"Mum?" Milly grabbed her arms firmly and guided her back down to the chair.

This wasn't good. This wasn't good at all.

She felt very strange. The world around her was blurred, and she could hear a voice talking to her urgently, but she had no idea where she was or what was going on.

She heard someone saying *Mum, Mum!*

And then everything went black.

23

Nicole

It was pain that woke her. The hammering in her head and sore, gritty eyes. The exhausted, emotional hangover that came from too much crying.

She groped for the water she always kept by the bed and then remembered that she wasn't in her little room in Milly's boathouse.

She opened her eyes and saw Joel dozing in a chair in the corner of the room.

She sat up, disorientated, and he opened his eyes and yawned.

"You're awake. Shame. I hoped you might sleep a little longer." His voice was gravelly from sleep, and he was obviously struggling to focus. "You look terrible, Wendy. I'd better call hair and makeup."

It was astonishing that even in her current state, with everything that had happened, he could still coax a smile from her. Or maybe she was just relieved to wake up and find she wasn't alone. Whenever there was a crisis in her life, she was almost always alone.

"My head is exploding. Have you been sleeping in the chair all night?"

He glanced at his watch. "We were still talking at two and it's only five now, so I wouldn't really call that a night. I generally need more than three hours' sleep to be able to function. I'll get you painkillers for your head, and maybe you'll go back to sleep again."

He levered himself out of the chair, and she noticed several dark smudges on his now crumpled shirt.

"What happened to your shirt?"

He glanced down at himself. "You cried on it. I think you were wearing mascara. Not that I'm an expert on such things, but I'm guessing it wasn't waterproof."

That's right. She'd cried on him. For hours.

She probably should have felt embarrassed and awkward, but for some reason she didn't. Maybe it was because he didn't seem bothered about it.

"I owe you a shirt."

"Forget it. I'll fetch those painkillers."

"No painkillers. But water would be great, thank you."

He left the room and returned moments later with a cool cloth for her head and a glass filled with ice water.

She sipped it gratefully and closed her eyes as he pressed the cloth to her forehead.

"I'm grateful to you."

"For what?"

"For answering your phone when I called. For letting me stay here. For listening." Her eyes filled again. "After Milly walked out I felt so bad. I didn't want to be on my own. It's not her fault, by the way, so don't blame her. It's my fault. All of it."

"Don't think about that now. We'll figure it all out, and you can stay here until we do."

She sniffed. "I'll book a flight later. I'll go home to California."

"Why would you do that?" He grabbed the box of tissues from the nightstand and put it on her lap. "You told me last night that you haven't slept a single night in your house since the intruder incident. You said that California doesn't feel like home. That you've been happier here than you've been anywhere."

She'd told him all that?

"That's true. But I can't exactly hang around Forest Nest, can I? I let Milly down. I wasn't there for her when she needed me." She'd failed her friend, and that was the worst feeling because Milly had been there for her when no one else was.

He took the cloth from her. "Let's see how that works out. No need to make any quick decisions."

He was so calm and measured, treating everything as if it wasn't that big a deal, that she started to feel her panic recede.

She pulled a tissue from the box and blew her nose.

"Why did you sleep in the chair?"

"Because you were upset, and I didn't want to leave you alone." He brushed damp strands of her hair away from her face. "Also, I figured that this way I could still tell my grandkids that I spent the night with a famous look-alike actress. You need to drink all that water, Wendy. Every drop."

"I don't even remember going to bed."

"I carried you. You cried for a long time. You were exhausted."

"You put a blanket over me."

"Yes. And I took your shoes off. I hope that's okay. I drew the line at undressing you."

She drank the water. "I don't know why you're being kind. I'm a stranger. You don't know anything about me. Just what you see in the movies." And she was used to that, of course. People who thought they knew who she was because they'd seen her on the big screen.

He took the empty glass from her and put it on the nightstand. "Exactly how much do you remember about last night?"

"Apart from the part where you carried me to bed, most of it. Why wouldn't I? I didn't drink or anything."

"You didn't drink because you're pregnant. I know." He nodded. "You told me."

"I *told* you that?" Her head reeled. She remembered sobbing onto his shoulder and blurting out words, but maybe her memory of what she'd said wasn't as clear as she'd thought. "When?"

He sat down on the edge of the bed. "When did you tell me

you were pregnant?" He thought for a moment. "I seem to remember it was in between the part where you told me how terrified you were of being a bad mother because of your own mother and the part when you said that Justin was a weak-minded, pathetic snake and you realized you didn't really love him at all, you just thought you loved him because you so badly wanted to have someone special in your life."

With a groan she leaned back against the pillows and covered her face with her hands. "What else did I say?"

"You want me to repeat it word for word? Because you talked without stopping for at least three hours. Maybe four. I wasn't watching the time."

She was mortified. "That must have been a delightful experience for you."

"It was enlightening. And after everything you told me, I happen to agree that Justin does seem like a weak-minded, pathetic snake. And it's brutally unfair that you've been lacerated in the press and dropped from your next movie while he appears to have enjoyed a career boost. By the way, if being pregnant is the reason you're not taking painkillers, I think the one I have in my cupboard is considered safe, but if you're worried, I can call my brother-in-law and ask. He's a doctor."

She rubbed her face and then lowered her hands and looked at him. "I'm sorry I subjected you to a total deluge of my emotions. I can't imagine what you must think of me."

"I think you've been through a lot and have some flaky, unreliable people in your life."

"But not Milly." Guilt pierced her heart. She'd hurt Milly badly, and still Milly had shown up for her. She'd put her own feelings aside to be there for Nicole, even when Nicole hadn't been there for her.

She couldn't work out what she should do next. She'd called him in a moment of desperation, but she knew it was only temporary.

"Where's my phone? I'll call a cab."

"You're not calling a cab. You're not going anywhere until you've had a shower, eaten something and given proper thought to what you want to do. Maybe it's time to stop running."

"What do you mean?"

"You were running when you called me last night," he said. "Running when you went to Milly. It seems to me it would be a nice change for you to start living your life on your own terms. Leave somewhere because you want to rather than because you feel you have to. There's no reason for you to rush off. No one knows you're here, not even Milly."

The mention of Milly's name had the tears flowing again.

"She is never going to forgive me. I've ruined the best and only real relationship in my life."

"Hey, enough." He sat down on the edge of the bed. "You have to stop this. We're going to figure it all out, I promise."

She sniffed. "I still don't know why you're helping me."

"You're looking for an ulterior motive, and after everything you said to me last night I understand why. Everyone in your life wants something from you, don't they?" His voice was gentle. "Must be impossible to filter out what's real. So let's address this."

"Address what?" She wasn't sure she wanted to examine her life too closely right now.

"Address why people try and get close to you. You listed it for me at one point last night. Number one was your influence in the industry—that's of no use to me at all. Number two was wealth." He counted them off on his fingers. "I am fortunate enough to be financially independent and I enjoy the life I've made for myself, so I'm not interested in your money. What else was there? Oh, your looks." He studied her for a moment, and a faint smile touched his mouth. "You look truly terrible, Wendy, and I'm still sitting here so I think we can strike that out as a possible reason I'm sticking around."

She scraped her fingers through her hair, trying to shape it. "I look terrible?"

"You do. But I don't care. It's good to know that even a movie star can get red eyes when they cry. And as we're being brutally honest with each other—"

"You're the one being brutally honest," she muttered. "No one has ever told me I look terrible before. But go on—don't hold back. What else do you have to tell me?"

"Are you sure you want to hear it?" He pulled a face. "This is a big one. It could possibly end our friendship."

Our friendship.

It was comforting to think of it that way and to know that he was thinking it too. When she'd called him in desperation she'd felt completely alone in the world, but now she didn't.

"If the fact that I ruined your shirt didn't end our friendship, then I'm sure it will survive whatever it is you need to tell me."

"Let's see." He took a deep breath. "I don't particularly enjoy going to the movies. I've taken my nieces to a few animated films, but generally I prefer spending my time outdoors or reading a good book. I'm not very familiar with your work." He cleared his throat. "I think I've seen one of your movies."

He'd seen just one of her movies.

He was watching her, waiting. "You're smiling. Why are you smiling? Say something."

"You think I'm ugly, and you don't like my movies."

He frowned. "I didn't exactly say you were ugly. And I didn't say I don't like your movies. I don't really like any movies. It's not personal. You need to pay closer attention, Wendy."

She grabbed the tissue he'd given her and blew her nose. "If you don't like movies, then obviously we can never be friends."

"I was afraid of that."

"Which is a pity because I'm a bit low on friends at the moment. Always, in fact." The reality of her situation hit again. "I've been a terrible friend to Milly, and she is never going to forgive me."

"Okay, enough self-pity." He stood up. "If you're not going back to sleep, then go and take a hot shower and get dressed, and

I'll make you some breakfast. Then we'll talk and work out a plan together."

"Thanks, but I'm not hungry." She glanced around her. "Where's my phone?"

"I confiscated it because you kept wanting to message Milly, and I thought maybe you both needed time."

"Time isn't going to fix this."

He paused by the door, sympathy in his eyes. "When things went wrong for my sister, she felt the same way. Her life was shattered, and she couldn't see how it would ever be right again. But you'll do what she did and make it right, piece by piece. And maybe your life won't end up looking the same as it used to, but there's a good chance it might even look better."

She didn't say that without Milly's friendship there was no way her life could be better.

"Did your sister ruin your shirt too?"

He smiled. "Take that shower, Wendy. I'll be in the kitchen when you're ready."

She did as he suggested and felt better for it.

Once she'd washed and dried her hair, she changed into a pair of fresh shorts and a T-shirt from her suitcase.

By the time she joined him in the kitchen, her head had stopped throbbing.

"Something smells good."

She noticed that the ends of his hair were still damp, so presumably he'd taken a quick shower too.

"Bacon, scrambled eggs, mushrooms. When we've eaten this, we can turn to strong coffee." He served it onto plates and put them on the table next to two glasses filled with juice. "I squeezed a couple of oranges so that you have vitamin C."

She took a mouthful of eggs and discovered she was hungrier than she'd thought, so she took another mouthful and then another and then put her fork down.

He raised an eyebrow. "Something wrong?"

"Nothing. It's delicious, but as I told you before, I can't put on weight in my job. It's just how it is."

"I get that, but from what you were saying last night you don't actually have a job at the moment, so maybe this is a good time to eat." He nudged the plate closer to her. "If you don't eat, you'll offend me."

She picked up her fork again. "So, you're saying that it's fine if I ruin your shirt and deprive you of sleep, but if I don't eat your bacon, then our friendship is over?"

"That sounds about right. And talking of friendship, I've been thinking about what you said last night. About Milly and Richard and what happened."

"A grisly story, don't you think?"

"It's a pretty sad story. But I think that in all the emotional upset, you're losing sight of the most important factor."

"Which is?"

"That the person in the wrong here is Richard."

It was true that she'd virtually wiped Richard from her thoughts. Her head was filled with Milly and the words she'd spoken. "I was in the wrong too because I wasn't there for Milly." It was painful to think about it. She so badly wanted to put the clock back and make different decisions. "I felt so bad about what I'd overheard and what I'd said to him. I was scared of what it would do to our friendship if I told her what had happened, and I just didn't know what to say. So I said nothing. I wasn't there for her."

"You're so hard on yourself. You were put in a horrible position."

"Yes." She could admit that now. She could also admit that she'd been a coward. "But I should have been there for her. The crazy thing is that I was afraid to tell her the truth in case it ruined our friendship, but I managed to ruin it anyway."

"I doubt that."

Nicole thought back to the night before. And she thought about what she knew about Milly. "The thing I forgot," she said slowly, "is that Milly has an almost visceral fear of being abandoned. I suppose it started when her dad left. Loyalty is everything to her.

Being able to depend on someone. Trust them. I knew that, and yet somehow I forgot it. I was focused only on myself."

"And that's understandable too. No one gets it right all the time, Nicole." He used her name for the first time. "We're not puppets. We bring our own life experiences and beliefs to every interaction, and what seems right to one person might be wrong to another. I think Milly will realize that when she has had time to reflect. Where did she go, anyway?"

"She went to stay with Connie."

"Well, there you go." He pushed his plate away. "Connie will help her figure it out. She's the wisest person I know. And if you don't want to go back to the boathouse, you can stay here. Make yourself at home in my spare room until you figure out what you want to do."

The offer overwhelmed her. "Thank you. I don't know how to repay your kindness."

"Friendship isn't transactional," he said. "No payment required."

She realized that, for her, friendship had always been transactional, apart from her relationship with Milly.

"I kept you awake for most of the night, and you'll be going to work soon. You must be exhausted."

"Nothing that strong coffee won't fix." He stood up and made them both coffee. "Do you love being an actor? Do you still enjoy it?"

She watched as he made two espressos and then foamed milk. She thought about how much fun she'd had rehearsing with Zoe. "I love acting. I hate the movie business. Not the same thing."

"Have you considered giving it up?"

"I think that decision may have been taken out of my hands. The movie business seems to have given me up." But she knew what he was asking. "Acting was my dream. And I wanted to be good at it. The best. I wanted to be famous." That was before she'd known what fame meant. What it brought with it.

"Because you wanted to make your mother proud. Prove that you were good at something." He put the coffee on the table and sat down opposite her. "That was something else you told me last night."

"That hasn't happened, and I've accepted that it never will. I'm just the wrong daughter for her. Square peg, round hole and all that. Maybe if I'd been a scientist or a mathematician . . ." She took a sip of coffee.

"Parental love isn't a movie award. It isn't something you win. You don't have to be voted the best at something to deserve it. And if you couldn't please her, then that's her failure, not yours. No child should be made to feel as if they have to earn a parent's love. They should grow up knowing they're loved for who they are, not who their parents want them to be. And if that doesn't happen, then the fault doesn't lie with you."

In her heart she knew that, but it was good to hear him say it.

"I grew up wanting her approval. Needing it. And every time I did well I'd think *This is it, this is the moment when she is going to say something warm and loving*, but she never did. And after a while it ceased to matter because the public gave me the approval I needed. And at the beginning the fame gave me confidence. It finally made me feel as if I was an okay person. As long as I had their good opinion, I felt validated. It was like a drug. Gave me a real high."

She waited for him to say something, but he sat quietly, paying attention, so she carried on.

"But then people turn on you. A rumor on social media. A photograph that's misinterpreted. A movie that tanks. And you realize how thin and shallow it all is. And it isn't real, of course, because they're judging the parts you play, not you. And producers and directors claim to love you, but all they really love is the money you bring in. All that flattery and attention from studio heads isn't about you but about your commercial value. And eventually you realize that the whole thing is empty and that despite all the fame and success you're lonelier than you've ever been." She felt awkward. "Sorry. I know how lucky I've been. I'm grateful for it."

He stirred. "Presumably one of the upsides of the success is that it has given you financial security. Financial security gives you a certain degree of freedom, but you don't feel free at the moment, do you?"

"No."

"In the end the only opinion that really matters is your own. Only you can decide what is right for you. What you really want to do with your life."

"Playing other people was a way of not thinking about who I was. I've done it for so long, I'm not sure I even know who I am anymore."

"Of course you do." He took a sip of his coffee. "Like many creative people, you're sensitive. You care what people think. You love the outdoors, and you're naturally adventurous, but the life you're living now has made you wary and afraid. You're sure of your talents because you know you're good at what you do, but despite that you worry that you're not enough. Everything you do, you have to be best at because you think that's the way to earn people's respect and love. You didn't feel that you were good enough as a daughter, and that created a lasting impact. It's the reason you feel you haven't been a good enough friend to Milly, even though it's obvious that you've been a great friend, despite this recent blip. It's the reason you're afraid you won't be good enough as a mother, when any child would be lucky to have you in their life. You're trusting and loyal by nature, but people have betrayed and used you so many times you no longer dare to be who you really are."

She swallowed, a little shaken by his insight. "I must have said a lot more last night than I remember saying."

"How would it feel to just be yourself and not have to try so hard? You put all your effort into being the best, becoming a star, being big—but what would life look like if it was smaller? If the only people who cared what you do and think and eat for breakfast are the people who love you?"

She stared into her coffee cup. "There aren't many of those."

"I think you'll find you're wrong about that, but either way isn't it better to live the life you choose rather than a life designed to please other people, whether it's your mother or an audience?"

"Acting was my dream."

"And in your case you made it a reality, but it doesn't sound like much of a dream anymore. Maybe it's time to find a new dream." He finished his coffee. "It's hard to give up something you've excelled at. I can see that. Why leave something when you're at the top of your game? But if it's no longer what you want to do, it's okay to let it go. Move on to something new."

"I wouldn't even know what to do if I wasn't an actor." She toyed with her cup.

"From what you've said you still enjoy acting, so maybe you can do something lower-key. Milly always says how good you are with Zoe. Maybe you could run drama workshops."

Milly had told him she was good with Zoe? That unexpected compliment raised her spirits a notch.

"Drama workshops? You mean for kids?"

"I don't know what I mean. I was just throwing ideas out there as a start." He glanced at his watch. "I need to go. Why don't you think about it today while I'm out? There's plenty of paper in the study, just through that door. Write down all the things that make you happy and all the things you'd like to delete from your life if you had the chance. We can look at it together tonight."

He stood up and reached for the plates, but she beat him to it.

"I'll clear up. It's the least I can do. You get ready."

"Are you sure? You'll be all right here today?"

"I'll be fine. I'm going to do what you suggested and imagine a different life." She loaded the dishwasher and wiped the table, and by the time she'd finished he was ready to leave.

"Call if you need anything."

"Thank you." She had no intention of calling him. He'd already given her what she needed most. A shoulder to cry on, a sympathetic ear, sanctuary. More importantly, he'd made her think and question. Now all she needed was some answers.

First she was going to put her California home on the market. That decision was one of the easy ones to make. She should have done it a long time ago. Perhaps by taking that first step, she'd feel as if she was a little more in control.

He paused by the door. "I know you don't believe me, but everything is going to be okay. I'm sure of it."

He left the house, and she immediately got to work.

Despite the lack of sleep and dull headache, she felt energized. Talking to Joel, hearing his thoughts on it, had clarified things for her.

She did as he suggested and made a list of all the things she loved about her life, and all the things she considered to be important.

Her baby (that went at the top of the list)

Her friendship with Milly (she was going to ignore the fact that it might no longer exist)

Her relationships with Connie, Nanna Peg, Zoe (and also Joel, but she didn't want to put that down on paper because she intended to show it to him later)

Acting (the actual process of acting, inhabiting a character)

Spending time outdoors

Physical activity

The list grew, and when she reached the bottom of the page she grabbed another sheet of paper, and this time she started listing all the things she would like never to have to deal with again.

The press

Reading about herself online (those two were linked but she decided they merited separate lines)

Always being watched

Never feeling safe, even with security

Interviews (she loved acting, but she hated talking about it)

That list was heading onto a second page when she heard the front door open and Joel's voice.

She was surprised. He'd been gone for less than an hour. "Did you forget something? I've made good progress here. I've already—" The words dried out when she saw his expression. "What?"

"Milly called. Check your phone."

She hadn't looked at her phone since the night before. "You took it away from me."

261

"You're right, I did." He disappeared through to the living room and reappeared holding her phone. "Here."

"What's this about?" She switched the phone on and saw the missed call from Milly and the voice mail waiting for her.

She pressed Play.

Nic, it's me. Mum has collapsed. There was a pause in the message, and it was obvious Milly was crying. *We're in the hospital. I just—I wanted to let you know in case you were wondering where I was.*

Connie in hospital?

Why? How?

Nicole played the message again as she grabbed her bag and a sweater.

Joel watched her. "What are you doing?"

She dropped her phone into the bag. "I have to go to her."

"She didn't ask you to do that."

"I know." But she'd called. That was what they did when one of them was in trouble, wasn't it? "I'm going anyway."

"Nicole, you can't."

"You heard her. She's terrified and upset. This is her mother, and they're so close. She will be worried sick."

She found her shoes and tugged them on.

"Wait." He put his hand on her arm. "You're not thinking this through. You came here to escape. To hide from all the attention. If you do this, that will be it. Everyone will see you."

Nerves rippled through her, and she felt a moment of sadness that her brief summer hideaway was over. She'd had a glimpse of how other people lived and she wanted more of it.

"This isn't about me." She picked up her bag. "It's about Milly. I let her down before, and there is nothing I can do about that, but I won't do it again. This time I intend to be there for her. I *want* to be there for her. Even if she's still angry. Even if she turns me away. I need to be there."

24

Milly

Milly paced the hospital corridor trying to stay calm and failing miserably. She kept reliving that moment when her mother had crumpled at her feet. Fortunately the ambulance had arrived quickly and so had Nanna Peg, who she'd called immediately after the ambulance.

"I'll stay with Zoe." For once Nanna Peg hadn't been smiling. "You go, pet. Follow that ambulance."

Milly had done that and rushed to the hospital, breaking speed limits on the way.

The reception staff had told her that her mother was being seen by doctors and that Milly couldn't see her yet because she was having tests.

What tests? And why couldn't anyone tell her anything more?

In those last terrifying moments before her mother had collapsed on the floor Connie had been incoherent and confused. She hadn't registered Milly's presence. Judging from the speed with which the paramedics had whisked her to hospital, they hadn't liked what they were seeing.

And Milly was beating herself up for not having noticed sooner how unwell her mother was. She'd been so lost in her own problems that when her mother had told her she was fine, she'd believed her.

She glanced at the clock on the wall. When was she going to hear something?

She'd drunk two cups of vile-tasting coffee, and in a weak moment she'd messaged Nicole, something she now regretted. Why had she done that? There was nothing Nicole could do, and Milly's call would have worried her. Whatever had or hadn't happened, Milly didn't doubt her friend's love for her mother.

Her eyes filled. She made yet another bargain in her head. *Please let her be okay, and I will be a good person for the rest of my life.*

But what if she wasn't okay? What would she do if something happened to her mother? How would she ever cope?

She wished she could switch off her feelings or at least turn down the dial. Her mind spiraled to darker and darker places, and finally, after what felt like a lifetime, a doctor appeared in the corridor, and she rushed toward him.

"Do you have news about my mother? Connie Beckworth?"

"You're a relative?"

"Her daughter." That word didn't begin to sum up their relationship. What her mother meant to her. "Is she going to be okay?"

"She has a head injury and a couple of fractured ribs—"

Fractured ribs?

"The ribs will heal by themselves, but we're not sure what other injuries she may have sustained so we're doing some more tests. She will probably be discharged later, so if you'd prefer to go home in the meantime—"

"I'll stay," Milly said immediately. "Can I see her?"

"Not yet. We'll let you know when you can."

The doctor strode away leaving Milly feeling more helpless than ever.

She sat down on one of the hard plastic chairs.

Next to her an elderly man was being reassured by his daughter.

The warmth between them intensified Milly's feeling of loneliness.

She wished there was someone she could lean on, but she couldn't call Nanna Peg because she was with Zoe, and anyway she didn't want to worry her. Brendan?

She almost laughed. No matter how good a time they'd had on Saturday (Was it only Saturday? It felt like a lifetime ago), their relationship definitely wasn't ready to survive a frantic phone call from a hospital.

She couldn't call anyone from work because they needed to get on with their jobs.

She was on her own. There was no one she could call. But she'd cope because that was what she did. And when she was finally able to see her mother she'd be stoic and calm.

Tiredness and anxiety started to press down on her, and she was considering going outside for a breath of air when she saw Nicole hovering at the end of the corridor.

For a moment she thought she was hallucinating.

And then Nicole saw Milly, and her expression changed. She sprinted down the corridor toward her, and they met halfway. Milly found herself hugged and held, and she hugged back, marveling at how this one moment of human contact could do so much to restore her strength.

Eventually she pulled away. "What are you doing here?"

"You left a message. I would have come sooner, but I didn't check my phone until this morning."

"I didn't mean for you to come. I just wanted to let you know." Milly sniffed and realized her friend wasn't wearing a wig or any type of disguise. "You shouldn't be here. Someone will recognize you."

"Never mind that. How is Connie? How bad is it?"

It was a relief to no longer be on her own with it. To have someone there to share the anxiety.

"She fell off a horse and has a head injury and broken ribs." Milly told her what she knew, which wasn't much. "How did you get here?"

"Joel." Nicole gestured over her shoulder. "He's parking the car."

"You came with Joel?"

"It's a long story."

Milly still couldn't believe she was here. "About what I said yesterday—"

"Let's talk about it later." Nicole gave her hand a squeeze. "I'm sorry I wasn't there for you last time you needed me, but I'm here for you now. If you want me, that is."

If?

Milly knew she should probably encourage her to leave right away. She'd spent enough time with Nicole to know that her presence was unlikely to go undetected.

And yet, even knowing that, her friend was here.

"Don't cry." Nicole pulled out a tissue and rubbed a smear of mascara from Milly's cheek. "You're emotional because you're tired. You've always been the same. If you don't get your eight hours, you're a mess."

"Says the woman who has been making me get up at five in the morning to run." Milly took the tissue from her. "You, on the other hand, look stunning as always. Why didn't you at least wear a wig or something?"

"It didn't cross my mind. I was thinking of you and Connie. Don't worry about it. The place is pretty empty, and everyone is too worried about their ailments or their relatives to notice me."

The doctor appeared again. "We've transferred your mother to the ward, so you can see her now. She'll be able to go home later today or tomorrow." He gave them directions to the ward and then hurried back to the department.

There was no sign that he'd recognized Nicole, so Milly wondered if maybe she was right and that people here were too focused on other things.

Joel appeared next to them, having parked the car. "What news?"

They gave him an update as they headed to the stairs.

"I think you should take Nicole home," Milly said as they took the stairs two floors.

Nicole shook her head. "I'm not going anywhere."

"Think about this." Milly caught her arm. "Eventually someone is going to recognize you. Call the press."

"And if they do, we'll figure it out. I'll stay in the room, which will make it less likely." Nicole pushed open the door that led to the ward, and they were directed to a side room.

"Connie doesn't need a room full of visitors. I'll go and find you both some coffee," Joel said and strode away down the corridor leaving the two of them to go into the room together.

Connie lay in the bed, the bruise on her face darker than it had been when Milly had seen her earlier.

"Mum!" She flew across the room and then stopped next to the bed. "I want to hug you, but you have broken ribs. Are you feeling terrible?"

"I feel foolish." Connie tried to sit up. "Brian wanted to take me to the hospital yesterday right after it happened, and I refused. And instead I gave you a scare. You poor thing."

Scare didn't cover it. It had been the single most terrifying moment of her life.

"Don't worry about that." The only thing she cared about now was that her mother was going to be okay. The relief was indescribable.

It was funny to think that only yesterday she'd been so wrapped up in the drama and distress of learning the truth about Nicole. It had dominated her world, and then her mother had collapsed, and suddenly all her other worries had shrunk to nothing. The horror she'd felt in that moment had put everything into perspective.

As long as my family are well, she thought, that's all that really matters.

Richard, Avery—all of that was stressful, but compared to the really important things in life it was nothing. How had she lost sight of that?

Her mother reached out and touched her face. "You look exhausted, honey. Have you been here all night on your own?" Her gaze shifted, and she saw Nicole hovering in the doorway. "Nicole!" She looked at Milly with a question in her eyes, and Milly nodded.

"I left her a message, and she came here to be with me."

"Hi, Connie. You look like an extra in a fight movie." Nicole stepped forward and kissed Milly's mother gently on the forehead.

Connie leaned back against the pillows, the smile on her face showing that she knew what such a gesture would have meant to Milly. "Thank you for coming. It's good that you're here."

Milly squeezed her hand. "Get some rest. We'll be here when you wake up."

Nicole sat down on the other side of the bed. "And when you wake up I want to hear all about this man Brian. Is he hot?"

Connie laughed and then winced. "Don't make me laugh. Oh, it's good to see the two of you here together. Like the old days."

Not really like the old days, Milly thought, because back then no one would have cared who Nicole was.

But now they did care, and this gesture of support was probably going to cost Nicole privacy and piece of mind, but she'd done it anyway because that was what friends did. And Milly felt bad that Nicole had put herself at risk like that, but also good because she'd done it for Milly, and with that one gesture she'd fixed what Milly had thought could never be fixed.

25

Nicole

Connie slept, and Nicole and Milly quietly lifted chairs to the far side of the room so that they could sit together and talk without waking her.

Nicole put her hand over Milly's and was relieved when she wasn't rejected. "I didn't know she'd collapsed in front of you. That must have been terrifying."

She knew how that would have affected Milly. She knew how close her friend was to her mother and grandmother.

Even now Milly couldn't look away from Connie. "I kept saying her name, and she didn't seem to hear me—and then she crashed to the ground. I thought she was going to die."

They talked in hushed voices, but that didn't diminish the emotional impact of the conversation.

Nicole was engulfed in a wave of her own emotion. Connie had been more of a mother to her than her own ever had. "I love her too."

"I know you do. Thank you for coming."

The tensions of the previous night seemed almost forgotten, but Nicole knew it had to be addressed. And maybe this wasn't the right place, but it felt like the right time. It had to be the right time because the urge to fix this, to make everything right, was so powerful it was beyond her control.

"I'm sorry I wasn't there for you after Richard left."

Milly was still looking at her mother. "You were put in a horrible situation. I'm sorry I didn't immediately see that. I wish you'd told me at the time."

This time Nicole was determined not to duck any of the issues. "Because then you and Richard might still be together."

"No." Milly turned her head to look at her. "Because then you wouldn't have had to carry the weight of what you heard on your own. We could have figured it out together, the way we always used to figure things out together. But I can see why you were afraid to tell me."

Nicole glanced quickly at Connie, wondering if they were disturbing her, but she was still asleep.

"I felt as if it was my fault. That he'd left because I'd given him that ultimatum. I wanted to be there for you because you were at your lowest point, but after what I'd said to him I felt like a hypocrite."

"That wasn't my lowest point," Milly said. "My lowest point was when I realized that as well as losing my husband, I'd lost my best friend."

Nicole kept hold of her hand. "You didn't lose me, but I didn't know how to make things right. And then my life blew up, and I had no one else to turn to. And the fact that you met me at the station that night and brought me back to the boathouse and gave me a safe place to stay confirmed what I'd always known. That you are a one-in-a-million friend."

The room was silent, but in the distance they heard the shriek of an ambulance siren. Nicole wondered who was in the ambulance. Someone's loved one. Someone's friend. Someone else whose life had probably changed in an instant.

"I wasn't a one-in-a-million friend," Milly said softly. "Yes, I picked you up, but I was determined to keep some distance. I was cold toward you."

"I assumed you didn't need me anymore. That you'd coped fine without me."

"I wasn't fine. And I did need you, but I was hurt and trying to protect myself. You'd shown that you didn't need me, so I was determined not to need you either. And the more distant I was, the more afraid you were of telling me the truth. I made everything harder, and I'm sorry."

The apology was unexpected.

"I should have told you the truth the night I arrived here, but I couldn't bear the thought of what that might do to us. I messed up."

"So did I. What you needed when I picked you up that night was a great big hug, and I didn't give you one." Milly sighed. "Friendship can be hard, can't it? I never knew that when we were young. It all seemed straightforward."

"Yes."

"Can we just forget it and move on?"

Nicole felt a surge of overwhelming relief. "Yes. I really want that." She felt Milly's hand tighten on hers.

"This is going to sound weird, but I'm almost glad your life blew up or maybe we wouldn't be here together now."

"I know exactly what you mean. I feel the same way."

"Thank you for coming to the hospital. That means a lot."

Before Nicole could answer, the door opened, and Joel appeared carrying two cups of coffee.

"Look who I found loitering in the waiting room." He propped the door open with his foot and Nanna Peg walked in with Zoe by her side.

Milly stood up and gave Zoe a hug. "You should be getting ready for school!"

"There's no way I'm going to school while Gramma is in hospital." Zoe clung to her mother. "Is she going to be okay?"

"The doctors say she's going to be fine."

"Can I stay?" Zoe pulled away. "I want to be here with you."

Milly nodded. "Yes. I'll call the school and explain."

Milly's attention was fixed on Zoe, and it was Nicole who noticed the look on Nanna Peg's face.

She moved her chair next to the bed. "Sit down, Nanna Peg."

Nanna Peg sank onto the chair gratefully just as Connie opened her eyes.

"Mum?"

"I'm here." Nanna Peg's voice was shaky. "What do you think you're doing, scaring us all?"

"I fell off a horse."

"I know. And who is this Brian chap that Milly mentioned? If you wanted to go on a date, why couldn't you just go to the movies like a normal person? Why horse riding?"

Connie managed a smile. "You know I don't go on dates. I like horses, and I like being outdoors. And Brian is just a friend."

"Whatever." Nanna Peg took her hand. "I'm too old for this type of stress. If you want to spend time outdoors, you can join my hiking group. We're in need of new members since Phyllis fell and broke her hip. And we might be losing Maureen soon."

Connie eased herself into a more comfortable position. "What has happened to poor Maureen?"

"Nothing yet, but if she doesn't stop boasting about her grand-children she is going to have an accident. Nothing fatal," Peg said darkly. "I was thinking maybe a twisted ankle. Enough to give us all a break."

Nicole smothered a smile. It was a relief to see Nanna Peg return-ing to her feisty self. "Your hiking group sounds exciting, Nanna Peg. I might join you."

Nanna Peg clutched Connie's hand. "We don't have room for your type."

"My type?" Nicole raised her eyebrows. "What exactly is my type?"

"Drama queen. You'll be rushing back to Hollywood and leav-ing us in the lurch."

Nicole sat down on the edge of the bed. "I won't be rushing back to Hollywood. I'm not going back at all."

There was a sudden silence in the room.

Connie spoke first. "You're not?"

"No." She thought about the lists she'd made when she was at

Joel's earlier. About how clear everything had seemed once she'd written it down. "I'm going to buy a traditional Lakeland stone cottage with roses round the door."

Nanna Peg scowled. "We don't love second-home owners. They drive up house prices and ruin a community."

"It won't be my second home. It will be my only home. And I intend to be part of the community." She turned her head briefly and met Joel's gaze.

He was smiling, as if he wasn't at all surprised by her announcement.

Connie, however, was definitely surprised. "But why? Did something happen, honey?" The kindness in her tone made Nicole wonder why it had taken her so long to realize that this was where she wanted to be.

This was where she felt most like her real self.

"Of course something happened." Nanna Peg gave a sniff of disapproval. "She was dating that man whose eyes are too close together. I blame myself. I should have warned you never to trust a man whose eyes are close together."

Nicole laughed. "A warning would have been useful. And to answer your question, Connie, yes, something happened. I'm pregnant." She paused, self-conscious and unsure about how that announcement might be received. "I'm having a baby. And before you ask, no, the father doesn't want anything to do with it, but honestly that's fine because I think I'll do better by myself. And I'm excited. Terrified, obviously, but also excited."

"You won't be by yourself." Milly joined them at Connie's bedside. "You'll have me."

"And me!" Zoe was beside herself with excitement. "I'm a brilliant babysitter."

"You'll have all of us," Nanna Peg said, "and we'll have you, which is good because it will give me something new to boast about. *My friend the world-famous actress*. Maybe I won't trip Maureen up just yet. I might need the audience."

"Talking of audiences," Joel said, "I was thinking that maybe

I should take you back to Forest Nest, Nicole, before the hospital gets too crowded and it's impossible to smuggle you out."

"That's a good idea," Milly said. "The doctor seemed confident that Mum will be discharged today, so I'll keep you updated and see you back home later. Maybe you shouldn't go back the way we came. The waiting room will be crowded by now."

Joel nodded. "I found a back entrance that comes out near the mortuary. It's very quiet."

"Dead people are usually quiet." Nanna Peg looked thoughtful. "We could smuggle you out, Nicole. You could lie on a trolley, and we could cover you with a sheet. I can sob and look bereft if you think that would add authenticity."

Joel was laughing too much to speak, and even Connie was smiling.

"Thanks, but I'll just walk out like a live person and take my chances," Nicole said hastily.

"You can wear my hoodie." Zoe handed it over to her. "Slouch and keep your head down. No one will notice you."

Nicole took the sweatshirt and put it on. She was exhausted. The stress of the night before and the lack of sleep were catching up on her.

"I'll see you later, Connie." She leaned down and kissed Connie and then gave Milly a hug. "Call if you need me."

"I will."

She left the room with Joel and headed down the stairs he'd found. There was no one else around, their footsteps echoing in the empty stairwell.

At the bottom, he paused with his hand on the door that led outside. "Did you mean what you said? About staying?"

"Yes. I'm going to sell my house and look for something here." She'd never been more sure of anything in her life. "Thank you for yesterday, and for last night. For listening. For being a good friend."

"You're welcome. And I'm glad you managed to sort everything out with Milly." His hand was still on the door, but he didn't open it. "So does that mean you'll be available for more hikes?"

She looked into his eyes and felt something she'd never expected to feel. "Yes, but naturally I'm going to join Nanna Peg's group. I feel I have to be there to protect Maureen."

"Understood." He smiled and opened the door. "Keep your head down, Wendy, or I'll have to sling you over my shoulder and pretend you're a corpse."

26

Milly

Her mother was discharged at lunchtime with instructions to rest for a few days and contact the hospital if there were any concerns.

"I'm not sure about these symptoms." Nanna Peg was studying the piece of paper that the doctor had given them. "I have most of them. Maybe I'm the one who should be in the hospital."

Milly unloaded the shopping she'd picked up on the way home. "I wish you'd come and stay with me at the boathouse, Mum."

"I'm better off in my own bed, honey, but thank you."

"You're not sleeping here alone."

"I'll be here," Nanna Peg said. "If we need you, we'll call. Now, enough talk of illness. Tell me about Nicole."

Milly put apples into the fruit bowl. "You mean about her being pregnant? Or the fact that she is thinking of moving here permanently?" That had come as a surprise to her, but it was a good surprise.

They had so much to talk about.

"Neither of those things. I'm talking about Joel."

"Joel?" Milly added oranges and plums to the bowl. "What about Joel?"

"Are you seriously pretending you don't know?" Nanna Peg glanced at Connie. "I despair of the younger generation. They spend so long online they don't understand human interaction when they see it."

Milly put the milk in the fridge. "If you're talking about their friendship, then yes. I know about that. She bumped into Joel on her first day here—" she decided not to give them the details of Nicole thinking he was an intruder "—and they became friends. He took her hiking yesterday."

"I've been hiking with people," Nanna Peg said, "and I don't look at them the way he looks at her. Or the way she looks at him."

Milly closed the fridge. "You see romance everywhere."

"I see romance where there's romance." Nanna Peg made a pot of tea and put it on the table in front of Connie. "Trust me—those two are more than hiking buddies, even if they don't yet know it themselves. Did you unload the chocolate biscuits, Milly, or are they still in the car?"

"Still in the car, I think." Could Nanna Peg be right? "She's pregnant."

"I don't see why that matters." Connie poured the tea. "But she's a world-famous actress, and he's a carpenter."

"Exactly." Nanna Peg added sugar to her tea. "And you have a perfect rom-com right there."

Milly rolled her eyes. "Your imagination is unbelievable. I'll leave you to it while I go and hunt for the chocolate biscuits. Try not to move or injure yourselves while I'm gone." But it was good to see the pair of them laughing and joking.

"I'll help you with the shopping." Zoe followed her to the car and Milly grabbed the last bag of groceries and rescued the packet of chocolate biscuits that had rolled under the car seat.

"Are you doing okay, Zoe? I'm sorry about last night." It had been playing on her mind. "Dragging you out to stay here. And the whole conversation with Nicole. You shouldn't have had to hear all that."

"It's fine. I'm an adult. Almost. You don't have to hide things from me. I prefer it if you don't." Zoe's cheeks were pink. "To be honest it gave me hope."

"Hope?"

"Hearing you and Nicole fall out and then seeing you fix it again. I've always thought you two had, like, the perfect, most amazing friendship. I didn't imagine that you ever exchanged an angry word. And then you did, but it was okay. And seeing that gave me courage to speak to Cally. I'm going to do that."

"Good." Milly leaned against the car door to close it, her arms full. She was relieved that Zoe didn't seem scarred by witnessing a surfeit of maternal emotion. And who would have thought that her problems with Nicole would have turned into a teachable moment? Usually she tried to smooth or sanitize everything, but maybe she needed to be a little more open. After all, her job as a mother was to prepare Zoe for a real version of life, not a polished version. "I hope she's receptive and that the conversation isn't too stressful. If you want to talk through how to approach it, I'm here." She took a step toward the house, but Zoe stopped her.

"Talking of not hiding things—"

"Mm?" Milly paused, her maternal radar on full alert.

"I kind of understood why it was hard for Nicole to tell you. About Dad, I mean—" Zoe stumbled over the words "—because it's not an easy thing, is it? Talking about something like that. When you overhear something you shouldn't. It's like holding something hot that is scalding you, and the last thing you want to do is hand it over and scald someone else."

Milly stayed still, waiting.

This was how it was with teenagers, she was discovering. You could sit them down and encourage them to talk and they gave away frustratingly little, but then you were standing in the blazing sunshine clutching a bag of groceries with a packet of chocolate biscuits melting in your hand and suddenly you knew that this conversation about not much was about something very important.

"Have you been in that position, sweetheart?"

Zoe gave her a desperate look. "I overheard Dad talking." The words fell out of her as if they'd been held inside for too long. "It was at home one night. When we were still in our old house. I came down for a glass of water. He didn't know I was there." She broke off. "I don't even know if I should be telling you this."

They were standing in full sunshine.

Milly was sweltering. Her clothes were sticking to her. The chocolate biscuits were turning liquid.

"You can tell me anything, honey. Anything at all."

Zoe swallowed. "He was talking to someone on the phone. And the moment he saw me he turned like a weird puce color and ended the call, and he told me off for creeping up on him. But I honestly wasn't. I just wanted a drink. And if he hadn't acted all guilty I probably wouldn't even have noticed."

Milly's mouth was dry. "When was this?"

"I don't know. But before we went to LA to stay with Aunt Nicole. And then I saw him on the balcony arguing with Aunt Nicole, and I guessed what might be going on. But I didn't know exactly. And I didn't know what to do. Or say. And last night you were so mad at Nicole that she hadn't told you—"

"Oh, sweetheart, no, that's not true. It was more complicated than that. And I'm so, so sorry you were put in that position." Milly put the biscuits in with the groceries and put the bag down on the ground. Then she held out her arms, and Zoe walked straight into them. "I wish you'd told me. Not for me, but for you."

Zoe clung to her. "I didn't want to hurt you. And I suppose a part of me hoped that if I ignored it, it might go away."

Milly stroked Zoe's hair. Her eyes were stinging. "That was a big thing to have to carry, and next time you're worried about anything at all, you're to tell me and we'll share it. That's what family does." She held her daughter tightly, and then there was a hammering at the window. "That's Nanna Peg."

"She wants her chocolate biscuits." Zoe gave a tearful laugh and pulled away. "You're not mad at me?"

"I could never be mad at you. I'm sorry this has been so hard on you. I feel terrible about all of it. The divorce. Moving house . . ." She couldn't believe they were having such an important conversation outdoors next to the car, clutching bags of shopping and risking sunstroke.

"Don't feel bad. None of it is your fault. And I love the boat-house." Zoe picked up the bag. "And Dad leaving was difficult, but I'm getting used to it. Avery has tried really hard to make me feel at home there, which can't be easy because she doesn't have kids or anything. She has started buying food she knows I like, even though she doesn't eat it herself." She said it tentatively, as if it was something she wasn't sure her mother would want to know, and Milly realized how tough it must have felt for her.

"I'm glad you like her, I really am. It's a relief to me."

"Truly?"

"Yes. And if your dad is happy with her, then I think that's good too."

Zoe shifted the weight of the bag. "Do you wish you'd never married him?"

There had been moments when she wished that, but now she thought differently.

"We had many happy years, and just because we've both moved on doesn't make those years worth less. It was a different phase of our lives, that's all. And now this is a new phase."

"I worry about leaving you alone on the weekends. Gramma and Nanna Peg want to sign you up to a dating app."

Milly thought about Brendan. "I don't think that will be necessary."

"I just want you to be happy, Mum."

Maybe it *was* time to be more open. "Well, it's funny you should say that, because I just may have gone on a date while you were staying with your dad and Avery this weekend."

Zoe gasped. "You did? Who with?"

"I'm going to tell you all about it another time or Nanna Peg will come out here searching for those biscuits herself."

"Okay, but answer me one question. What did you wear?"

Milly laughed. She definitely should be sharing more of her life with her daughter. "A dress that Nicole found tucked at the back of my wardrobe. And a pair of shoes that gave me a blister." Milly headed back toward the house, Zoe next to her looking decidedly more cheerful.

She poached some salmon and made a light salad for supper, and by the time they all went to bed, Connie was looking a lot better.

Milly was settling down to sleep when a message pinged on her phone.

It was from Brendan.

Joel updated me. I'm here if you need me so call.

She replied with a thank you and a row of kisses, and then deleted two of the kisses in case it was too much.

Then she lay back and smiled into the darkness. She wasn't going to call, but she was pleased that he'd suggested it.

And suddenly she felt lighter, as if the world had opened up in front of her. Her mother was going to be okay, things were good with Nicole, and she was finally in a better place about her own situation. Putting her marriage to Richard firmly in the past and letting go of all the regrets and questions she'd had left her feeling free.

She thought about the date she'd had with Brendan. The fun they'd had.

She wished now that she'd gone with him to his cabin. Next time, she would. And she was determined there would be a next time.

She went to sleep smiling, and that feeling of contentment lasted until her phone woke her the following morning.

It was Joel.

"Hi." Milly's voice was groggy from sleep. "Everything okay?"

"Not exactly. I'm calling to warn you not to come near Forest Nest."

"What?" She sat up and rubbed her eyes. "I was going to drop Zoe at school and then come straight over. What has happened?"

"There are photographers everywhere. Mostly men with cameras. They're swarming all over the boathouse."

Milly's stomach dropped. "Nicole—"

"Fortunately she stayed over with me last night. I went into work early this morning and saw a man with a long lens in the bushes. Then another group arrived. We have a problem."

Milly registered briefly that Nicole had stayed the night with Joel, then pushed it out of her mind. She'd think about that later. There were more urgent things to deal with.

This had happened because Nicole had come to the hospital to give her support. She needed to try and fix it.

"Don't let her leave the house." She was out of bed and pulling on clothes as she spoke. How on earth were they going to extract Nicole from this? "I'll drop Zoe at school early and come straight over. Nanna Peg will stay with my mother." She comforted herself with the fact that her mother had seemed fine the evening before.

"Be careful," Joel said. "They might follow you."

"I doubt they know who I am, but just to be sure I'll park far away from your house and approach from the trail. No one will see me."

An hour later she was driving back to the village, wondering why photographers would be at the boathouse. That didn't make sense. If someone had followed Nicole from the hospital then they'd be outside Joel's cottage, surely?

She checked her mirrors constantly, but there was no sign of anyone following her, so she pulled over and parked outside an outdoor store at the edge of the village, grabbed her bag and headed up the narrow unmarked trail that passed behind Joel's cottage.

She slipped in through the gate, crossed his sunny garden and tapped gently on the French doors.

Joel opened them, and she stepped inside.

"I didn't see anyone. And this doesn't make sense to me. If someone at the hospital saw her, why would they be at the boathouse?"

"I don't think it was anything to do with the hospital. We're assuming it might be the couple we met the day before yesterday on our walk. They recognized me." Nicole was tucked into one corner of the sofa. Her legs were smooth and tanned and endless from beneath cutoff shorts, and everything about her seemed so perfect it was hard to believe that less than ten minutes' drive away a crowd of photographers and journalists were hovering in the hope of uncovering some scandal they could expose.

"You should have tried harder to behave like a normal person, Wendy," Joel said. "You're a terrible actor."

The two of them exchanged a smile, and Milly had no idea what they were talking about, but she was relieved Nicole didn't seem more stressed.

"I'll make us coffee," Joel said and headed to the kitchen.

Milly sat down next to Nicole. "I'm sorry this happened. We were trying so hard to hide you and protect you."

Nicole gave a brief shake of her head. "It's not your fault. We'll figure it out. How is your mother doing?"

"Her ribs hurt, but I think she's doing okay. Nanna Peg is staying with her today."

The door opened again, and Joel paused, three brimming cups of coffee on a tray. "I had an idea." He put the coffee down on the table. "I was thinking we could find a photo of Nicole at Heathrow and post it as a sighting. Throw them off the scent. Send them in another direction."

"Not a bad idea." Milly picked up one of the mugs and handed it to Nicole. "Or I could drive home innocently and look blank when they tell me they're looking for you and say, *Nicole who?*"

Joel settled himself on the chair opposite them. "But someone must have followed us to know she was staying in the boathouse. So that probably won't work."

"We could just say nothing," Milly said. "I don't talk to them. They don't know you're here, so you just stay indoors. They'll get bored."

"I have a better idea." Nicole finally spoke. "I use their presence to announce my retirement from acting. Or at least the fact that I'm taking a break."

Milly looked at her. "So all those things you said at the hospital—"

"About moving here? Yes, I meant them."

It seemed like such a huge step. "Are you sure you're not rushing this decision? Shouldn't you let the idea sit for a while in case you change your mind?"

"I won't change my mind. I already emailed my agent."

"Won't she be upset?"

"Possibly, although I'm not exactly hot property at the moment." Nicole didn't seem at all stressed about that fact. "But it doesn't really matter what she thinks. This is about me. What I want. What I need."

Milly put her cup down. "But acting is all you've ever wanted to do. This was your dream."

"Dreams can change." Nicole exchanged a brief glance with Joel, and Milly wondered exactly what had happened between the two of them.

Something had, that much was obvious.

"What will you do?"

Nicole curled her legs under her, totally at home on Joel's sofa. "What will I do?" A slow smile spread across her face. "I intend to take a little time off and do the things I enjoy most. I'm going to go hiking, read a few books on how to be a good mother, see a doctor or midwife or whatever it is I'm supposed to do, eat proper meals, maybe learn to cook, help Zoe rehearse for her play." She drew breath. "I was also thinking that maybe I could help out at her drama group."

This was a whole new version of Nicole. Closer to the person she'd been when they were growing up.

"You're going to learn to cook?" Milly kept her tone light. "If you're going to do that, at least let me give you some basic lessons. So you don't poison yourself or chop off your fingers."

Nicole laughed. "Sounds like a plan."

"I love your idea of helping at the drama group. They'd be delirious with excitement, and I know you'd be good at it. I'm happy you'll be sticking around." Her mood lifted. "All we need to do now is get rid of the press."

Nicole's smile dimmed a little. "I just need to accept that they're not going to leave me alone. At least for a while, until they get bored. But once they find out I'm pregnant, there will be a lot of speculation, and I hate that."

"We need them to lose interest before you start looking pregnant." Milly thought about it but couldn't see a solution. "It's maddening that they can't respect your right to privacy and leave you alone."

Nicole finished her coffee and put the mug down. "I'll give an interview about retiring and hope that will keep them at bay for a while."

Milly frowned. "I just don't see that it's any of their business." It bothered her that Nicole seemed to think she had a duty to make parts of her life public. "Surely your agent can put out a statement saying that you're taking a break. That's enough."

Nicole shrugged. "It isn't enough, though, is it? They're going to want to know what I was doing here. I need to give them a reason or they will never leave me alone."

A reason for being here.

Milly stared at her. An idea came into her head.

No. It would never work. Would it?

"What?" Nicole looked at her expectantly. "What are you thinking? Tell me."

"I'm not sure if it's a terrible idea."

But they had to do something, so surely it was worth a try?

27

Nicole

This was a terrible idea." Nicole paced across Joel's living room and back again. "I can't remember ever feeling this tense about anything."

"Could you sit down? You're making me nervous too." Milly checked the time. "Why hasn't he called? It has been four hours. He said he'd call and update us."

"Probably means it has all gone horribly wrong." Nicole sat down for two seconds, but it was impossible to relax so she stood up again. "We shouldn't have asked him to do this. It wasn't fair."

"Don't say that." Milly threw her a look. "It was my idea, and now I'm doubting myself."

"What are you two worrying about now?" Joel walked into the room carrying a plate of sandwiches and a jug of ice water.

Milly blinked. "Sandwiches? It's eleven in the morning."

"The day started early. I've adjusted mealtimes accordingly. Also, eating stops me from falling asleep." He put the sandwiches down on the table.

"Maybe I should call and tell him not to do it." Milly stared at her phone, as if she was willing it to ring.

"You two are overthinking this. If he didn't want to do it, he would have said no." Joel topped up Nicole's glass of water. He caught her eye briefly and smiled, and she smiled back.

He was so attentive, and Nicole was having to make a real effort not to watch him the whole time. He'd been such a good friend to her.

Fortunately Milly didn't seem to be paying much attention to them. "I didn't exactly give him much of a choice. He probably hates me now. It will be the end of a short but beautiful relationship."

"And you hadn't even had sex." Nicole gave her an apologetic look. "Next time, seize the moment. Life is too short not to grab fun whenever you can." She saw Milly turn scarlet, and Joel raised an eyebrow.

"There don't seem to be a lot of secrets left between the four of us, so don't worry." His gaze slid to the garden. "But if you want us to clear the room and leave you and Brendan alone, you need to tell us. Because he's here."

"Definitely don't clear the room." Milly turned an even deeper shade of red and smoothed her hair.

Brendan tapped on the doors, and Joel opened them.

"Welcome. You took so long we were worried you'd been devoured by the press pack."

"I got lost trying to find the trail." He glanced at Milly. "For the record, your directions are terrible."

"I told you to turn left at the outdoor shop."

"Yes, but you omitted to tell me that after that I had to climb a gate and dodge a herd of cows. Hi, Nic. Good to see you." He crossed the room to Nicole, and she hugged him.

"Brendan. It has been a while." She'd worked with so many people over the course of her career, some good and some bad. Fortunately Brendan landed firmly in the Good column.

"I didn't know you were staying here. The owner of Forest Nest is the soul of discretion."

Joel raised his eyebrows. "You two know each other?"

"I played the part of the detective from one of his books," Nicole said, "which you'd know if you ever went to the movies."

"Now, why would I want to waste my life doing something like that?" Joel helped himself to one of his sandwiches. "Sorry, but I need to eat. All this drama is making me light-headed."

"Please," Milly begged, "will you put us out of our misery and tell us what happened? I feel physically sick."

"In that case, is it okay if I eat your share of the sandwiches?" Brendan accepted the plate Joel was offering and loaded it with sandwiches. "Put the TV on, and all your questions will be answered. I know you're not a big screen lover, but you do have a TV, don't you, Joel?"

"Sarcasm is an unattractive feature." Joel moved a couple of books on the coffee table and retrieved the remote control. He pointed it at the TV in the corner of the room.

"You don't find me attractive? I'm gutted. That's the last beer we share together." Brendan bit into a sandwich. "What's in this? What am I eating?"

"I don't know. Various bits from my fridge." Joel was channel-flicking. "What am I looking for?"

"The news."

Nicole's stomach lurched, and she exchanged looks with Milly. "It has made the news? I thought you were just going to get rid of them in a low-key way."

"I was, but then I decided I might as well get some prime-time promotion for myself while I was at it. I have a new book coming out next month. Also, if you go big, then it stops the story escalating because it has nowhere else to go. They recorded a very nice piece to camera—now we just need to see how much they edited." He finished the sandwiches on his plate. "I don't suppose you have any of Milly's chocolate cake? I would kill for her chocolate cake."

"Shh. Here we go, this is it." Joel turned up the volume, and all four of them stared at the screen as the presenter talked through all the serious news of the day.

"I write suspense for a living, and even I'm struggling with the tension." Brendan helped himself to a sandwich from Joel's plate. "Oh look, she's smiling. That means they're about to do their light-hearted piece. That's how it works. They give you half an hour of all the different ways the world is ending, and then give you two minutes of fluffy kittens to stop you cutting your throat when you turn it off."

The presenter smiled at the camera.

"And finally, best-selling crime writer Brendan Scott confirmed today that he and Nicole Raven are in the early stages of negotiations to bring another of his books to the big screen."

The camera cut from the presenter in the studio to a shot of Forest Nest, the sun glinting through the trees.

"Looks good, Milly." Joel's eyes were fixed on the screen. "Your bookings are going to go up."

"According to Scott, he and Raven have been scouting possible locations around the UK, including Yorkshire and the Lake District. Scott refused to confirm or deny rumors that Raven may be setting up her own production company, but the two have worked together in the past, and Scott admitted that he was excited about the possibility of another collaboration."

"A production company?" Nicole looked at him. "You told them I was setting up a production company?"

"Pay attention. She said I refused to confirm or deny rumors." Brendan was still watching the report. "Gives them something else to think about. Shh. This is my big moment."

The camera cut to Brendan, looking relaxed and handsome by one of the trails in the resort. *"Nicole Raven is that rare thing, a global superstar. I'm a long-time fan of her work, and I'm looking forward to see-ing her bring one of my most popular fictional characters to life."*

"Scott, who has notched up fifteen number-one bestsellers in the last decade . . ."

"Sixteen," Brendan muttered. "I told them it was sixteen."

"Be quiet!" Milly caught his arm, her focus on the TV.

". . . will be back in the US next month for the launch of his next book. Raven has already left the country and was unavailable for comment, but Scott dismissed rumors that recent revelations about her alleged affair with Justin Fisher had sent her into hiding. 'She's been working hard, finding her own projects for development,' Scott said as he confirmed that more

meetings were planned. 'She's one of the new breed of actors who aren't afraid to take control of their own destiny, and that can only be good news for authors like me and for moviegoers everywhere.'"

"They cut the part where I told them the title of my next book!" Brendan scowled.

"They think I've already left the country?" Nicole felt light-headed with relief. "Do they believe that?"

"Yes. I said you were far too busy and important to spend time hanging around here with me. But you probably should lie low for a couple of days, just to be safe."

Nicole felt a soaring sense of gratitude. "I can't believe you did that for me."

"I know, I'm a hero. And I didn't even get anything out of it for myself because they cut the mention of my book." Brendan winked at her. "If I'm not careful there will be rumors that I'm a good guy, and I can't have that. I work hard at making my life seem murky and mysterious, in keeping with my author persona."

Nicole laughed. "Does this mean that I actually have to set up a production company?"

Brendan helped himself to the last sandwich on Joel's plate. "I don't know, but I've heard worse ideas in my time. Shame you're not still in the country or we could have a meeting about it."

Milly sank onto the edge of the sofa. "So now what?"

Joel picked up the empty plate. "Now I make more sandwiches, given that Brendan has eaten them all. After that, you go back to work and do whatever you do. We don't want to raise suspicions. Nicole stays here. Brendan goes back to editing his book."

"You mean I go back to staring out the window. That's how writers spend their day."

"Why don't I cook dinner for us all tonight?" Milly made the suggestion tentatively. "Zoe is spending the evening with my mother and Nanna Peg. I can do it here, so that Nicole doesn't have to leave the house."

Brendan looked at Milly, and his expression softened. "I'd rather have you to myself than share you with these two, but I suppose it depends on what you're cooking. Is it lemon chicken?"

Nicole saw Milly blush.

"It could be lemon chicken."

"Great. In that case I'll bring the wine. Tonight will be dinner with friends. Our date can wait until tomorrow."

Dinner with friends.

Nicole looked at the three of them.

Milly had given her sanctuary, and Joel had done the same. Brendan had willingly stepped in to protect her from the press. And she knew without doubt that she could trust every person in this room.

A lump formed in her throat. "I thought I was going to have to do this on my own. Handle it on my own."

"No chance," Joel said, and Milly shook her head.

"We are all in it together."

"I wasn't in anything at all," Brendan said, "until Milly threatened never to make me her lemon chicken again. Now I'm all in."

Nicole didn't know whether to laugh or cry.

"I've never had three friends before. Not three real friends." They all turned to look at her, and she felt suddenly awkward. "I mean friends who would put themselves out. Friends who would do something for me without getting anything in return."

There was an emotional silence, and then Joel spoke.

"I want something in return," he said finally. "I want you to help me make the next round of sandwiches because I'm starting to feel as if I'm running a catering company."

"And I want you to mention my book on social media," Brendan said, "because you have more followers than I do."

Nicole laughed and walked with Joel to the kitchen, feeling as if she was poised on the edge of something exciting. A baby, good friends and a home in a place she'd always loved. It was a million miles from her old life, but it felt exactly right. Exactly where she wanted to be.

It was a clarity of thinking that was long overdue.

28

Milly

Milly sat in the café, hoping this wasn't a mistake. She'd chosen somewhere that was neutral territory, halfway between Forest Nest and the city where Richard now lived with Avery.

She nursed the single black coffee she'd ordered on arrival, and to distract herself from what was to come, she thought about the evening before.

As requested, she'd made her lemon chicken, and Brendan had opened chilled champagne (Joel had provided a chilled elderflower mocktail for Nicole), and the four of them had sat in Joel's pretty garden, eating, drinking, laughing, talking about everything and nothing, and breathing in the sweet smell of honeysuckle until the sun dipped behind the fells.

Milly had noticed that Joel had kept calling Nicole *Wendy*, but when she'd asked about it they'd both smiled and said it was a private joke, and Milly had suppressed her curiosity because she was just pleased to see Nicole relaxed and happy and confident enough to share a private joke with someone who wasn't her.

Milly and Nicole had been friends forever, of course, but by the end of the evening it had felt as if the four of them were a unit.

As Milly watched Joel place his arm protectively onto the back of Nicole's chair, she'd been sure of it.

And a few hours ago Nicole had messaged her to give her the time of the doctor's appointment she'd arranged so that Milly could meet her there. She said that Joel had offered to go with her (earning him major plus points), but she really wanted Milly, and Milly was so excited at being part of Nicole's baby journey that she'd agreed instantly.

And then there was Brendan . . .

"Milly?" Richard's voice made her jump, and she almost spilled her coffee.

"Sorry. I didn't see you arrive. I was thinking about something."

"Something good, judging from the smile on your face." He sat down opposite her. "I was surprised to get your message. I didn't think you'd ever speak to me again after the other night."

She didn't know quite what reaction she'd expected from him, but it wasn't that.

"What? You think I don't know when I've been an idiot?" He put his phone and car keys down on the table. "I have a lot to apologize for, so do you want to go first or shall I?"

"You—you want to apologize?"

"*Want* to apologize?" Richard gave a faint smile. "No. I hate admitting I'm wrong, you know that. But do I need to? Yes. But first I need coffee. Can I get you another?"

She hadn't finished the one sitting in front of her, but she nodded, mute, and he stood up and ordered at the counter and then sat back down again.

"I suppose I should start with the other night. I didn't expect to see Nicole. It was a shock. And I know that doesn't excuse anything—" he lifted a hand before she could say anything "—but it brought back a lot of emotions, stresses—"

"Because she confronted you and made you choose."

"No. Well, yes, I suppose there's some of that in there, but mostly because I felt terrible at the time, and seeing her brought it all back."

"You felt terrible?"

"Yes. I already felt terrible about what I was doing, and she made me feel worse, and rightly so. I behaved badly. And I knew it. I was conflicted." He paused while their coffees were delivered. "I loved you, Milly. Maybe you don't believe that, but I did. I loved our life. I didn't intentionally look for anyone else. But when I met Avery at those yoga classes . . ." He shook his head. "I don't know. It just felt—it was powerful."

Milly never would have thought she could have sat still and listened to him talk like this, but here she was, listening, and it didn't feel as hard as she'd thought it would. Something had changed. She'd changed.

"So you cheated on me."

"And I regret that every day." His cheeks were flushed. "I should have done the brave thing and told you right away that I was having doubts, that I'd met someone. Maybe we could have worked it through. I don't know."

Milly sighed. "Richard, this is history now—"

"Not really, because it's always between us. In every conversation you're hurt and punishing me, and I'm defensive and snappy and behaving like an idiot because I'm eaten up with guilt."

Was she punishing him? Yes, she probably was.

Bringing the past into the present, as her mother would say.

"That's why you've been behaving the way you have? You feel guilty?"

"I've felt guilty from day one." He muttered the words and glanced briefly at the table closest to them. "And the more accommodating and patient you were, the guiltier I felt. Given what I put you through, you were a saint."

"I thought I was a martyr."

He flushed. "I shouldn't have said that."

She was trying to absorb what he was telling her. "So you behaved badly in response to me behaving reasonably. And then when that changed and I stood my ground . . ." she tried to make sense of it ". . . you're saying you preferred the annoyed version of me?"

"The annoyed version of you is easier to handle than the sad version. The sad version breaks me up." He looked at her then, and for a moment she saw the man she'd married. The man she'd trusted, the man she'd laughed and cried and made a child with.

It was good to know that man still existed. That she hadn't imagined it all.

She felt an ache of sadness for what they'd once had and lost, but also a sense of peace because she knew that whatever things were like now, they'd been good once. And maybe it was time to focus on that.

"It's helpful to know that." She picked up her coffee and looked at him over the edge of her cup. "I thought you'd just turned into a monumental idiot."

His eyes gleamed. "At least you haven't lost your sense of humor."

But she had, hadn't she? At least for a while. But she was going to forgive herself for that. She put her cup down. "I didn't know you felt guilty."

"Of course I did. We had all those happy years together. And we had Zoe. Our girl. And you probably won't believe me, but Avery felt terrible too. For a while I didn't think our relationship was going to work because the guilt kept coming between us."

"But it did work."

He looked at her for a long time, trying to decide whether to say something or not. "I'm happy, Milly. I know you think it was a midlife-crisis thing, and there's the age difference, but I love Avery. And she loves me. And I'm sorry if that hurts."

"It doesn't. Not anymore. I'm pleased for you both, really." Milly decided that the time had come to build a bridge so that they could both move forward. "Zoe likes Avery. And she has obviously made an effort—she has upended her life and let a teenager invade her immaculate single-person space, so she gets points for that."

Richard reached out and touched her hand. "I don't regret our marriage, although I'm sure you do."

She stared down at his hand, covering hers. It was the first time they'd touched since he'd left her. And she thought about the early days. The fun they'd had. The way they'd been by each other's sides through everything. Zoe. "I don't regret anything. We had plenty of good years together, Richard. Maybe it's time to celebrate those."

He studied her face for a long moment, searching for something. "You've changed. Something has happened."

Milly thought about Nicole, about all the conversations they'd had over the past few weeks. She thought about Brendan and the night they'd spent together.

Her mother had made a full recovery, and once Milly was confident that things were steady again, she'd rearranged her date with Brendan. This time she'd told Zoe about it, and that might have been a mistake because Zoe had sat with her nose pressed to the window to see whether Brendan was hot (or *buff* to quote Zoe exactly) until Nicole had hauled her away to rehearse her part.

And when Brendan had invited her back to his cabin she'd said yes without hesitation, relieved that she'd had the foresight to arrange for Zoe to sleep over at her grandmother's house. Connie, predictably, had been delighted to facilitate this new development in her daughter's sex life, and Milly had tried not to think about the interrogation she would be facing in the coming days.

They'd drunk more champagne (Brendan had no food in his fridge, but he seemed to have plenty of beer and bubbly) and they'd sat and talked in soft voices for hours, and she wasn't sure exactly when, but at some point they'd turned to each other and then they were kissing again, only this time it hadn't stopped at kissing.

And the whole thing had been so deliciously exciting, so breathtakingly perfect that she'd never wanted the night to end.

And now, thinking back, she remembered how romantic it had been. She remembered the whisper of breeze through the open doors of his cabin cooling her heated skin, the sound of the lake lapping gently against the reeds beneath his deck, the feel of his fingers and the skilled brush of his mouth.

And as she'd lain there afterward, her legs tangled with his, she'd felt as if everything had changed. But it hadn't, of course, not really. The only thing that had changed was her.

"I think I've just moved on." She answered Richard's question finally. "And it was about time. We need to find a way to function well in our new relationship." The door to the café opened again, and Milly glanced up. "Which is why I asked Avery to join us."

Richard almost fell off his chair. "Avery?"

"Hi." Avery arrived at the table, a wary look in her eyes, and Milly stood up.

"I'm glad you came." The whole situation felt painfully awkward, but she kept her tone warm. "I wanted to thank you for your kindness to Zoe."

"Oh—" Avery looked thrown "—of course. She's a special girl. A credit to you." Her gaze skidded to Richard, as if to check what he was making of all this.

"She loved the performance of *A Midsummer Night's Dream*. It made her day. And it also made her determined not to give up drama, so I'm grateful to you for that."

Avery sat down at the table. "She enjoyed it. I saw her mouthing the words. And we talked about it a little bit afterward. She told me about her friend and how difficult it has been."

Milly delved into her bag and pulled out two tickets to Zoe's play. "It's an outdoor performance, so we're hoping the weather holds, but I do hope you'll both come. There will be a group of us there cheering her on. I think it would be lovely for Zoe if you were both there too. United front and all that. Family."

Avery glanced at Richard, who looked nervous.

"When you say a group of you, will that include your mother?"

"Yes." Milly smiled. "But I'm sure you're not afraid of my mother, are you, Richard?"

"She's a formidable woman," he muttered. "Are you sure she won't try and kill me in public?"

"We're watching a performance of *A Midsummer Night's Dream*, not *Macbeth*," Milly said. "There will be no murders, and I'm sure you'll be fine. Things change, Richard. Relationships change. It's part of life. My mother knows that."

And now she knew it too, and not only because her blossoming relationship with Brendan had given her a glimpse of a future she hadn't envisaged for herself.

At some point she'd finally realized that she wasn't to blame for Richard leaving, any more than she was to blame for her father leaving. People were complicated, and often unpredictable, and sometimes what they wanted changed, and you couldn't control that. Sometimes you needed to accept the way things were instead of wishing for something different or trying to turn the clock back.

"I do hope you'll come." She stood up, keen to get back to her life now that this final job was done. "I think it will be a special evening."

29

Milly

"Are you sure I can't kill him? Not just for what he did to you, but also for what he did to Nicole. There are foxgloves over there in that pretty border. I could grind them down and drop them into his wine. How much would you need, I wonder?" Nanna Peg clutched her handbag as they stood together and watched as Richard walked toward them along the path. Avery was next to him, wearing a floor-length summer dress in a pale shade of blue. "She looks very plain and washed-out next to you, Milly. You look gorgeous."

Milly decided that inviting the whole family might have been a mistake. Much as she adored Nanna Peg and appreciated her steadfast support, she was already seeing the potential for many embarrassing moments. And on top of that stress, she felt sick with nerves for Zoe. She'd worked so hard on the part, and Milly knew how disappointed she'd be if it didn't go well.

Still, it was a comfort to know that Nicole was with her backstage, and Nicole would be far more use in this situation than Milly would have been.

She knew nothing about first-night nerves.

"The dress was a gift from Nicole." Milly glanced down at herself, wondering if she was slightly overdressed. "I wasn't sure."

"It's stunning. Fuchsia pink is perfect with your coloring." Nanna Peg narrowed her eyes. "You look a little like a foxglove yourself. Maybe it's a metaphor. You could be the death of—"

"It's not a metaphor," Milly said quickly. "It's just a dress."

"I don't know about foxgloves, but I hope Avery doesn't drop the strawberries on that blue dress. Wearing something so pale to an outdoor performance in a garden might be a mistake," Connie muttered, but Milly noticed something other than the dress.

She saw that Avery was gripping Richard's hand and casting wary glances around her.

"She's nervous. It must have taken a lot of courage to come," Milly said, "and I'd like you both to be friendly. This is how our family looks now. Different. Maybe a little messy. But it's still our family."

Nanna Peg stuck her jaw out. "I'm not sure that—"

"You're going to do it for my sake, Nanna Peg." Milly leaned in and kissed her grandmother on the cheek. "And for the sake of your great-granddaughter. We are going to move on. We are all evolved people here."

"Are we?" Nanna Peg blinked. "I suppose I can pretend to be evolved. As long as she doesn't try and turn me into a vegetarian. I have limits." She sniffed. "It will be easier to stomach now that you're seeing that extremely hot young guy yourself."

"Nanna Peg!" Milly felt her face turn pink. Why had she thought a family gathering would be a good idea? She must have been crazy.

"What? He has strong shoulders. I love a man with strong shoulders. It means he can—"

"Mum," Connie intervened, "you're embarrassing Milly."

"What's wrong with that? What is a grandmother for? Also the fact that she is embarrassed proves that I'm right. And now I want all the details."

Milly wished she'd brought her grandmother to a different performance. "Please be quiet! He and Joel went to get wine. They'll be back any moment."

Right on cue, Brendan appeared carrying glasses of wine for Connie and Nanna Peg. "Joel and Brian are right behind me with more drinks."

"Thank you." Nanna Peg beamed up at him. "Can I ask you something, Brendan?"

Milly almost groaned.

Say no, she thought, but Brendan smiled.

"Ask me anything."

"If you had to murder someone using only what is available in these gardens, what would you do? I was thinking foxglove."

To give him credit, Brendan didn't flinch. He glanced around him, his gaze lingering on the flower-filled borders and the stream that wound its way along the end of the garden.

"Foxglove would probably work," he said and turned back to Nanna Peg, "but if I wanted to use a plant and be absolutely sure of the end result, I'd choose hemlock—*Conium maculatum*. It's deadly. The highest alkaloid concentration is in the seeds, but every part of the plant is toxic."

Nanna Peg listened to him with rapt attention. "Goodness, what an interesting and knowledgeable young man you are. I could talk to you for hours. I don't suppose you and Milly would like to join an old lady for dinner one night, would you? Now that my roof is fixed, I'm entertaining again."

"I don't know." Brendan's eyes were bright with laughter. "Will you be cooking, Peg?"

Nanna Peg laughed so hard that Milly started smiling too.

They were still laughing when Richard and Avery reached them, and the wave of good humor seemed to dilute the potentially awkward moment.

Milly greeted them warmly, and Richard was so starstruck to see Brendan Scott again that he could barely stammer out a sentence.

And she had to admit that the whole encounter was so much

easier with Brendan and Joel there and also Brian, her mother's new "friend" (Milly still didn't totally understand the nature of their friendship, but her mother seemed happy, and that was all that mattered).

They were a large and happy group, and she felt a slight sense of smug satisfaction when Brendan put a protective hand on her back, and Richard's eyes almost popped out of his head.

Maybe she wasn't as evolved as she liked to think.

Richard cleared his throat. "Where's Nicole? I was hoping to have a word."

"She's backstage. She has been helping them all week," Milly said. *And also staying out of the way so that she didn't draw attention to herself.* The focus of tonight was the children. "I'm sure she'll be around afterward if there was something you felt you wanted to say to her."

She knew he wanted to apologize, and she wasn't going to stop him. He and Nicole had been friends once, and even if they couldn't reach that point again, she hoped they could at least find some sort of harmony.

"She'll be with me," Joel said calmly, "so we'll come and find you."

His message was clear. That Nicole wasn't going to be on her own for any part of the evening. That there was a whole gang of people who loved her and had her back.

Fortunately, at that moment a bell rang to indicate that they should take their seats, and they all moved to the chairs that had been laid out in front of the stage.

"I never noticed it before," Nanna Peg said as she settled next to Milly, "but Richard's eyes are really close together. I don't trust a man whose eyes are close together. And he certainly doesn't have Brendan's sex appeal."

"Shh." Milly sent a mortified glance at Brendan, who was seated the other side of her. "Sorry. I'm so sorry."

"Don't be sorry." He was laughing so hard he was almost crying. "Your grandmother is priceless. And she's given me an idea for my next book."

"Oh please, no, don't tell her that. She'll never stop going on about it." She held her breath as the lights came on and everyone's attention was directed to the stage.

The set was an enchanted forest, lit by what seemed like thousands of tiny lights.

And suddenly Milly was terrified. There was a huge number of people in the audience, far more than she'd anticipated.

"I hope this doesn't go horribly wrong. It's so important to Zoe." She couldn't remember ever feeling so nervous, and when Brendan reached for her hand, she didn't pull away.

But she needn't have worried because the play was wonderful, and not just because she'd known so many of the children (she still thought of them as children, even though they were teenagers now) for years. And Zoe was without doubt the star, acting the part that Milly had heard her and Nicole rehearsing over and over again.

Brendan tightened his grip on her hand and leaned closer to her. "She has talent," he whispered. "Maybe she's a star in the making."

Milly thought about Nicole and the positives and negatives of her career and wasn't sure she wanted that for Zoe, but she wasn't going to worry about that now. If there was one thing that the last couple of years had taught her, it was that it was best to focus on today if you could, because no one really knew what the future was going to bring. Chance played such a big role in what happened in life.

So for now she watched her daughter and enjoyed the moment, and she felt pride and love and gratitude, and she realized that being a parent, despite all the worry and sense of responsibility that came with it, was the best thing in the world, and even on the very worst day she wouldn't change it for anything.

It was the perfect way to spend a moonlit summer evening, and afterward the cast joined them in the gardens, and Milly hugged Zoe so tightly she protested that her ribs were going to crack.

"You were brilliant. I was so proud."

"Did you see the part where I fell over the tree stump? Agh!" But Zoe was clearly on a high with it all, dizzy with the rush of adrenaline that came after a performance. She was still wearing the floaty dress she'd worn on stage and had flowers in her hair. "Nicole was amazing. Everyone agrees having her there made such a difference."

Nicole joined them at that moment. She'd dressed discreetly in the hope of not attracting attention, but of course it would have been impossible for Nicole Raven not to attract attention. There had been a ripple of excitement through the whole audience as word had spread that they were in the presence of Hollywood royalty, and every now and then one of Zoe's friends would drag an embarrassed adult over to them with a *Can I just introduce you to my mum and dad?* and Nicole would smile and be gracious as she shook hands and signed whatever was thrust in her direction.

Joel didn't leave her side once, standing like a sentry, his eyes on the crowd.

"Nicole is going to help with our drama group." Zoe's eyes were shining. "Isn't that amazing? She's going to talk to the staff about doing some special sessions."

"That's great." Milly looked around and searched the crowd. "Where's Cally? Is everything all right between the two of you now? Did you manage to have that talk?"

"Yes, thanks to Nicole." Zoe gave Nicole a grateful look. "She spoke to the whole cast about what it is really like making a career of being an actor. She said, 'The parts you get will come and go, but if you're lucky the friendships you make will last forever,' and Cally got this weird look on her face, and then she asked if she could talk to me, and she said how ashamed she was and how she is never going to let anything come between us again."

"That's good to hear." Milly was sure that at some point something would challenge their friendship because that was just life, but for now she was just relieved that everything was back to normal. She glanced at Nicole, intending to thank her, but Nicole was laughing at something Joel had said and didn't even notice.

"Oh, there's Dad! I should go and talk to him, and to Avery." Zoe paused. "Is that okay?"

"Of course it is. This is a family event." Milly watched her speed across the grass to her father and saw Avery hesitate and then hug Zoe and make what appeared to be a great big fuss of her.

And Milly realized that she no longer felt anxious or sick at the thought of sharing Zoe, and she decided that as long as Avery was kind to her daughter, then she was going to be grateful for that, and they would make this work.

"So here we are." Nicole appeared by her side and slid her arm into Milly's.

"Here we are." Milly moved closer to her friend. "Thank you for everything you did for Zoe."

"It was nothing. It was fun working with them. It reminded me how much I love acting. And I'm glad things are better with Richard." Nicole raised her hand to gently fend off a bee that had taken a wrong turn on its hunt for pollen. "He apologized to me, by the way."

"Good."

"You seem much better about it all. Happier. I'm assuming that's all the sex with Brendan."

Milly half gasped and half laughed. "Could you speak a little louder? I think only the north of England heard you. You're worse than Nanna Peg."

"I do hope so. It's a definite life goal of mine." Nicole's gaze rested on Nanna Peg, who was deep in conversation with Brendan once again, and then on Connie. "Who is that guy with your mother? The tall one with dark hair."

"That," Milly said, "is Brian."

"That's Brian?" Nicole tilted her head to one side. "He actually *is* hot, for an older guy. Do you think they—"

"I have no idea, and I'm not asking. She asked if she could bring him tonight, and I got him a ticket. That's the end of my interference. Although, I did overhear them talking about a possible trip to Australia. Brian's daughter is there."

Nicole studied them for a moment. "Do you think they're romantically involved?"

"I don't think so. I think it really is friendship. And that's what my mother wants."

"I can understand that." Nicole leaned her head against Milly's shoulder. "Friendship is important. Possibly the most important thing of all, don't you think?"

Milly felt her throat thicken. "I don't know about that." Her voice was husky. "I mean, sex is pretty important."

"True."

"And talking of sex, how is it going with Joel?"

"You're getting ahead of yourself. My situation is a little bit complicated, if you remember. But I admit I like him." Nicole sighed. "I like him so much. He's brilliant in every way, which is why I'm taking it slowly. I thought I might rent a place nearby while I look for somewhere permanent, but he suggested I stay with him for now. Not make any quick decisions."

Milly decided that Joel was possibly an even better person than she'd always thought. "That's good. He's your built-in security."

"Yes. But it's more than that. The scary thing is that he seems to really know me and understand me."

"Why is that scary?"

"Because I haven't been me for a long time. I've spent most of my life not being me."

Milly was one of the few people who was able to understand the truth in that statement. "Then, this should be a refreshing change."

They both watched as Joel brought Connie and Nanna Peg another drink.

"I like being with him. I'm terrified of messing it up," Nicole said, "the way I have messed up every other relationship I've ever had."

"You're not going to mess it up."

Nicole turned to look at her. "How can you be so sure?"

That was easy to answer. "Because this isn't like any other relationship you've ever had."

Nicole stared at her for a long moment and then smiled. "That's true. It isn't."

They were both silent for a moment, watching the crowd, enjoying each other's company.

And then Nicole tightened her hold on Milly. "If you could have three wishes—"

"That's easy. I only need one." Milly smiled as Zoe sprinted across the grass to Connie and Nanna Peg, the flowers that had been carefully wound into her hair now trailing down by her shoulders. "I would wish that for five minutes life could stay as it is right now. No changes. No challenges. Nothing traumatic to deal with."

"That would be good." Nicole pulled her closer. "But when things do change, because they will, at least we'll have each other."

And Milly knew that was true.

Through the ups and downs, the highs and lows, the challenges, arguments, hugs, laughter, gossip, support—through the whole bumpy journey of friendship, they'd be there for each other.

"I'm glad you're staying." Although she knew now that their friendship would survive no matter what, she was honest enough with herself to admit that she would have missed Nicole if she'd left. "You haven't changed your mind?"

"Why would I change my mind? At Joel's suggestion, I made a list of everything I'd like to have in my life. And it turns out that all of it is right here. Including you."

Milly's heart felt full. "That's interesting, because if I were to make a list of everything I'd like to have in my life, all of it would also be right here. Including you."

Nicole pressed closer, and Milly stood with her friend and watched her family together, then met Brendan's gaze across the crowded gardens and marveled at how life could seem so hard and impossible one minute, and yet so exciting and full of possibilities the next.

Change could be difficult, particularly when it was forced on you, but it could also be positive.

You had to keep going, she thought. No matter how tough things were. You had to keep going because you never knew what might be around the next corner, and you had to believe it might be something good.

"About you staying—"

"Mm?"

"Are you going to give up being a drama queen?"

Nicole laughed. "Never. That's one thing that is never going to change. You can be sure of that."

★ ★ ★ ★ ★

Acknowledgments

Writing is mostly a solitary endeavor, but once the book is finished it becomes a team effort. So many books are published each week, and I am always grateful and excited to see my book on the shelves because I know it's the result of the hard work and dedication of my publishing teams. Canary Street Press in the US and HQ Stories in the UK work hard to get the book into the hands of readers everywhere. I owe a debt of gratitude to every individual—if I listed them, this book would be too fat to fit on the shelves—but I'm particularly grateful to Michele Bidelspach, who edited this book and whose helpful insight helped shape the final version, and also to Margaret Marbury and Susan Swinwood for their ongoing support. Lisa Milton and Manpreet Grewal are a treat to work with, and I'm constantly in awe of their creativity and dedication. I know I'm lucky to work with such inspirational people.

I'm grateful to my agent Susan Ginsburg for all her wisdom and support, and also to Catherine Bradshaw and the rest of the brilliant team at Writers House.

I'm fortunate to have a wonderful family who have grown accustomed to the strange fictional world I inhabit and are endlessly supportive, and also to my writer (and nonwriter!) friends.

My biggest thanks goes to all the booksellers, bloggers and reviewers who support my writing and to the readers who send kind messages and continue to buy and post beautiful photographs of my books being read in various places around the world. (I often think that my books live a much more exciting life than I do.) I am lucky to have such a loyal, enthusiastic and kind bunch of readers.

Turn the page for a
SNEAK PEEK
from the new feel-good festive novel from

SARAH MORGAN

All Together for Christmas

Coming
October 2025

1

Becky

Standing in the airport terminal surrounded by too much noise and too many stressed people, Becky decided that she didn't love Christmas anywhere near as much as she'd always thought.

Usually she looked forward to it, but there was nothing usual about this particular year.

And now this.

She glanced at the departures board. Everything was red, and not a happy Santa red. Cancelled flight red. *You're-not-going-anywhere* red.

'Nothing?' She gripped the counter. 'Are you seriously telling me nothing is flying?'

'That's right. Everything is delayed or cancelled because of the snow. I'm sorry.' The immaculate woman behind the airport check-in desk gave her a smile that was polite rather than warm.

Becky imagined it being part of the uniform policy. *Knee length skirt, smooth hair, wide smile.*

'This trip isn't optional.' If it was, she wouldn't be going. She'd be avoiding a family gathering, the way she'd been avoiding all family gatherings lately. Not that she felt good about it. On the contrary, she felt horribly guilty. Even more so because just last week her mother had confessed how much she was looking forward to finally having everyone together. 'I *have* to get home.'

'I understand your frustration.'

Becky was confident she did not understand. There was no way this woman would have any insight into Becky's current emotional state. If her hair was any indication, she was the type who had every aspect of her life firmly under control.

She tried to stay calm. She reminded herself how lucky she was. She had a job, somewhere to live, and she was healthy. She had nothing to complain about. The fact that her inner world was in turmoil didn't count. She could almost hear her brother saying *first world problems, Becks.*

'How about Edinburgh? I booked a flight to Newcastle, but Edinburgh would be fine. I can drive to Northumberland in just over an hour from there.'

'Nothing is flying. Not to Newcastle, and not to Edinburgh. I wish I could help, but sadly we can't control the weather.'

What *can* we control, Becky wondered? In her experience, not much at all. But maybe that was just her messy, complicated life.

'I need to get home to my family.'

'You and several million other people. It's Christmas and as I said,' the emphasis was gentle but unmistakeable, 'nothing is flying. Have you considered taking a train?'

'The trains are on strike.' It was as if the entire world of public transport had conspired to make her Christmas as difficult as possible.

'In that case I suggest a car rental, but you'd better make it fast because everyone here is going to have the same idea. And now if you'll excuse me –' the uniformed woman transferred her smile and her attention to the person who was next in the queue.

Becky knew she should feel sorry for her. It couldn't be fun having to deal with a transport crisis guaranteed to put a dent in everyone's Christmas cheer or to be expected to soothe and placate thousands of irate and upset travellers armed with nothing more than charm and a very red lipstick. But she was too tired to dredge up the necessary sympathy. Also the woman's composure was annoying. How did she tame her hair into something so smooth and perfect? Was it part of the training course? No matter what Becky did, her hair ended up in a tangle of curls which was why she'd had it cropped short. There weren't enough hours in the day to waste a chunk of them drying and styling her hair every day as her twin sister Rosie did.

'You don't understand. If I don't make it home it will look as if I'm –' how would it look? It wasn't as if any of her family knew the real reason she didn't want to be there. No one did. Not even Rosie. It was her secret, which in itself wasn't too much of a problem because she generally kept her feelings to herself. Growing up, Rosie had expressed enough feelings for both of them and Becky let her get on with it.

And now she thought about it she realised that the weather and the train strike gave her a perfect excuse not to show up for Christmas at all. For a wild moment she pictured herself sprinting from the airport and heading back home for a quiet Christmas of video games and walks in one of London's snowy parks.

But then the image faded and she thought instead of her mother's roast turkey and the tiny cinnamon flecked cookies she baked simply because she knew they were Becky's favourite. She thought of the cheerful red stocking her mother would have hung on the fireplace even though Becky had insisted they were all too old for a stocking (she wasn't too old for a stocking, but she was old enough to understand how much work went into filling it and felt a responsibility to demur). She thought about her father insisting 'just one more game of Scrabble, Becky' and the warm, comforting weight of their ancient Irish setter Percy as he lay on her feet.

She felt homesick for Northumberland with its windswept empty beaches and imposing castles.

She was scared to go home and yet she longed to go home.

'Could you look again? One more time? I really need to get home,' she said. 'It's not just about Christmas. My brother is having a special party – he's making an announcement. I assume that means he's getting engaged –' she frowned, 'and I'm not sure how I feel about that. He only met her two months ago. That's fast don't you think?' But she wasn't a great judge of what was normal when it came to relationships. She wasn't the sort who fell in and out of love easily.

The woman in the queue adjacent to her nodded. 'It is fast. My sister was married after four months and she was divorced a year later. She discovered all these things about him that she wished she'd known before.'

'Exactly.' Becky turned to face her, relieved that at least *someone* seemed to understand her concerns. 'That's what worries me. You need time to get to know a person. Also, my brother hasn't dated anyone seriously since his last girlfriend walked out. That was six years ago, and they'd been together for eight years. Since medical school. It left him a bit broken. We've all been worried about him. Mum, most of all, obviously, because she worries all the time even when we're fine. For years he has dated no one, and then suddenly he went on a business trip and he met this girl and now, two months later, he has an announcement to make. Tomorrow night. He has ordered champagne. I'm assuming it's a sign.'

'Sounds like it. Same thing happened to my cousin Martha,' the man standing behind her in the queue took a step forward. 'We'd all given up on her meeting someone, hadn't we Ginny?'

Bored with queuing, the woman he'd addressed the question to hauled her case forward so that she could join in the conversation. 'We had. Her boyfriend refused to propose, said they were fine as they were and didn't want to get married, but then a new receptionist started at his work and a month later he left Martha and was getting married. Turns out it wasn't that he didn't want to get married, but he didn't want to marry Martha. He said it wasn't personal, but how much more personal can you get?' She exchanged looks with her husband.

'Heartbreaking,' he said. 'We thought Martha would be single forever after that, but three years later she was walking the dog and that was it.'

'That was what?' Becky was struggling to keep up. People were so complicated. They made her head hurt, which was why generally she preferred to work with computers.

'She met Roland. A month later they were married.'

'Oh.' Maybe that was reassuring. 'A month is fast. And they're happy together?'

'No. They're divorced too.'

So not reassuring at all.

She was beginning to wish she hadn't started this conversation because it was doing nothing to soothe her anxiety about her brother. 'So you're saying it's best to take your time over falling in love.'

'Maybe, but you don't always have a choice.' Ginny leaned closer. 'Sometimes you can be going along living your life, minding your own business and then wham.'

'Wham? As in you walk into something and fall over?'

'No, wham as in you fall in love. Love at first sight. And you can't help it.'

Becky was about to say that she didn't believe in love at first sight, but then she thought about her twin sister, now married to Declan, Becky's long time work colleague (now ex-colleague). Becky had introduced them and that had definitely been a 'wham' moment. One minute Becky had been talking to both of them and the next they'd been talking to each other, mesmerised, her existence forgotten. She'd cleared her throat a few times, then banged her glass on the table. Nothing. They'd been so absorbed in each other she'd had a feeling that they wouldn't have noticed her even if she'd danced on the table. She'd always considered Declan to be a sensible human being, but after that encounter all he'd talked about was her sister. Rosie this. Rosie that. *Tell me more about Rosie.*

They were married eight months later.

Was that what had happened to Jamie? What was *wrong* with her family?

'I'm happy for my brother, obviously, but also worried. Although I suppose if I'm honest I didn't totally love his first girlfriend. She was a bit judgy.'

Perhaps if you tried to make yourself look a little more feminine, Becky. I get that you work in a mostly male environment and you want to fit in, but maybe you could wear a dress sometimes, or a touch of lipstick. A shoe that doesn't look as if it has passed the health and safety rules of a construction site.

'Try not to worry.' Ginny patted her arm. 'I'm sure he knows his own mind.'

Becky didn't share her confidence. She felt very protective towards her older brother.

She'd been in love once in her life and it hadn't been a quick process. It had crept over her stealthily, like an emotional weight gain, layer upon layer going unnoticed until one day you woke up and took a long hard look at yourself and realised something about you was different. It had come as a shock to her, and not a good one.

But she'd disciplined herself not to think about that.

Her phone rang and a name flashed up.

Rosie.

After a moment's hesitation she rejected the call and a moment later a message popped up on her screen.

Declan and I are on our way! Can't wait to see you.

Becky's fingers hovered over the keyboard but in the end she just sent a couple of emojis.

Rosie was married now. She didn't need to get into lengthy exchanges with her twin sister. And at this precise moment Becky didn't feel robust enough to handle Rosie cooing over how fantastic Declan was – how he'd fixed her laptop again (Becky had often fixed her sister's laptop and had never be on the receiving end of even a fraction of the love and appreciation that Declan was shown for performing the same task) or how perfect Declan was (he certainly hadn't been perfect when Becky had worked with him, and not just because he always left the milk out of the fridge). And honestly Becky was happy for her. She adored her sister, and she believed that if there was ever a moment when life wasn't dumping crap in your lap, then you should make the most of it.

But being relegated to the second most important person in her sister's life wasn't easy, and training herself not to contact her sister at all hours of the day required a discipline that was exhausting.

Emojis were okay weren't they? Emojis didn't intrude on her twin's personal space.

She could hardly register the fact that Rosie was married, even though she'd been at the wedding. This was going to be the first time the whole family had been together since that day in February. Their first family Christmas with an extra member of the family (two extra members if you counted Jamie's girlfriend). Rosie's first Christmas married to Declan. The first Christmas that Becky and Rosie wouldn't be up at dawn poking presents together. Rosie would be in bed with Declan. Sleeping. Or not. Maybe she'd be doing more exciting things than sleeping. Jamie would be in bed with his girlfriend, probably not sleeping.

And she'd be in bed on her own. Or maybe with the dog if she could sneak him into her room without her mother seeing.

Becky felt horribly flat. Not gloomy exactly, but close to it.

Christmas was going to be different. And not in a good way, at least for her.

She wasn't sure she wanted to go at all.

But if she stayed in London she'd break her mother's heart. And very possibly her own. Also, she needed to check out this woman Jamie had met. Turned out the sibling bond was stronger than the need for self-preservation.

She'd be okay. Her superpower was hiding her feelings, not just from other people but also from herself. She worked on the principle that if you didn't acknowledge something, then you could pretend it wasn't there.

She zipped up her hoodie, tightened the laces on her winter

boots and clomped her way through the terminal building, dragging her large suitcase and dodging passengers as she followed the signs for car rental. Thanks to the party her flatmate had thrown the night before, she was tired (she'd worn earplugs and noise cancelling headphones and still the entire building had vibrated), and the last thing she needed was to navigate pre-Christmas traffic for seven hours or longer, but it seemed as if she didn't have a choice. If necessary, she'd pull over and take a nap.

She almost laughed.

She was twenty-eight years old and, if she was to believe the article she'd read on her phone the week before, in the prime of her life. If she hadn't been told, she wouldn't have known. She didn't feel as if she was in the prime of anything.

She'd started a new job eight months earlier and so far it wasn't going well. She was good at what she did and had no problems with the job itself, but in this new place being good at your job wasn't enough. You had to socialise. It wasn't about the work, it was about schmoozing with the right people. She hated playing those complicated political games and she wasn't good at it, mostly because she wasn't interested. Taking the job had been a mistake, she could see that now. One of many she'd made lately.

These days even home was stressful, because she was no longer living with her sister and she'd underestimated how hard that would be. She'd always known she'd miss her, at least at first, but not this much.

She paused just long enough to buy herself a strong coffee, hoping it might give her flagging energy a boost. Juggling suitcase, scarf and coffee, she walked past a giant Christmas tree glowing with lights and no doubt designed to put people in a festive mood. Twinkling stars cascaded from the roof of the terminal building.

Most people were too desperate about the travel situation to take any comfort from twinkling stars. What they wanted was transport. No one was where they wanted to be.

It felt like a metaphor for her life.

It crossed her mind briefly that if Rosie and Declan hadn't yet left she could grab a ride with them, but she dismissed the thought instantly. She wasn't a good passenger at the best of times, and being trapped in the car with those two lovebirds would finish her off. Christmas would be bad enough. She didn't need a preview.

As the woman had predicted the queue for car rental was long and crackling with impatience and tension.

The man and the woman in front of her were locked in an argument.

'What if we make it to the front and then there are no cars left?'

Good question, Becky thought. *What then?*

'They will have cars.'

'You don't know that. Look at the length of the queue! I think we should head out of London and try somewhere less busy.'

Becky considered that suggestion even though it hadn't been directed at her.

Maybe that wasn't the worst idea. But what if she did that and there were still no cars? She'd be stranded outside London. No, she was staying put and hoping for some luck.

Honestly, could things be any worse?

'Becky?'

The deep voice almost made her drop her coffee.

Oh no. Please no.

She conjured up a smile – if the woman behind the check in desk could do it then so could she – and turned.

He stood directly behind her, drawing interested glances from the many bored women standing in the queue.

'Will! This is a surprise. What are you doing here?'

He was living proof of the fact that just when you thought things couldn't get any worse, they got worse.

'Same as you I imagine. I was hoping for a quick journey home, but it doesn't look as if that's going to happen.' He pulled her in for a hug, which was a standard greeting between them and it gave her a chance to bury her very red face in his coat.

Typical. It was snowing outside and her cheeks were blazing like a furnace.

She never would have thought she could feel uncomfortable with Will, but that was before she'd embarrassed herself at her sister's wedding. Embarrassed was probably too tame a word. Embarrassed was when you were late for a dental appointment, or you forgot someone's birthday. This was bone deep humiliation. The sort of humiliation that made you wonder if you should emigrate, have plastic surgery and change your name.

She was just going to ignore it. Pretend it had never happened.

Hopefully he'd do the same.

She stepped back. 'I thought I'd hang out in an airport for a while. Soak up some of the festive spirit.'

'I'm pleased you haven't lost your sense of humour.' He studied her for a moment, his hands still on her shoulders. 'It's good to see you. It has been a while.'

'Oh, you know – new job, busy, busy –'

He nodded. 'Are you okay? You look – I don't know. Upset?'

And she thought that hiding her feelings was her superpower. Not from Will, apparently. 'I'm fine. It's just airport stress.'

'I can tell you're not fine, Becky. Talk to me.'

She almost told him that she didn't feel remotely festive. That she was dreading going home for Christmas. *That she was a mess.* But she managed to stop herself. 'You know those train announcements – the ones where they tell you to mind the gap between the train and the platform? It's the same for Christmas. I try not to fall into the chasm between expectation and reality.'

He gave her a speculative look. 'Okay. Well if you want to talk about whatever it is that's bothering you, you know where I am.'

'You know me. I'm not big on talking about things. I leave that to my sister.'

'Hopefully your reality will improve a little once you get out of this place.' His gaze shifted from her face to the queue. 'You're hiring a car?'

'Yes.' What else could she say? That she was standing in line to see Santa? 'That seems to be the only way to get up north today. Unless a certain person in a red suit with a white beard can find room for me on his sleigh as he flies past. I didn't see any mention of his flight being grounded.'

'I don't have a sleigh, but I do have a car and I'm parked here, at the airport. You can come with me if you like. We can drive up together.'

She didn't like. She absolutely did not like.

'That's a kind offer, but it will be easier if we do our own thing. I might need to stop on the way, make a few work calls –' she stumbled under his questioning gaze.

'If you need to make a work call from my car, you can make a call Becks.' He was the only person other than her brother, who called her Becks.

'It's confidential.'

He raised an eyebrow. 'I'm not exactly known as a gossip.'

And given what he'd witnessed that was lucky for her, although right now she didn't feel lucky.

She felt as if the universe hated her.

From behind her she heard a woman mutter *if she doesn't want to get into his car then I will,* and for a fleeting moment she saw Will as a stranger might.

He was tall and he radiated calm confidence. He was a doctor, a cardiologist, and she was sure that any patient who saw him approach the bedside would instantly feel reassured. A smart wool coat emphasised the width of his shoulders and a pair of glasses with a bold tortoiseshell frame accentuated the lean lines of his face. He looked as if he'd stepped directly from a photoshoot for 'sexy academic man'.

She was conscious of her faded jeans and her favourite hoodie that she all but lived in. What did he see when he looked at her?

His best friend's little sister.

The thought was annoying. She shouldn't care. She didn't care! She'd known him all her life and he was the one of the few people she always felt comfortable with, but that had all changed the day of the wedding.

The memory of that had her reaching behind her for her hood. She tugged it over her head in the hope that it might act as a shield.

He frowned. 'Are you cold? Because you can have my coat.' He was already starting to shrug it from his shoulders but she stopped him.

'I'm not cold. My coat is in my luggage because I always overheat in airports. It's just my head. My head gets cold. You lose most of your heat through your head. You're a doctor. You should know that.'

'Um –' he pulled a face and pushed his glasses up his nose. 'That's a myth.'

'It is? That isn't a thing?'

'Not exactly, although of course it's important to bear in mind the effects that cooling the face and head can have on systemic cardiovascular reflex responses, particularly in elderly people.'

She loved it when he delivered random facts. 'Elderly? I'm twenty-eight.'

'I know how old you are, Becks.'

Of course he did. He knew everything about her.

She shifted her weight from one leg to the other, wishing she was more comfortable in awkward social situations. This was one of those occasions where, given the choice, she would have shut herself away with just her laptop for company.

'I'm keeping my hood up anyway. In case my head is the exception. I might be suffering from premature ageing. Or maybe my head gets colder because my hair is short.'

'It's cute. You look good with short hair.'

He was trying to make her feel better. Trying to ease the embarrassment he knew she was feeling.

Since the wedding she'd avoided him as much as she could. The last thing she'd expected was to come face to face with him in a busy airport but given her current run of bad luck she probably should have anticipated it.

It was time to implement her extraction protocol.

She was great at melting away without anyone noticing, mostly because she wasn't the sort of person people noticed in the first place but in this case melting anywhere wasn't easy because Will was looking at her in a slightly strange way and it was unsettling because he always seemed to see so much more than most people.

'Honestly, I'm fine. I'll need a car when I'm up there anyway. I was going to hire one at the airport so that I can be independent because my mother's car has a habit of breaking down at inconvenient moments.'

'Is this about what happened at the wedding?' He reached out and brushed a strand of hair away from her face and if it had been anyone else but Will she would have slapped his hand away but he'd been hauling her out of ditches and shunting her up trees in the forest near where they lived since she was five years old.

She didn't mind him touching her hair, but she did mind about the question.

She didn't want to think about the wedding. She'd tried to block the whole thing from her mind. But now he'd reminded her and every painful detail came flooding back, including all the emotions she'd been trying to ignore.

'The wedding? No, of course not. It feels like a lifetime ago, doesn't it? I can barely remember a thing about it, apart from the scratchy dress Rosie made me wear. No, this is about what's practical. Anyway, good to see you Will. I hope you have a good journey home and have a great Christmas. Maybe we'll bump into each other at some point.' She was tempted to step away but then she would have lost her place in the queue, so she waited for him to do it. *Leave. Please, just leave.*

He didn't leave.

'We're going to be bumping into each other tomorrow. You do know I'm going to the party at your house?'

No, she hadn't known that. If she'd known she would have looked harder for an excuse to stay in London.

This was promising to be the most excruciating Christmas on record.

'Jamie invited you?' Of course he had. Will was Jamie's closest friend. They'd known each other since kindergarten. They'd gone to the same medical school, although once qualified they'd chosen different specialities and their paths had diverged. But if Jamie was having a celebration, Will was going to be there.

'Yes. He said he had something big to announce. I assume it's an engagement?'

'I'm assuming the same.'

'I'm happy for him. I know things were rough there for a while.' He adjusted his glasses. 'So you're going to be a bridesmaid again.'

Her gaze met his briefly and she knew they were both thinking about the last time she was a bridesmaid.

Not her finest moment.

'Looks that way. Woohoo. Lucky me. I just hope he doesn't expect me to dress as a fairy like Rosie did. I'm not fairy material.'

'You looked stunning in that dress, Becks.'

He was just being kind, because he'd sensed she was in a low mood.

'Yeah, right. It gave me a rash, but – thanks.' Another thing she wasn't good at. Accepting compliments. 'Anyway, you should get going. I'm guessing the snow is going to make the driving difficult.'

Will glanced from her to the long line of people ahead of her, as if trying to understand her decision. 'If you're sure . . .'

'I'm sure.'

But just at that moment there was a commotion at the front of the queue.

'What do you mean there are no more cars?' A man spoke in a loud voice. 'There has to be something.'

A ripple of consternation passed through the line of people.

'No cars?'

'*Did he say no cars?*'

'*What's supposed to happen now?*'

It was obvious what had to happen now, at least for Becky.

She closed her eyes and tried a few seconds of mindfulness.

When she opened them Will was still standing there, waiting. She had to admire his staying power.

With a sigh, she swallowed her pride. 'If your offer of sharing your car still stands –'

'It still stands, and I promise not to listen when you make your important phone call.'

She wished she'd never mentioned a phone call. Not only would she now need to find someone to call, but she was going to have to make it sound important.

'Thanks.'

He nodded and stretched out his hand. 'Do you want help with that suitcase?'

'Do I look weak and feeble? Thanks, but I'm fine.' She grabbed it firmly and tugged it closer to her, wondering how she was going to survive this. As well as dreading the impending family gathering, she was now also dreading the journey.

'I thought your muscles might have atrophied given the time you spend glued to computer screens.'

He was teasing her the way he'd always teased her. It should have felt natural, but nothing felt natural anymore.

'I could still beat you in an arm-wrestling match.'

His eyebrow lifted. 'If you're referring to that incident on your fifteenth birthday, I let you win.'

'No you didn't, but we'll pretend you did if that protects your ego.'

'I let you win because you were trying to impress that boy who

329

played in the school orchestra with you. The one with red hair and freckles. Tom.'

'Tim.' How on earth had he remembered that? 'Tim Tucker. I haven't thought about him in years.'

'I seem to remember the strategy backfired. He was too scared to go near you after that.'

'So you're the reason that relationship didn't work out.'

He nodded slowly. 'Probably, although in my defence I couldn't see you being happy with a man who was scared to arm wrestle you. But relationships are complicated. So are feelings.'

And didn't she know it. She wasn't good at showing her feelings, but that didn't mean she didn't have them. And she wished she didn't. Feelings were so *annoying*. There were plenty of days when she thought life would be a lot easier if the human body had been designed to include an on/off switch for feelings. At least then when it all got too much she could have rebooted the system.

She gestured towards the sign directing them to the car park. 'We should probably get moving.'

'Yes. If we're lucky we'll be there by late afternoon.'

She hoped his luck was better than hers otherwise there was no chance of that.

He was checking the weather and the route on his phone. 'Mm. If this forecast is correct, the journey might not be easy. It's saying nine hours.'

'Nine hours? *Did you say nine hours?*'

'It's snowing. Broken down vehicles. Lane closures. Don't worry. We'll stock up with snacks and you can choose the music.'

The way she felt at the moment her first choice would be a funeral march.

She should have trusted her instincts and refused his offer.

Because it wasn't true that no one knew the real reason she didn't want to go home for Christmas. That no one knew her secret.

Will Patterson knew. And now she was going to be trapped in a car with him for nine hours.

Merry Christmas Becky.

Will this Christmas finally bring comfort and joy?

A painful secret

Imogen loves her job as an events organiser, and her colleagues are in awe of her. But Imogen isn't the person she pretends to be, and she's hiding painful truths about her past. But as long as she can keep on top of her work, Imogen can put everything else to one side.

An act of kindness

And then Imogen makes a catastrophic mistake at work, and finally realises it's time to reset. When her favourite client, Dorothy, invites her to spend Christmas with her and her family, in her cottage in the Cotswolds, it sounds like the perfect way for Imogen to take stock.

Finding happiness at christmas

Imogen soon settles into idyllic cottage life, especially with the prospect of a new romance on the horizon ... but when long-buried secrets and unwanted faces from the past resurface, Imogen's new peace is threatened. Will Imogen end up alone this Christmas, or can she find it in her heart to forgive and move on?

Could this Christmas be the start of a whole new chapter?

A long-lasting friendship

Every year, Erica, Claudia, and Anna reunite for their book club holiday. They're bonded by years of friendship and a deep love of books, but there is still so much they keep from each other . . .

A perfect Christmas escape

At the cosy Maple Sugar Inn, Hattie specialises in making her guests' dreams come true, but this Christmas all she wants is to survive the festive season. Between running the inn and being a single mother, Hattie is close to breaking point.

The start of a brand-new story . . . ?

Over the course of an eventful week, Hattie sees that the friends are each carrying around unspoken truths, but nothing prepares her for how deeply her story will become entwined in theirs. Will this Christmas be the end of the book club's story or the start of a whole new chapter?

Can you find new beginnings with old friends?

Joanna Whitman's high-profile marriage held more secrets than she cares to remember, so when her ex-husband dies, she doesn't know what to feel. But when she discovers that he's left behind a pregnant young woman, Joanna is forced to act. She knows exactly how brutal the spotlight on them both will be...unless she can find a way for them to disappear.

Ashley Blake is amazed when Joanna suggests they lie low at her beach house in her sleepy Californian hometown. Joanna should be hating her, not helping her. But alone and pregnant, Ashley needs all the support she can find.

Joanna's only goal for the summer is privacy. All Ashley wants is space to plan for her and her baby's future. But when an old flame reappears, and secrets spill out under the hot summer sun, this unlikely friendship is put to the test...

'A PERFECT SLICE OF JOYFUL SUMMER ESCAPISM'
Clare Pooley

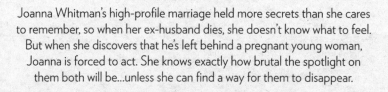

It's never too late
for adventure...

Kathleen is eighty years old. After a run-in with an intruder,
her daughter wants her to move into a residential home.

Liza is drowning under the daily stress of family life. The last
thing she needs is her mother jetting off on a wild holiday.

Martha is having a quarter-life crisis. Unemployed, unloved and uninspired,
she just can't get her life together. When Martha sees Kathleen's advert
for a driver and companion to take an epic road trip across America, she
decides this job might be the answer to her prayers. Besides, how much
trouble can one eighty-year-old woman be?

'THE ROAD TRIP
OF A LIFETIME
– TERRIFIC FUN'
Veronica Henry

It's never too late to start over again . . .

A summer escape

When Cecilia Lapthorne's 75th birthday celebrations take an unexpected turn, she seeks solace away from the festivities and escapes to Dune Cottage – without telling her family where she's going.

A new friendship

Lily Thomas, a struggling artist, has secretly been staying in the unoccupied cottage. When Cecilia discovers Lily during a late-night visit, an unexpected bond forms between the two women.

A chance to start over

Then Cecilia's grandson, Todd – and Lily's unrequited crush – shows up, sending a shockwave through their unlikely friendship. Will it inspire Lily to find the courage to live the life she wants? Can Cecilia finally let go of the past to find a new future? Because as surely as the tide erases past footprints, this summer is offering both Cecilia and Lily the chance to swap old dreams for new . . .

ONE PLACE. MANY STORIES

Bold, innovative and
empowering publishing.

FOLLOW US ON:

@HQStories